Guy Delisle

WORLD RECORD HOLDERS

**Translated by
Helge Dascher and Rob Aspinall**

Drawn & Quarterly

THE FIRST PANEL

ON THE VERGE OF A
NERVOUS BREAKDOWN,
I FINALLY GOT UP THE
COURAGE TO HAND
IN MY LETTER OF
RESIGNATION TO THE
VIDEO GAME COMPANY
I WAS WORKING FOR.

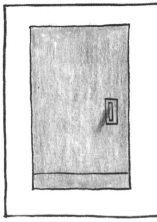

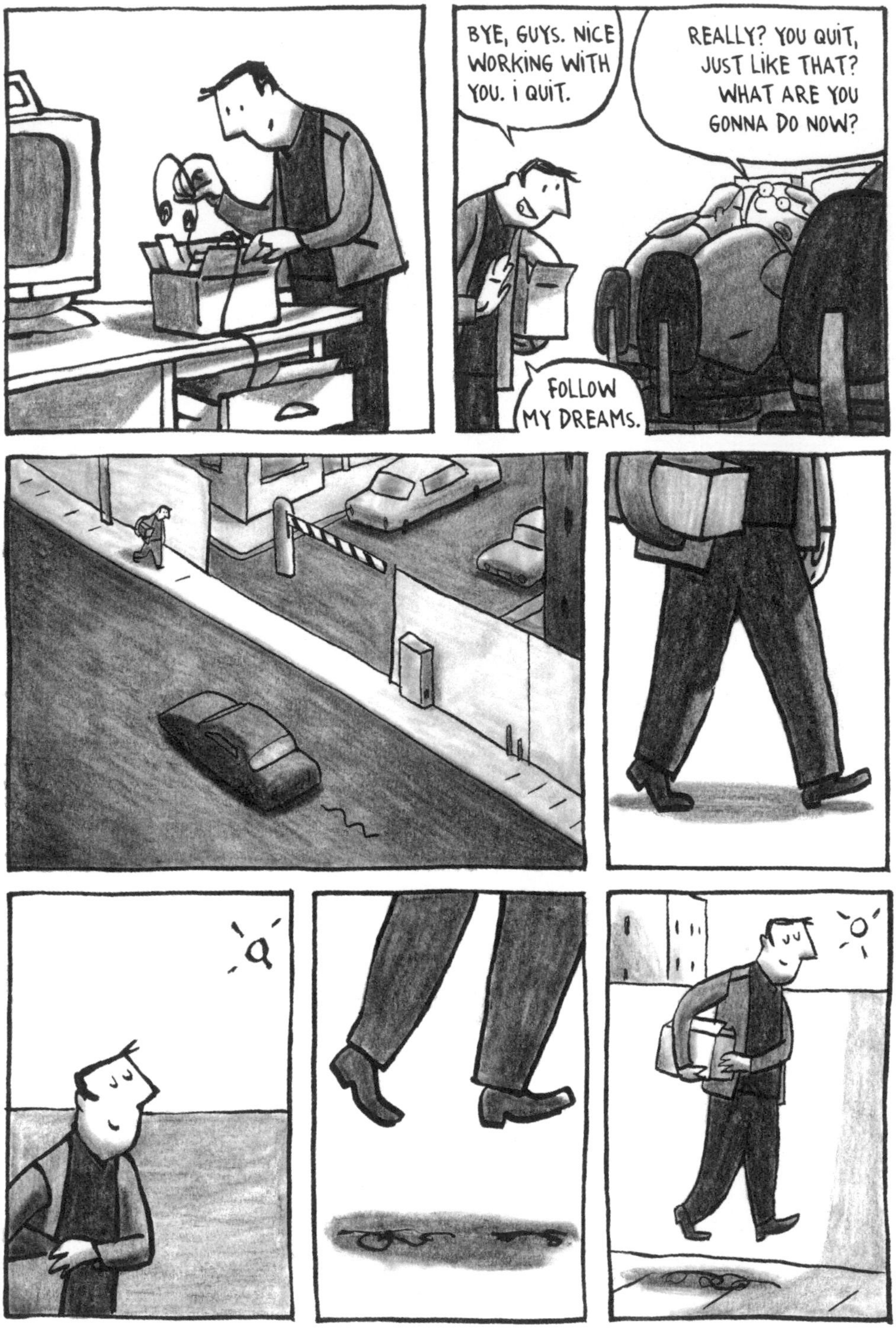
BYE, GUYS. NICE WORKING WITH YOU. I QUIT.
REALLY? YOU QUIT, JUST LIKE THAT? WHAT ARE YOU GONNA DO NOW?
FOLLOW MY DREAMS.

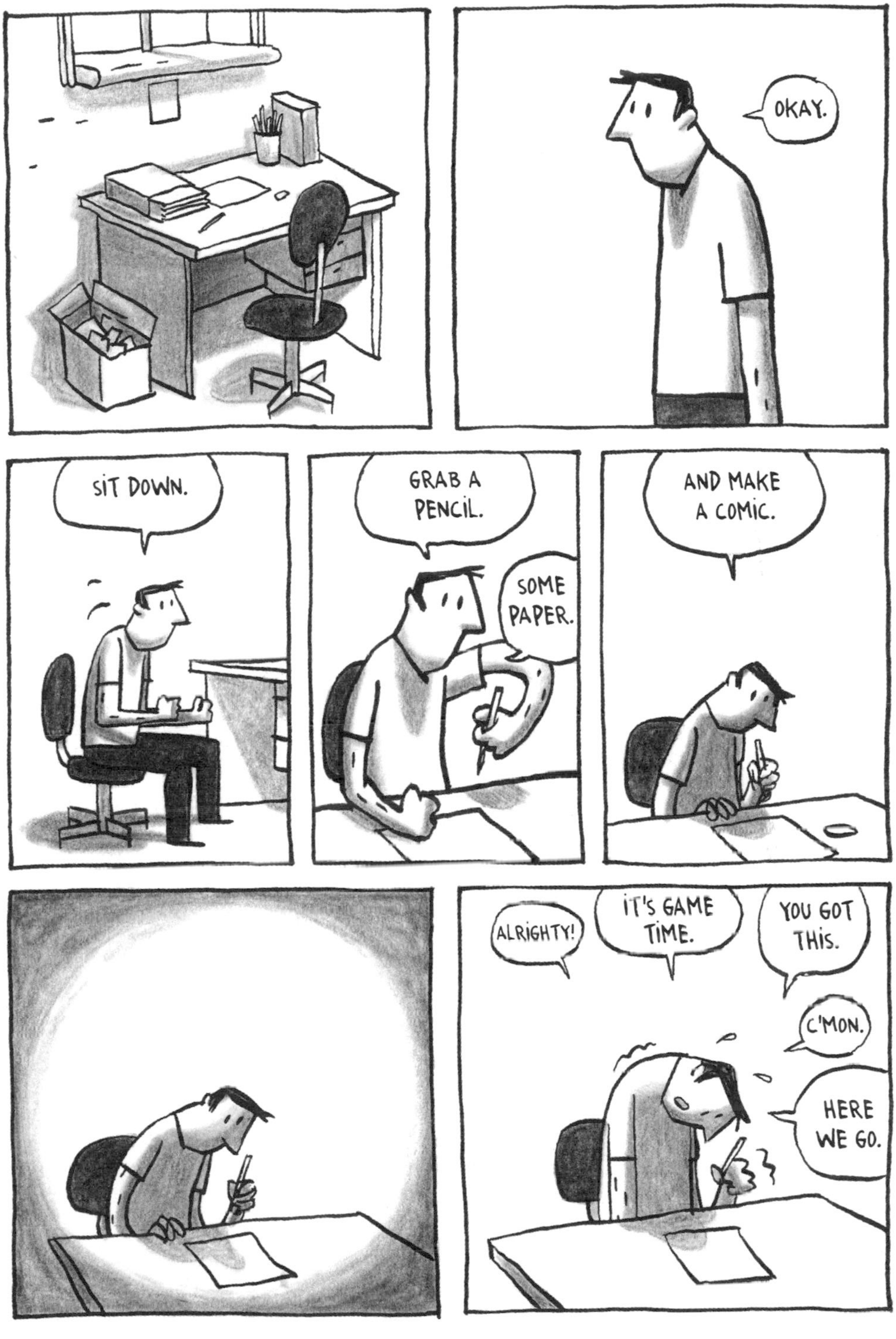
OKAY.
SIT DOWN.
GRAB A PENCIL.
SOME PAPER.
AND MAKE A COMIC.
ALRIGHTY!
IT'S GAME TIME.
YOU GOT THIS.
C'MON.
HERE WE GO.

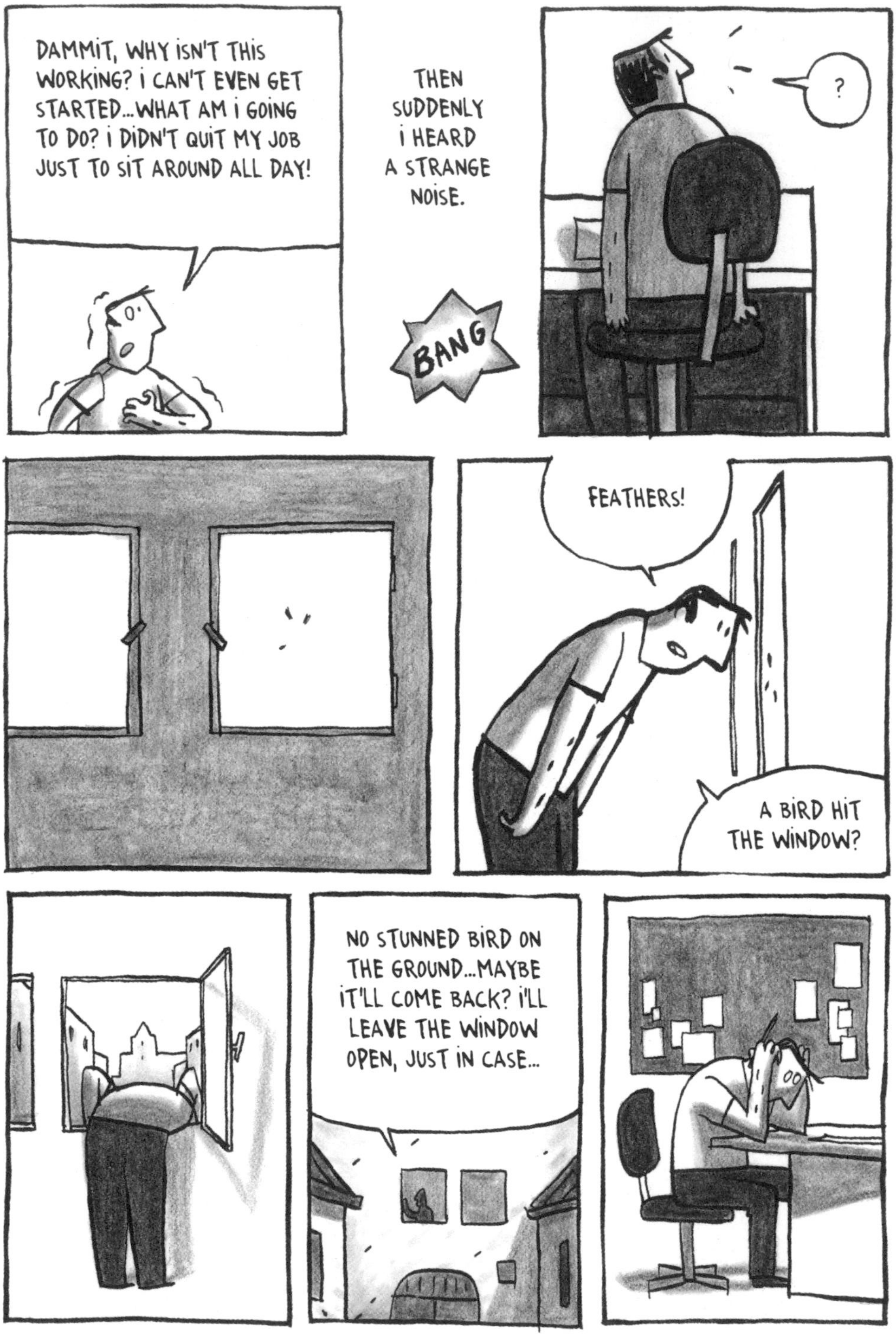
DAMMIT, WHY ISN'T THIS WORKING? I CAN'T EVEN GET STARTED...WHAT AM I GOING TO DO? I DIDN'T QUIT MY JOB JUST TO SIT AROUND ALL DAY!
THEN SUDDENLY I HEARD A STRANGE NOISE.
BANG
?
FEATHERS!
A BIRD HIT THE WINDOW?
NO STUNNED BIRD ON THE GROUND...MAYBE IT'LL COME BACK? I'LL LEAVE THE WINDOW OPEN, JUST IN CASE...

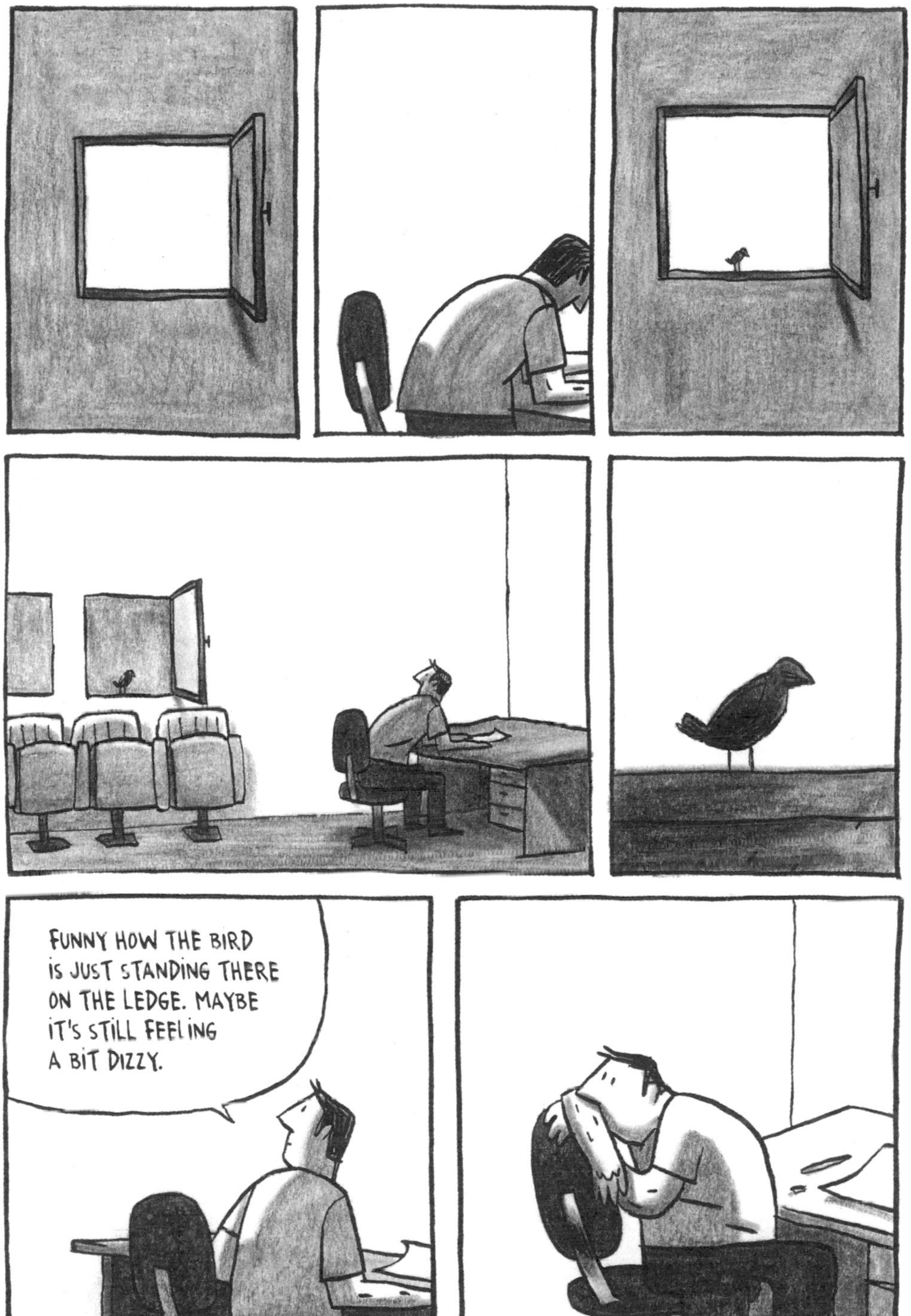
FUNNY HOW THE BIRD IS JUST STANDING THERE ON THE LEDGE. MAYBE IT'S STILL FEELING A BIT DIZZY.

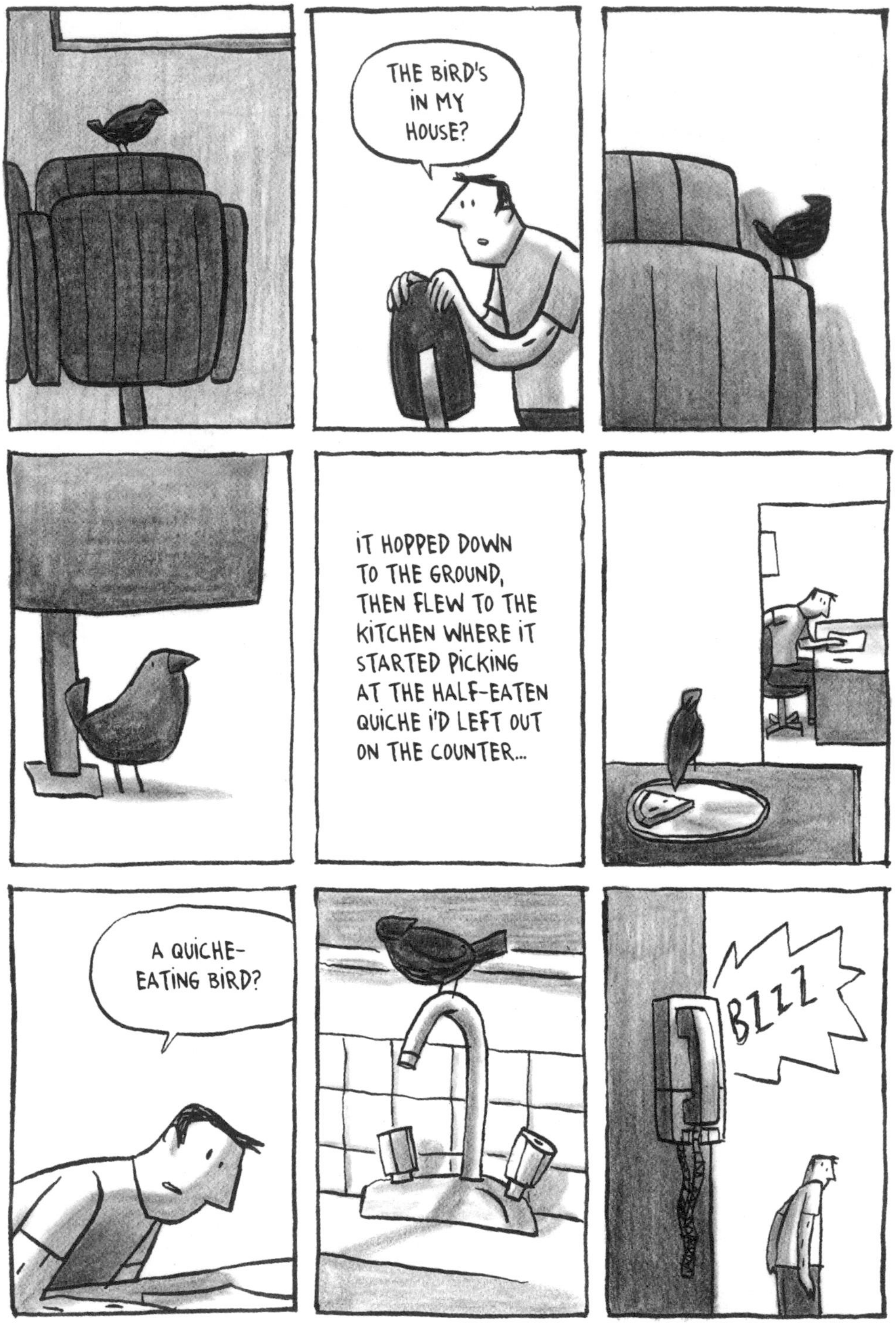
THE BIRD'S IN MY HOUSE?
IT HOPPED DOWN TO THE GROUND, THEN FLEW TO THE KITCHEN WHERE IT STARTED PICKING AT THE HALF-EATEN QUICHE I'D LEFT OUT ON THE COUNTER...
A QUICHE-EATING BIRD?
BZZZ

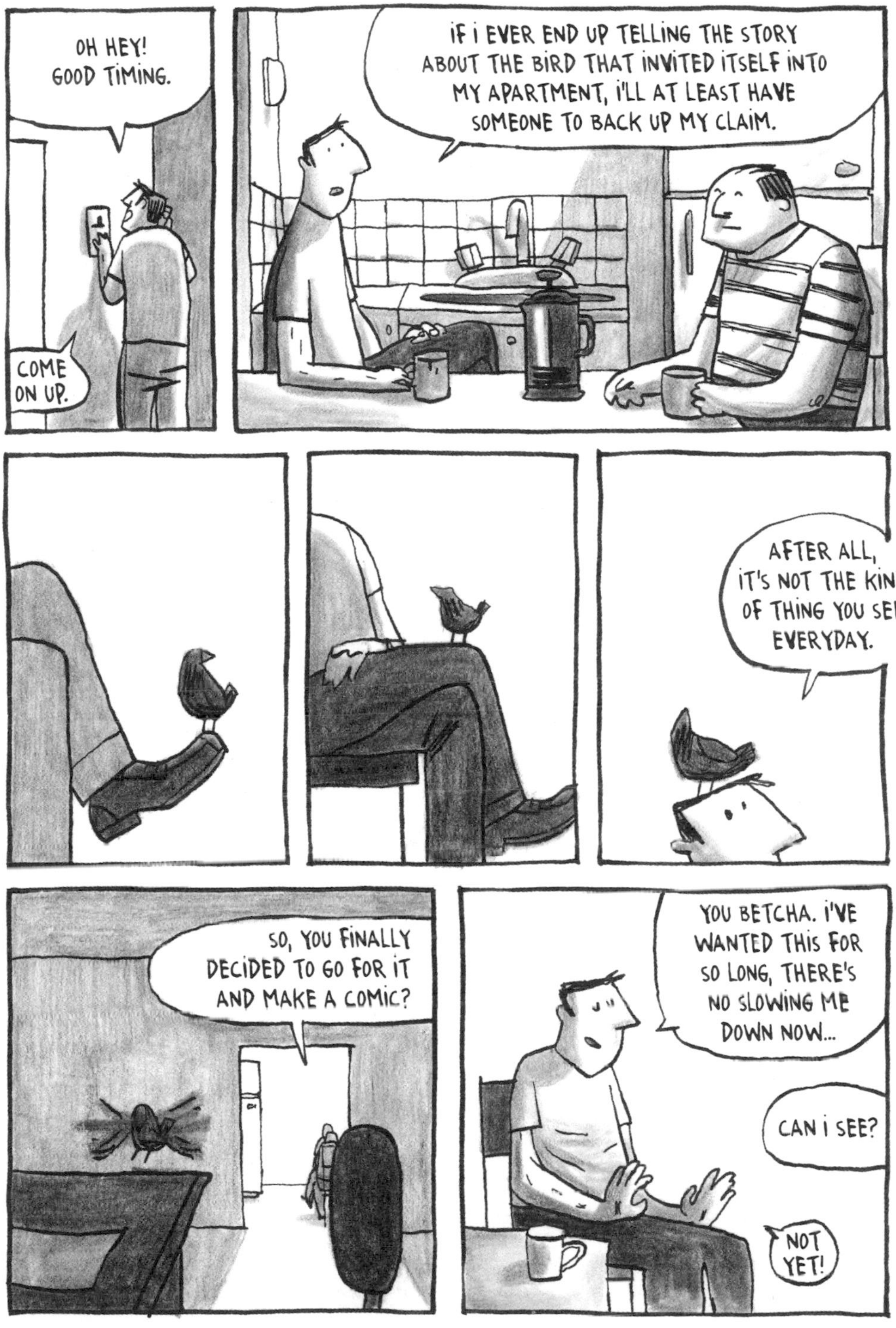
OH HEY! GOOD TIMING.
COME ON UP.
IF I EVER END UP TELLING THE STORY ABOUT THE BIRD THAT INVITED ITSELF INTO MY APARTMENT, I'LL AT LEAST HAVE SOMEONE TO BACK UP MY CLAIM.
AFTER ALL, IT'S NOT THE KIND OF THING YOU SEE EVERYDAY.
SO, YOU FINALLY DECIDED TO GO FOR IT AND MAKE A COMIC?
YOU BETCHA. I'VE WANTED THIS FOR SO LONG, THERE'S NO SLOWING ME DOWN NOW...
CAN I SEE?
NOT YET!

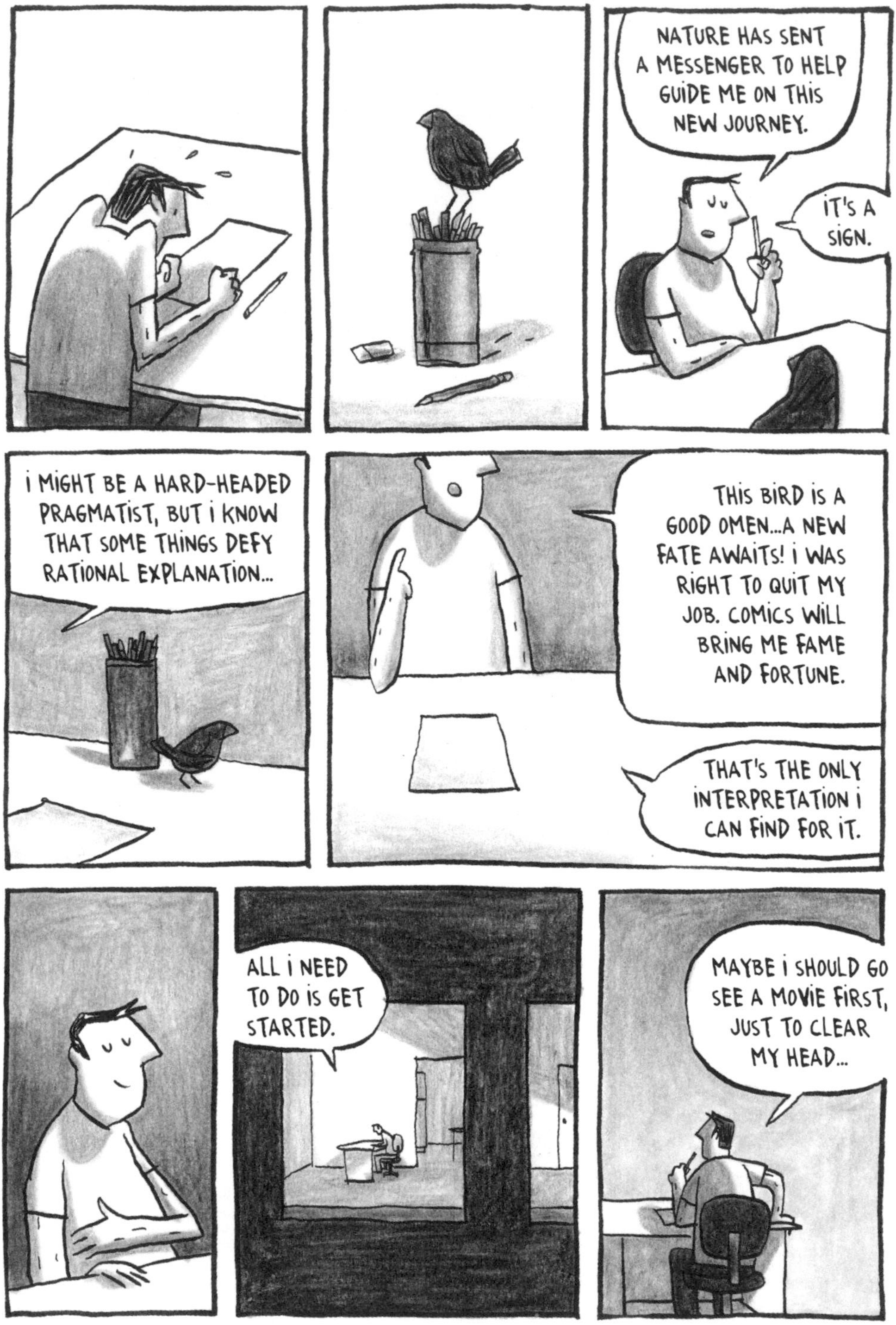
NATURE HAS SENT A MESSENGER TO HELP GUIDE ME ON THIS NEW JOURNEY.
IT'S A SIGN.
I MIGHT BE A HARD-HEADED PRAGMATIST, BUT I KNOW THAT SOME THINGS DEFY RATIONAL EXPLANATION...
THIS BIRD IS A GOOD OMEN...A NEW FATE AWAITS! I WAS RIGHT TO QUIT MY JOB. COMICS WILL BRING ME FAME AND FORTUNE.
THAT'S THE ONLY INTERPRETATION I CAN FIND FOR IT.
ALL I NEED TO DO IS GET STARTED.
MAYBE I SHOULD GO SEE A MOVIE FIRST, JUST TO CLEAR MY HEAD...

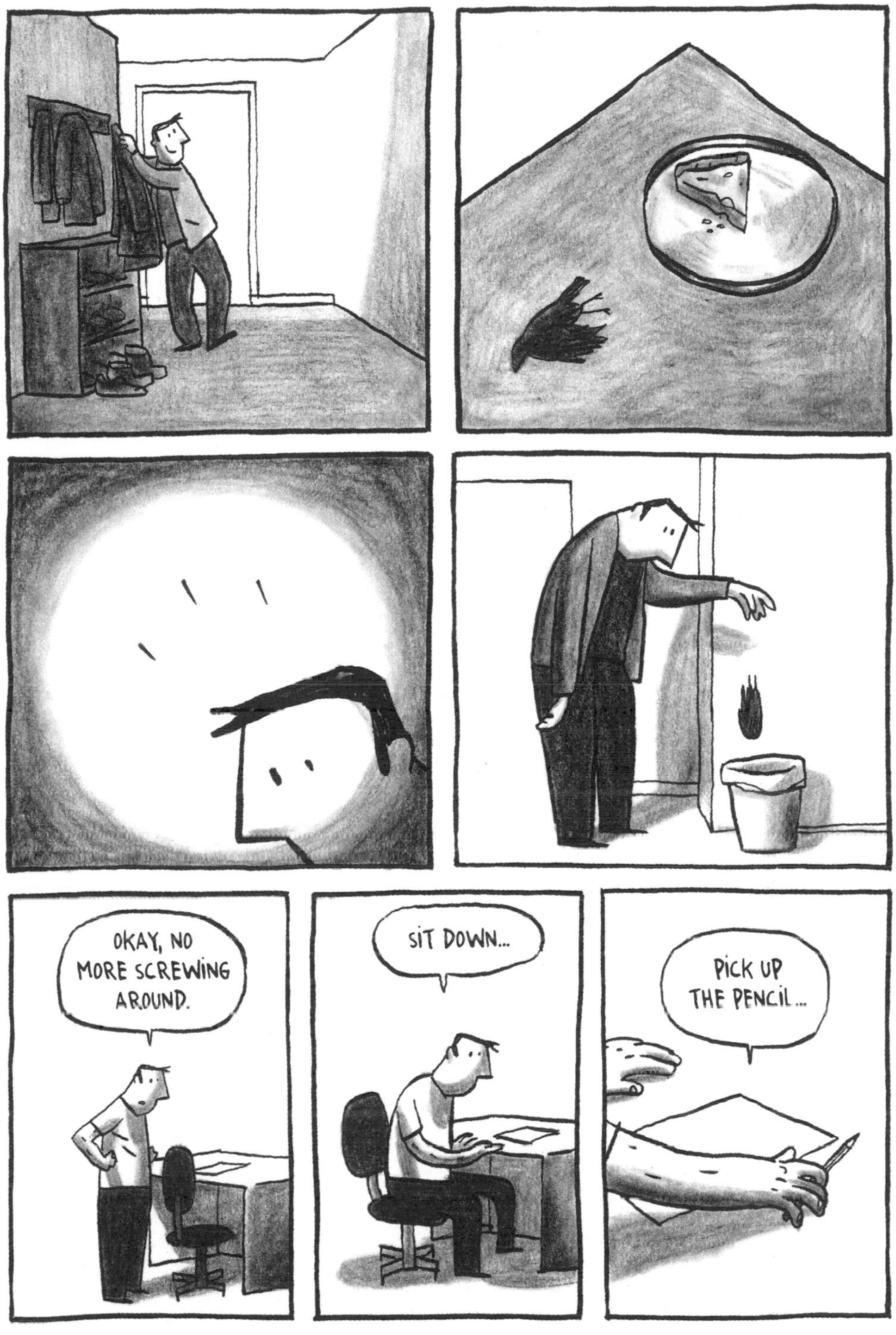
OKAY, NO MORE SCREWING AROUND.
SIT DOWN...
PICK UP THE PENCIL...

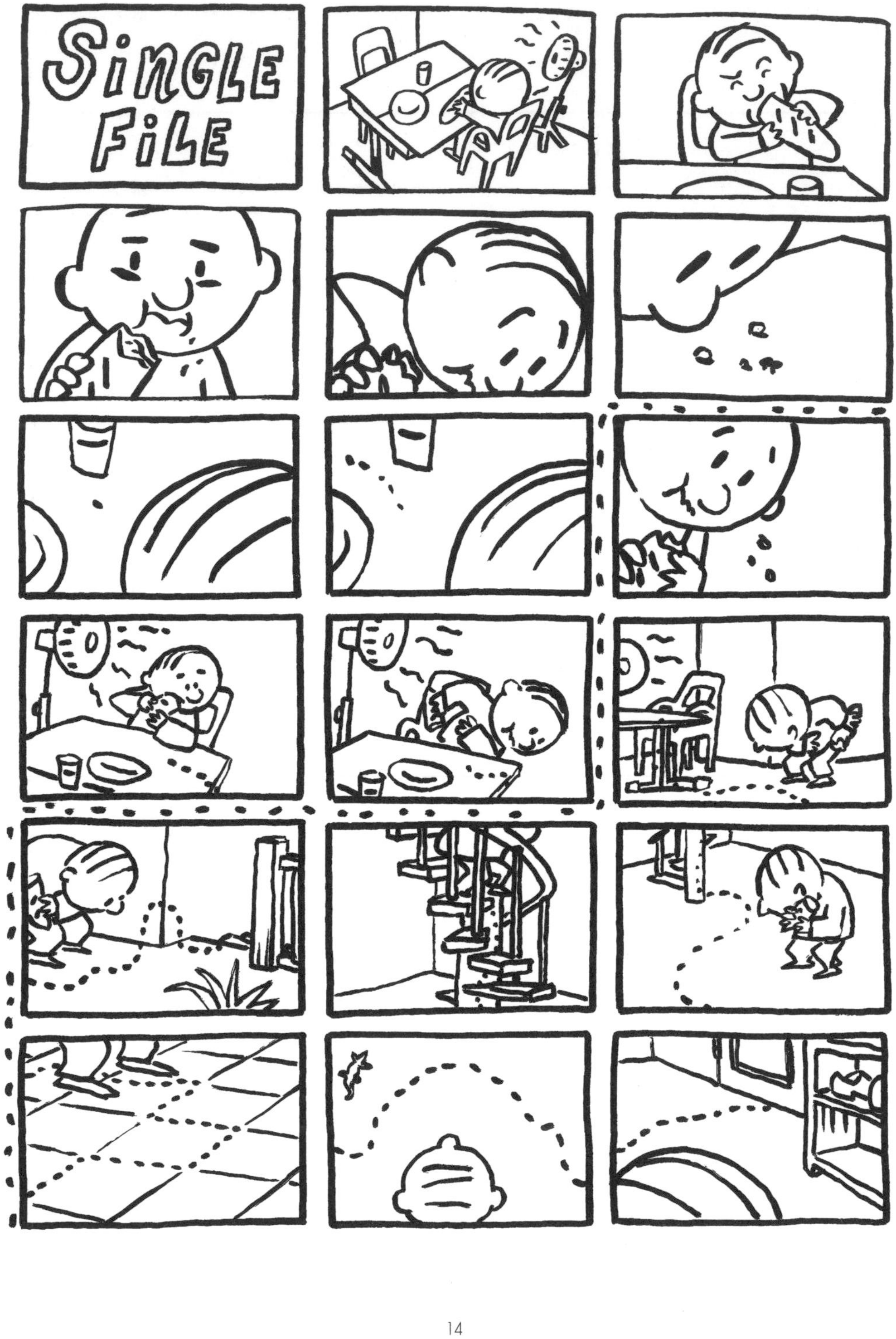
SINGLE FILE

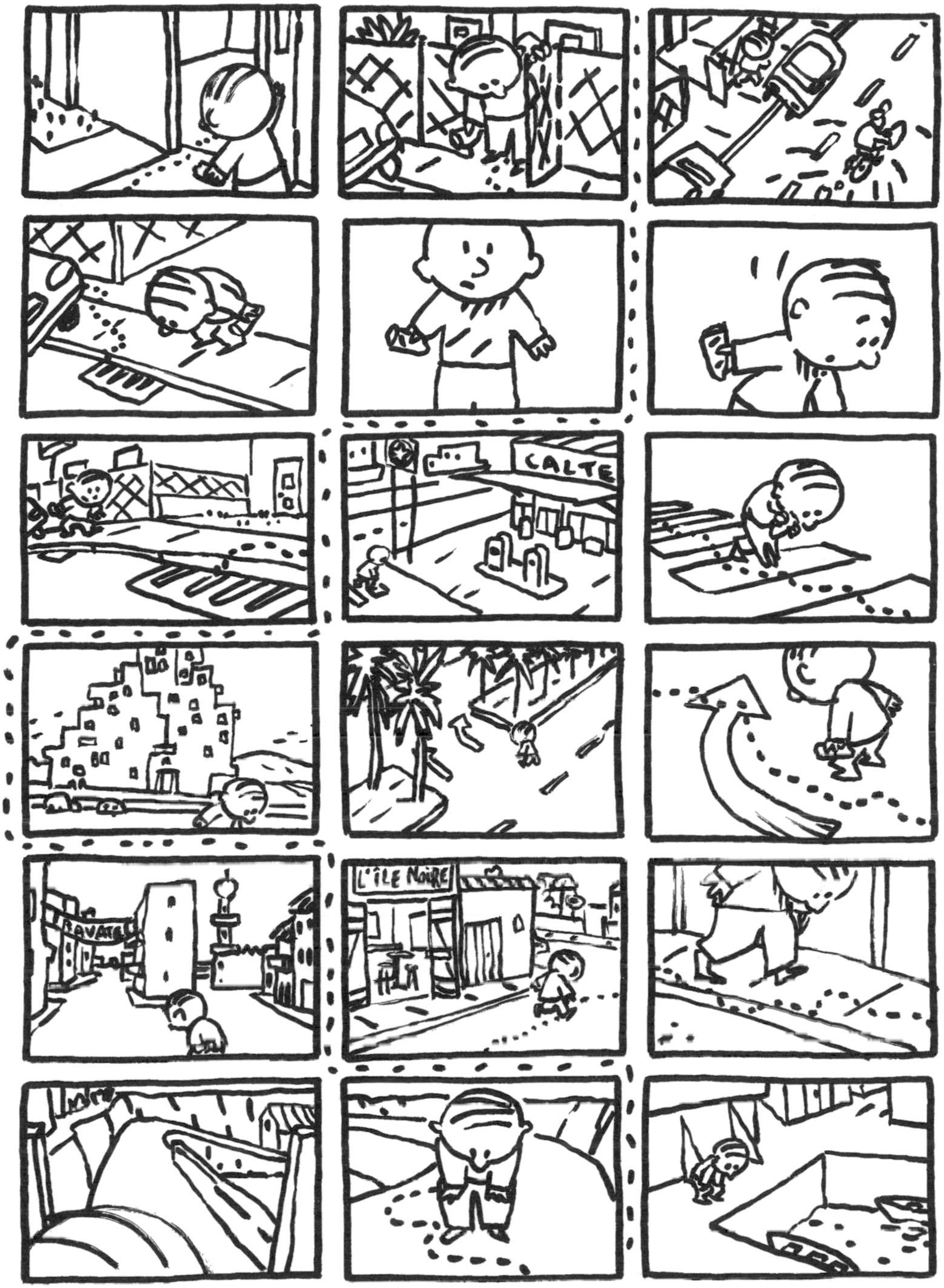
CALTE
RAVATE
L'ÎLE NOIRE

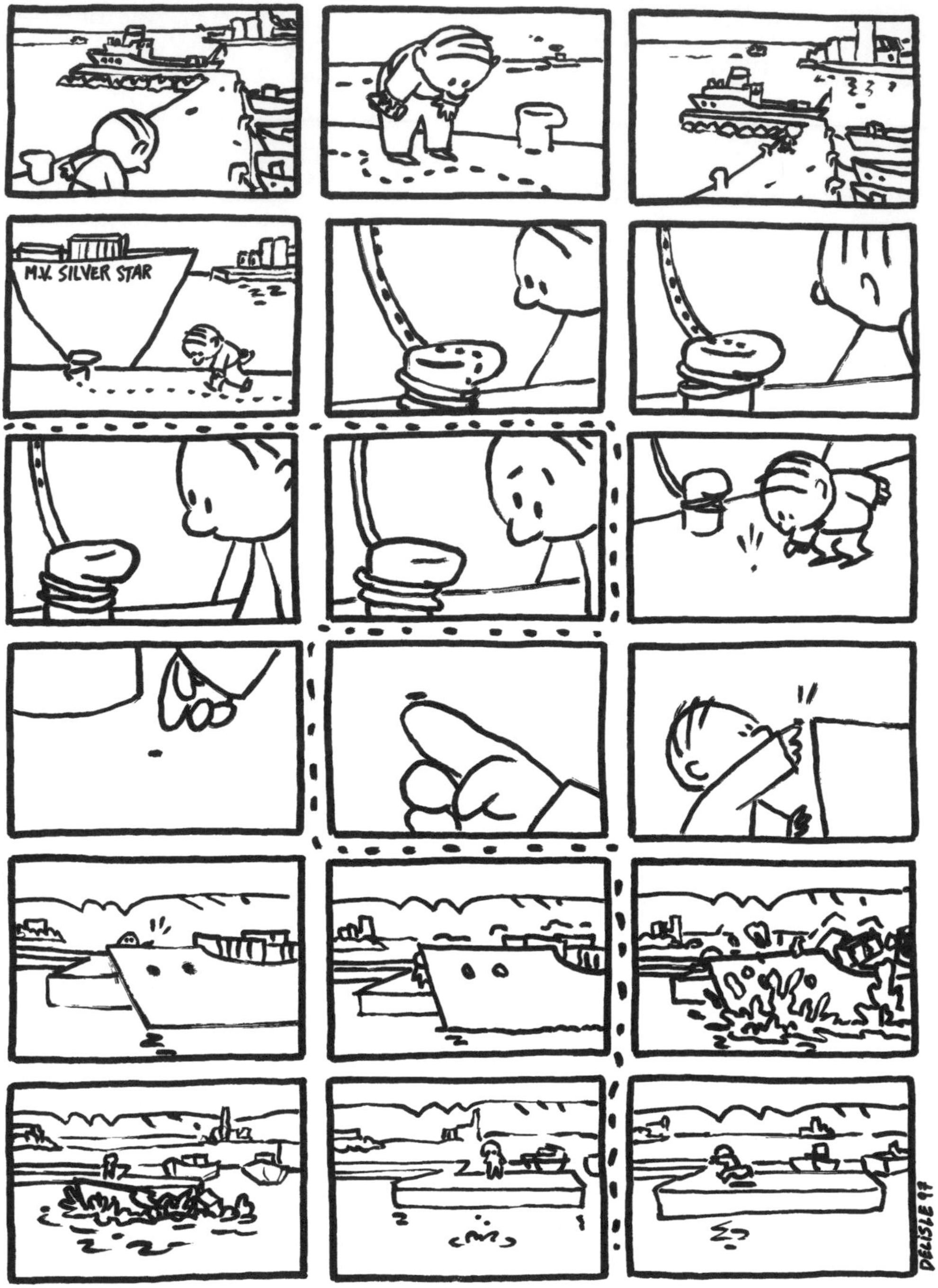
M.V. SILVER STAR
DELISLE 97

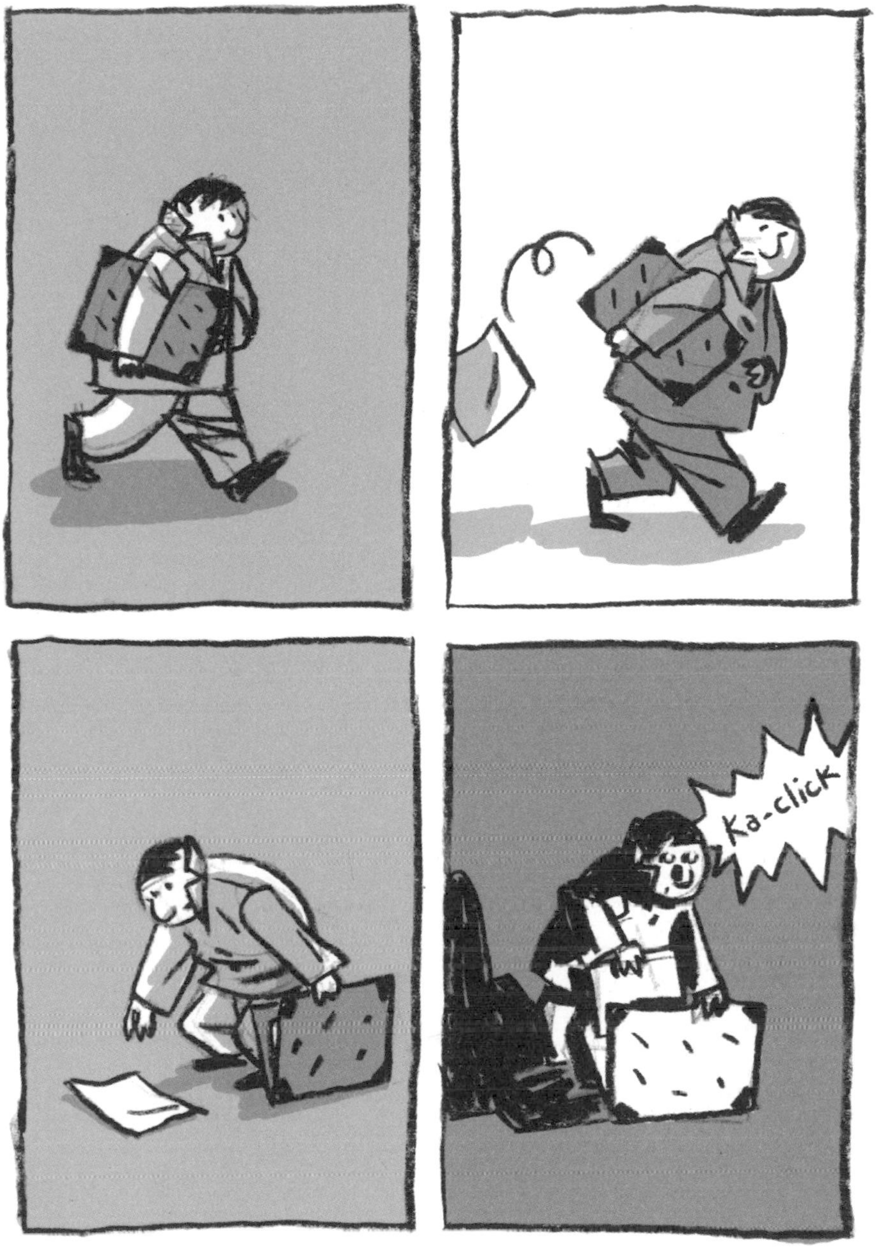
Ka-click

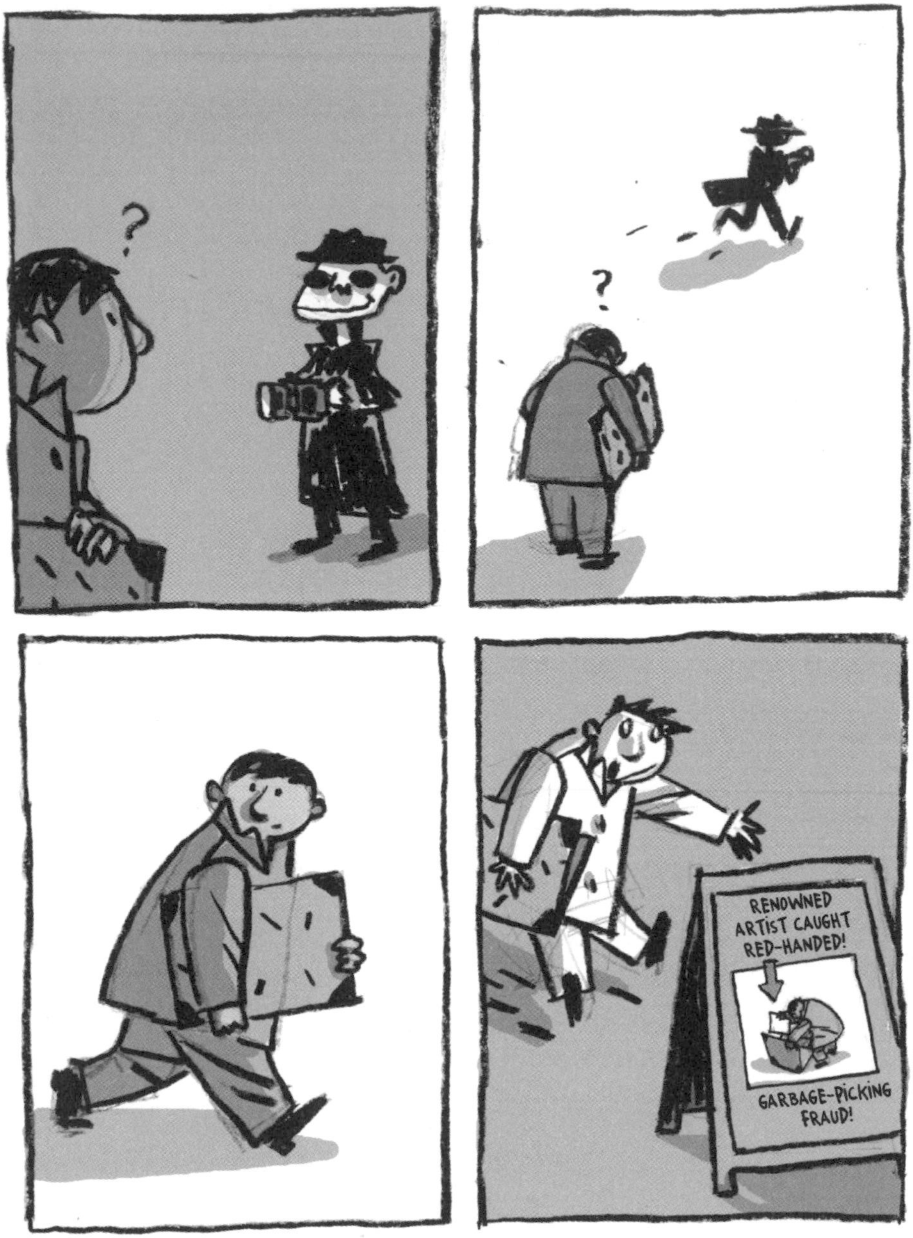
?
?
RENOWNED ARTIST CAUGHT RED-HANDED!
GARBAGE-PICKING FRAUD!

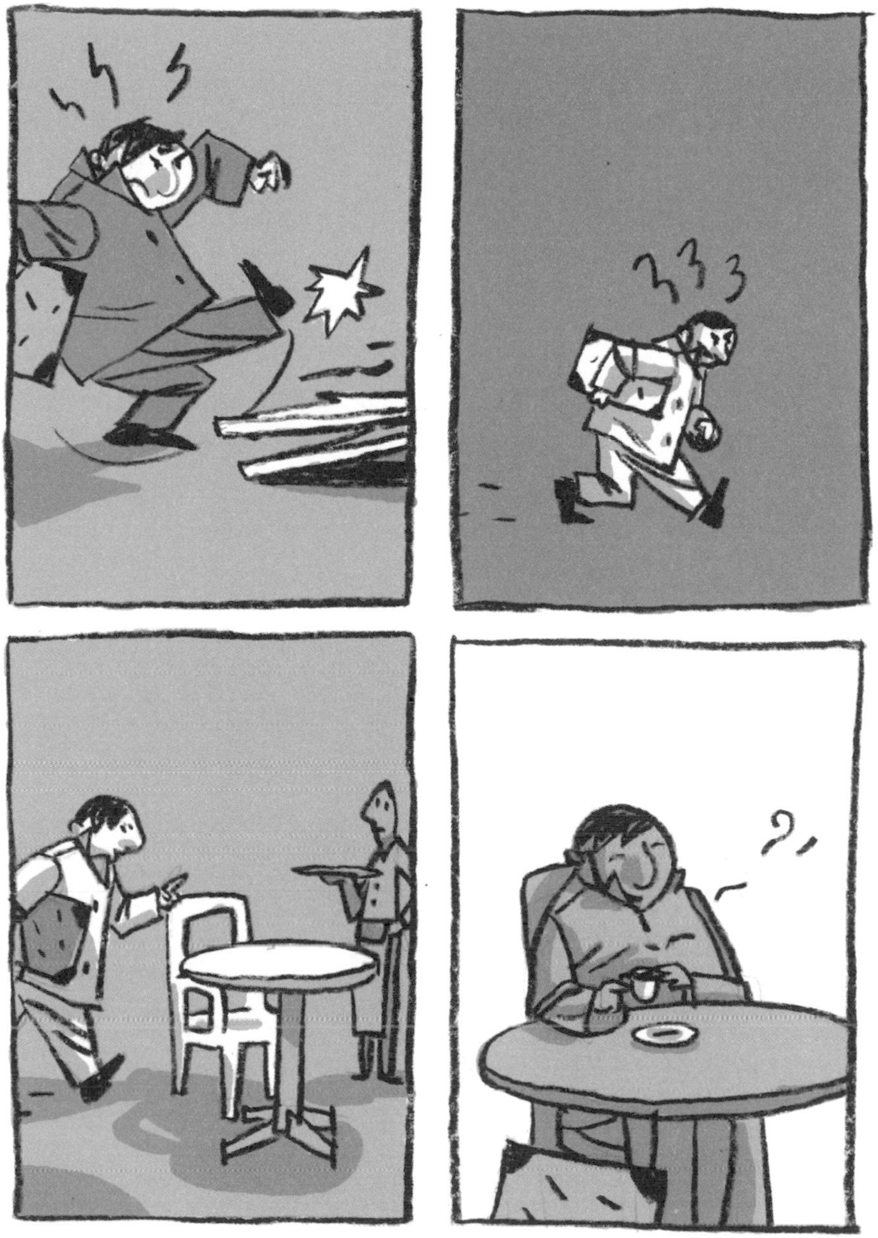

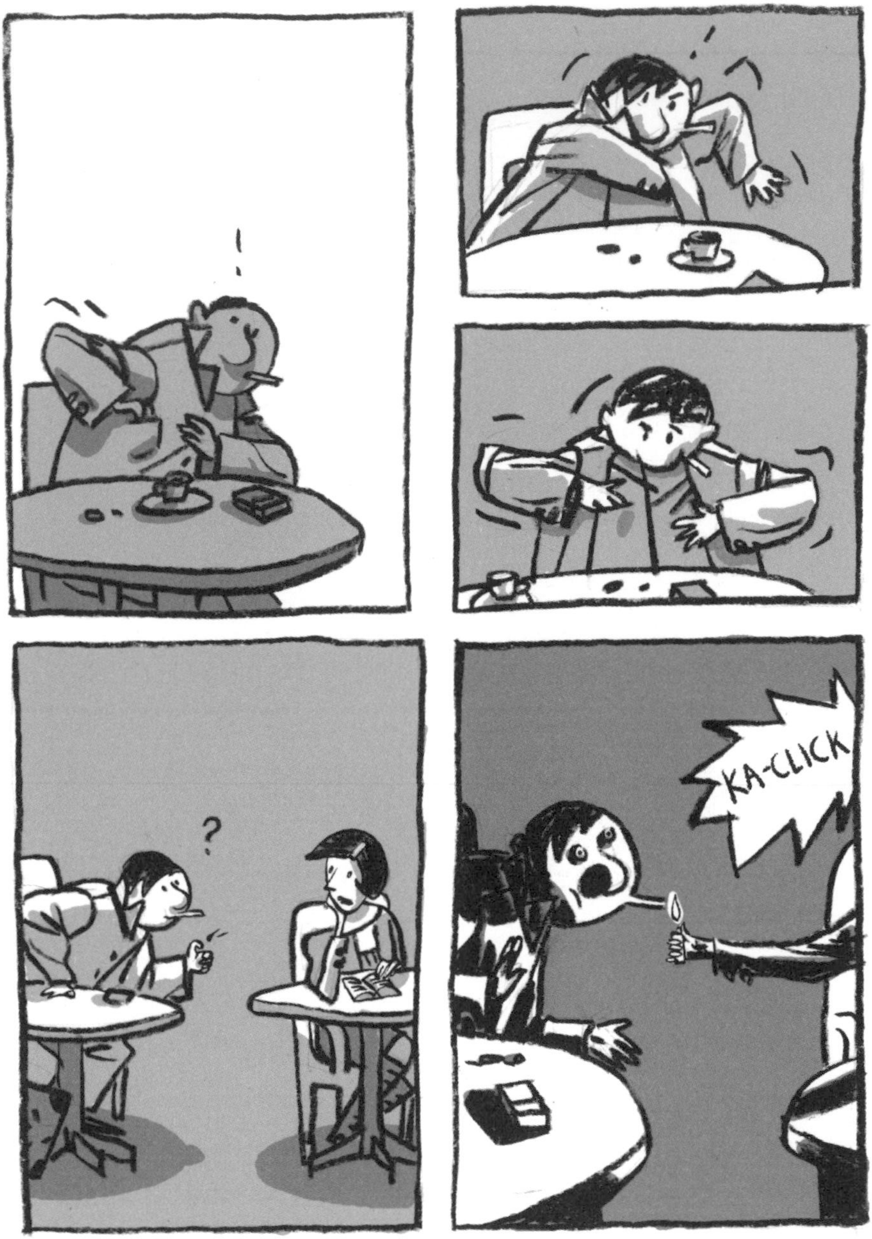
?
KA-CLICK

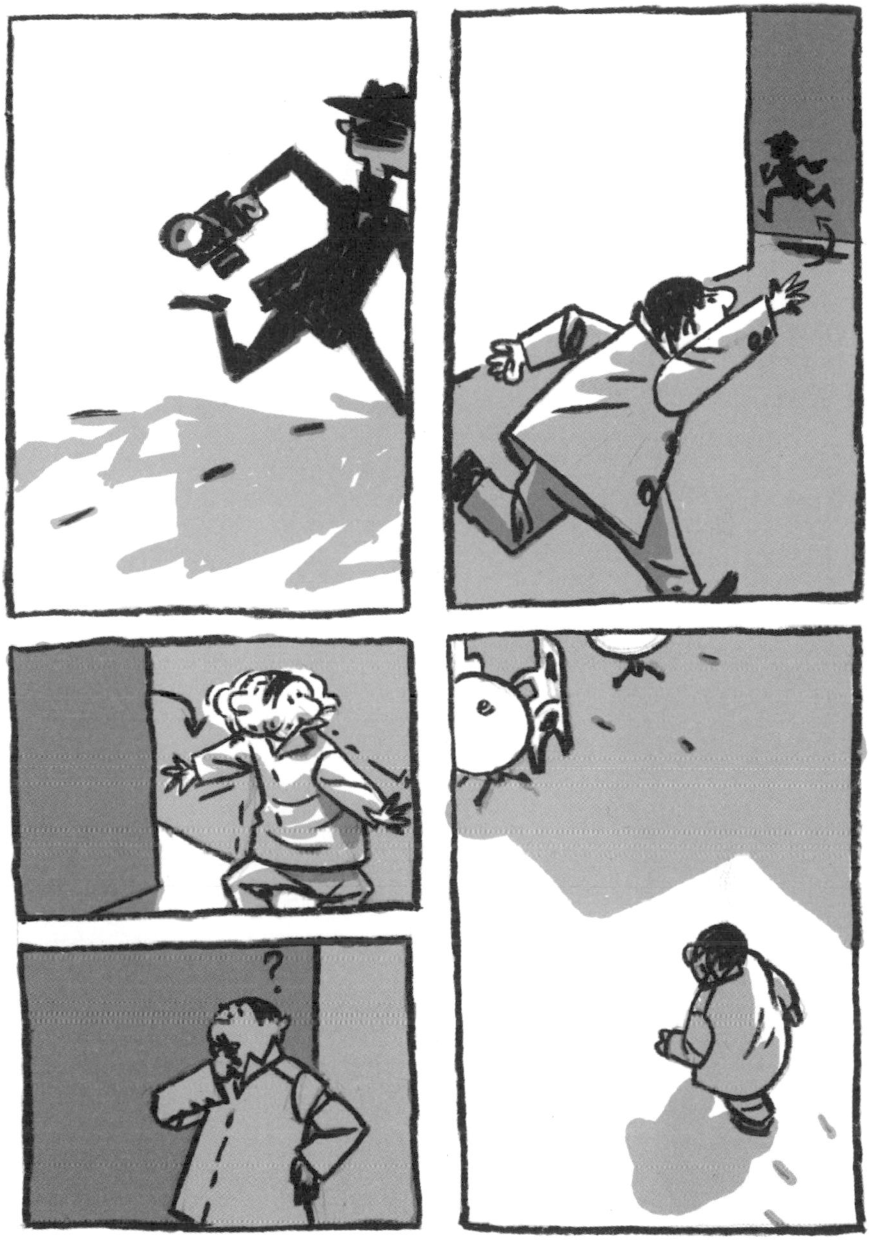
?

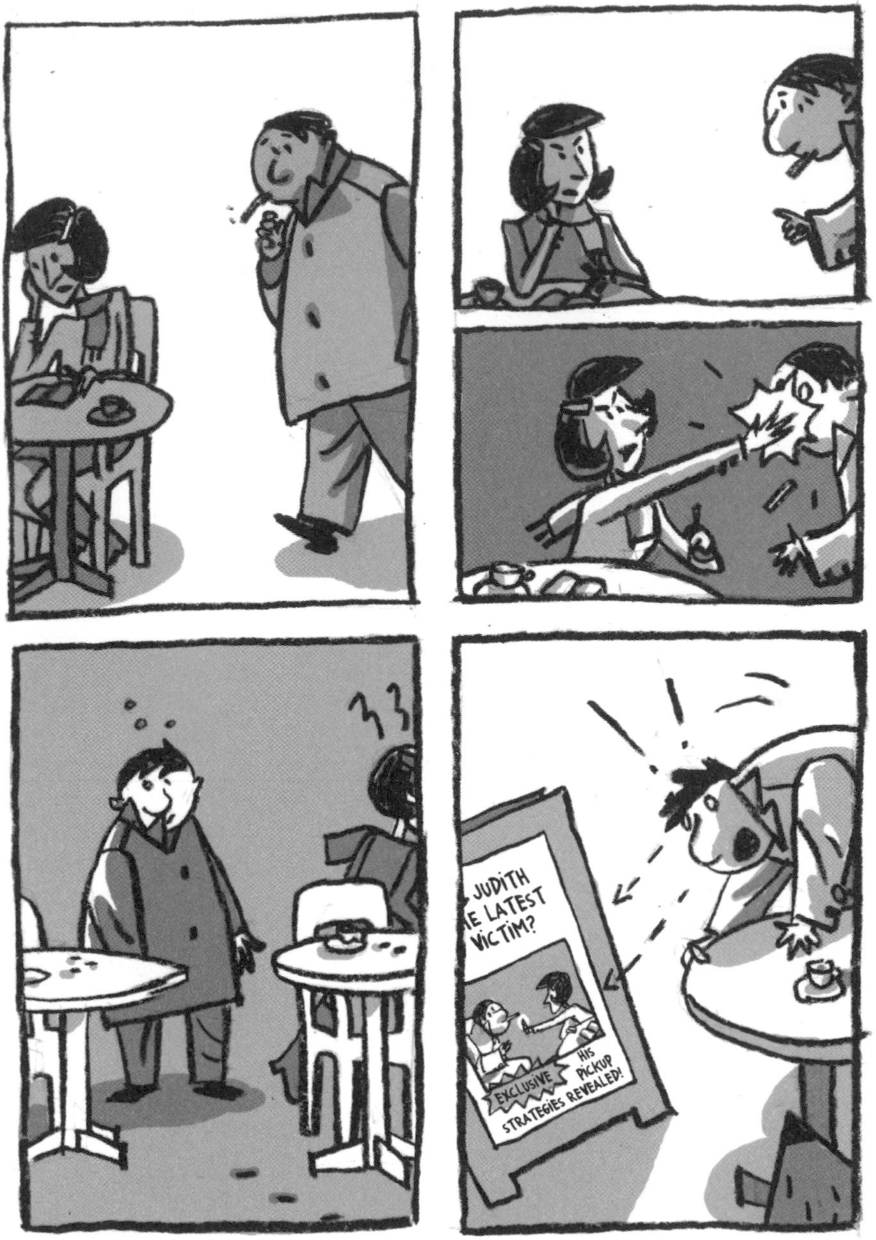
JUDITH
E LATEST
VICTIM?
EXCLUSIVE
HIS PICKUP STRATEGIES REVEALED!

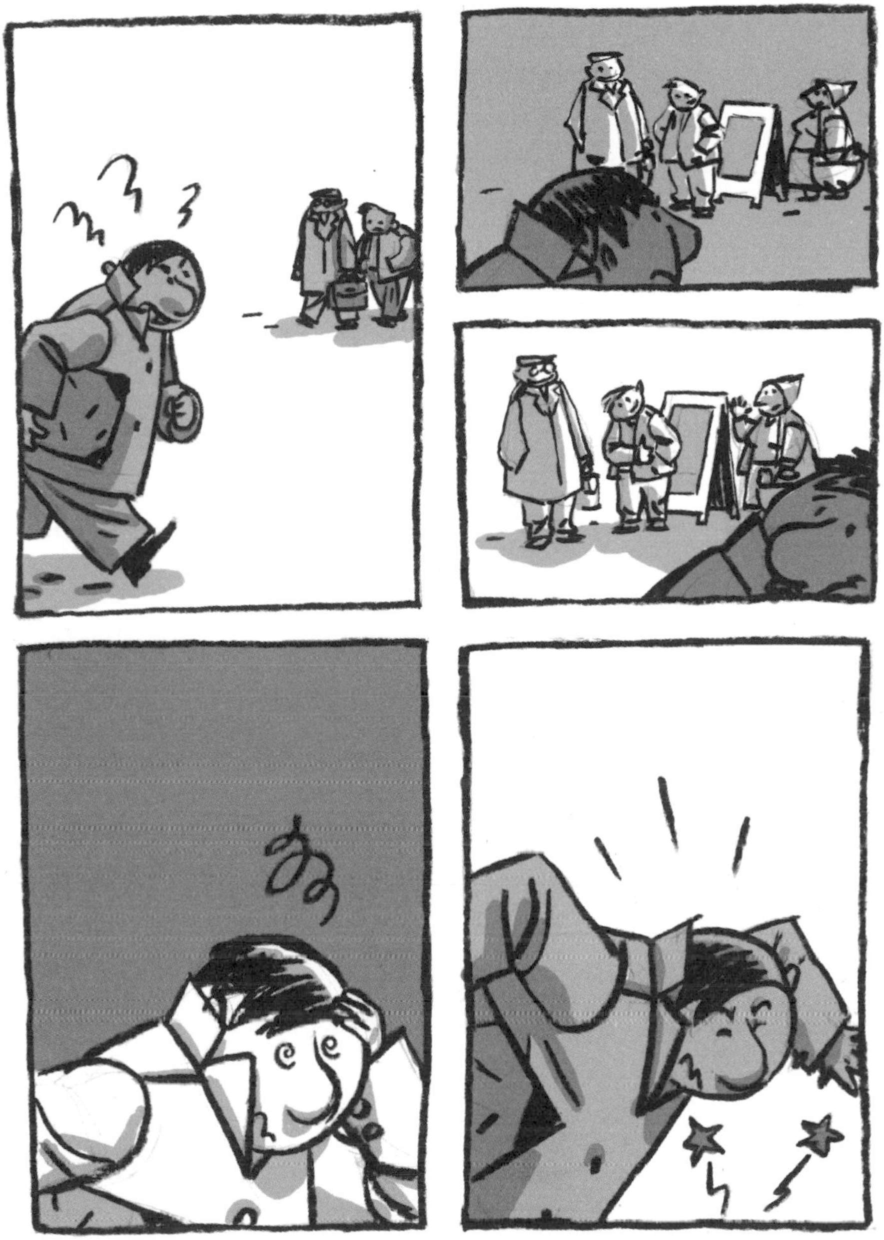

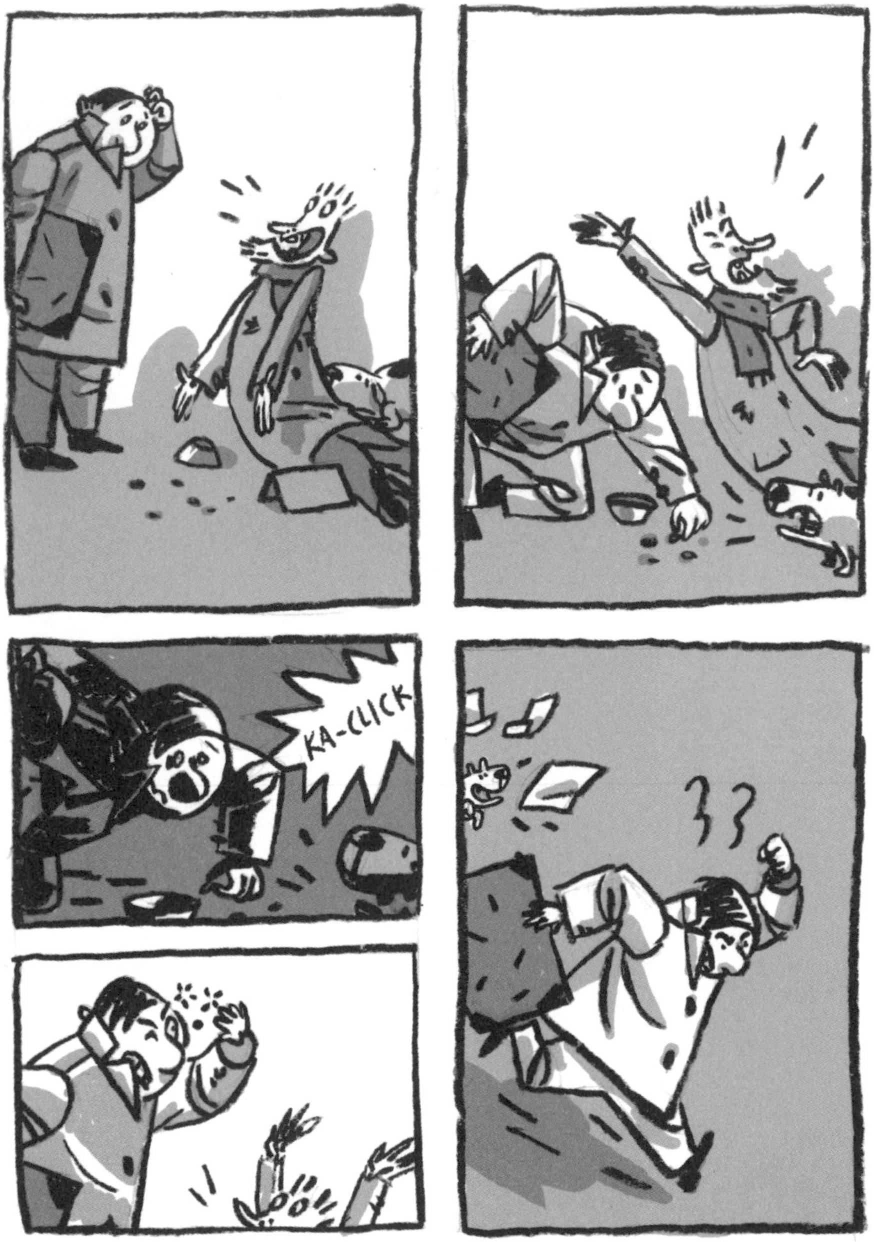
KA-CLICK

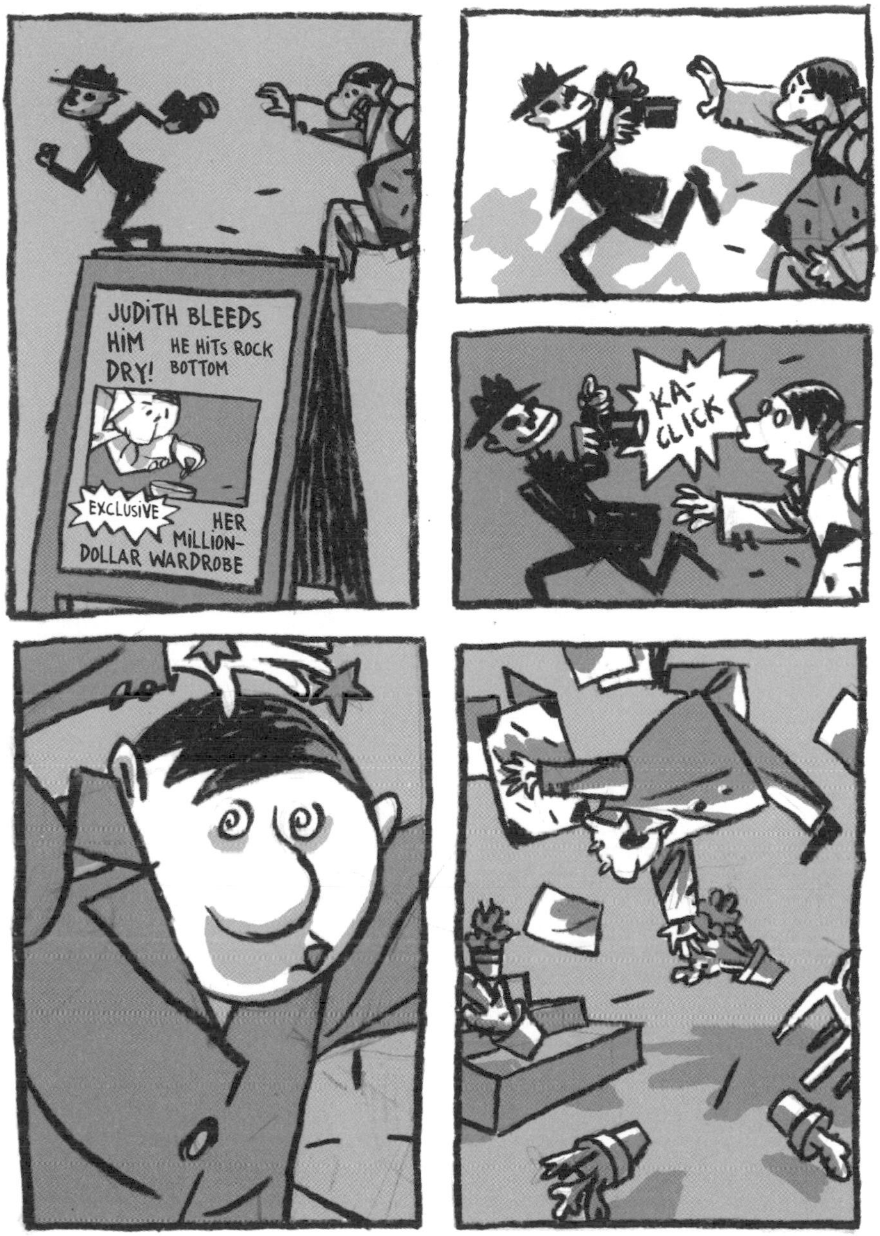
JUDITH BLEEDS HIM DRY!
HE HITS ROCK BOTTOM
EXCLUSIVE
HER MILLION-DOLLAR WARDROBE
KA-CLICK

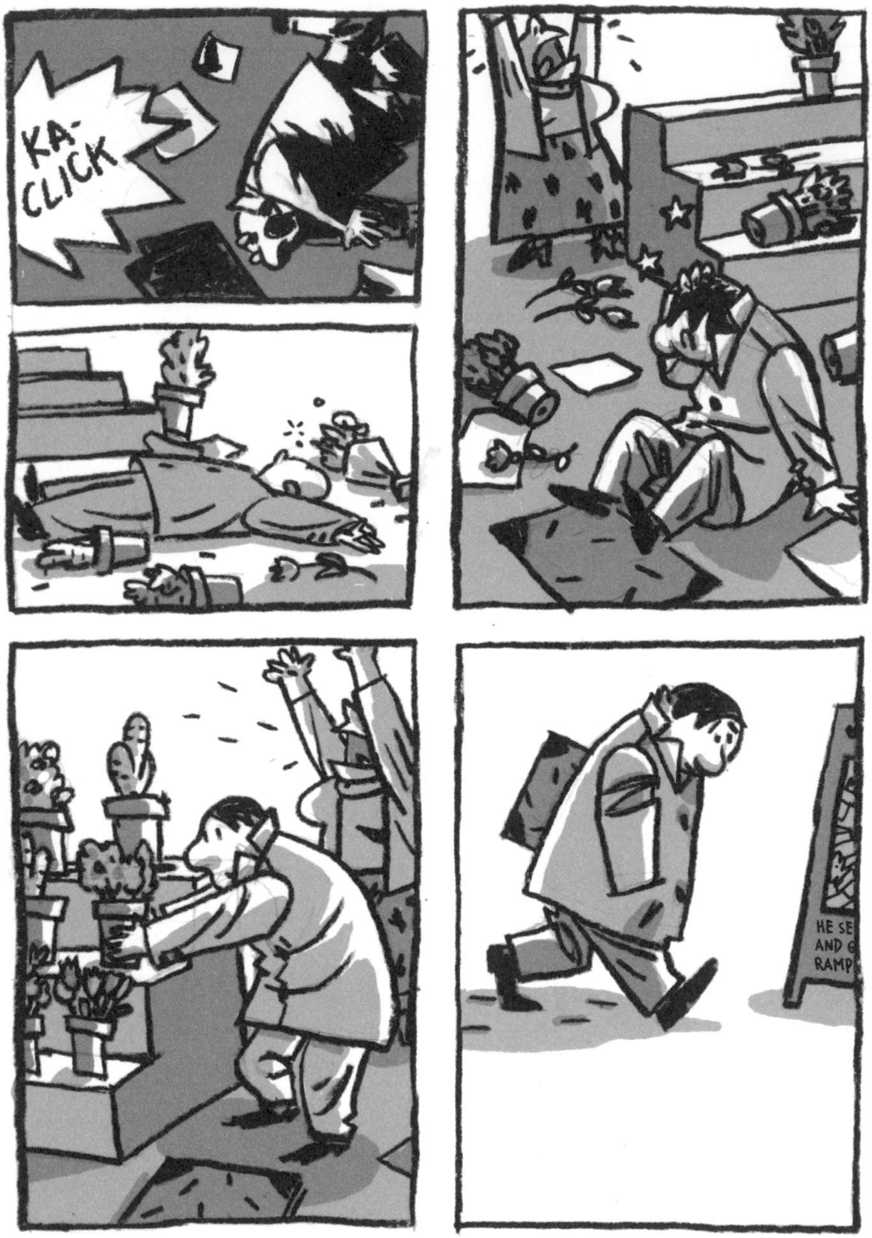
KA-CLICK

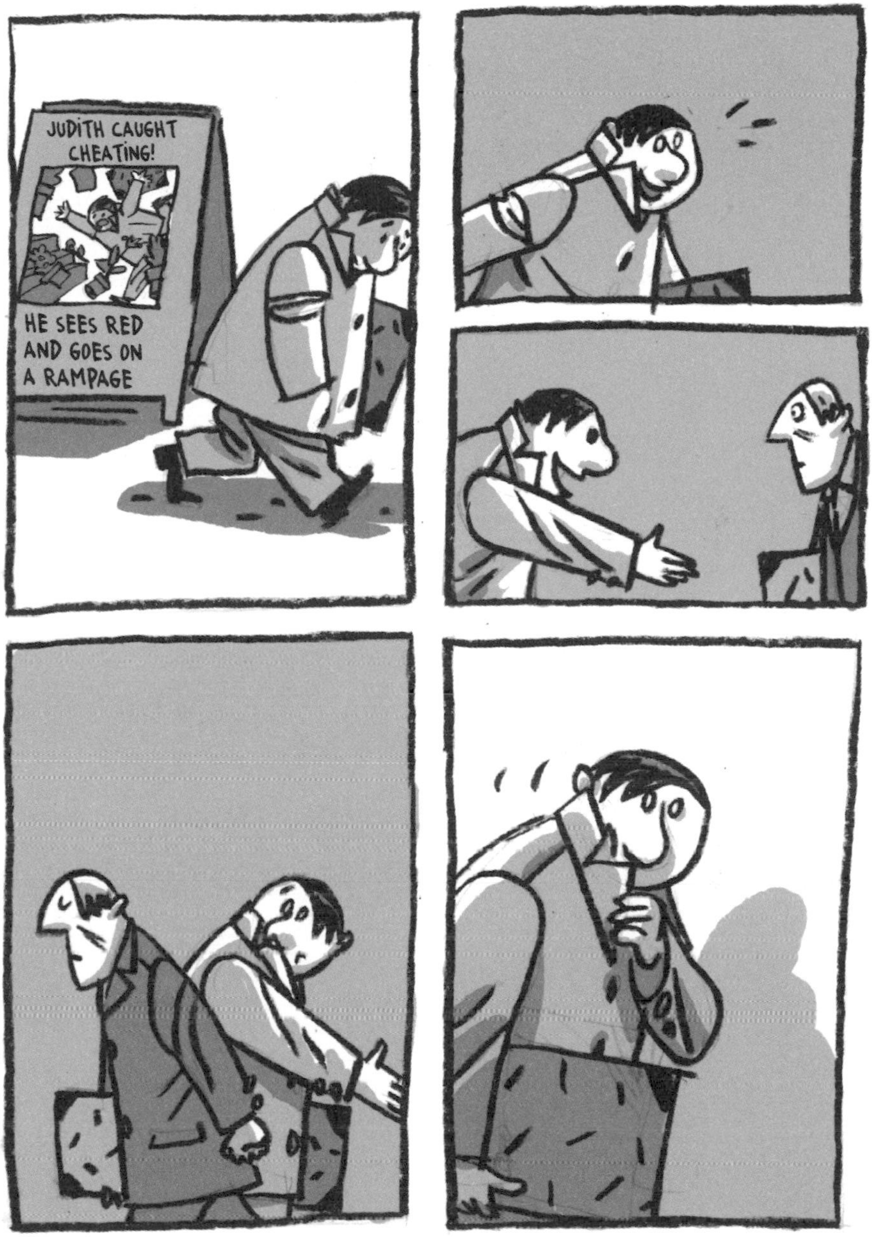
JUDITH CAUGHT CHEATING!
HE SEES RED AND GOES ON A RAMPAGE

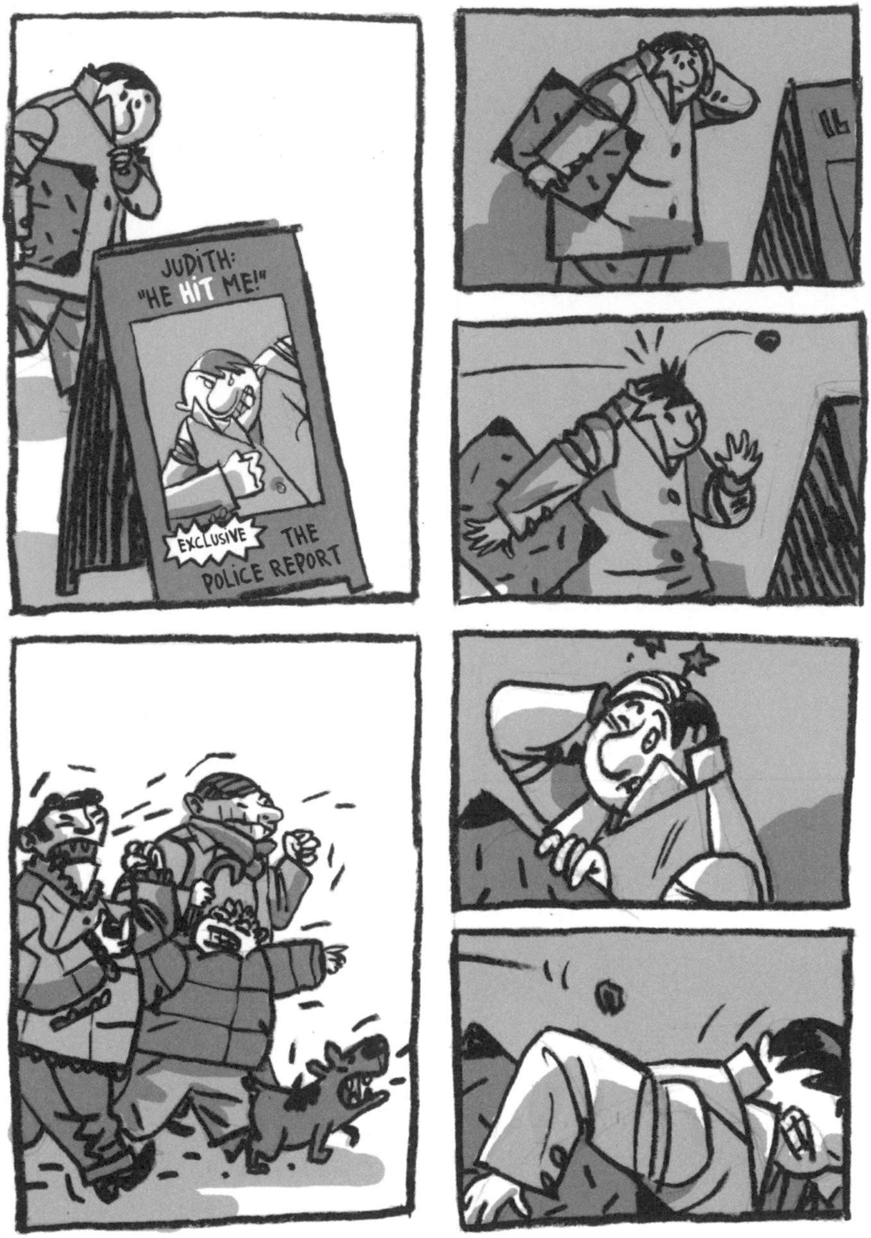
JUDITH:
"HE HIT ME!"
EXCLUSIVE
THE POLICE REPORT

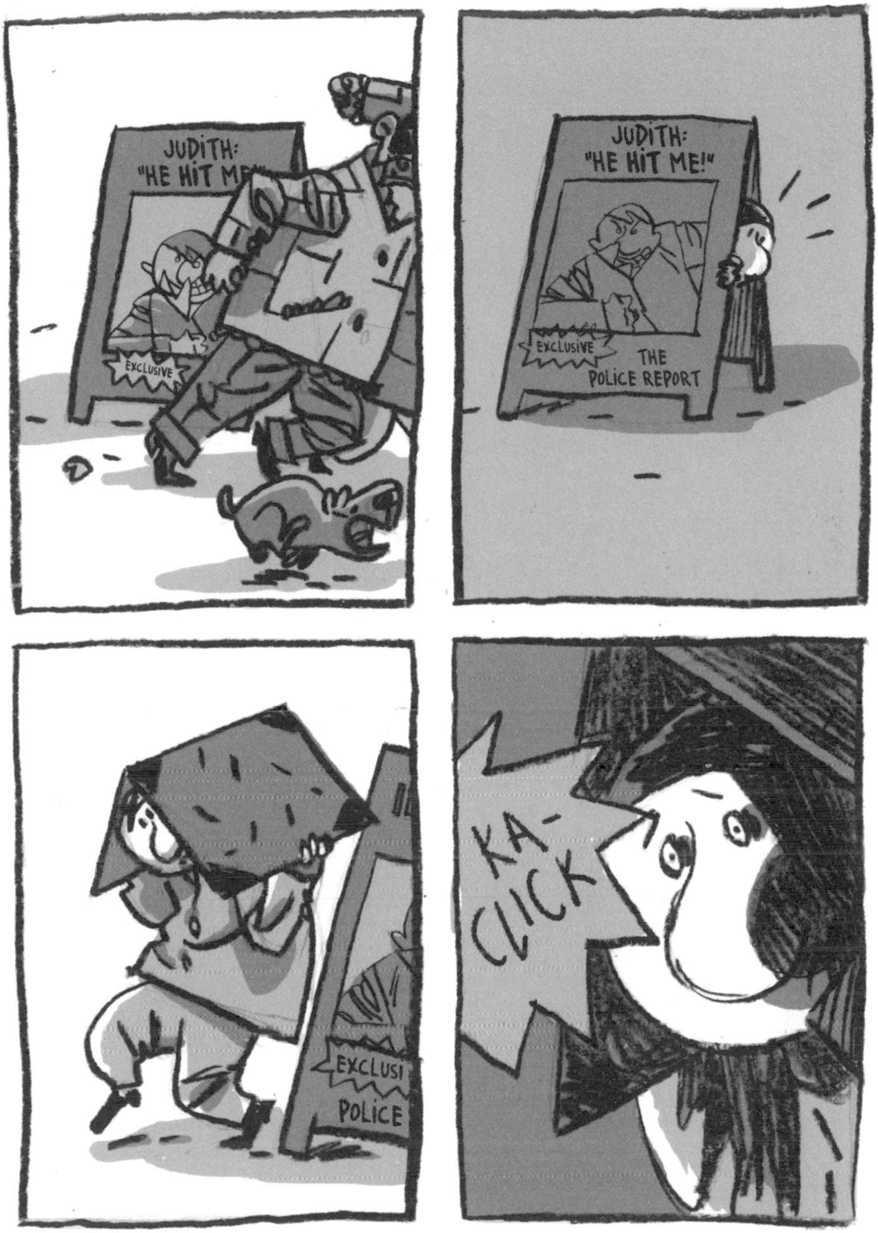
JUDITH:
"HE HIT ME!"
EXCLUSIVE
THE POLICE REPORT
EXCLUSI
POLICE
KA-CLICK

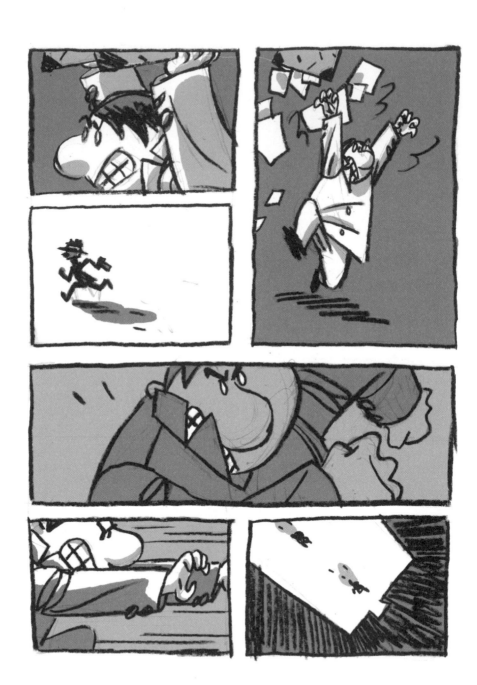

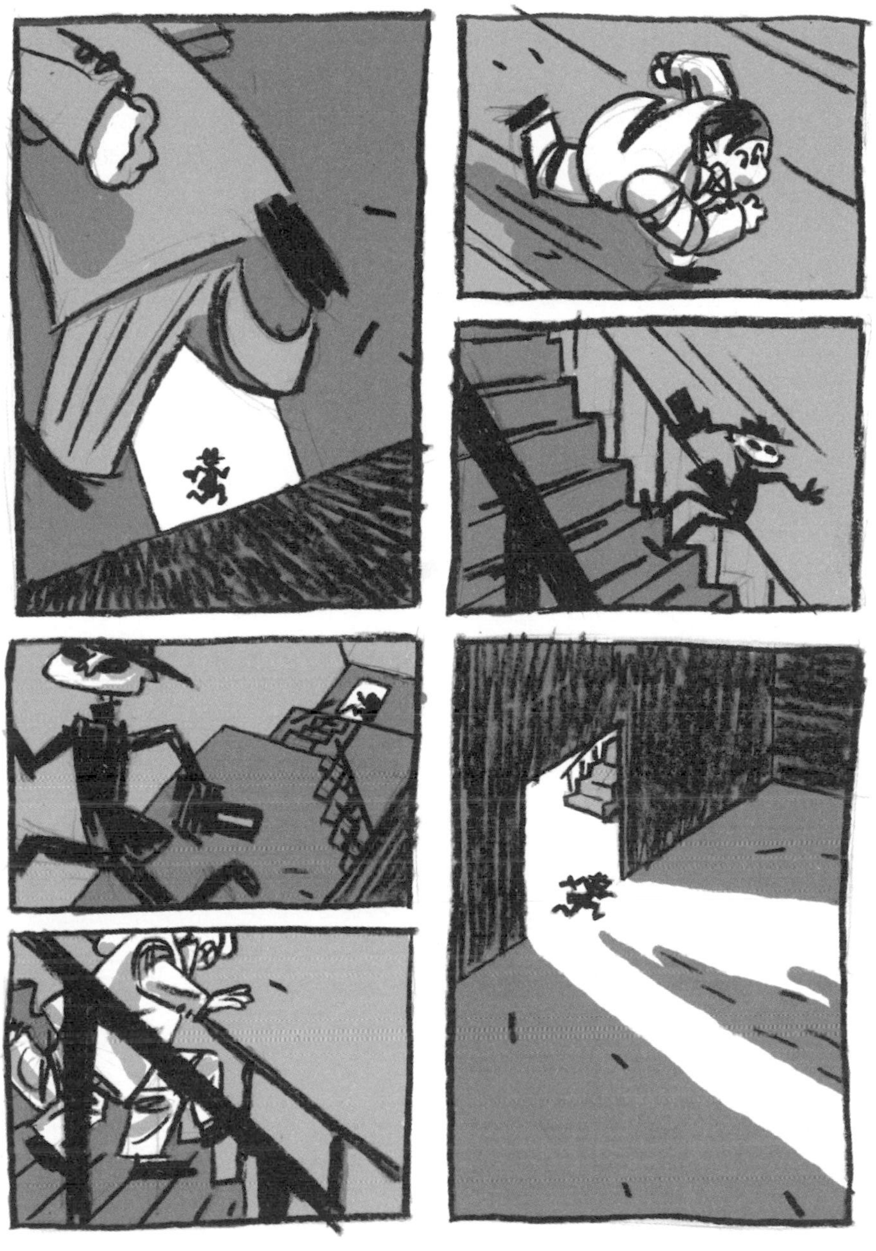

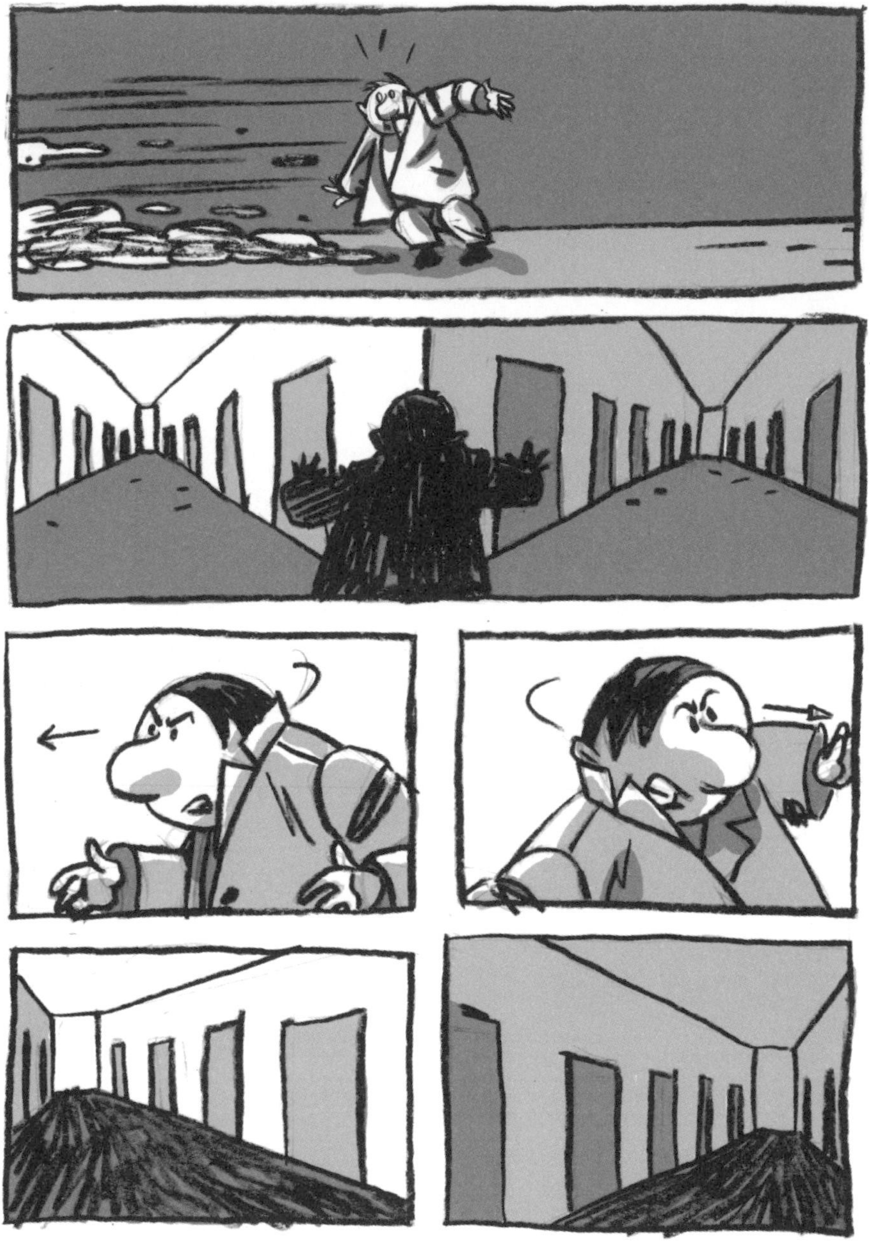

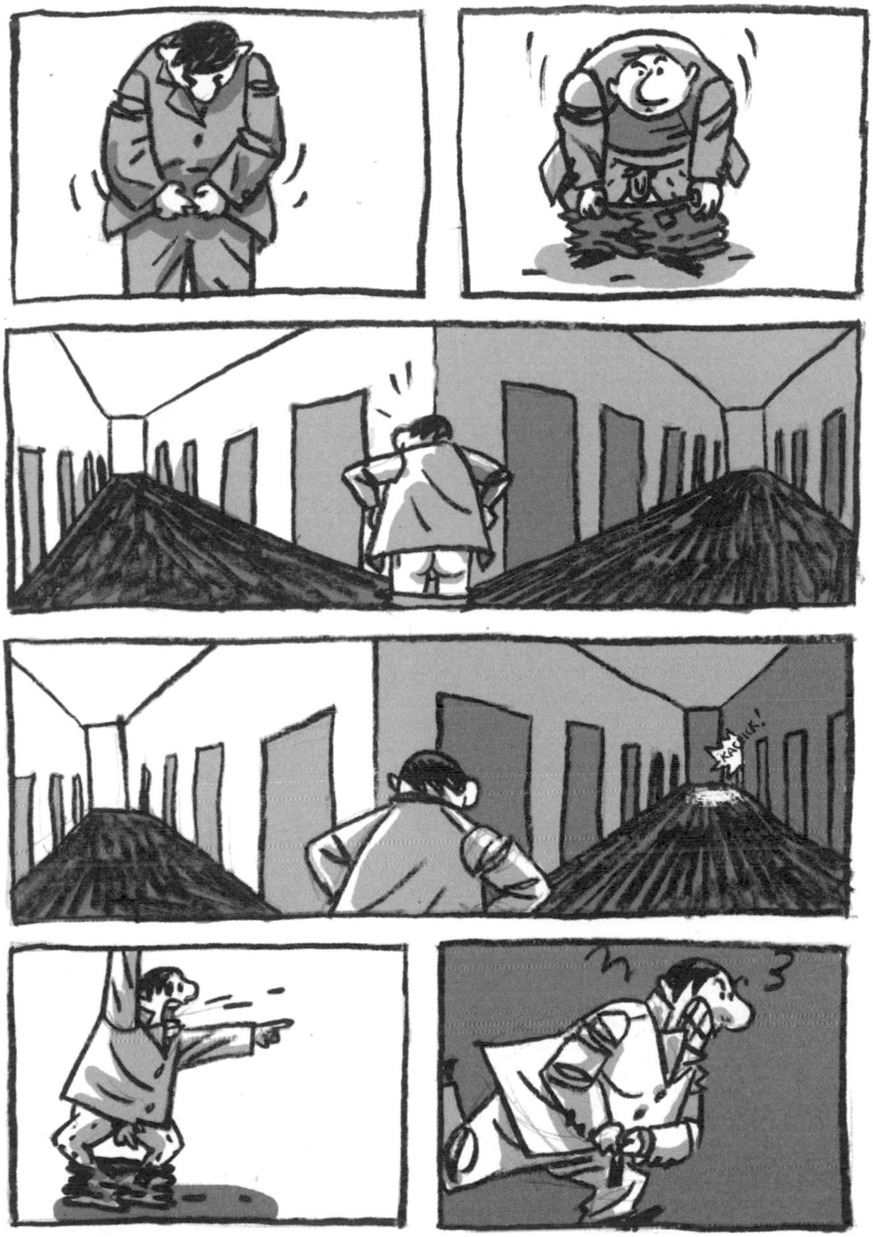
KAC ICK!

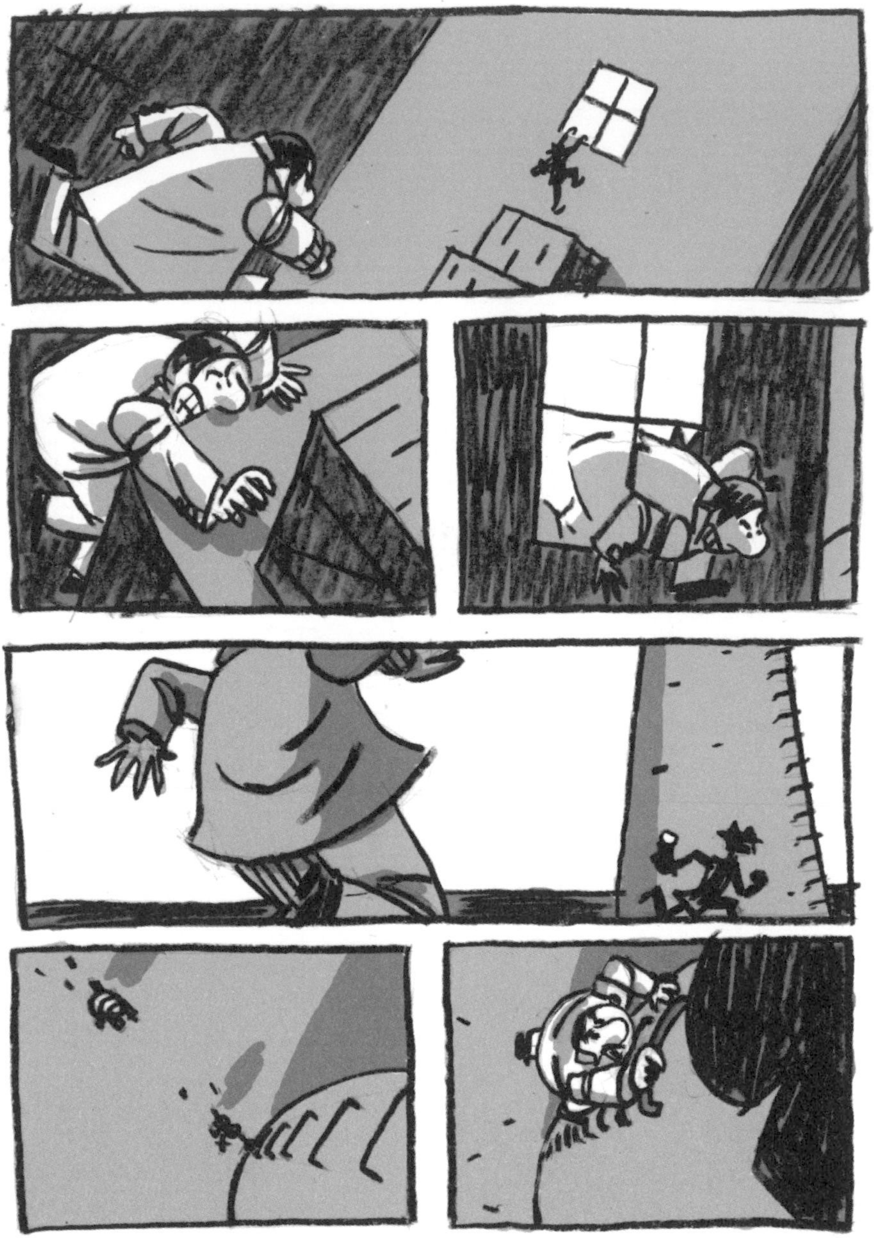

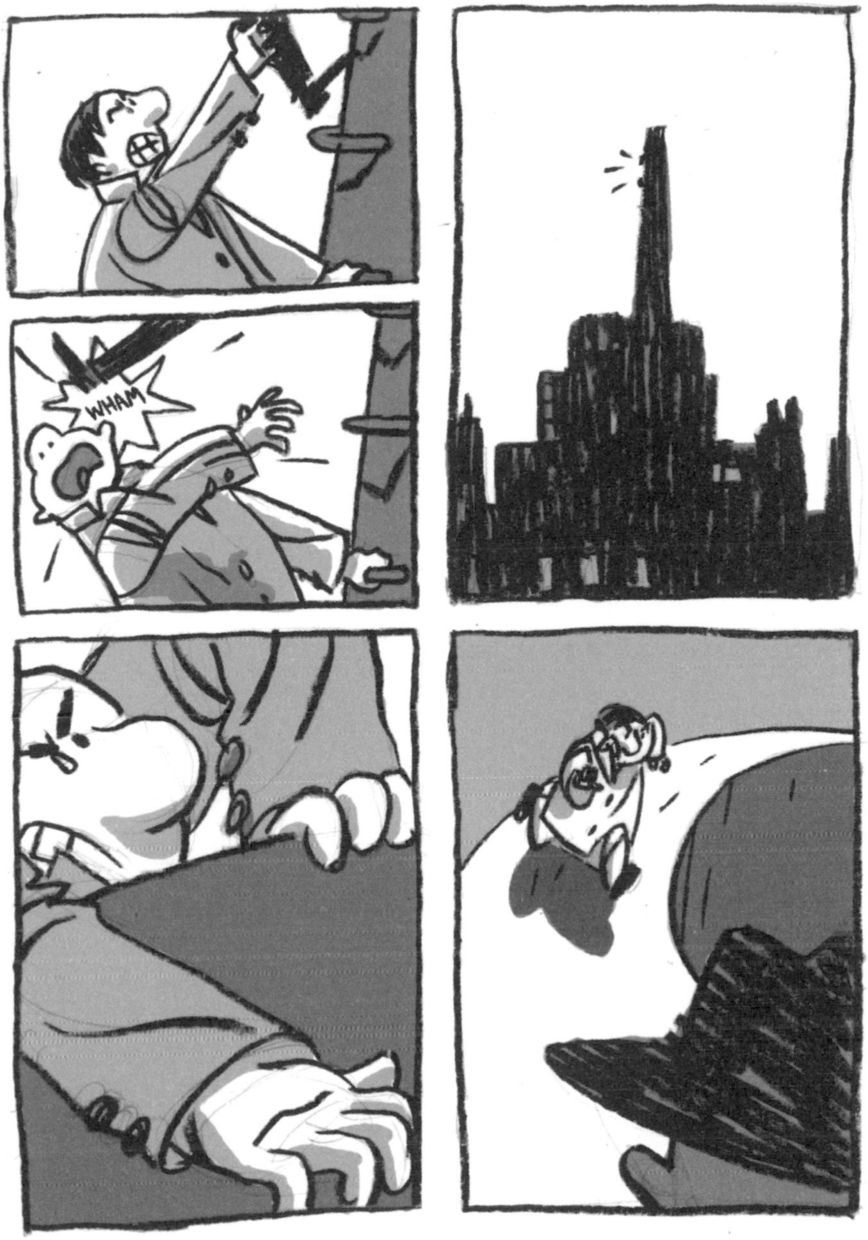
WHAM

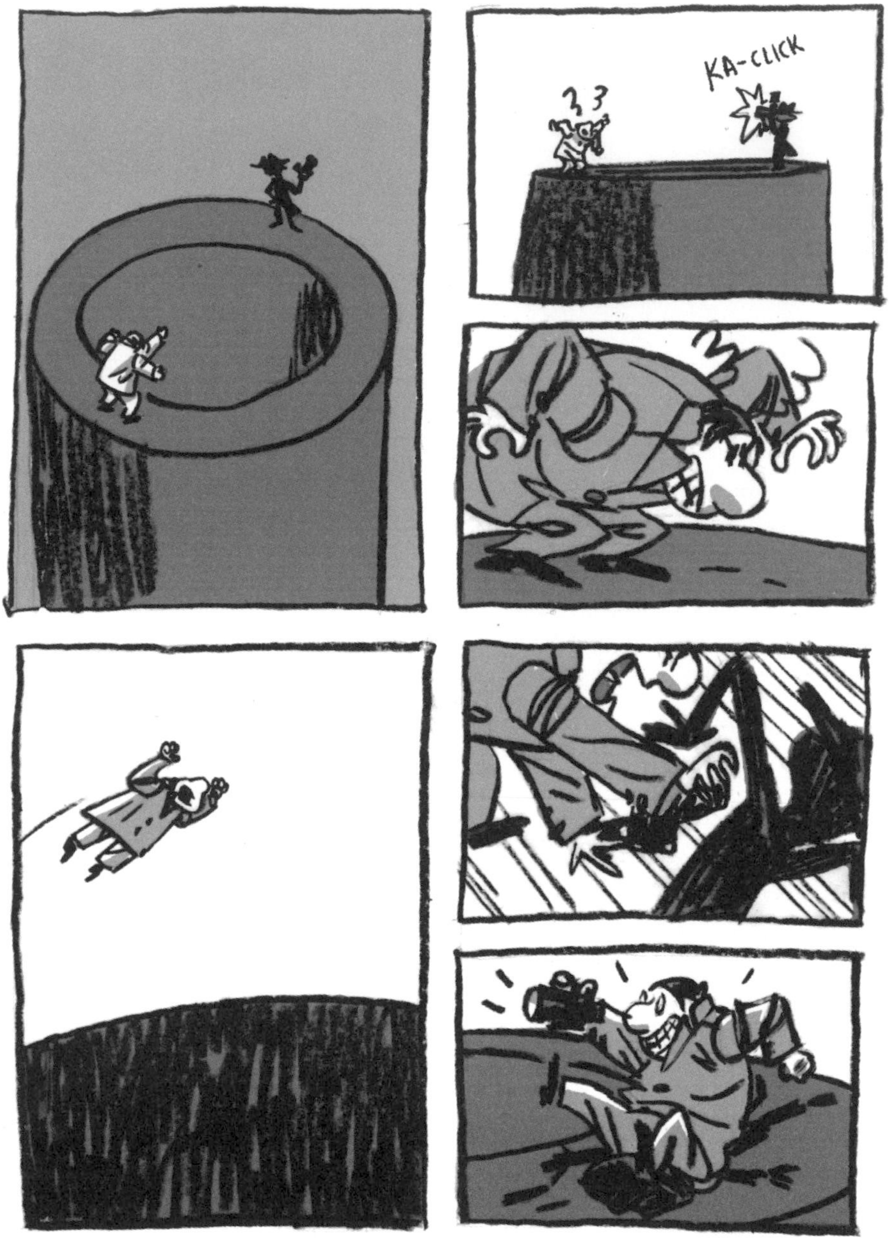
KA-CLICK

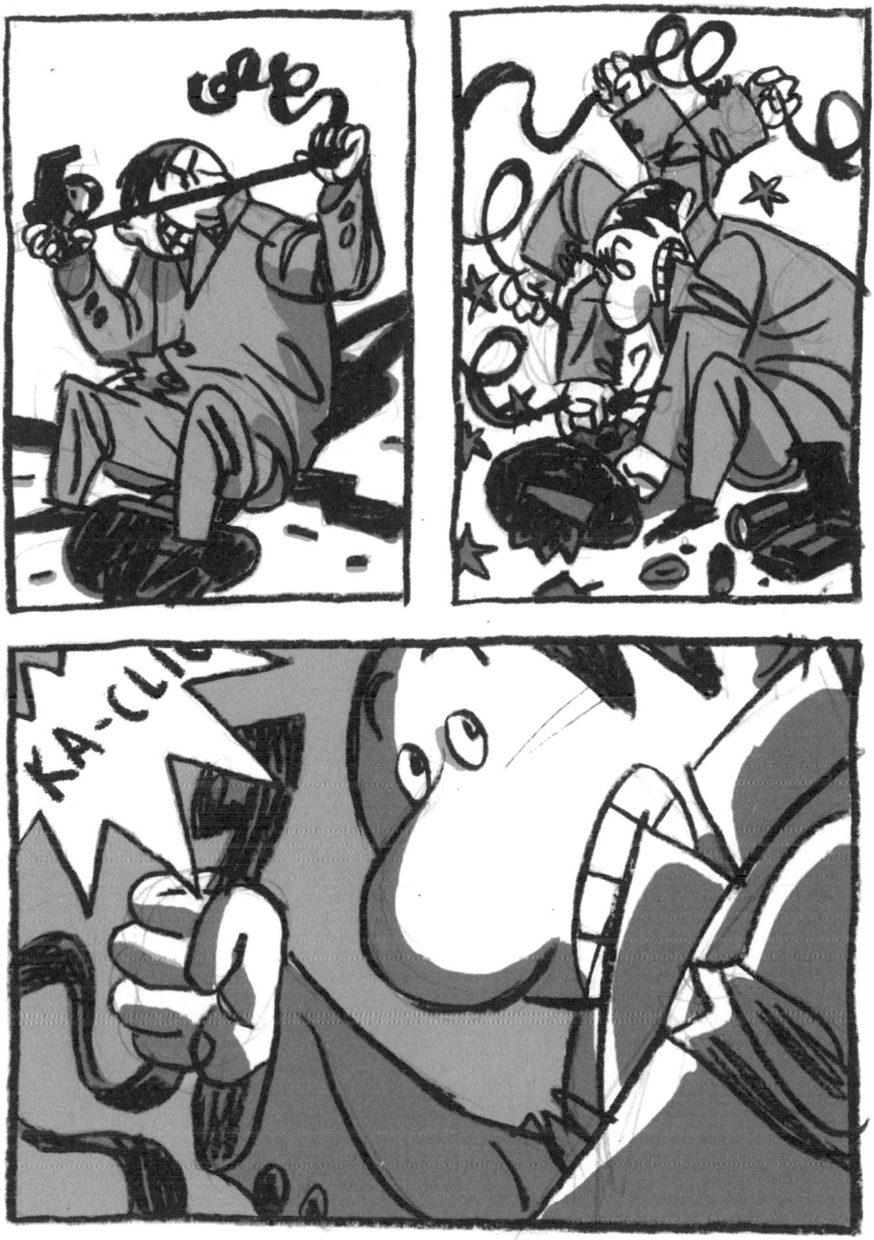
KA-CLI

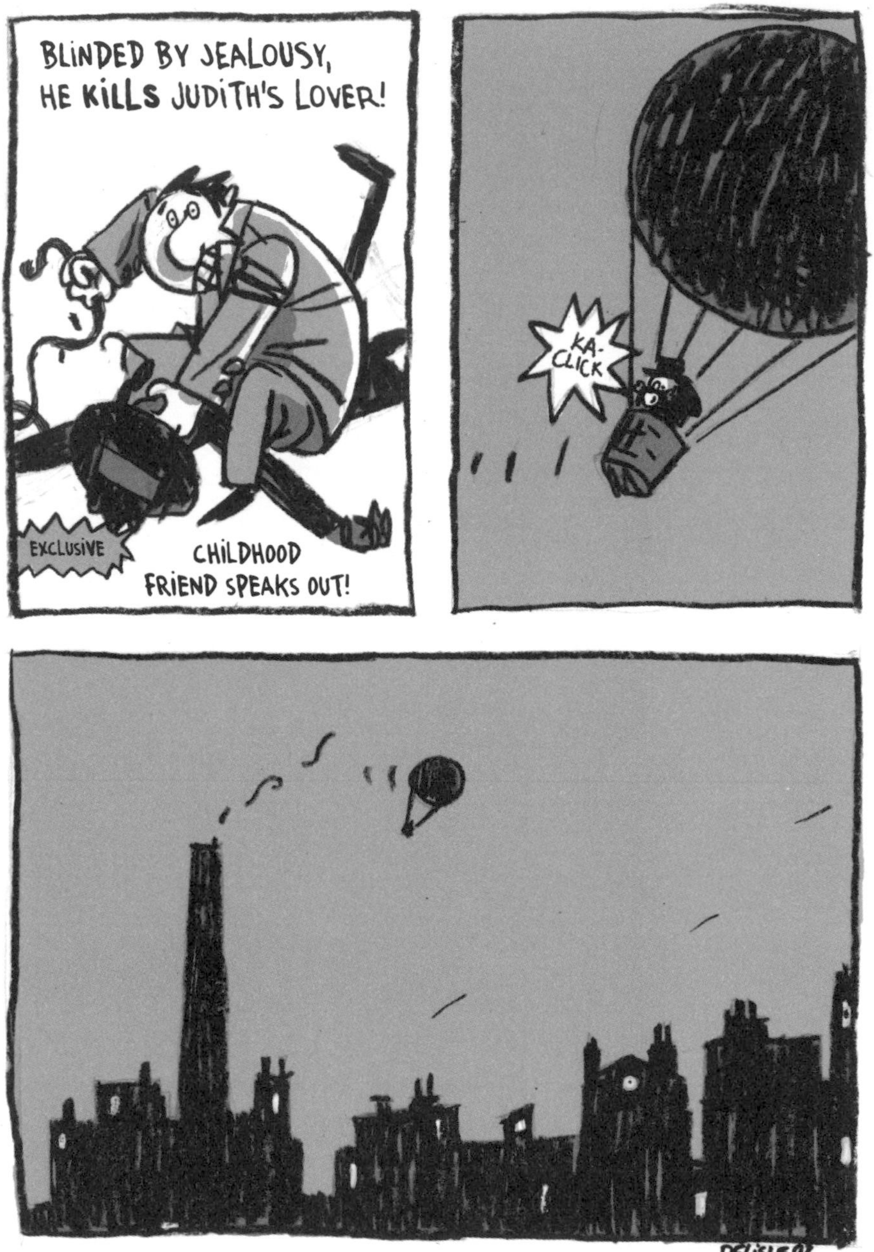
BLINDED BY JEALOUSY, HE KILLS JUDITH'S LOVER!
EXCLUSIVE
CHILDHOOD FRIEND SPEAKS OUT!
KA-CLICK
DELISLE 96

The Floating Dog's Tale

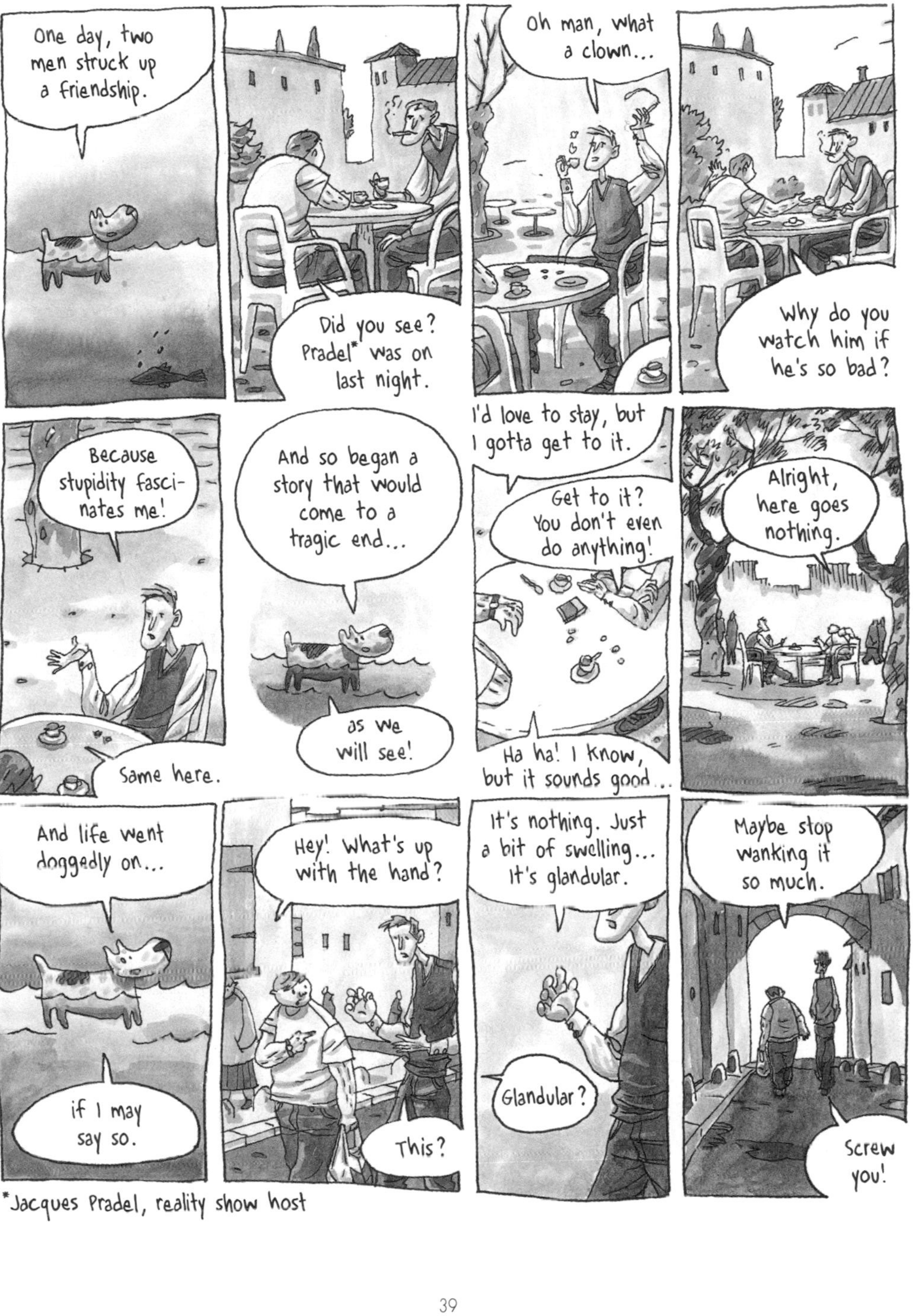
One day, two men struck up a friendship.
Did you see? Pradel* was on last night.
Oh man, what a clown...
Why do you watch him if he's so bad?
Because stupidity fasci-nates me!
Same here.
And so began a story that would come to a tragic end...
as we will see!
I'd love to stay, but I gotta get to it.
Get to it? You don't even do anything!
Ha ha! I know, but it sounds good...
Alright, here goes nothing.
And life went doggedly on...
if I may say so.
Hey! What's up with the hand?
This?
It's nothing. Just a bit of swelling... It's glandular.
Glandular?
Maybe stop wanking it so much.
Screw you!

*Jacques Pradel, reality show host

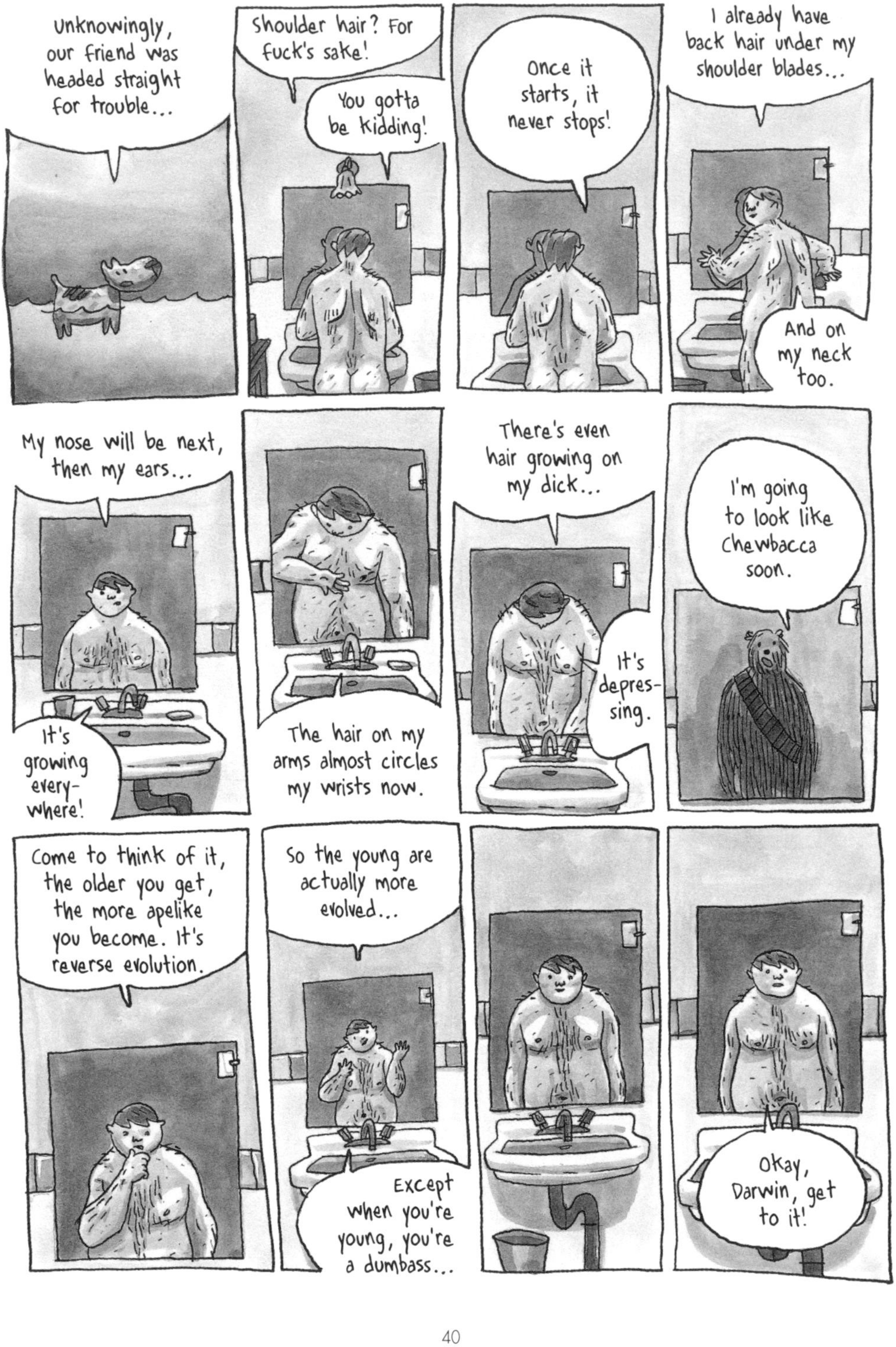
Unknowingly, our friend was headed straight for trouble...
Shoulder hair? For fuck's sake!
You gotta be kidding!
Once it starts, it never stops!
I already have back hair under my shoulder blades...
And on my neck too.
My nose will be next, then my ears...
It's growing every-where!
The hair on my arms almost circles my wrists now.
There's even hair growing on my dick...
It's depres-sing.
I'm going to look like Chewbacca soon.
Come to think of it, the older you get, the more apelike you become. It's reverse evolution.
So the young are actually more evolved...
Except when you're young, you're a dumbass...
Okay, Darwin, get to it!

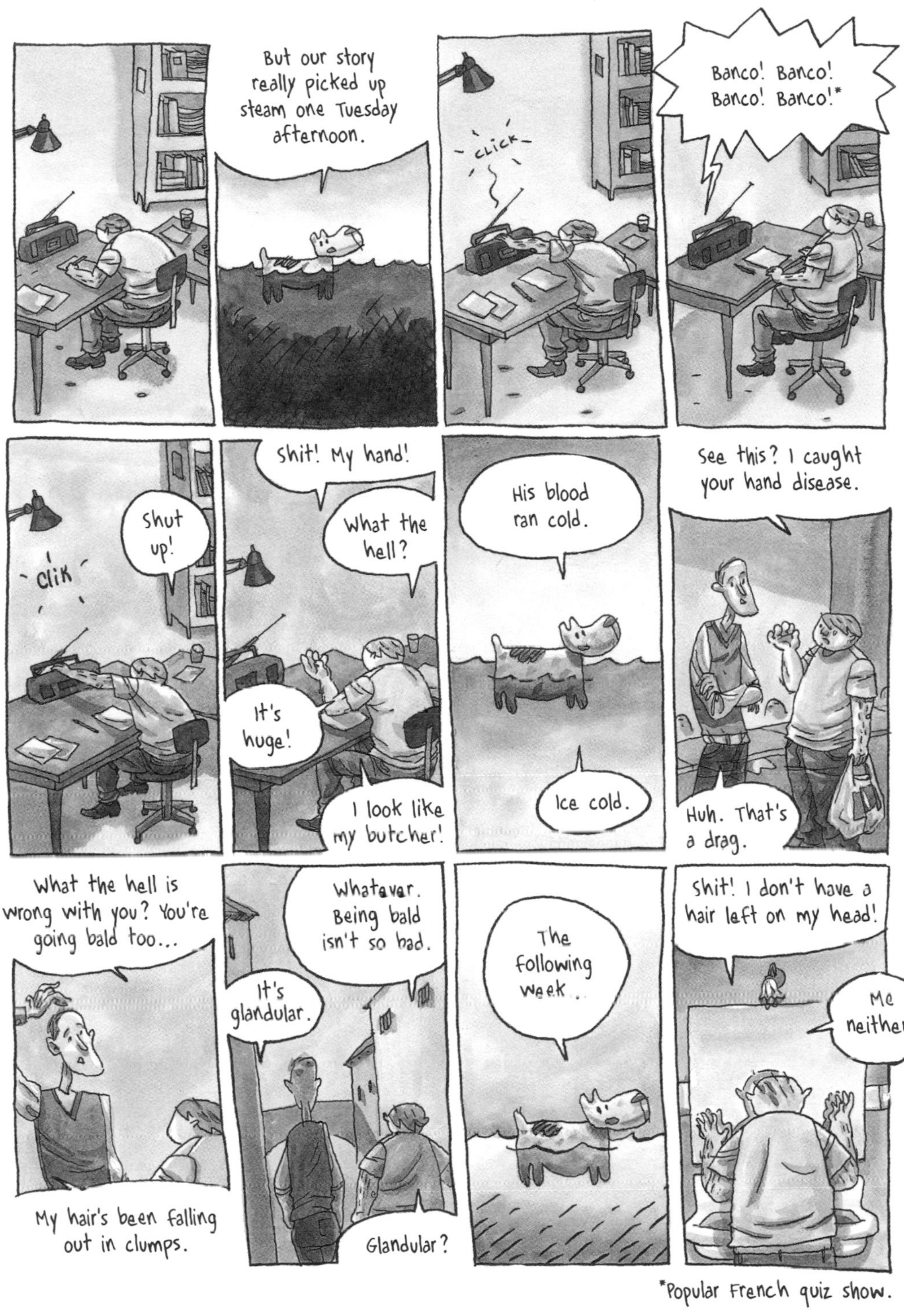
But our story really picked up steam one Tuesday afternoon.
CLICK
Banco! Banco! Banco! Banco!*
CLIK
Shut up!
Shit! My hand!
What the hell?
It's huge!
I look like my butcher!
His blood ran cold.
Ice cold.
See this? I caught your hand disease.
Huh. That's a drag.
What the hell is wrong with you? You're going bald too...
My hair's been falling out in clumps.
Whatever. Being bald isn't so bad.
It's glandular.
Glandular?
The following week...
Shit! I don't have a hair left on my head!
Me neither!

*Popular French quiz show.

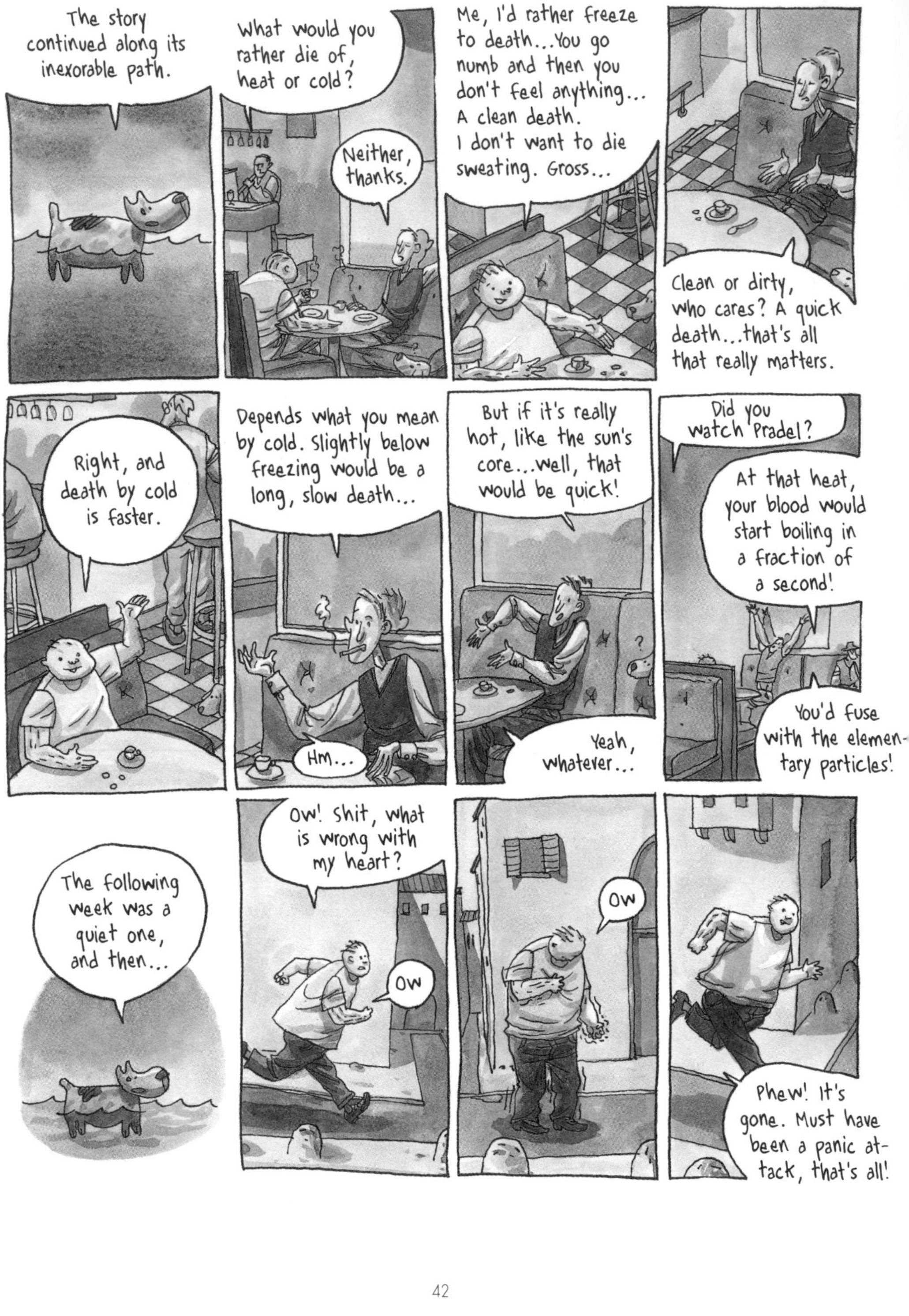
The story continued along its inexorable path.
What would you rather die of, heat or cold?
Neither, thanks.
Me, I'd rather freeze to death... You go numb and then you don't feel anything... A clean death. I don't want to die sweating. Gross...
Clean or dirty, who cares? A quick death... that's all that really matters.
Right, and death by cold is faster.
Depends what you mean by cold. Slightly below freezing would be a long, slow death...
Hm...
But if it's really hot, like the sun's core... well, that would be quick!
Yeah, whatever...
Did you watch Pradel?
At that heat, your blood would start boiling in a fraction of a second!
You'd fuse with the elementary particles!
The following week was a quiet one, and then...
Ow! Shit, what is wrong with my heart?
OW
OW
Phew! It's gone. Must have been a panic attack, that's all!

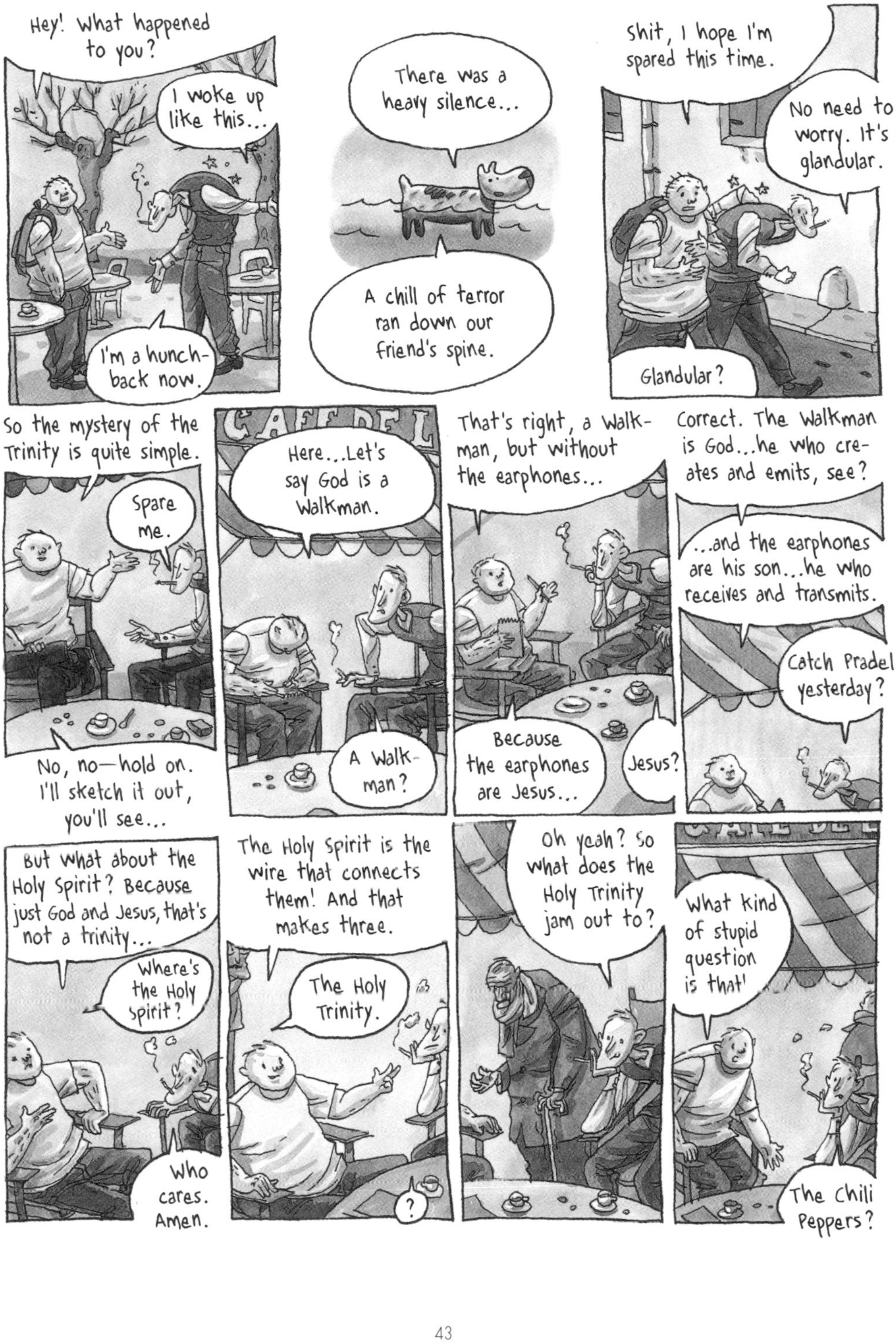
Hey! What happened to you?
I woke up like this...
I'm a hunch-back now.
There was a heavy silence...
A chill of terror ran down our friend's spine.
Shit, I hope I'm spared this time.
No need to worry. It's glandular.
Glandular?
So the mystery of the Trinity is quite simple.
Spare me.
No, no—hold on. I'll sketch it out, you'll see...
Here...Let's say God is a Walkman.
A Walk-man?
That's right, a Walk-man, but without the earphones...
Because the earphones are Jesus...
Jesus?
Correct. The Walkman is God...he who cre-ates and emits, see?
...and the earphones are his son...he who receives and transmits.
Catch Pradel yesterday?
But what about the Holy Spirit? Because just God and Jesus, that's not a trinity...
Where's the Holy Spirit?
Who cares. Amen.
The Holy Spirit is the wire that connects them! And that makes three.
The Holy Trinity.
?
Oh yeah? So what does the Holy Trinity jam out to?
What kind of stupid question is that!
The Chili Peppers?

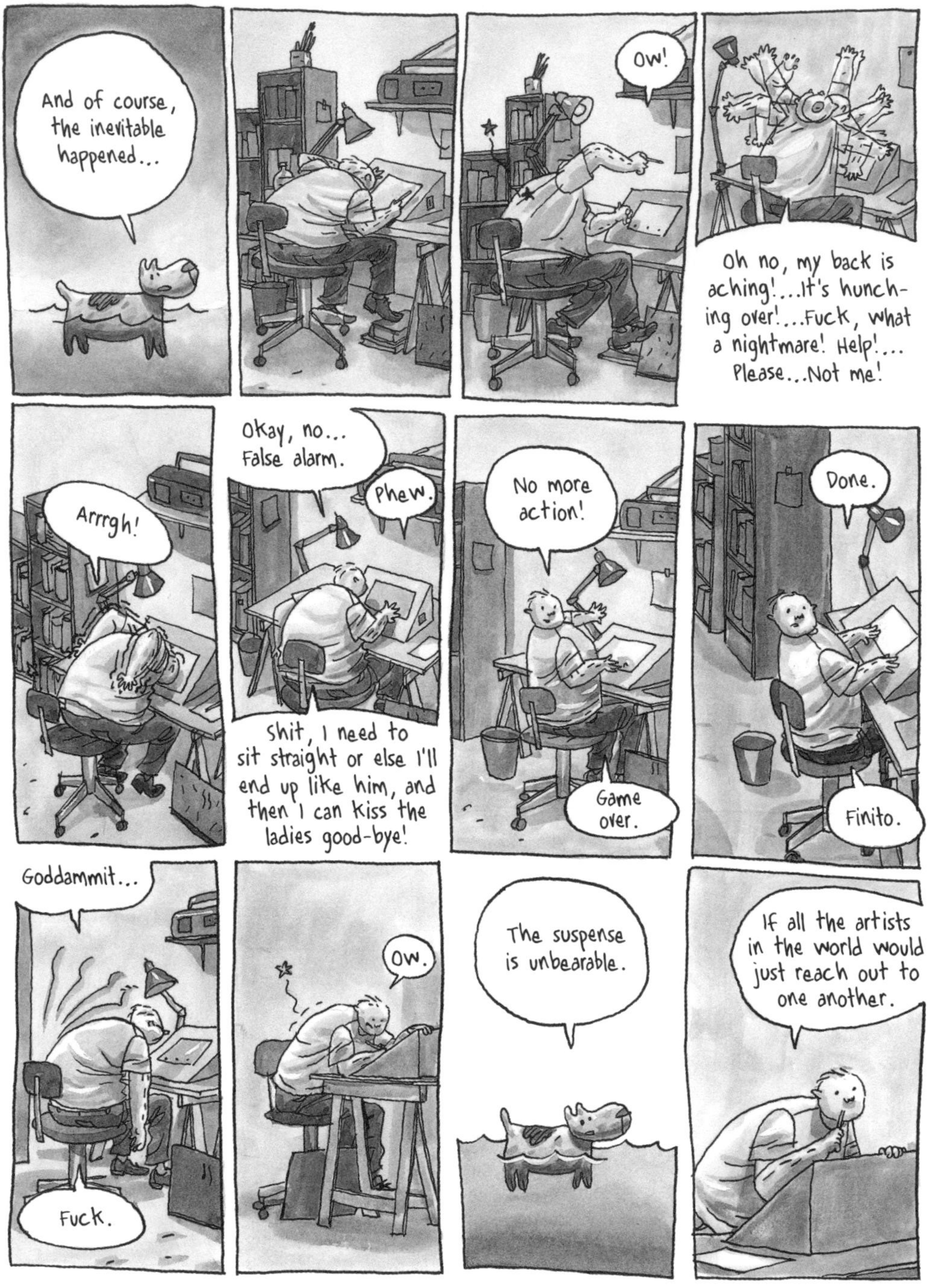
And of course, the inevitable happened...
Ow!
Oh no, my back is aching!...It's hunching over!...Fuck, what a nightmare! Help!... Please...Not me!
Arrrgh!
Okay, no... False alarm.
Phew.
Shit, I need to sit straight or else I'll end up like him, and then I can kiss the ladies good-bye!
No more action!
Game over.
Done.
Finito.
Goddammit...
Fuck.
Ow.
The suspense is unbearable.
If all the artists in the world would just reach out to one another.

"Bad things come in threes." That old saying hung over our friend's head like a dark cloud.

Sometimes I'll almost drop something, but then I manage to catch it...

That's really interesting, honestly. I'm dying to hear more...

Well...I saw a great movie the other day.

By whom? I don't know.

Starring? I forget.

Where? Uh...

Anyway, it was great...You need to see it...

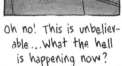

But misfortune was about to wreak havoc...

Oh no! This is unbelievable...What the hell is happening now?

I can barely move!!!

I'm done with this shit. That guy is bad luck!

I need to keep away from him.

The less I see of him, the better.

He's worse than the plague.

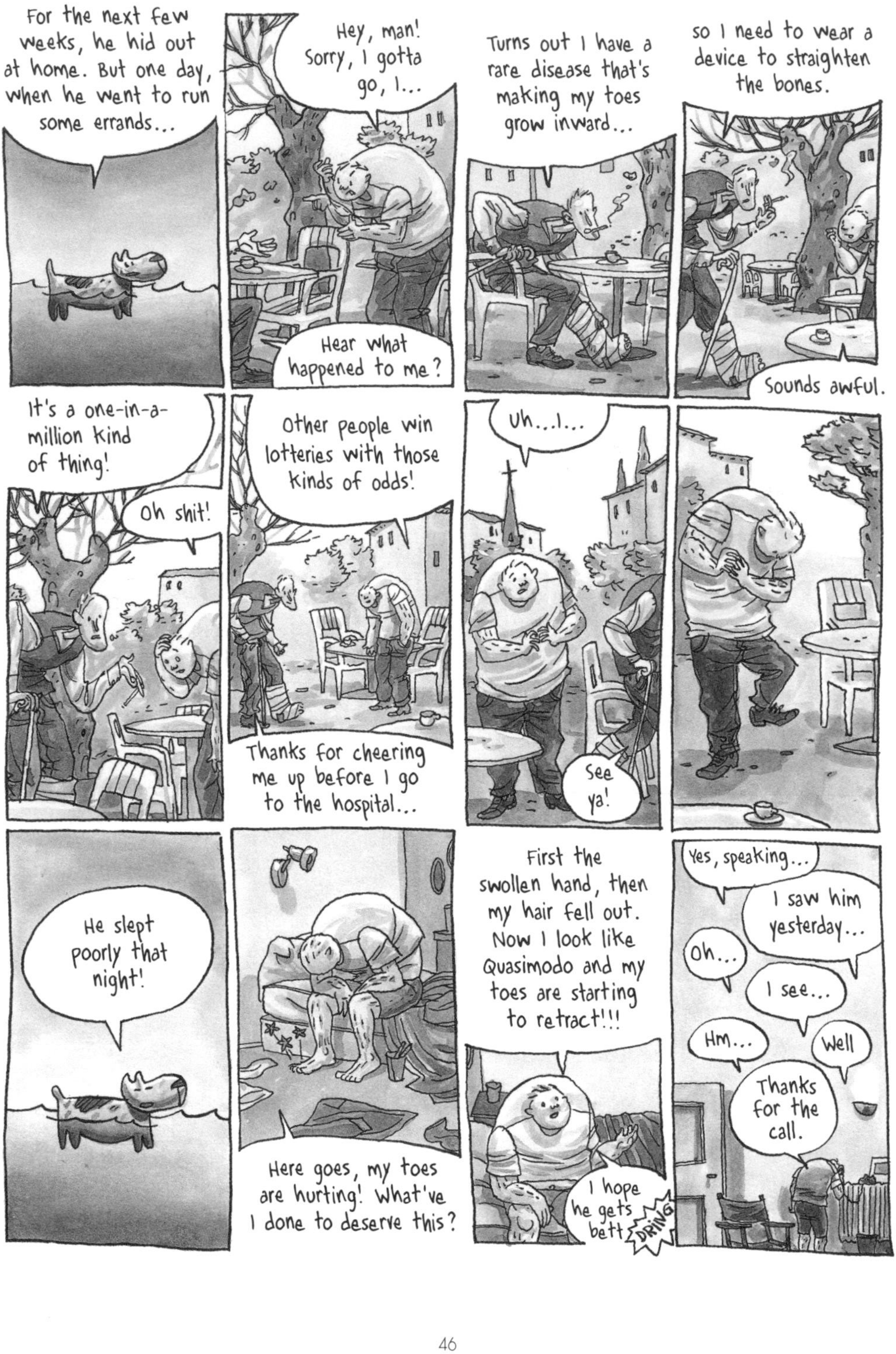
For the next few weeks, he hid out at home. But one day, when he went to run some errands...
Hey, man! Sorry, I gotta go, I...
Hear what happened to me?
Turns out I have a rare disease that's making my toes grow inward...
so I need to wear a device to straighten the bones.
Sounds awful.
It's a one-in-a-million kind of thing!
Oh shit!
Other people win lotteries with those kinds of odds!
Thanks for cheering me up before I go to the hospital...
Uh...I...
See ya!
He slept poorly that night!
Here goes, my toes are hurting! What've I done to deserve this?
First the swollen hand, then my hair fell out. Now I look like Quasimodo and my toes are starting to retract!!!
I hope he gets bett
DRING
Yes, speaking...
I saw him yesterday...
Oh...
I see...
Hm...
Well
Thanks for the call.

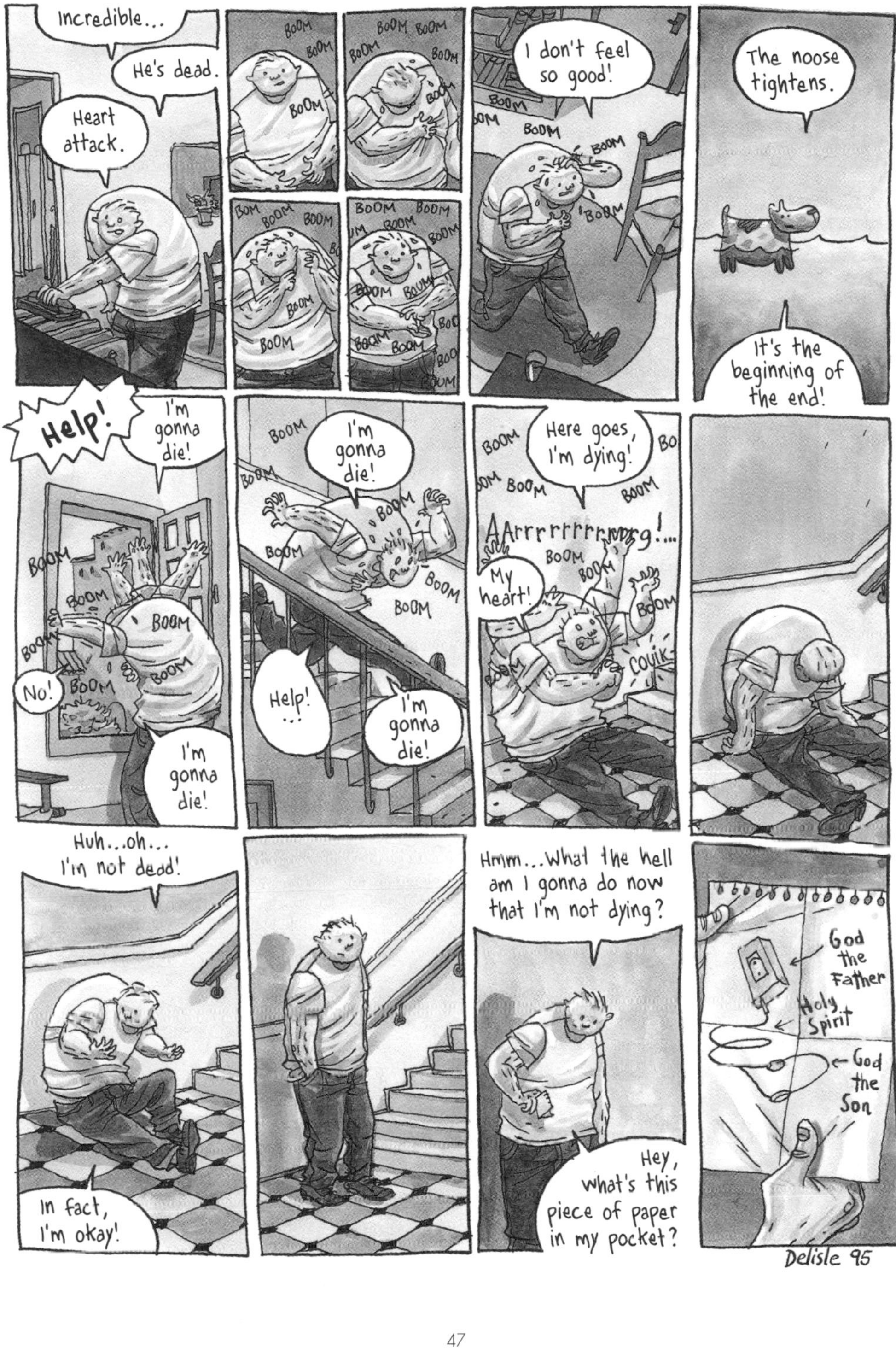
Incredible...
He's dead.
Heart attack.
BOOM BOOM
BOOM
BOOM BOOM BOOM
BOOM
BOOM BOOM BOOM
BOOM
BOOM
BOOM BOOM BOOM
BOOM BOUM
BOOM
I don't feel so good!
BOOM
BOOM
BOOM
BOOM
The noose tightens.
It's the beginning of the end!
Help!
I'm gonna die!
BOOM
BOOM
BOOM
BOOM
No!
BOOM
BOOM
I'm gonna die!
BOOM
I'm gonna die!
BOOM
BOOM
BOOM
BOOM
BOOM
Help! ...
I'm gonna die!
BOOM
Here goes, I'm dying!
BOOM BOOM
BOOM
Aarrrrrrrrrg!...
My heart!
BOOM
BOOM
BOOM
COUIK
Huh...oh... I'm not dead!
In fact, I'm okay!
Hmm...what the hell am I gonna do now that I'm not dying?
Hey, what's this piece of paper in my pocket?
God the Father
Holy Spirit
God the Son
Delisle 95

THE BOLD AND THE BEAUTIFUL

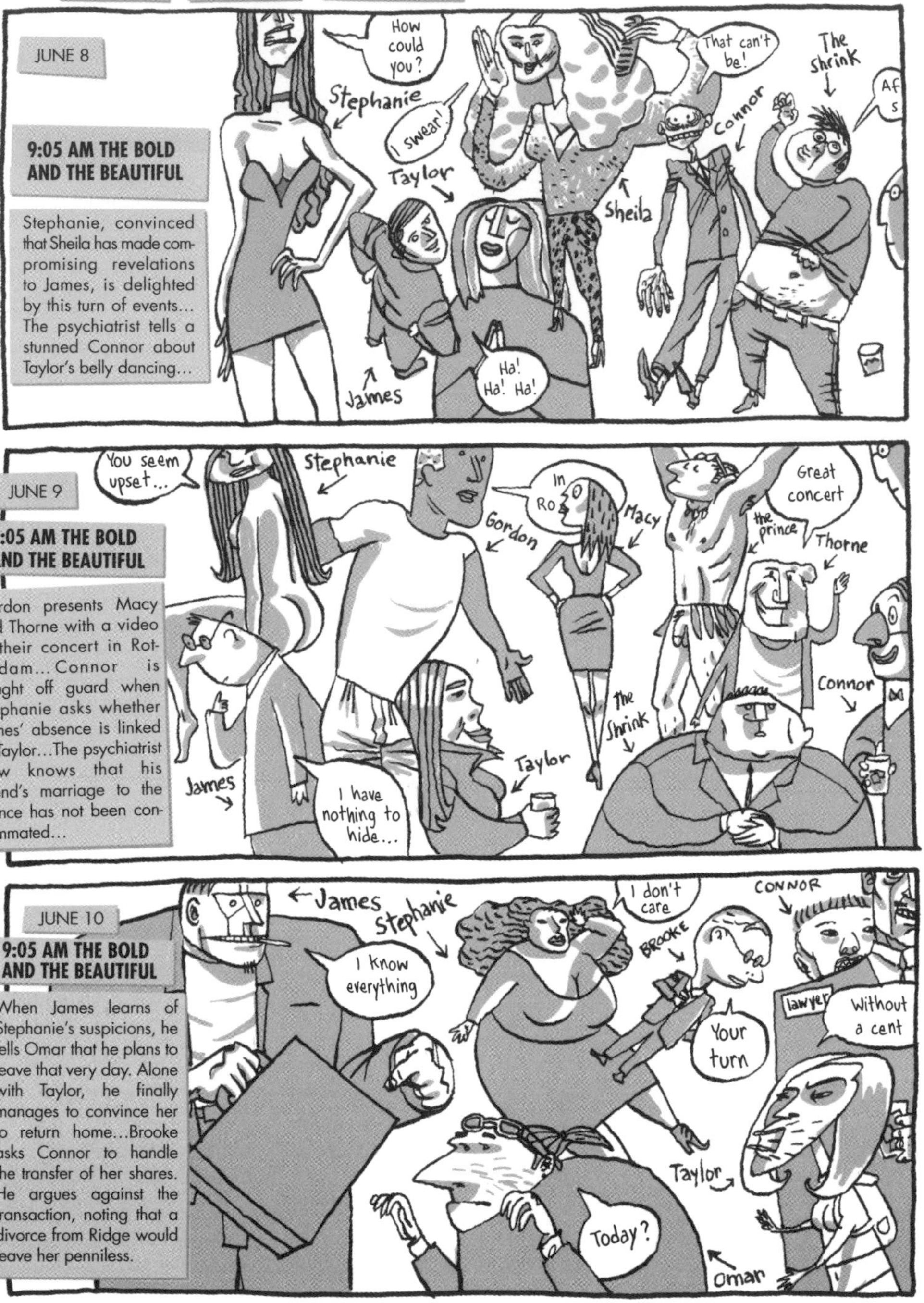
JUNE 8
9:05 AM THE BOLD AND THE BEAUTIFUL
Stephanie, convinced that Sheila has made compromising revelations to James, is delighted by this turn of events... The psychiatrist tells a stunned Connor about Taylor's belly dancing...
How could you?
Stephanie
I swear!
Taylor
That can't be!
Sheila
Connor
The Shrink
Af
s
Ha! Ha! Ha!
James
JUNE 9
9:05 AM THE BOLD AND THE BEAUTIFUL
Gordon presents Macy and Thorne with a video of their concert in Rotterdam... Connor is caught off guard when Stephanie asks whether James' absence is linked to Taylor... The psychiatrist now knows that his friend's marriage to the prince has not been consummated...
You seem upset...
Stephanie
Gordon
In
Ro
Macy
Great concert
the prince
Thorne
the Shrink
Connor
James
I have nothing to hide...
Taylor
JUNE 10
9:05 AM THE BOLD AND THE BEAUTIFUL
When James learns of Stephanie's suspicions, he tells Omar that he plans to leave that very day. Alone with Taylor, he finally manages to convince her to return home... Brooke asks Connor to handle the transfer of her shares. He argues against the transaction, noting that a divorce from Ridge would leave her penniless.
James
Stephanie
I know everything
I don't care
BROOKE
CONNOR
lawyer
Without a cent
Your turn
Taylor
Today?
Omar

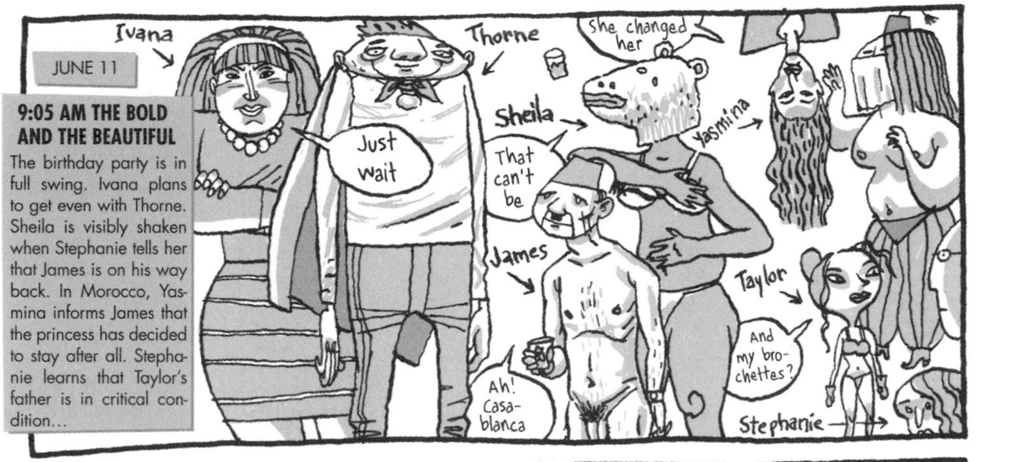
JUNE 11
9:05 AM THE BOLD AND THE BEAUTIFUL
The birthday party is in full swing. Ivana plans to get even with Thorne. Sheila is visibly shaken when Stephanie tells her that James is on his way back. In Morocco, Yasmina informs James that the princess has decided to stay after all. Stephanie learns that Taylor's father is in critical condition…
Ivana
Thorne
Just wait
She changed her
Sheila
That can't be
Yasmina
James
Ah! Casablanca
Taylor
And my brochettes?
Stephanie

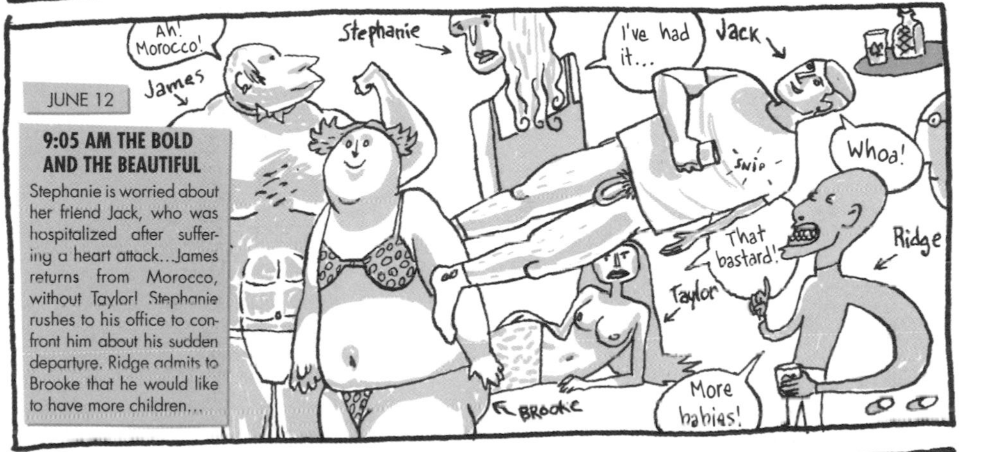
JUNE 12
9:05 AM THE BOLD AND THE BEAUTIFUL
Stephanie is worried about her friend Jack, who was hospitalized after suffering a heart attack…James returns from Morocco, without Taylor! Stephanie rushes to his office to confront him about his sudden departure. Ridge admits to Brooke that he would like to have more children…
Ah! Morocco!
James
Stephanie
I've had it…
Jack
SNIP
Whoa!
That bastard!
Ridge
Taylor
BROOKE
More babies!

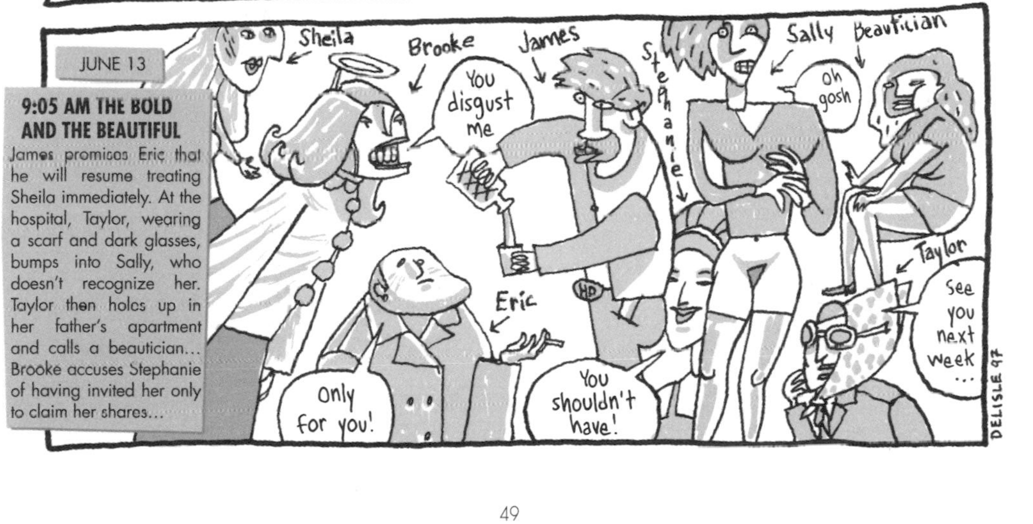
JUNE 13
9:05 AM THE BOLD AND THE BEAUTIFUL
James promises Eric that he will resume treating Sheila immediately. At the hospital, Taylor, wearing a scarf and dark glasses, bumps into Sally, who doesn't recognize her. Taylor then holes up in her father's apartment and calls a beautician… Brooke accuses Stephanie of having invited her only to claim her shares…
Sheila
Brooke
James
Stephanie
Sally
Beautician
You disgust me
Oh gosh
Taylor
Eric
See you next week…
Only for you!
You shouldn't have!
DELISLE 97

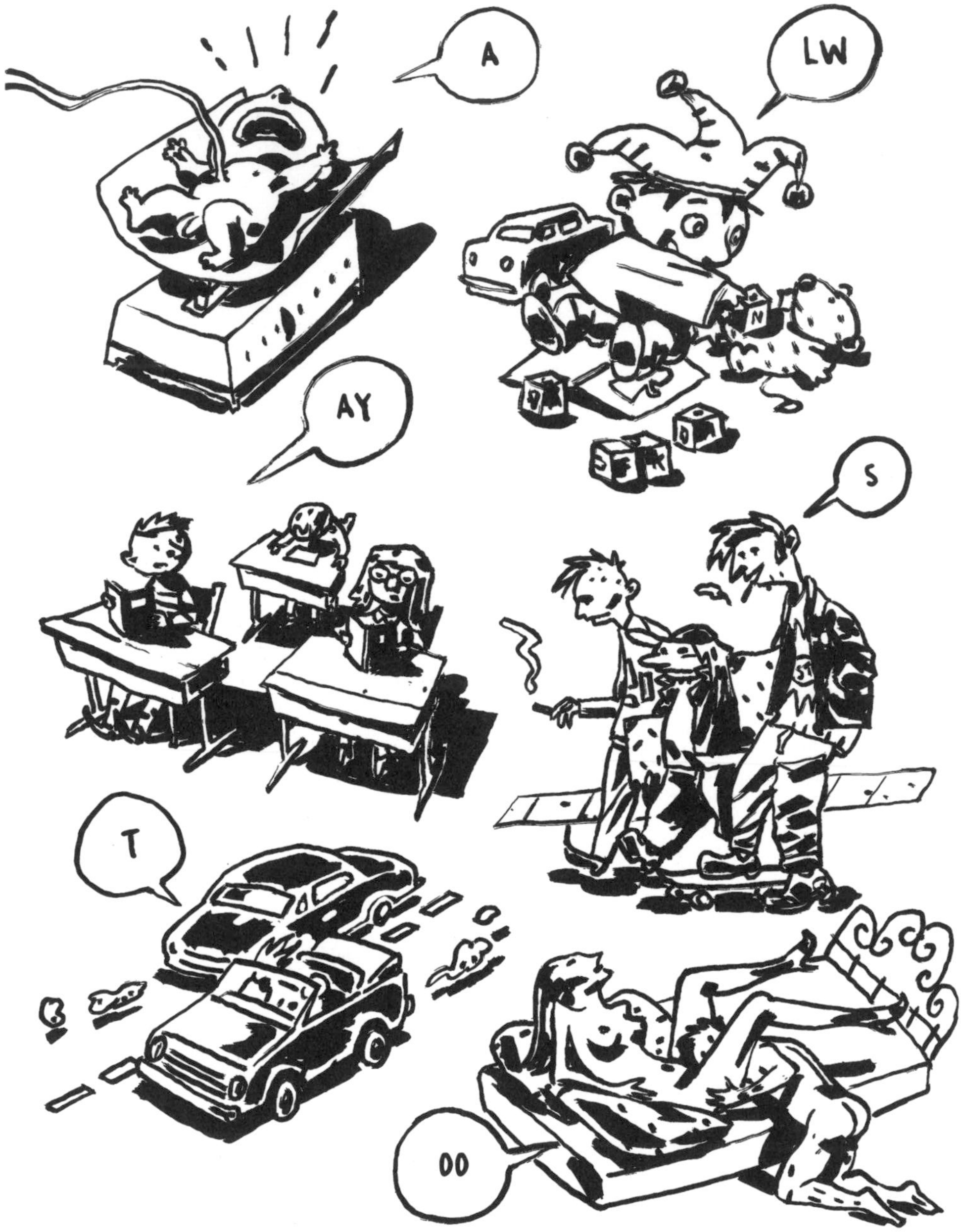
A
LW
AY
S
T
OO

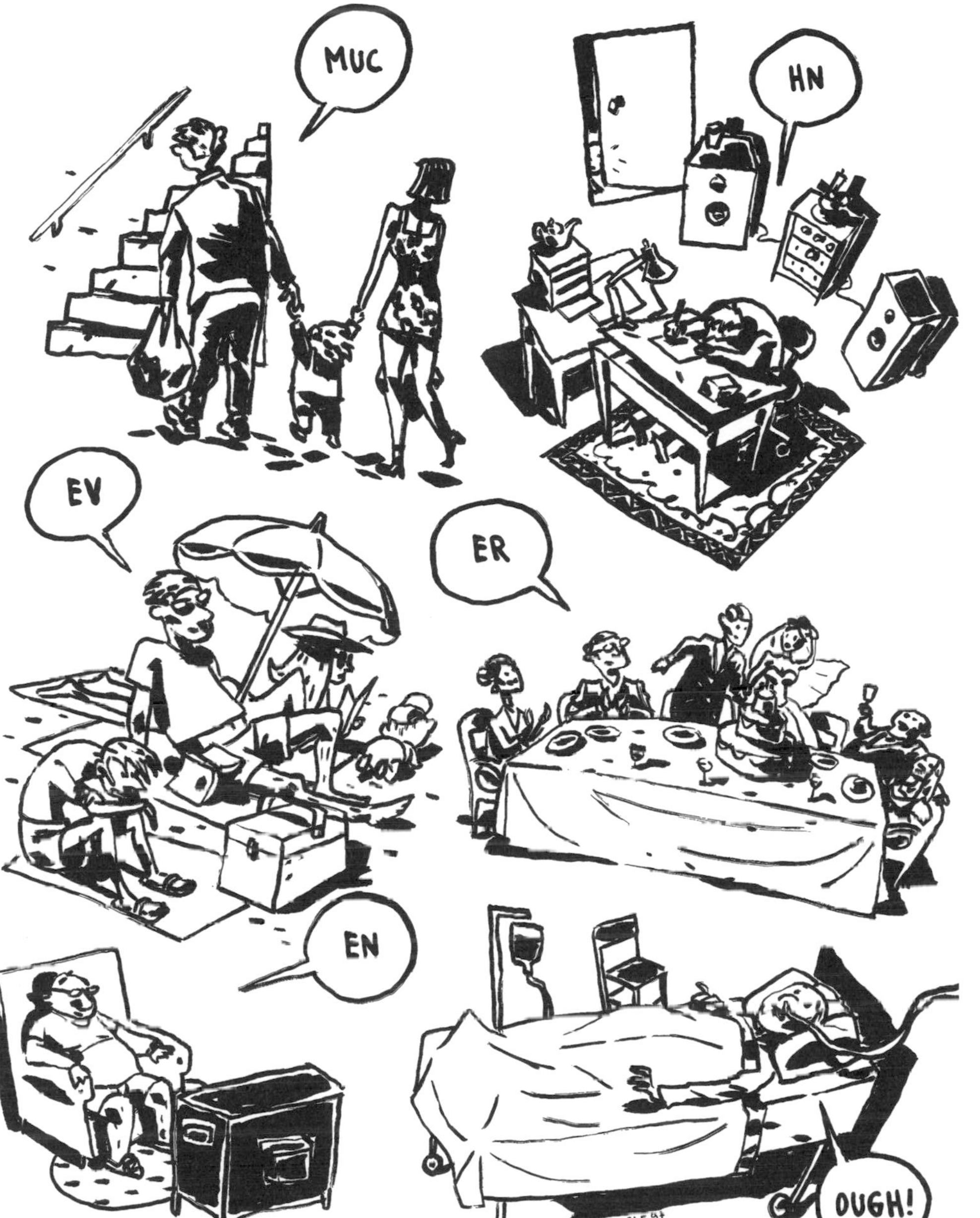
MUC
HN
EV
ER
EN
OUGH!
DELISLE 97

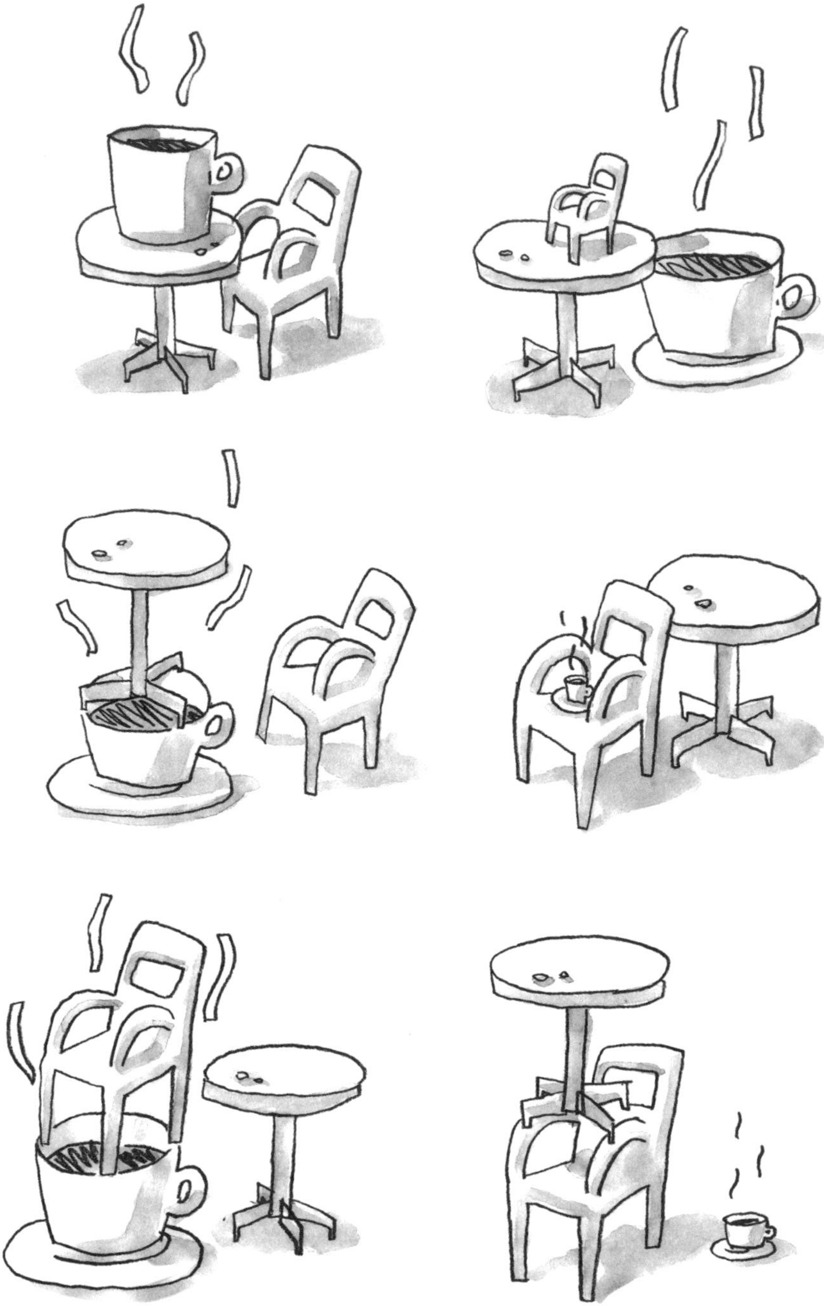

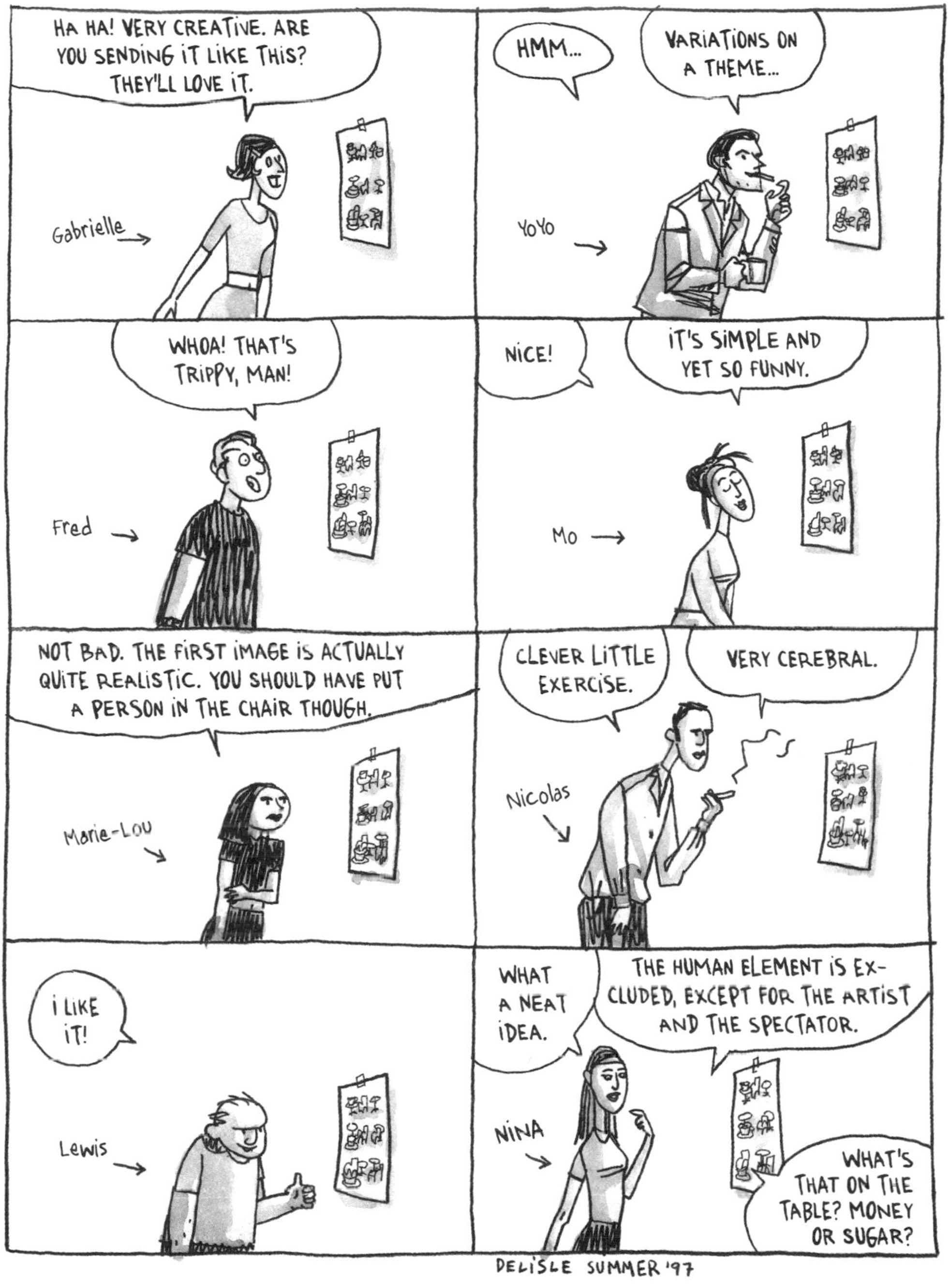
HA HA! VERY CREATIVE. ARE YOU SENDING IT LIKE THIS? THEY'LL LOVE IT.
Gabrielle
HMM...
VARIATIONS ON A THEME...
YoYo
WHOA! THAT'S TRIPPY, MAN!
Fred
NICE!
IT'S SIMPLE AND YET SO FUNNY.
Mo
NOT BAD. THE FIRST IMAGE IS ACTUALLY QUITE REALISTIC. YOU SHOULD HAVE PUT A PERSON IN THE CHAIR THOUGH.
Marie-Lou
CLEVER LITTLE EXERCISE.
VERY CEREBRAL.
Nicolas
I LIKE IT!
Lewis
WHAT A NEAT IDEA.
THE HUMAN ELEMENT IS EXCLUDED, EXCEPT FOR THE ARTIST AND THE SPECTATOR.
NINA
WHAT'S THAT ON THE TABLE? MONEY OR SUGAR?
DELISLE SUMMER '97

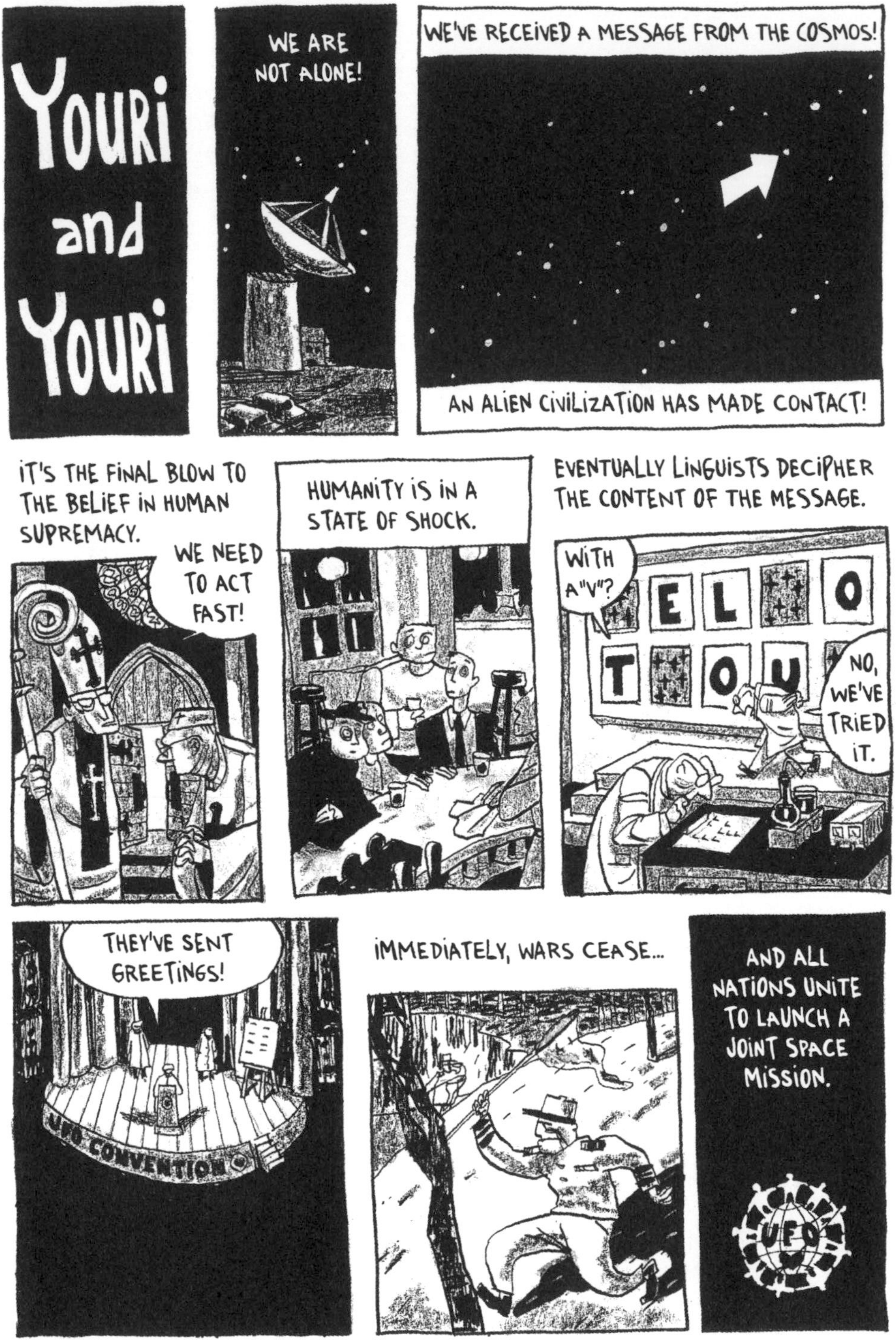
Youri and Youri
WE ARE NOT ALONE!
WE'VE RECEIVED A MESSAGE FROM THE COSMOS!
AN ALIEN CIVILIZATION HAS MADE CONTACT!
IT'S THE FINAL BLOW TO THE BELIEF IN HUMAN SUPREMACY.
WE NEED TO ACT FAST!
HUMANITY IS IN A STATE OF SHOCK.
EVENTUALLY LINGUISTS DECIPHER THE CONTENT OF THE MESSAGE.
WITH A "V"?
E L O
T O U
NO, WE'VE TRIED IT.
THEY'VE SENT GREETINGS!
UFO CONVENTION
IMMEDIATELY, WARS CEASE...
AND ALL NATIONS UNITE TO LAUNCH A JOINT SPACE MISSION.
UFO

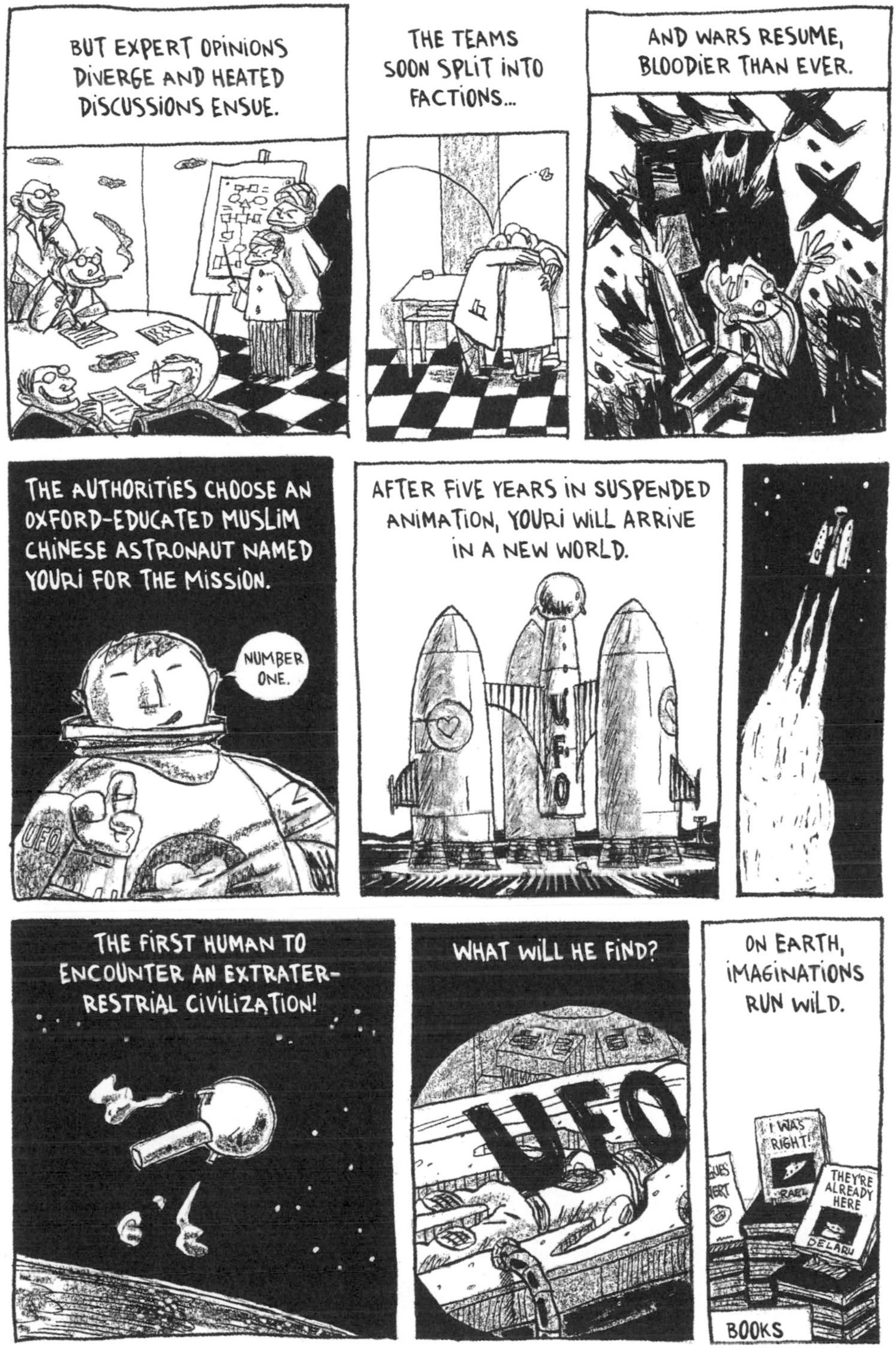

BUT EXPERT OPINIONS DIVERGE AND HEATED DISCUSSIONS ENSUE.
THE TEAMS SOON SPLIT INTO FACTIONS...
AND WARS RESUME, BLOODIER THAN EVER.
THE AUTHORITIES CHOOSE AN OXFORD-EDUCATED MUSLIM CHINESE ASTRONAUT NAMED YOURI FOR THE MISSION.
NUMBER ONE.
UFO
AFTER FIVE YEARS IN SUSPENDED ANIMATION, YOURI WILL ARRIVE IN A NEW WORLD.
UFO
THE FIRST HUMAN TO ENCOUNTER AN EXTRATERRESTRIAL CIVILIZATION!
WHAT WILL HE FIND?
UFO
ON EARTH, IMAGINATIONS RUN WILD.
I WAS RIGHT!
RAEL
THEY'RE ALREADY HERE
DELARU
BOOKS

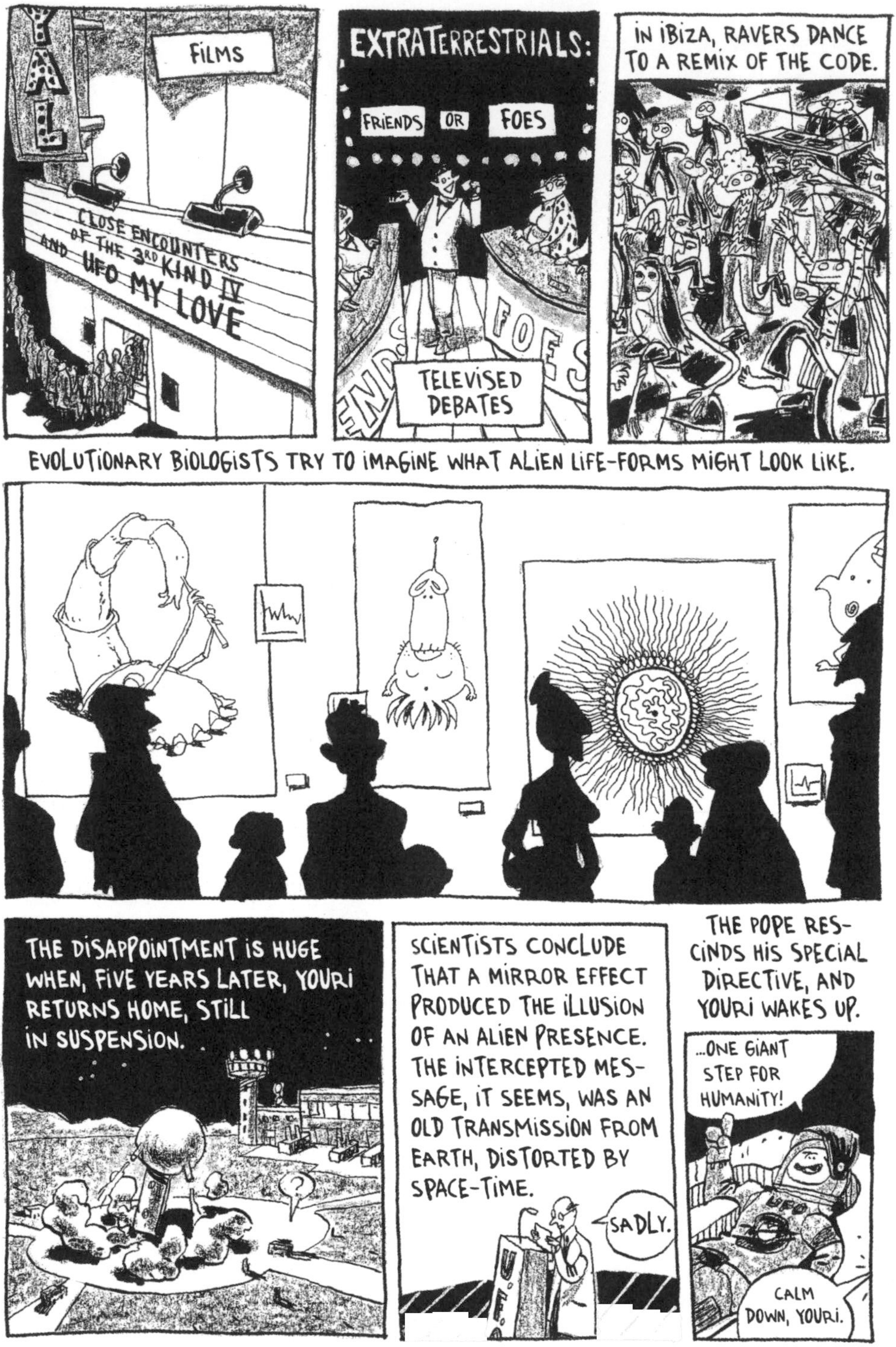
FILMS
CLOSE ENCOUNTERS OF THE 3RD KIND IV AND UFO MY LOVE
EXTRATERRESTRIALS:
FRIENDS OR FOES
TELEVISED DEBATES
IN IBIZA, RAVERS DANCE TO A REMIX OF THE CODE.
EVOLUTIONARY BIOLOGISTS TRY TO IMAGINE WHAT ALIEN LIFE-FORMS MIGHT LOOK LIKE.
THE DISAPPOINTMENT IS HUGE WHEN, FIVE YEARS LATER, YOURI RETURNS HOME, STILL IN SUSPENSION.
?
SCIENTISTS CONCLUDE THAT A MIRROR EFFECT PRODUCED THE ILLUSION OF AN ALIEN PRESENCE. THE INTERCEPTED MESSAGE, IT SEEMS, WAS AN OLD TRANSMISSION FROM EARTH, DISTORTED BY SPACE-TIME.
SADLY.
THE POPE RESCINDS HIS SPECIAL DIRECTIVE, AND YOURI WAKES UP.
...ONE GIANT STEP FOR HUMANITY!
CALM DOWN, YOURI.

WHAT NOBODY WILL EVER KNOW IS THAT YOURI ACTUALLY ACHIEVED HIS OBJECTIVE!

AMAZINGLY, THE ALIEN CIVILIZATION HAD FOLLOWED THE EXACT SAME EVOLUTIONARY PATH AS OUR OWN!

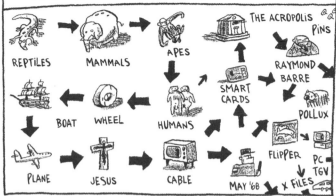

REPTILES → MAMMALS → APES → THE ACROPOLIS → PINS → RAYMOND BARRE

BOAT ← WHEEL ← HUMANS   SMART CARDS   POLLUX

PLANE → JESUS → CABLE   MAY '68 → X FILES   FLIPPER   PC TGV

AND SINCE THEY, TOO, HAD SENT OUT A SPACESHIP...

ZZZZ...

ZZZ

THEY WERE EQUALLY DISAPPOINTED TO SEE IT COME BACK, AND CONCLUDED THAT A MIRROR EFFECT HAD OCCURRED.

...ONE GIANT STEP FOR HUMANITY!

CALM DOWN, YOURI.

BUT AT NIGHT, LIGHT YEARS FROM ONE ANOTHER...

THE TWO YOURIS NO LONGER RECOGNIZE THE CONSTELLATIONS.

THEY MENTION IT AT HOME, BUT THEIR WIVES ARE TOO BUSY WITH THE KIDS TO LISTEN...

57

The proof is in: plants have feelings! Botanists have long studied the question, and now photo documentation provides irrefutable evidence. (A Drawn & Quarterly exclusive!)

In the silence of this forest, a tragedy is unfolding before our eyes... For almost a century, jealousy has consumed this mulberry tree.

It began with an unfortunate misunderstanding involving a nearby maple that, according to witnesses, behaved inappropriately toward the mulberry's fiancée. Even after the incident was resolved, the mulberry's resentment lingered...

Some ten years later, an axe was left lying nearby. The mulberry, still holding its grudge, directed all its energy toward growing out a branch to take posession of the tool.

A rising and falling movement has since been detected, occurring in three-year cycles and having continued now for more than eighteen years.

If time and weather don't erode the handle, and if no neighbouring tree intervenes to bring the mulberry to its senses, scientists predict that the mulberry will finish off the maple in about thirty-eight years. We will continue to monitor the situation as it evolves...

DELISLE 97

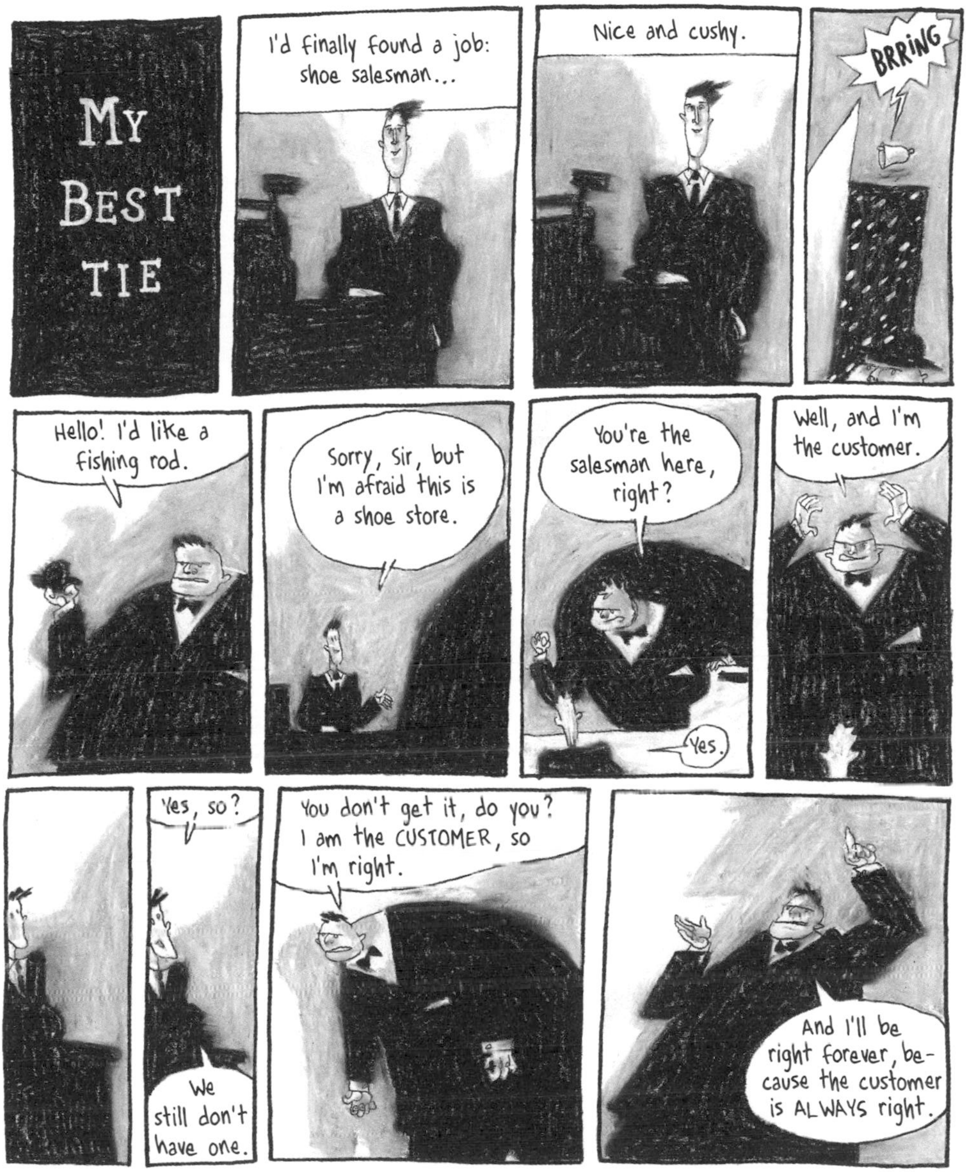
My Best Tie
I'd finally found a job: shoe salesman...
Nice and cushy.
BRRING
Hello! I'd like a fishing rod.
Sorry, Sir, but I'm afraid this is a shoe store.
You're the salesman here, right?
Yes.
Well, and I'm the customer.
Yes, so?
We still don't have one.
You don't get it, do you? I am the CUSTOMER, so I'm right.
And I'll be right forever, because the customer is ALWAYS right.

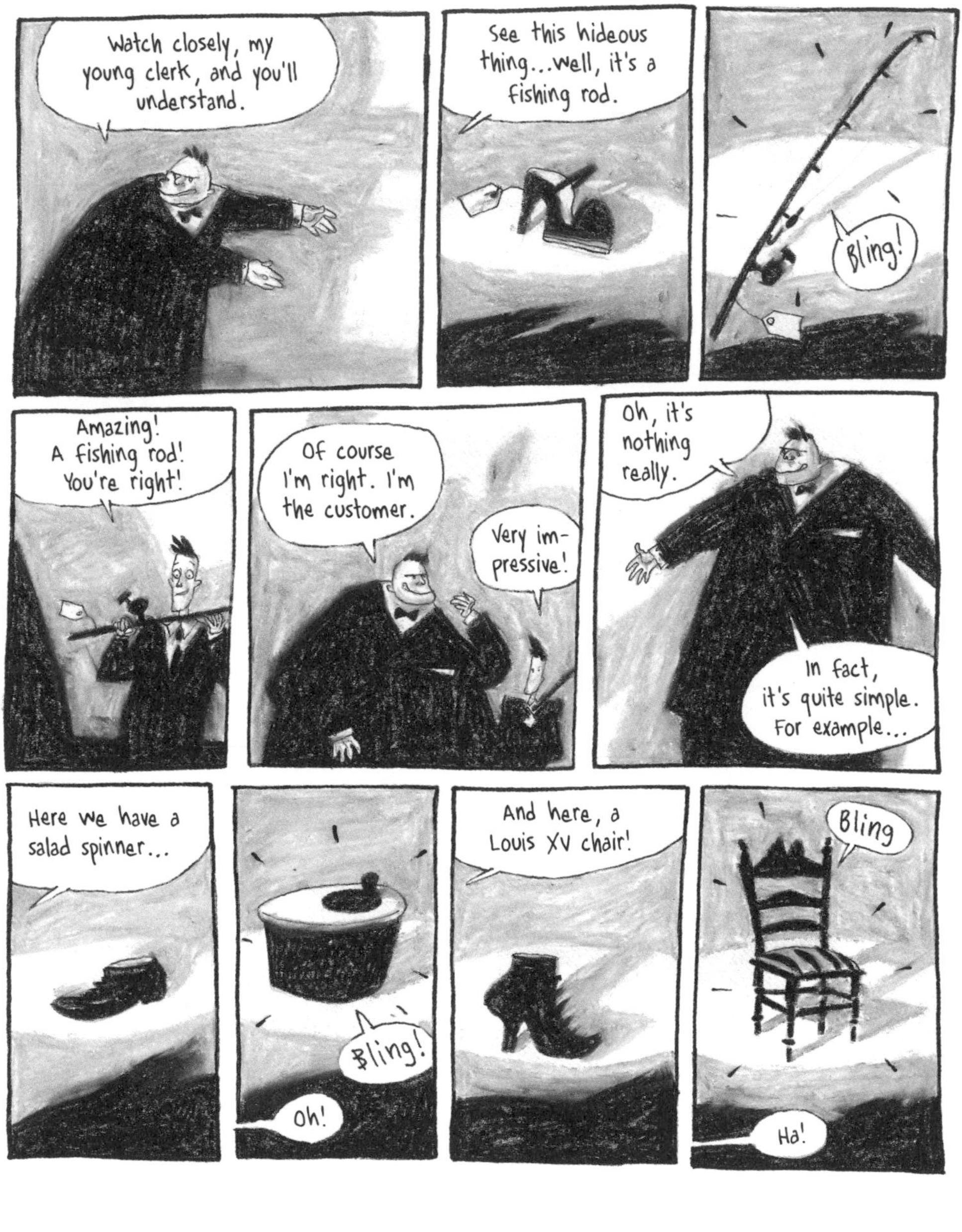
Watch closely, my young clerk, and you'll understand.
See this hideous thing...well, it's a fishing rod.
Bling!
Amazing! A fishing rod! You're right!
Of course I'm right. I'm the customer.
Very impressive!
Oh, it's nothing really.
In fact, it's quite simple. For example...
Here we have a salad spinner...
Bling!
Oh!
And here, a Louis XV chair!
Bling
Ha!

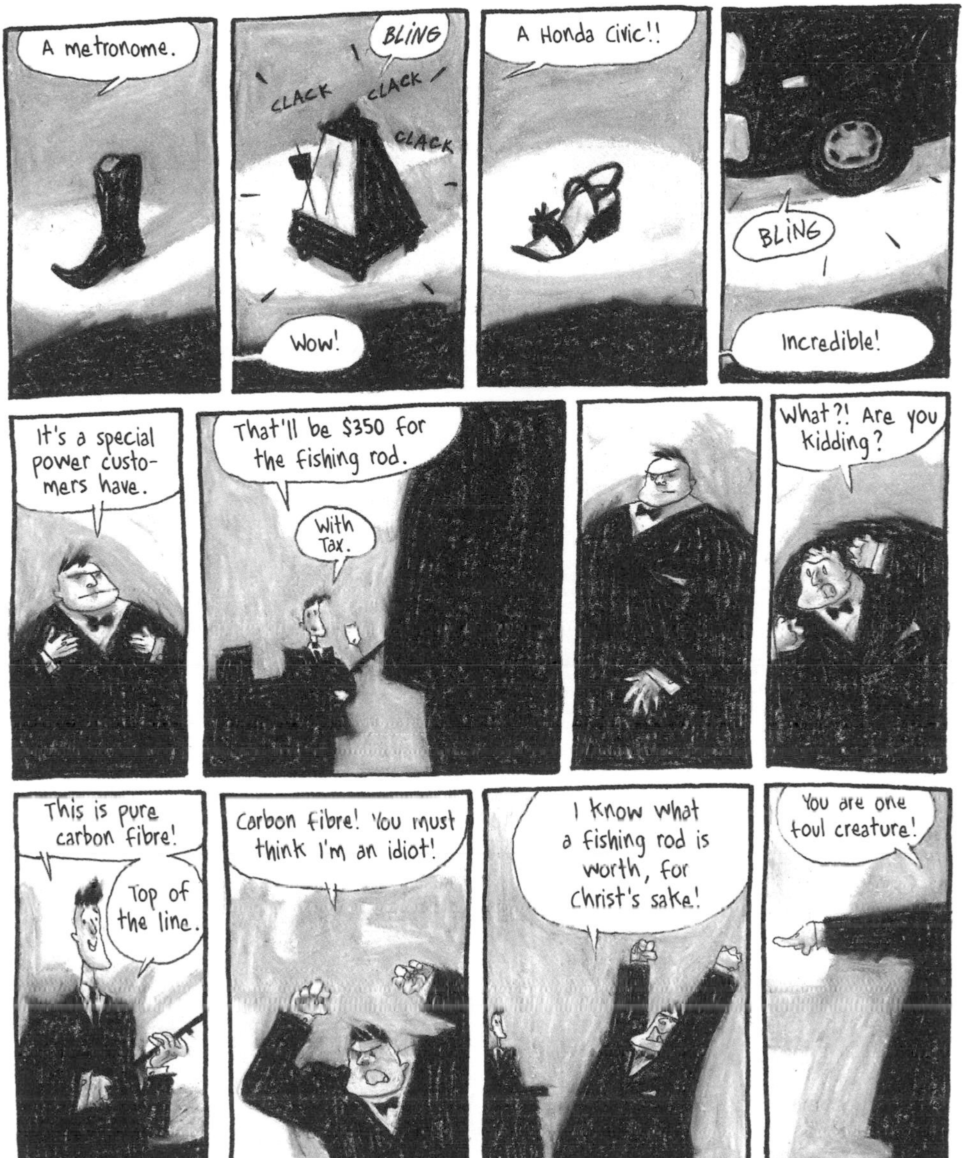
A metronome.
BLING
CLACK
CLACK
CLACK
Wow!
A Honda Civic!!
BLING
Incredible!
It's a special power customers have.
That'll be $350 for the fishing rod.
With Tax.
What?! Are you kidding?
This is pure carbon fibre!
Top of the line.
Carbon fibre! You must think I'm an idiot!
I know what a fishing rod is worth, for Christ's sake!
You are one foul creature!

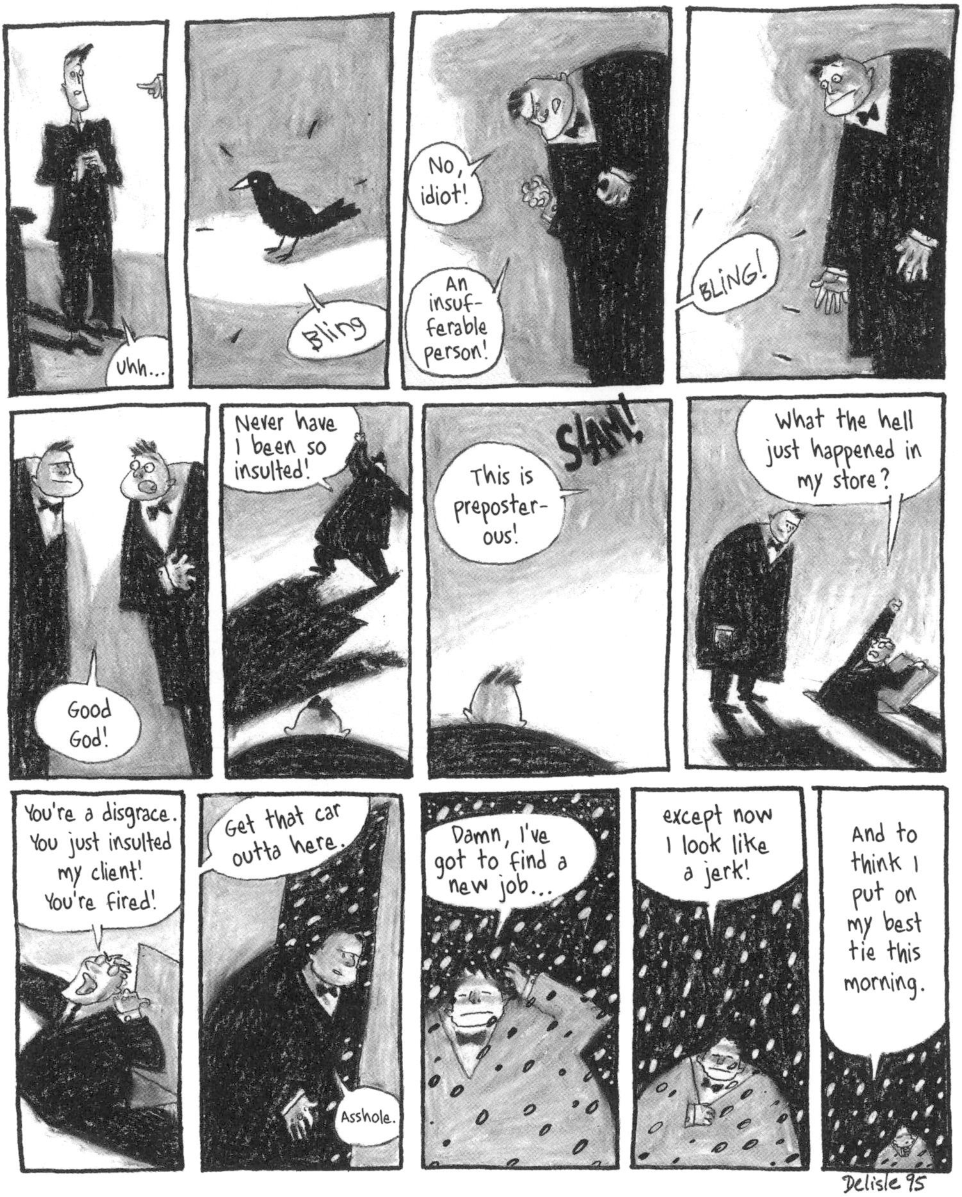

Uhh...
Bling
No, idiot!
An insufferable person!
BLING!
Good God!
Never have I been so insulted!
SLAM!
This is preposterous!
What the hell just happened in my store?
You're a disgrace. You just insulted my client! You're fired!
Get that car outta here.
Asshole.
Damn, I've got to find a new job...
except now I look like a jerk!
And to think I put on my best tie this morning.
Delisle 95

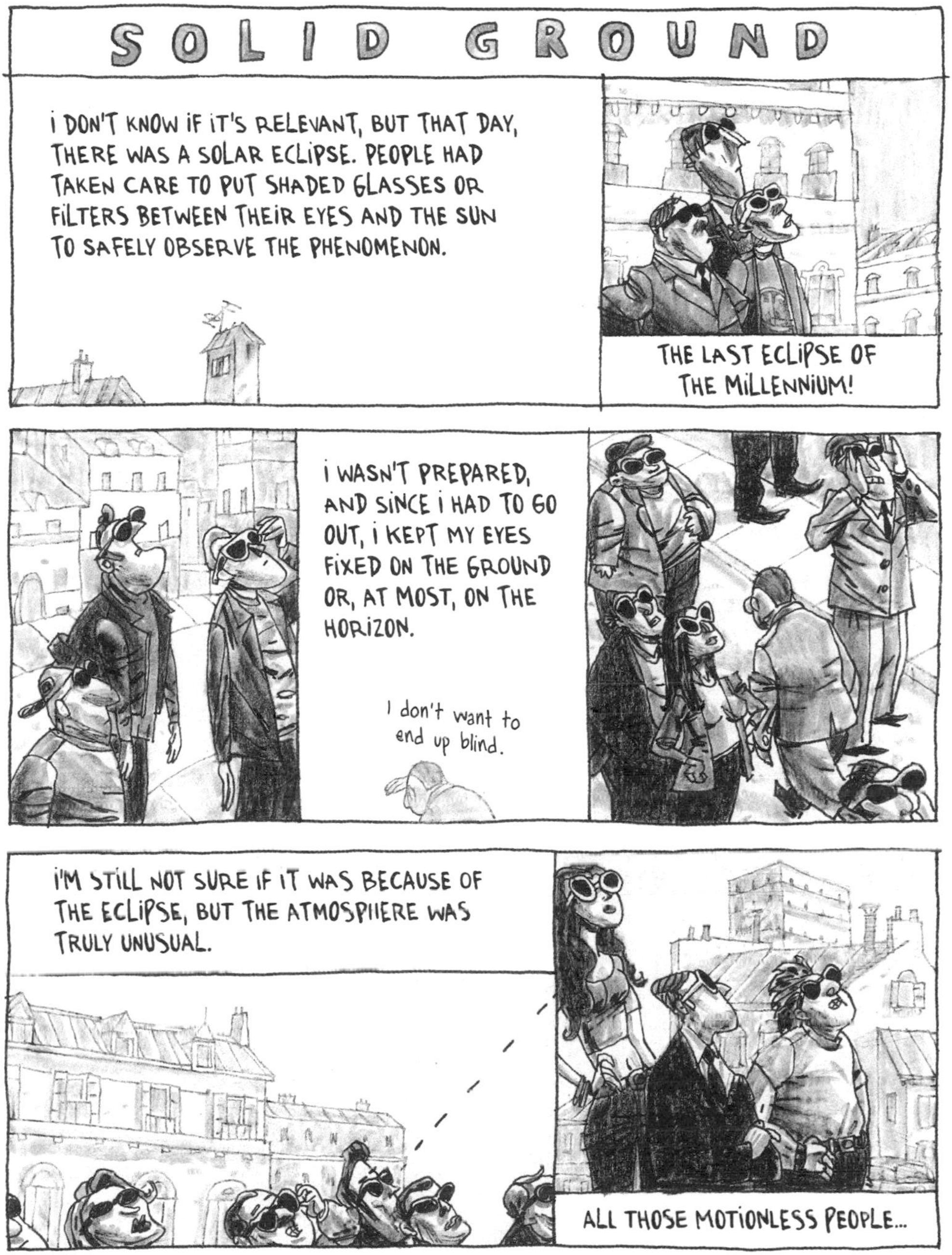
SOLID GROUND
I DON'T KNOW IF IT'S RELEVANT, BUT THAT DAY, THERE WAS A SOLAR ECLIPSE. PEOPLE HAD TAKEN CARE TO PUT SHADED GLASSES OR FILTERS BETWEEN THEIR EYES AND THE SUN TO SAFELY OBSERVE THE PHENOMENON.
THE LAST ECLIPSE OF THE MILLENNIUM!
I WASN'T PREPARED, AND SINCE I HAD TO GO OUT, I KEPT MY EYES FIXED ON THE GROUND OR, AT MOST, ON THE HORIZON.
I don't want to end up blind.
I'M STILL NOT SURE IF IT WAS BECAUSE OF THE ECLIPSE, BUT THE ATMOSPHERE WAS TRULY UNUSUAL.
ALL THOSE MOTIONLESS PEOPLE...

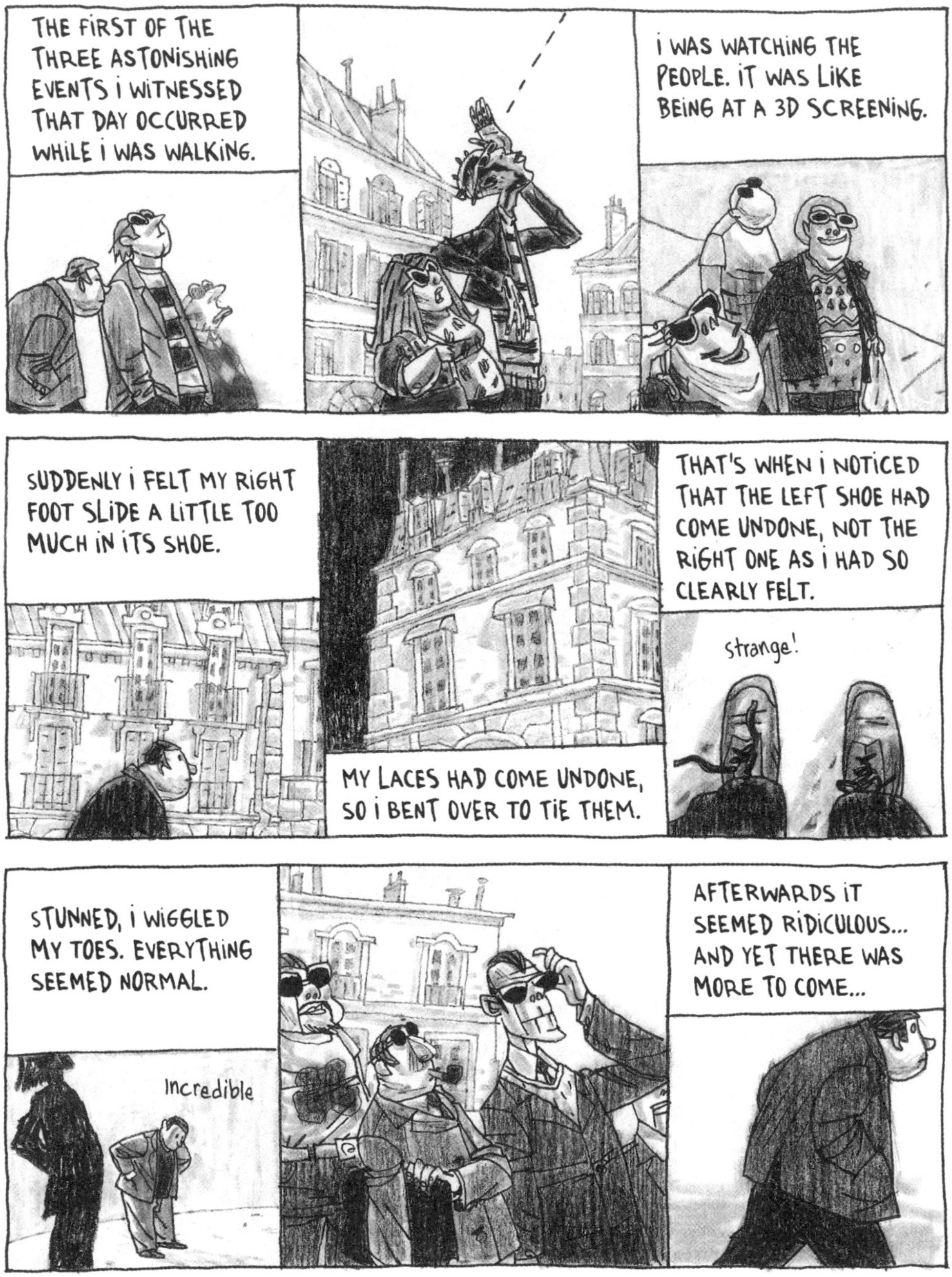
THE FIRST OF THE THREE ASTONISHING EVENTS I WITNESSED THAT DAY OCCURRED WHILE I WAS WALKING.
I WAS WATCHING THE PEOPLE. IT WAS LIKE BEING AT A 3D SCREENING.
SUDDENLY I FELT MY RIGHT FOOT SLIDE A LITTLE TOO MUCH IN ITS SHOE.
MY LACES HAD COME UNDONE, SO I BENT OVER TO TIE THEM.
THAT'S WHEN I NOTICED THAT THE LEFT SHOE HAD COME UNDONE, NOT THE RIGHT ONE AS I HAD SO CLEARLY FELT.
strange!
STUNNED, I WIGGLED MY TOES. EVERYTHING SEEMED NORMAL.
Incredible
AFTERWARDS IT SEEMED RIDICULOUS... AND YET THERE WAS MORE TO COME...

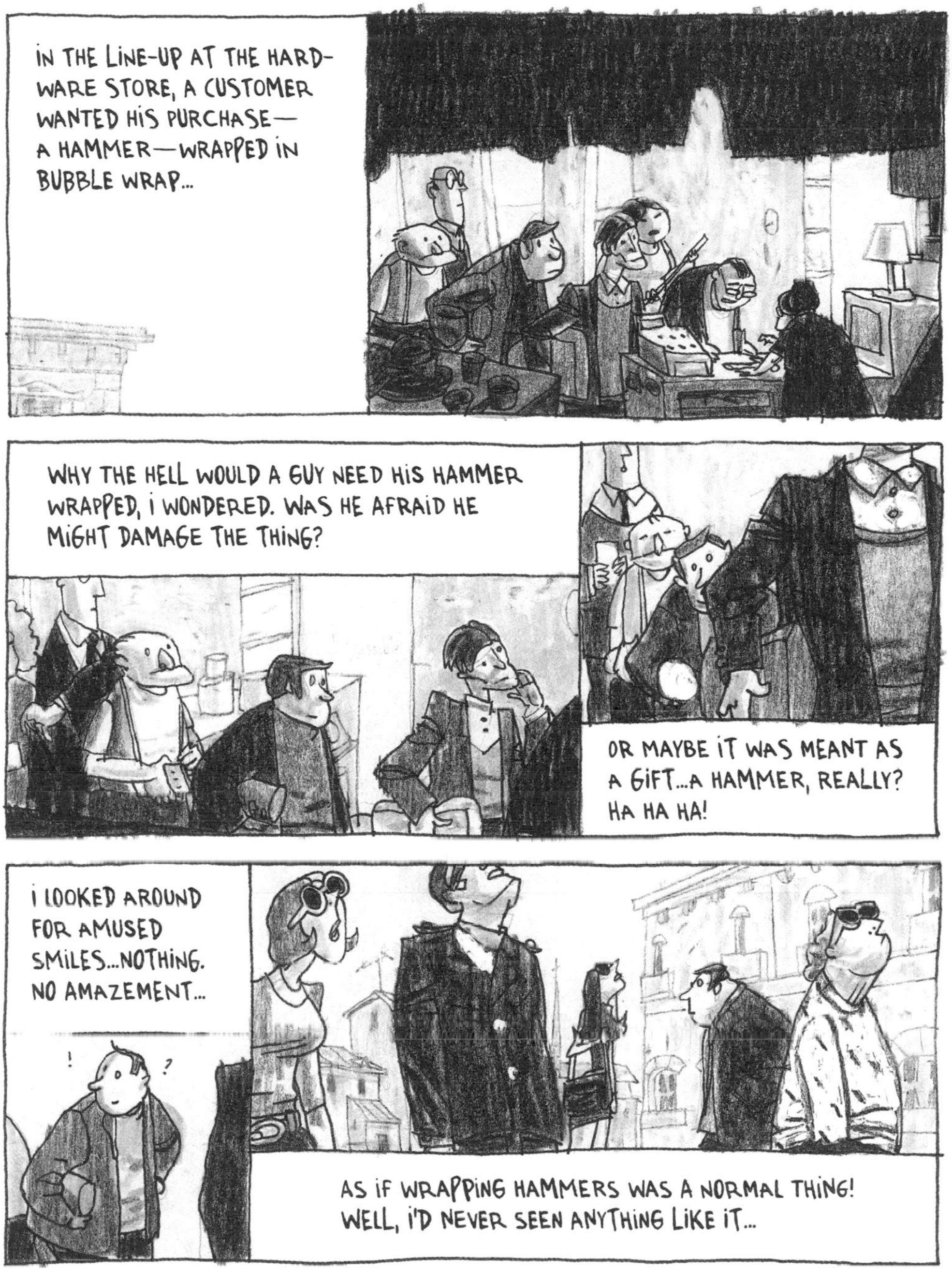
IN THE LINE-UP AT THE HARD-WARE STORE, A CUSTOMER WANTED HIS PURCHASE—A HAMMER—WRAPPED IN BUBBLE WRAP...
WHY THE HELL WOULD A GUY NEED HIS HAMMER WRAPPED, I WONDERED. WAS HE AFRAID HE MIGHT DAMAGE THE THING?
OR MAYBE IT WAS MEANT AS A GIFT...A HAMMER, REALLY? HA HA HA!
I LOOKED AROUND FOR AMUSED SMILES...NOTHING. NO AMAZEMENT...
!
?
AS IF WRAPPING HAMMERS WAS A NORMAL THING! WELL, I'D NEVER SEEN ANYTHING LIKE IT...

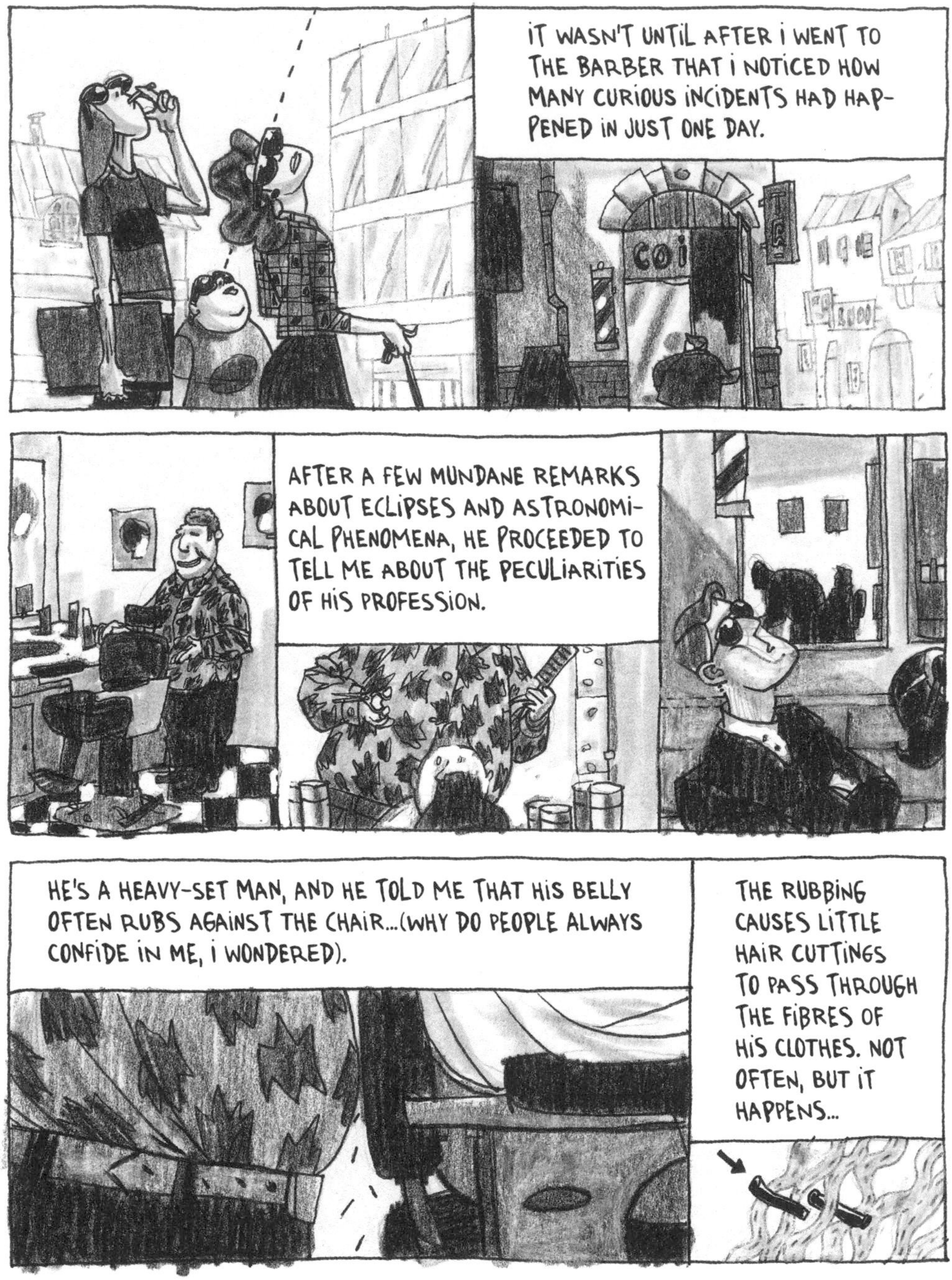
IT WASN'T UNTIL AFTER I WENT TO THE BARBER THAT I NOTICED HOW MANY CURIOUS INCIDENTS HAD HAPPENED IN JUST ONE DAY.
COI
AFTER A FEW MUNDANE REMARKS ABOUT ECLIPSES AND ASTRONOMICAL PHENOMENA, HE PROCEEDED TO TELL ME ABOUT THE PECULIARITIES OF HIS PROFESSION.
HE'S A HEAVY-SET MAN, AND HE TOLD ME THAT HIS BELLY OFTEN RUBS AGAINST THE CHAIR...(WHY DO PEOPLE ALWAYS CONFIDE IN ME, I WONDERED).
THE RUBBING CAUSES LITTLE HAIR CUTTINGS TO PASS THROUGH THE FIBRES OF HIS CLOTHES. NOT OFTEN, BUT IT HAPPENS...

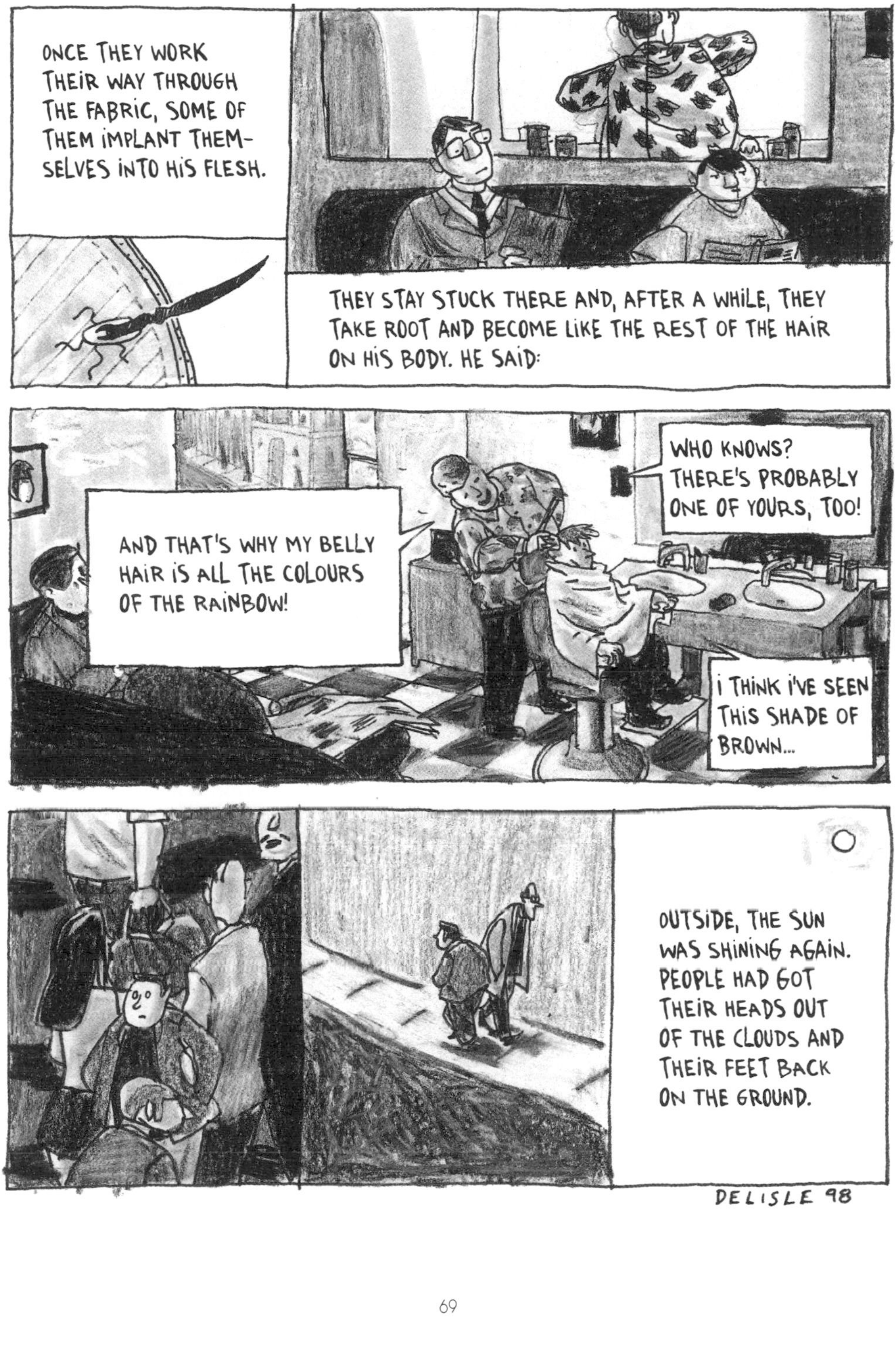
ONCE THEY WORK THEIR WAY THROUGH THE FABRIC, SOME OF THEM IMPLANT THEMSELVES INTO HIS FLESH.
THEY STAY STUCK THERE AND, AFTER A WHILE, THEY TAKE ROOT AND BECOME LIKE THE REST OF THE HAIR ON HIS BODY. HE SAID:
AND THAT'S WHY MY BELLY HAIR IS ALL THE COLOURS OF THE RAINBOW!
WHO KNOWS? THERE'S PROBABLY ONE OF YOURS, TOO!
I THINK I'VE SEEN THIS SHADE OF BROWN...
OUTSIDE, THE SUN WAS SHINING AGAIN. PEOPLE HAD GOT THEIR HEADS OUT OF THE CLOUDS AND THEIR FEET BACK ON THE GROUND.
DELISLE 98

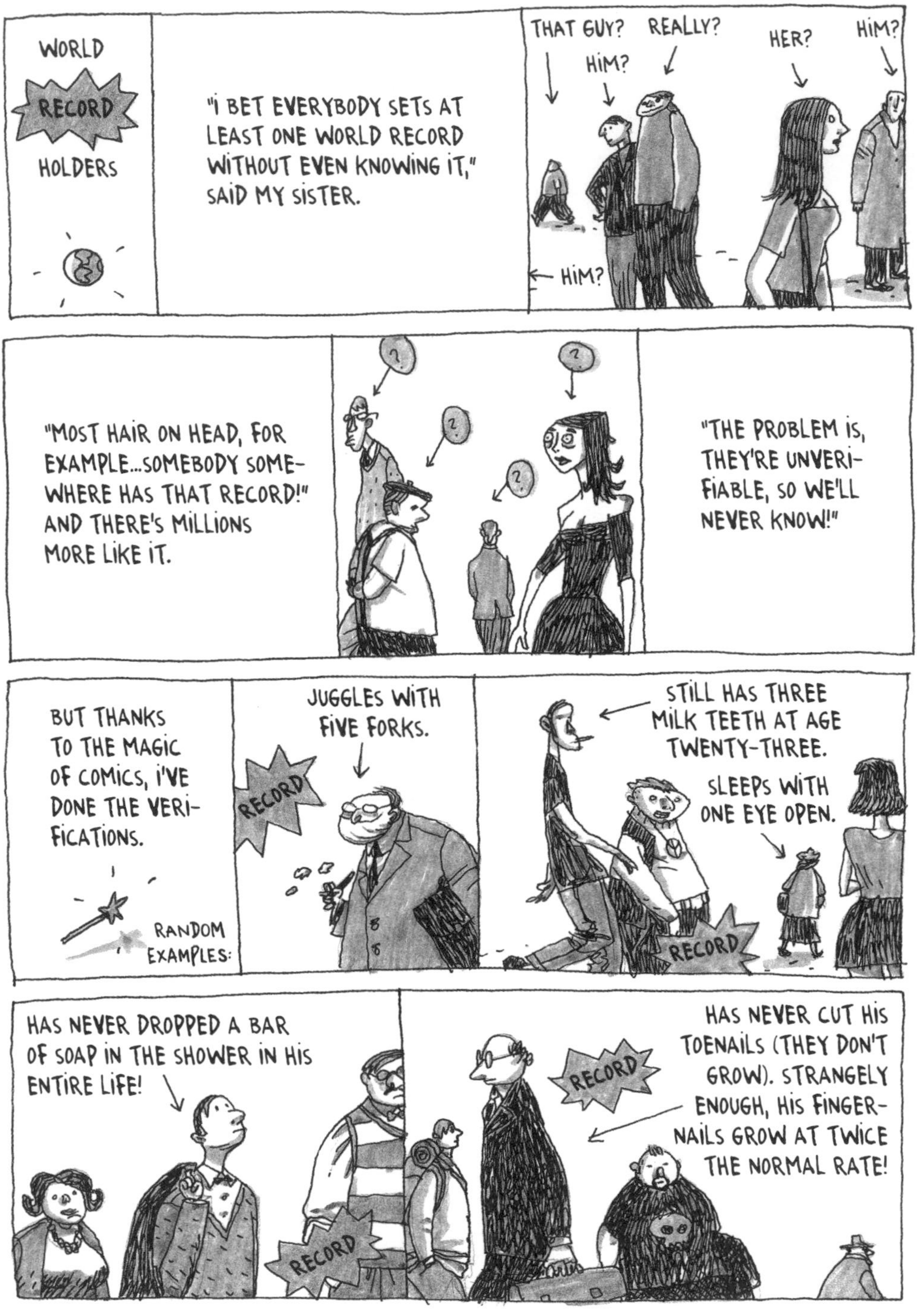
WORLD
RECORD
HOLDERS
"I BET EVERYBODY SETS AT LEAST ONE WORLD RECORD WITHOUT EVEN KNOWING IT," SAID MY SISTER.
THAT GUY?
HIM?
REALLY?
HER?
HIM?
HIM?
"MOST HAIR ON HEAD, FOR EXAMPLE...SOMEBODY SOME-WHERE HAS THAT RECORD!" AND THERE'S MILLIONS MORE LIKE IT.
"THE PROBLEM IS, THEY'RE UNVERI-FIABLE, SO WE'LL NEVER KNOW!"
BUT THANKS TO THE MAGIC OF COMICS, I'VE DONE THE VERI-FICATIONS.
RANDOM EXAMPLES:
JUGGLES WITH FIVE FORKS.
RECORD
STILL HAS THREE MILK TEETH AT AGE TWENTY-THREE.
SLEEPS WITH ONE EYE OPEN.
RECORD
HAS NEVER DROPPED A BAR OF SOAP IN THE SHOWER IN HIS ENTIRE LIFE!
RECORD
HAS NEVER CUT HIS TOENAILS (THEY DON'T GROW). STRANGELY ENOUGH, HIS FINGER-NAILS GROW AT TWICE THE NORMAL RATE!
RECORD

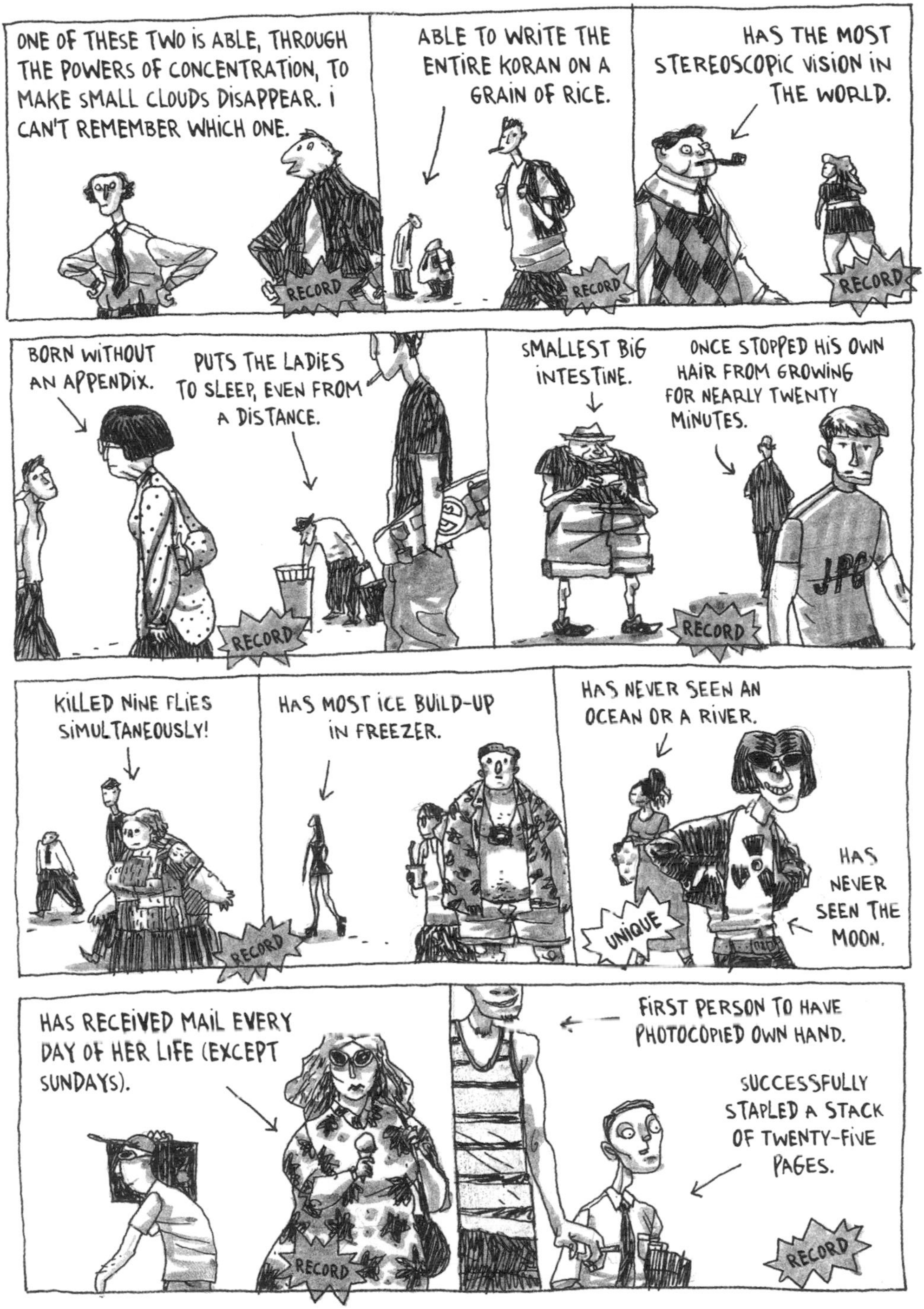
ONE OF THESE TWO IS ABLE, THROUGH THE POWERS OF CONCENTRATION, TO MAKE SMALL CLOUDS DISAPPEAR. I CAN'T REMEMBER WHICH ONE.
RECORD
ABLE TO WRITE THE ENTIRE KORAN ON A GRAIN OF RICE.
RECORD
HAS THE MOST STEREOSCOPIC VISION IN THE WORLD.
RECORD
BORN WITHOUT AN APPENDIX.
PUTS THE LADIES TO SLEEP, EVEN FROM A DISTANCE.
RECORD
SMALLEST BIG INTESTINE.
ONCE STOPPED HIS OWN HAIR FROM GROWING FOR NEARLY TWENTY MINUTES.
RECORD
KILLED NINE FLIES SIMULTANEOUSLY!
RECORD
HAS MOST ICE BUILD-UP IN FREEZER.
HAS NEVER SEEN AN OCEAN OR A RIVER.
UNIQUE
HAS NEVER SEEN THE MOON.
HAS RECEIVED MAIL EVERY DAY OF HER LIFE (EXCEPT SUNDAYS).
RECORD
FIRST PERSON TO HAVE PHOTOCOPIED OWN HAND.
SUCCESSFULLY STAPLED A STACK OF TWENTY-FIVE PAGES.
RECORD

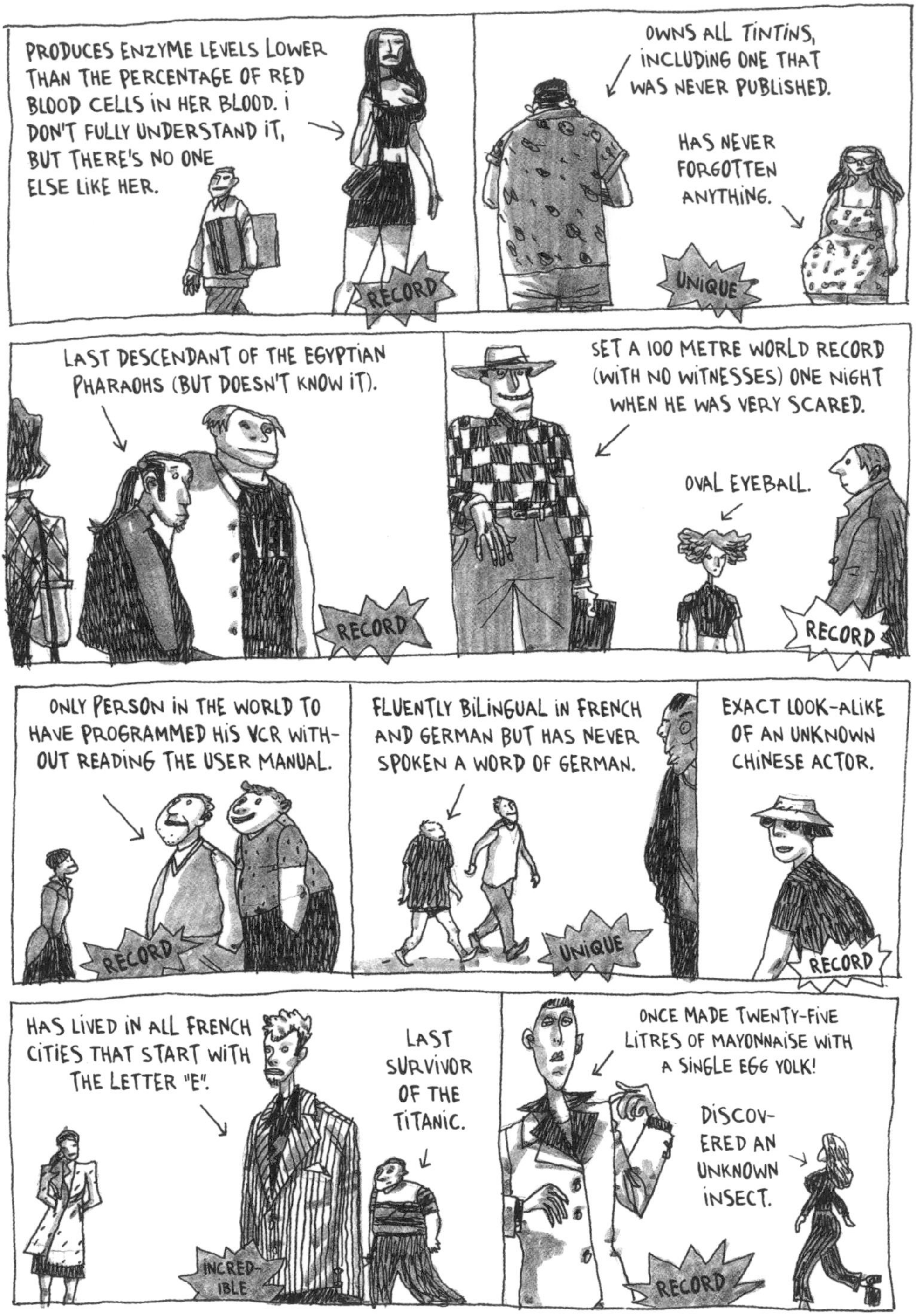
PRODUCES ENZYME LEVELS LOWER THAN THE PERCENTAGE OF RED BLOOD CELLS IN HER BLOOD. I DON'T FULLY UNDERSTAND IT, BUT THERE'S NO ONE ELSE LIKE HER.
RECORD
OWNS ALL TINTINS, INCLUDING ONE THAT WAS NEVER PUBLISHED.
HAS NEVER FORGOTTEN ANYTHING.
UNIQUE
LAST DESCENDANT OF THE EGYPTIAN PHARAOHS (BUT DOESN'T KNOW IT).
RECORD
SET A 100 METRE WORLD RECORD (WITH NO WITNESSES) ONE NIGHT WHEN HE WAS VERY SCARED.
OVAL EYEBALL.
RECORD
ONLY PERSON IN THE WORLD TO HAVE PROGRAMMED HIS VCR WITH-OUT READING THE USER MANUAL.
RECORD
FLUENTLY BILINGUAL IN FRENCH AND GERMAN BUT HAS NEVER SPOKEN A WORD OF GERMAN.
UNIQUE
EXACT LOOK-ALIKE OF AN UNKNOWN CHINESE ACTOR.
RECORD
HAS LIVED IN ALL FRENCH CITIES THAT START WITH THE LETTER "E".
LAST SURVIVOR OF THE TITANIC.
INCRED-IBLE
ONCE MADE TWENTY-FIVE LITRES OF MAYONNAISE WITH A SINGLE EGG YOLK!
DISCOV-ERED AN UNKNOWN INSECT.
RECORD

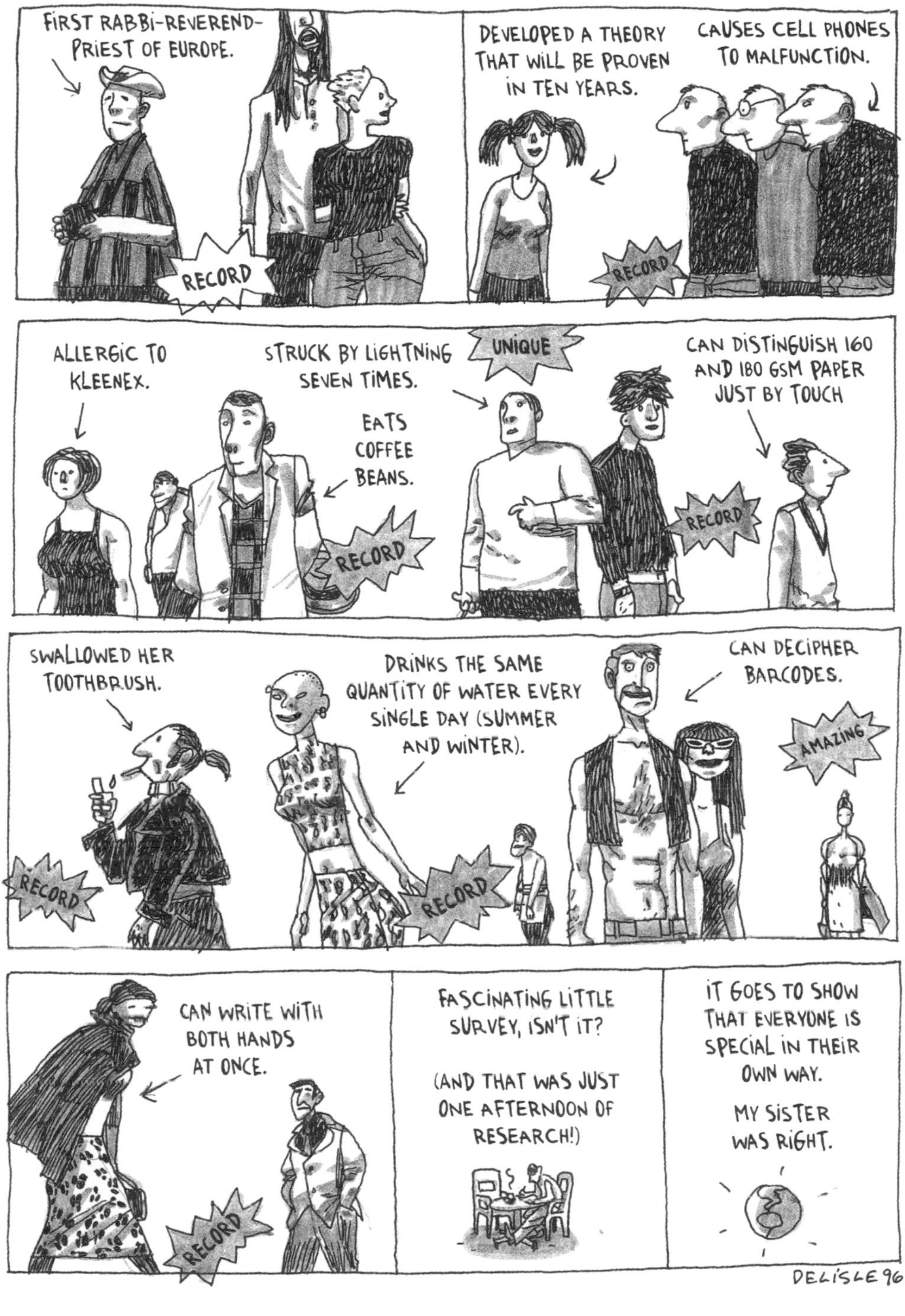

FIRST RABBI-REVEREND-PRIEST OF EUROPE.
RECORD
DEVELOPED A THEORY THAT WILL BE PROVEN IN TEN YEARS.
CAUSES CELL PHONES TO MALFUNCTION.
RECORD
ALLERGIC TO KLEENEX.
EATS COFFEE BEANS.
RECORD
STRUCK BY LIGHTNING SEVEN TIMES.
UNIQUE
CAN DISTINGUISH 160 AND 180 GSM PAPER JUST BY TOUCH
RECORD
SWALLOWED HER TOOTHBRUSH.
RECORD
DRINKS THE SAME QUANTITY OF WATER EVERY SINGLE DAY (SUMMER AND WINTER).
RECORD
CAN DECIPHER BARCODES.
AMAZING
CAN WRITE WITH BOTH HANDS AT ONCE.
RECORD
FASCINATING LITTLE SURVEY, ISN'T IT?
(AND THAT WAS JUST ONE AFTERNOON OF RESEARCH!)
IT GOES TO SHOW THAT EVERYONE IS SPECIAL IN THEIR OWN WAY.
MY SISTER WAS RIGHT.
DELISLE 96

THE SLEEPING GIANT

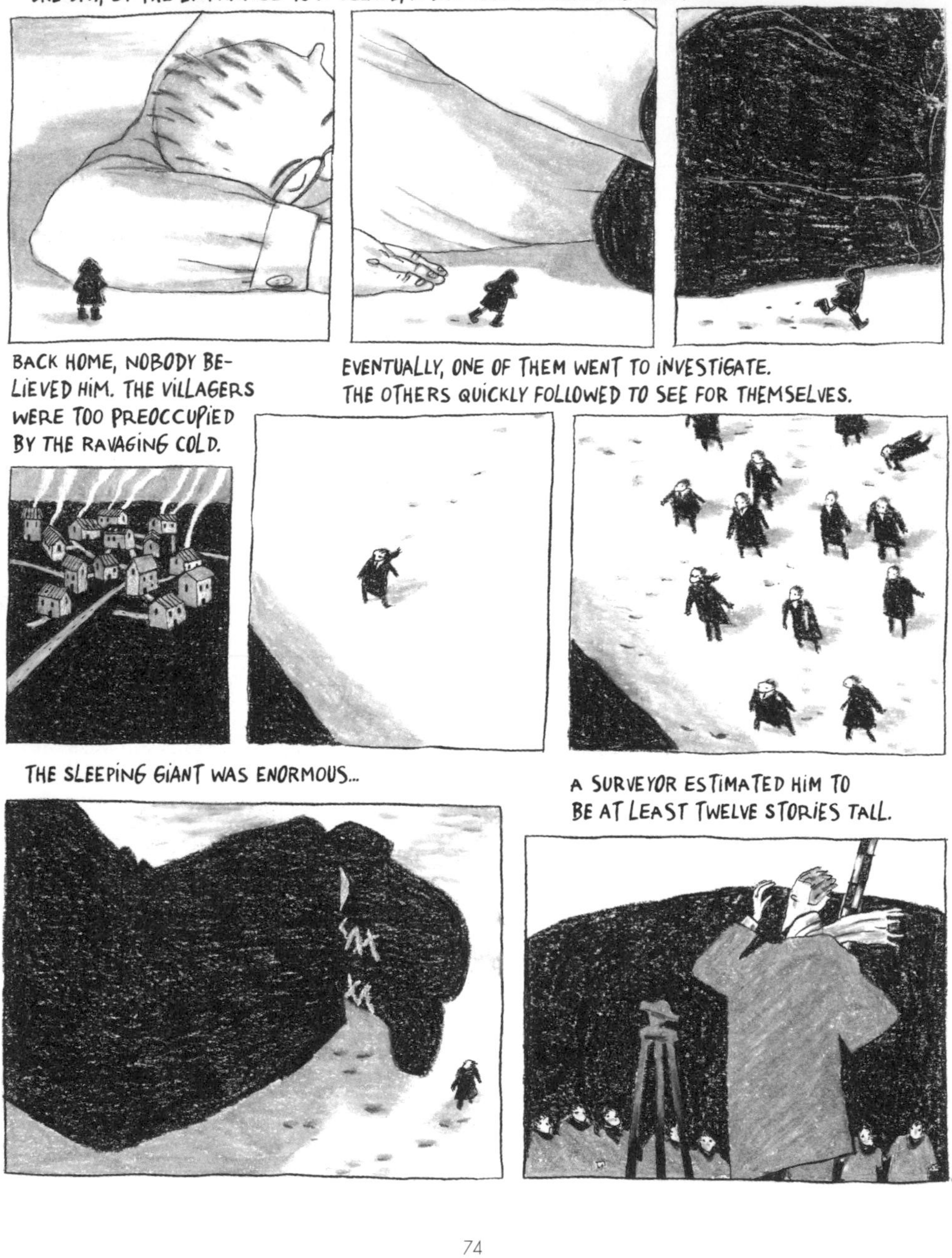

ONE DAY, BY THE ENTRANCE TO A VILLAGE, A BOY FOUND A SLEEPING GIANT...
BACK HOME, NOBODY BELIEVED HIM. THE VILLAGERS WERE TOO PREOCCUPIED BY THE RAVAGING COLD.
EVENTUALLY, ONE OF THEM WENT TO INVESTIGATE. THE OTHERS QUICKLY FOLLOWED TO SEE FOR THEMSELVES.
THE SLEEPING GIANT WAS ENORMOUS...
A SURVEYOR ESTIMATED HIM TO BE AT LEAST TWELVE STORIES TALL.

A WAVE OF FEAR SWEPT THROUGH THE VILLAGE.

"WHAT IF THE GIANT WAKES UP AND GOES ON A RAMPAGE? WE'D BE DOOMED!"

"MAYBE HE'S FRIENDLY," SOMEONE SUGGESTED.

THEY DECIDED TO TIE THE GIANT DOWN ANYWAY, JUST TO BE SAFE.

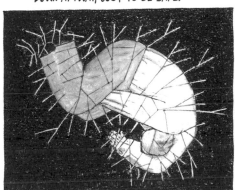

AND THEN THEY AGREED TO WAKE HIM UP IN ORDER TO ASK HIM A FEW QUESTIONS.

THEY TRIED FOR DAYS WITHOUT SUCCESS.

MEANWHILE THE CHILDREN PLAYED ON HIM.

AND PEOPLE CAME TO HIM FOR WARMTH.

THE HOMELESS ARRIVED FROM ALL OVER AND SET UP CAMPS.

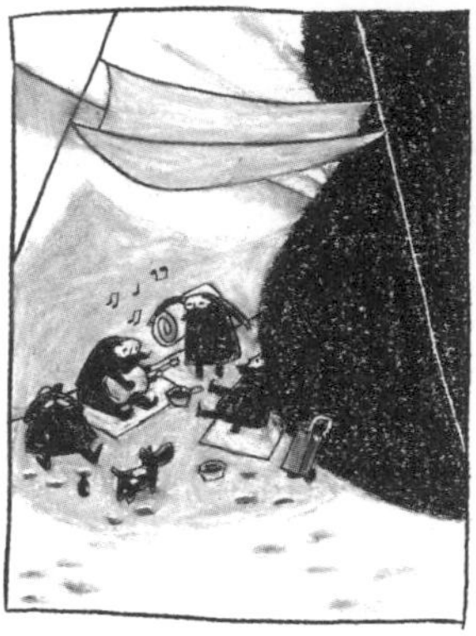

BUT THEY WERE DISPERSED, AND THE FIRST GIANT-HEATED HOUSE WAS BUILT.

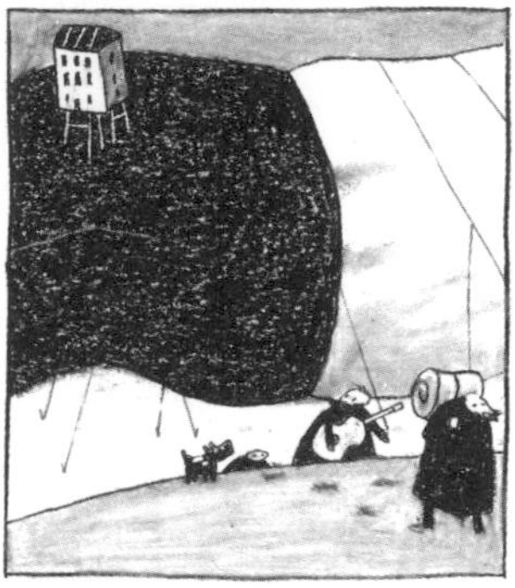

THE IDEA CAUGHT ON QUICKLY...

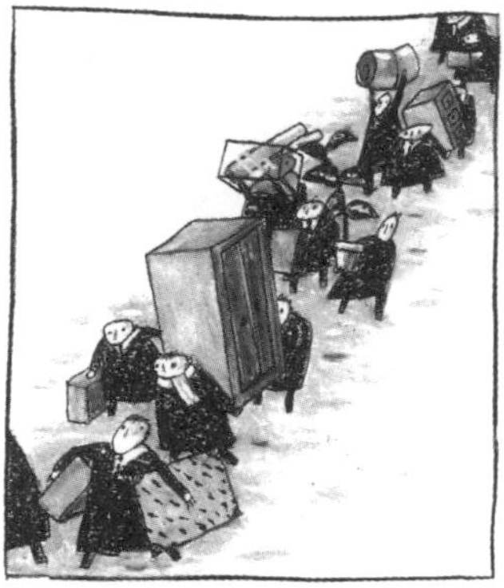

THE VILLAGE WAS ABANDONED... AND RAPIDLY CLAIMED BY THE HOMELESS.

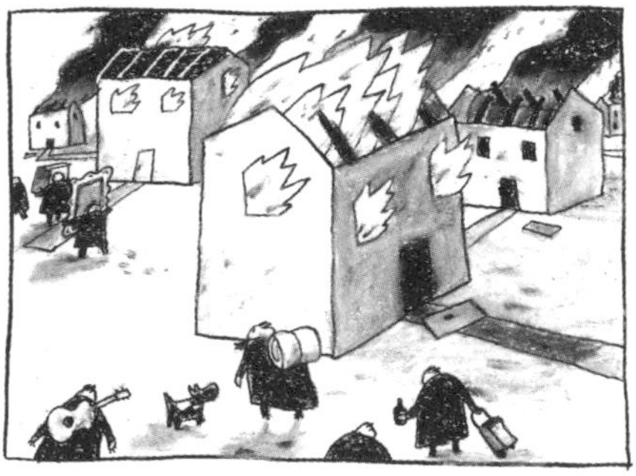

THE SLEEPING GIANT NOW LOOKED LIKE AN ISLAND FORTRESS.

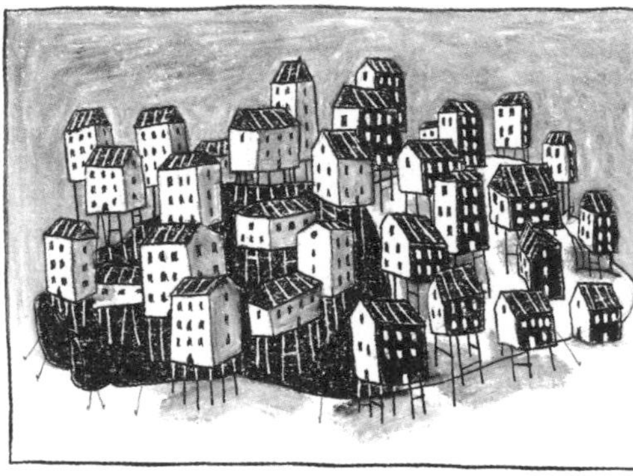

SPACE SOON RAN OUT... A SUBURB WAS BUILT.

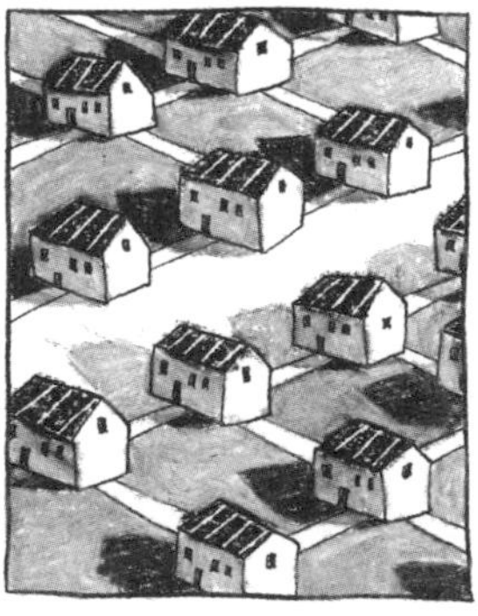

BLOOD WAS TRANSFUSED FROM THE GIANT'S ARM TO BRING HEAT TO THOSE LIVING ON THE OUTSKIRTS.

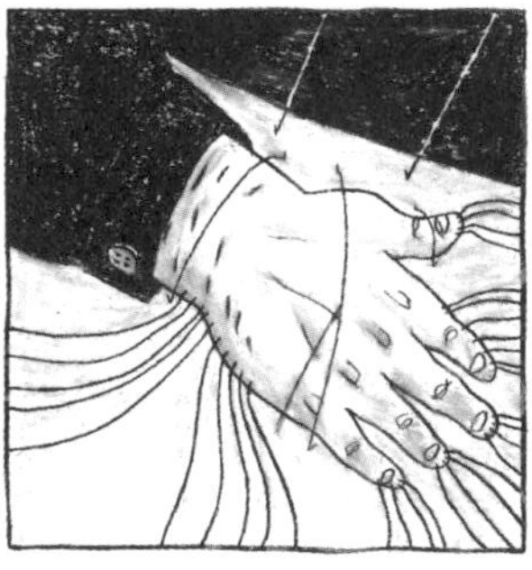

LIFE HAD IMPROVED GREATLY SINCE THE GIANT'S DISCOVERY.

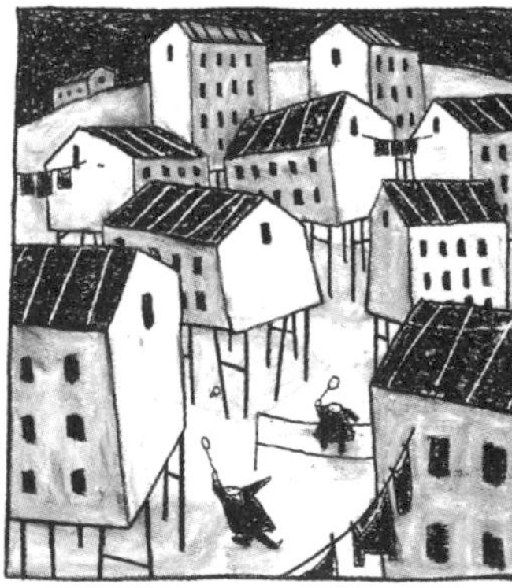

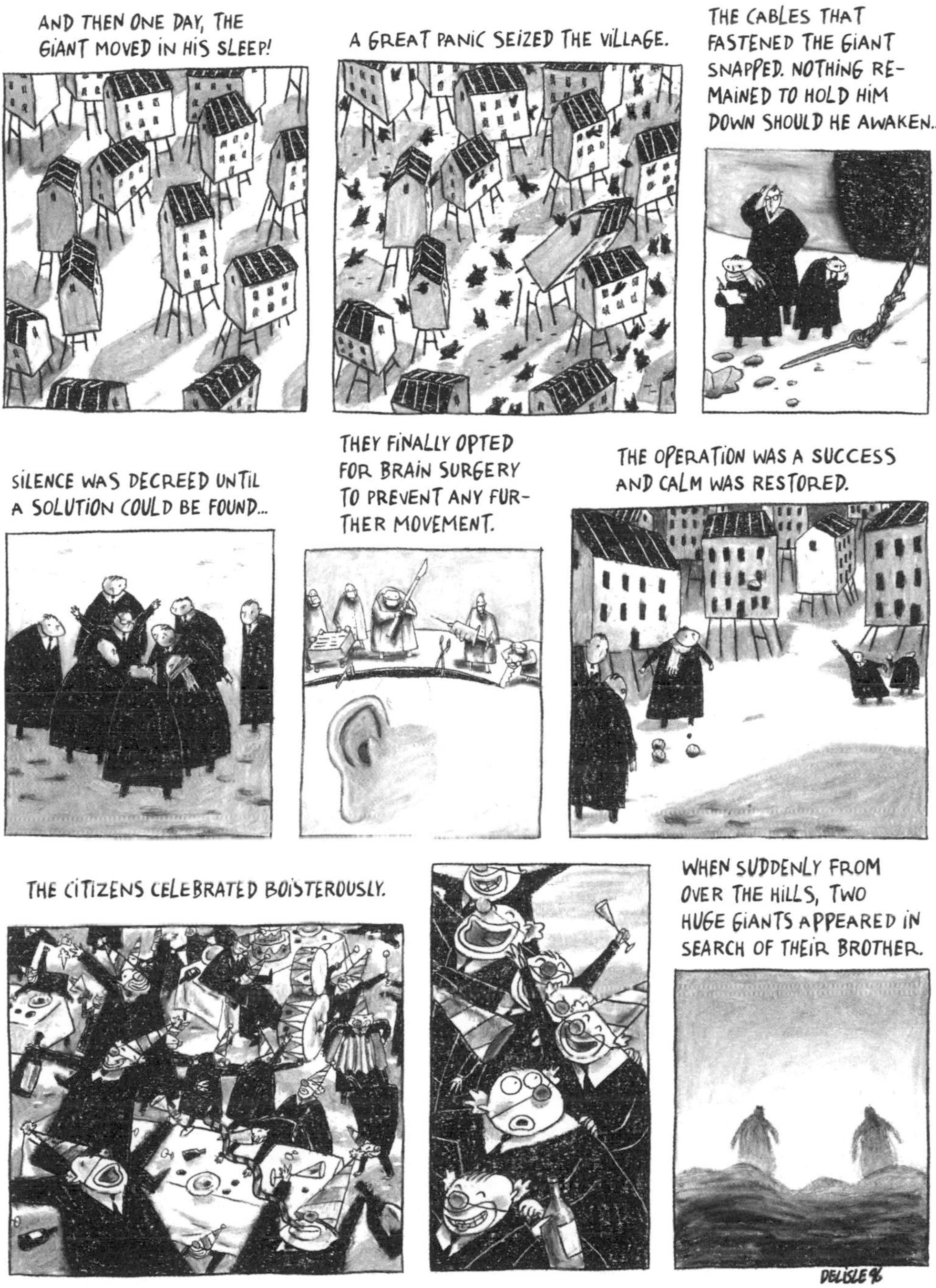
AND THEN ONE DAY, THE GIANT MOVED IN HIS SLEEP!
A GREAT PANIC SEIZED THE VILLAGE.
THE CABLES THAT FASTENED THE GIANT SNAPPED. NOTHING REMAINED TO HOLD HIM DOWN SHOULD HE AWAKEN...
SILENCE WAS DECREED UNTIL A SOLUTION COULD BE FOUND...
THEY FINALLY OPTED FOR BRAIN SURGERY TO PREVENT ANY FURTHER MOVEMENT.
THE OPERATION WAS A SUCCESS AND CALM WAS RESTORED.
THE CITIZENS CELEBRATED BOISTEROUSLY.
WHEN SUDDENLY FROM OVER THE HILLS, TWO HUGE GIANTS APPEARED IN SEARCH OF THEIR BROTHER.
DELISLE 96

SUMMER VACATION

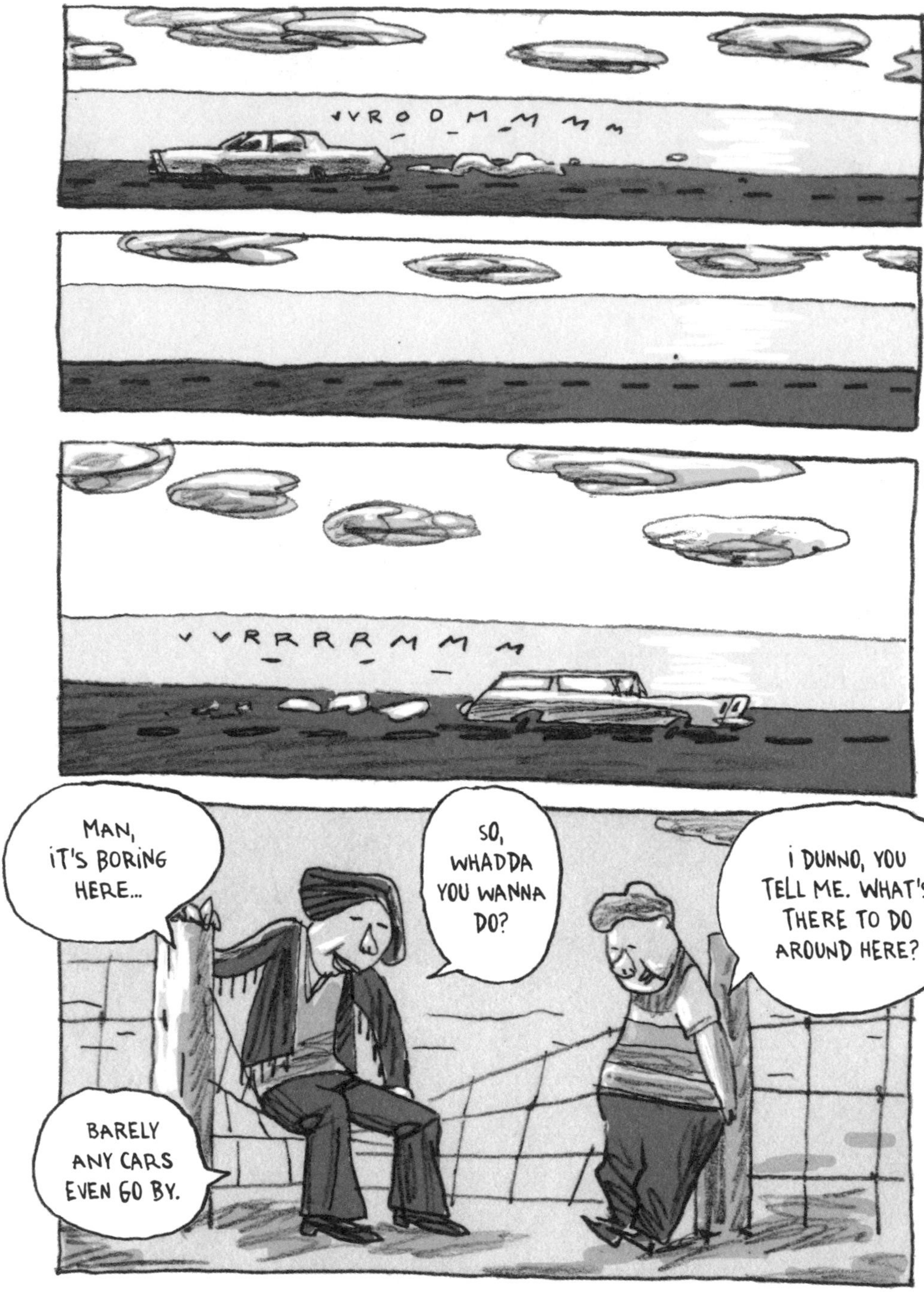
VVROOMMMM
VVRRRRMMM
MAN, IT'S BORING HERE...
BARELY ANY CARS EVEN GO BY.
SO, WHADDA YOU WANNA DO?
I DUNNO, YOU TELL ME. WHAT'S THERE TO DO AROUND HERE?

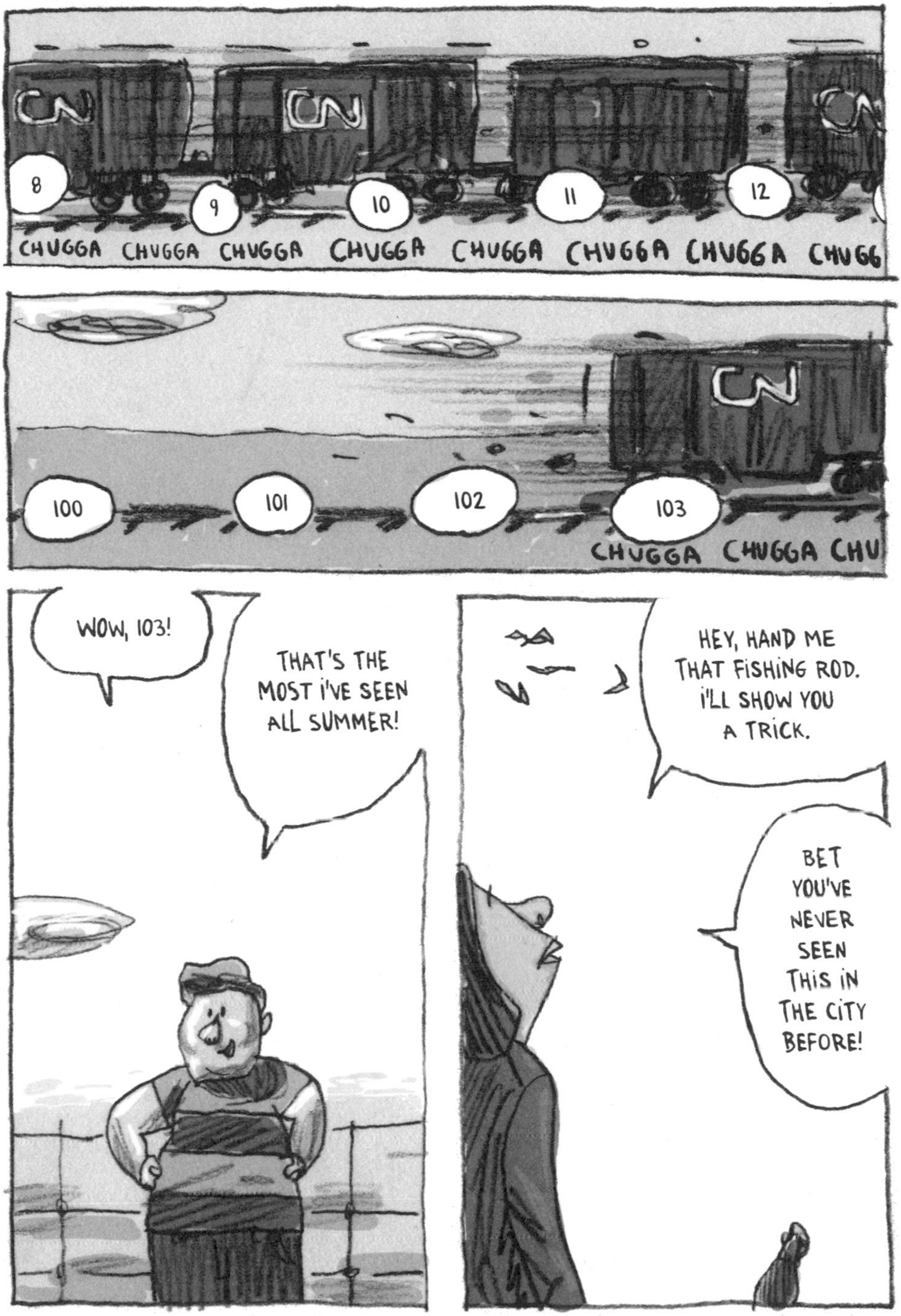
8
9
10
11
12
CHUGGA CHUGGA CHUGGA CHUGGA CHUGGA CHUGGA CHUGGA CHUGG
100
101
102
103
CHUGGA CHUGGA CHU
WOW, 103!
THAT'S THE MOST I'VE SEEN ALL SUMMER!
HEY, HAND ME THAT FISHING ROD. I'LL SHOW YOU A TRICK.
BET YOU'VE NEVER SEEN THIS IN THE CITY BEFORE!

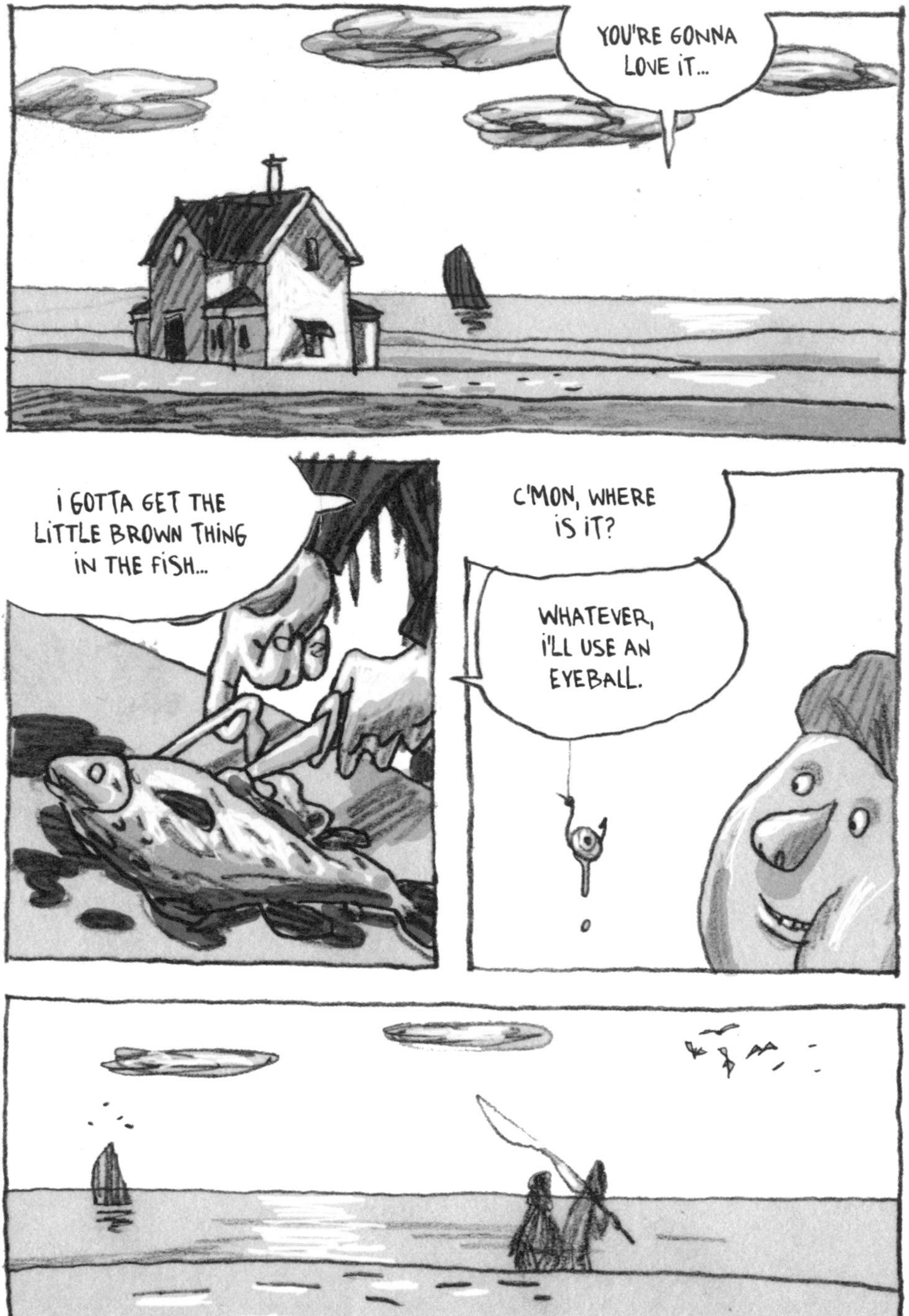
YOU'RE GONNA LOVE IT...
I GOTTA GET THE LITTLE BROWN THING IN THE FISH...
C'MON, WHERE IS IT?
WHATEVER, I'LL USE AN EYEBALL.

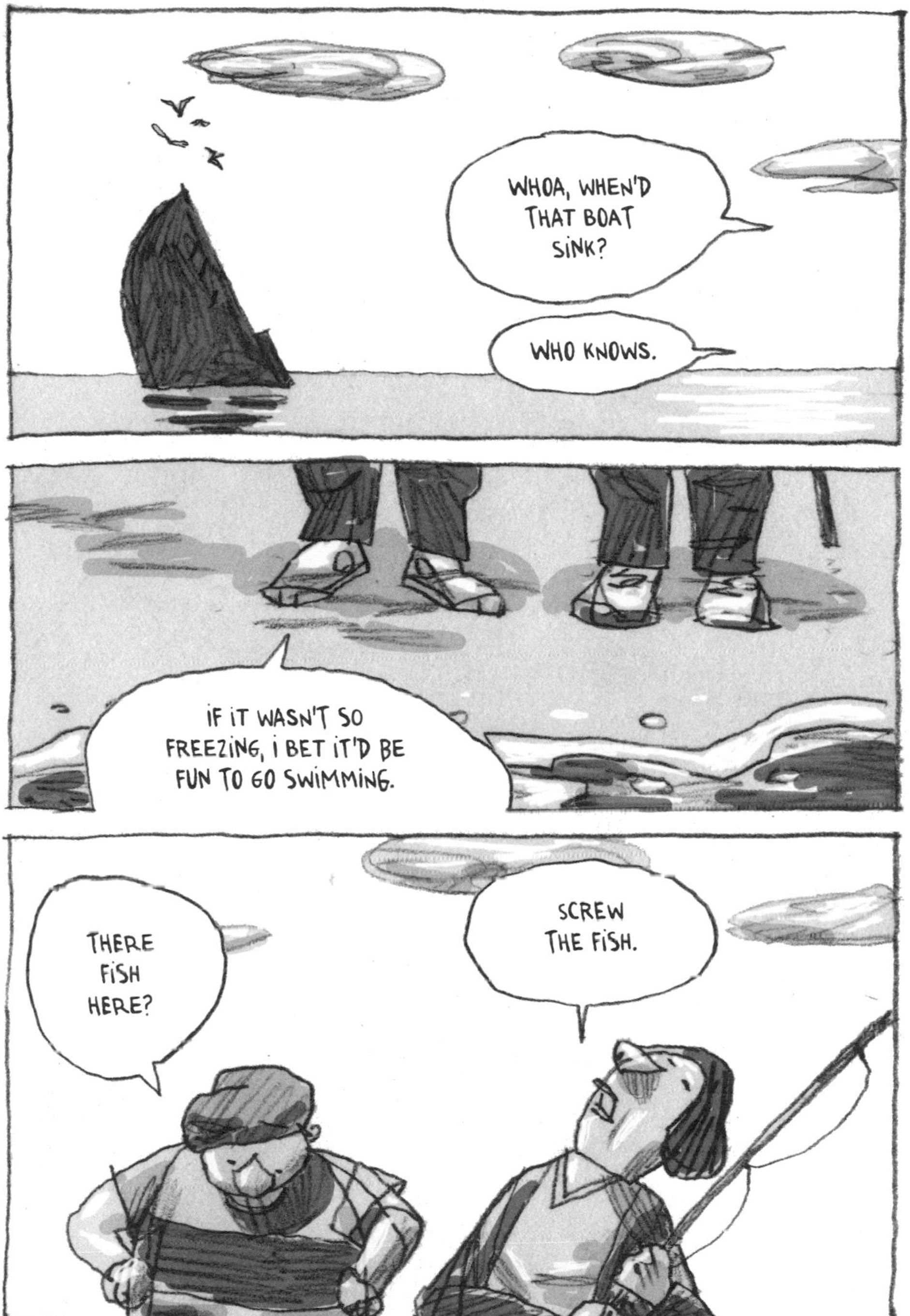
WHOA, WHEN'D THAT BOAT SINK?
WHO KNOWS.
IF IT WASN'T SO FREEZING, I BET IT'D BE FUN TO GO SWIMMING.
THERE FISH HERE?
SCREW THE FISH.

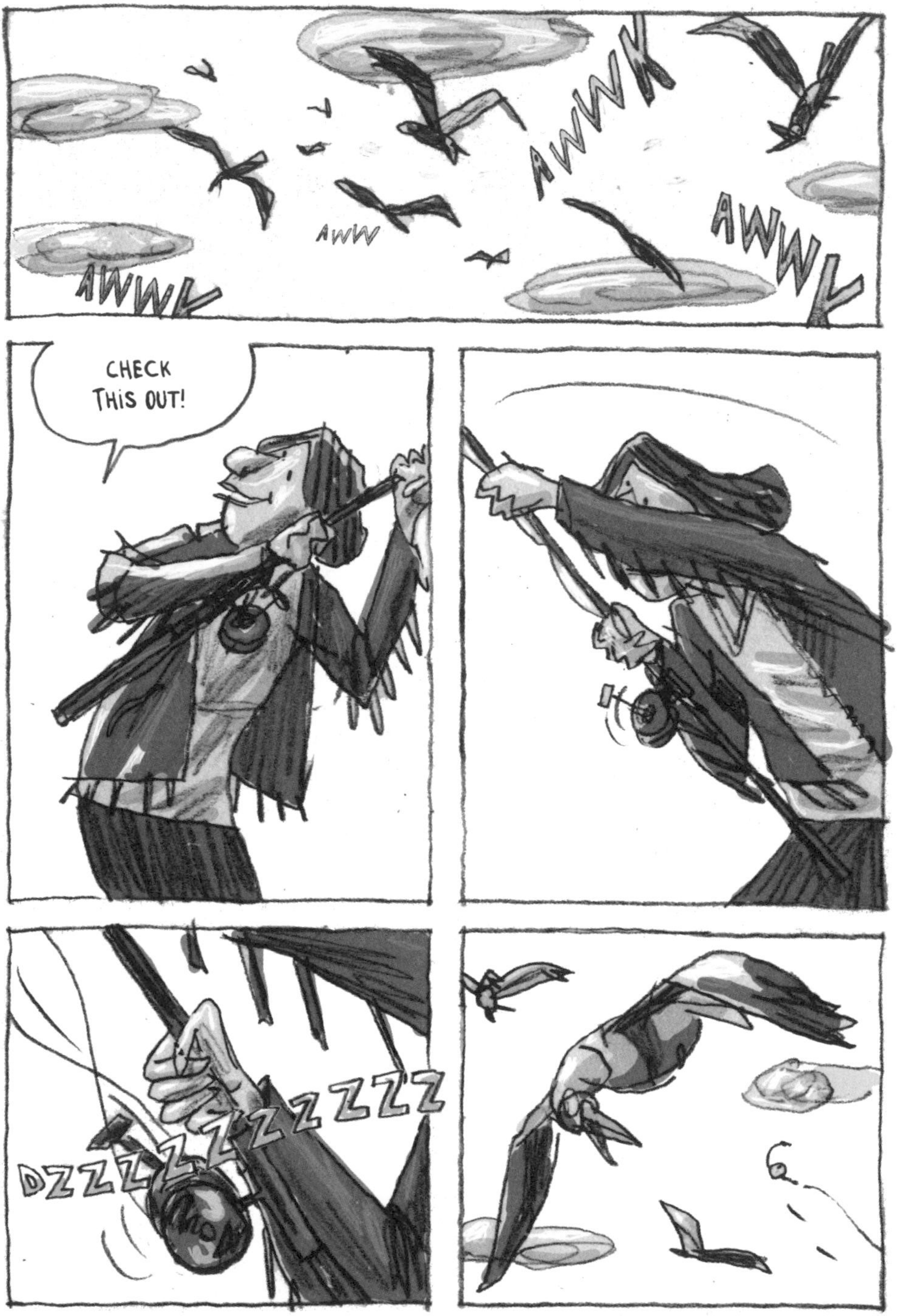
AWWK
AWWK
AWW
AWWK
AWWK
CHECK THIS OUT!
DZZZZZZZZZZZ

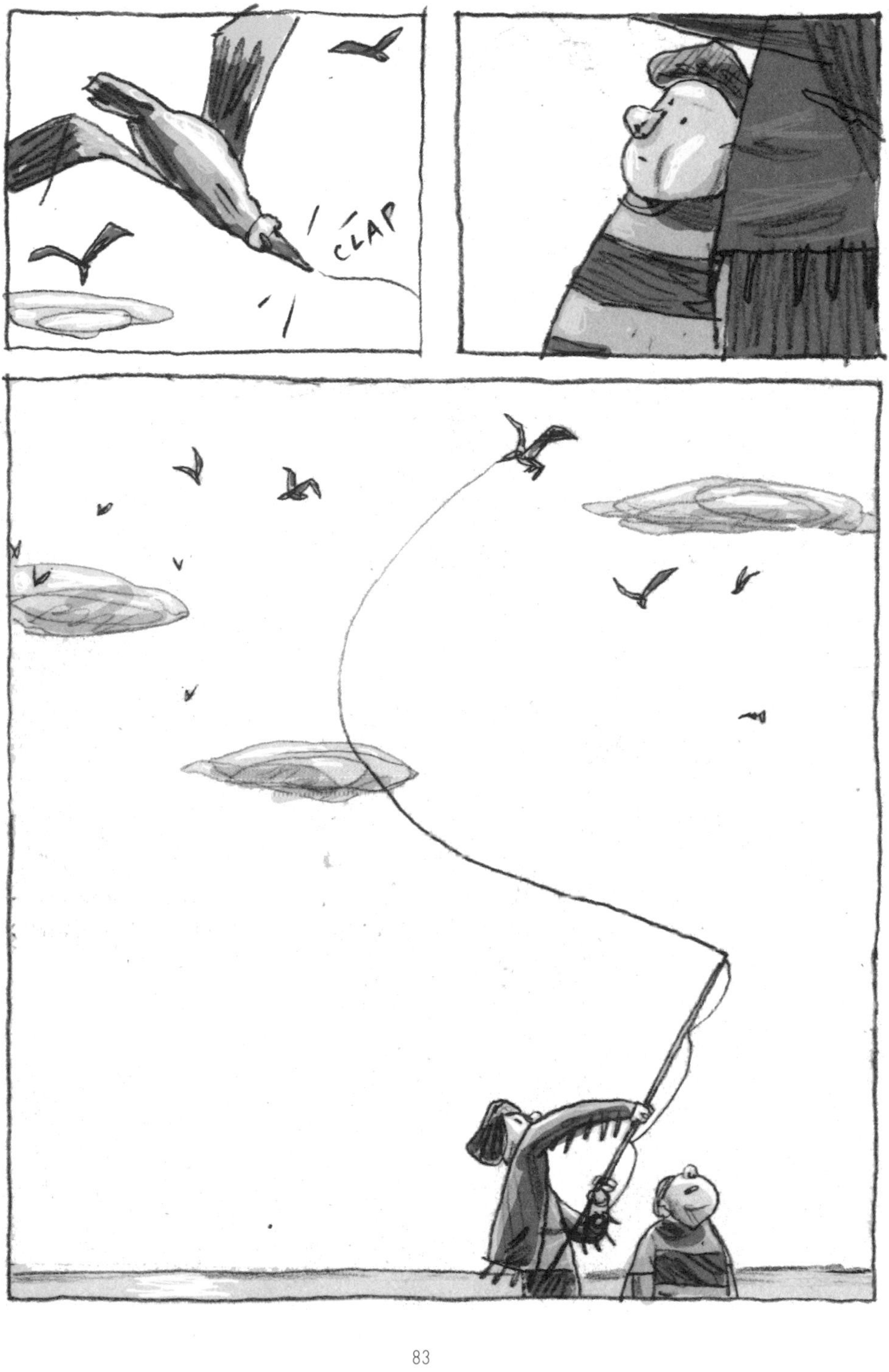
CLAP

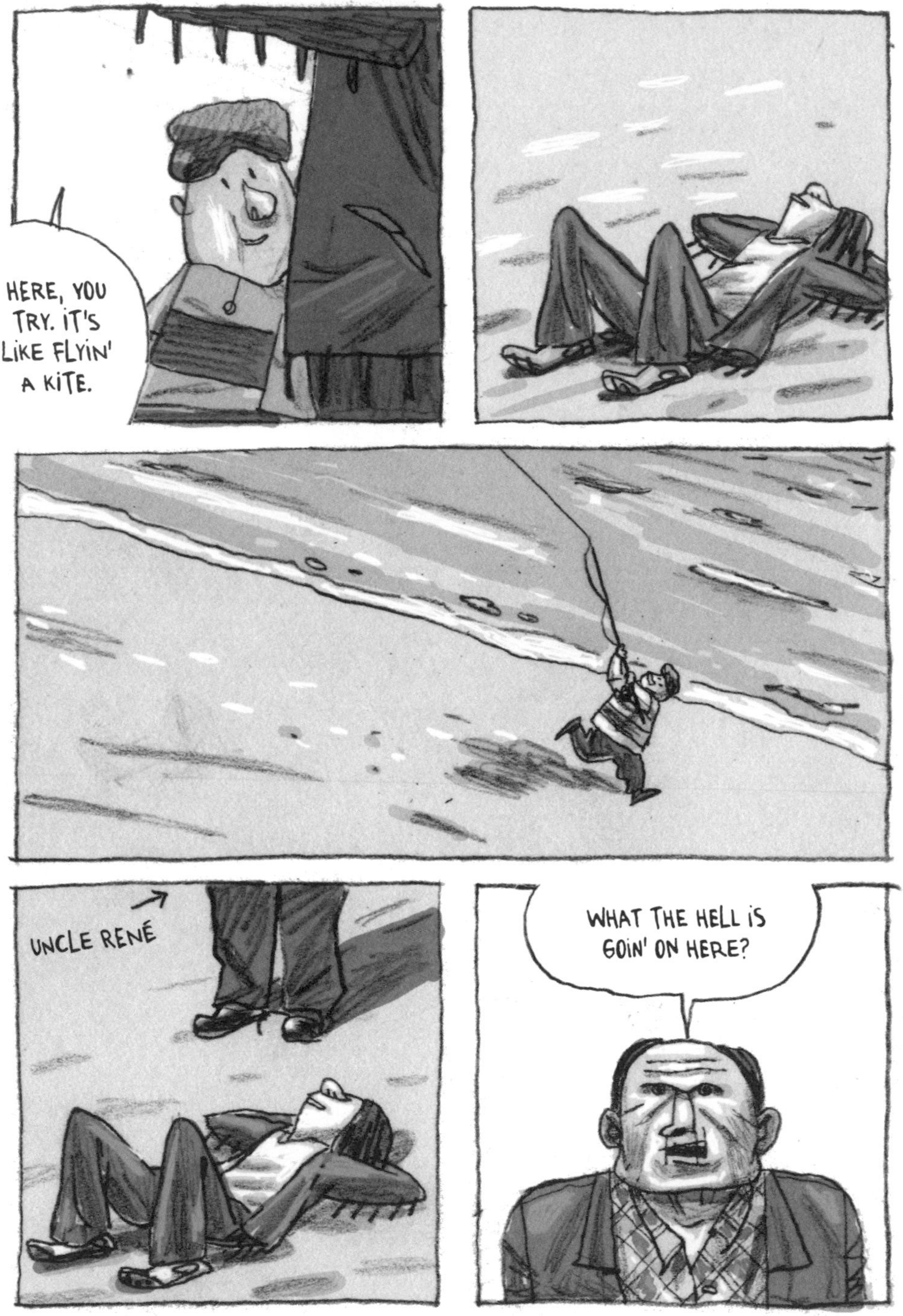

HERE, YOU TRY. IT'S LIKE FLYIN' A KITE.
UNCLE RENÉ
WHAT THE HELL IS GOIN' ON HERE?

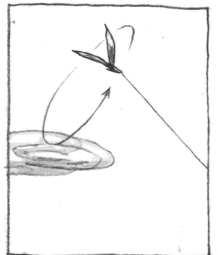

YOU'RE DOIN' IT ALL WRONG!

SNAP

i WAS A PRO AT STUPID STUFF LIKE THIS WHEN i WAS YOUR AGE!

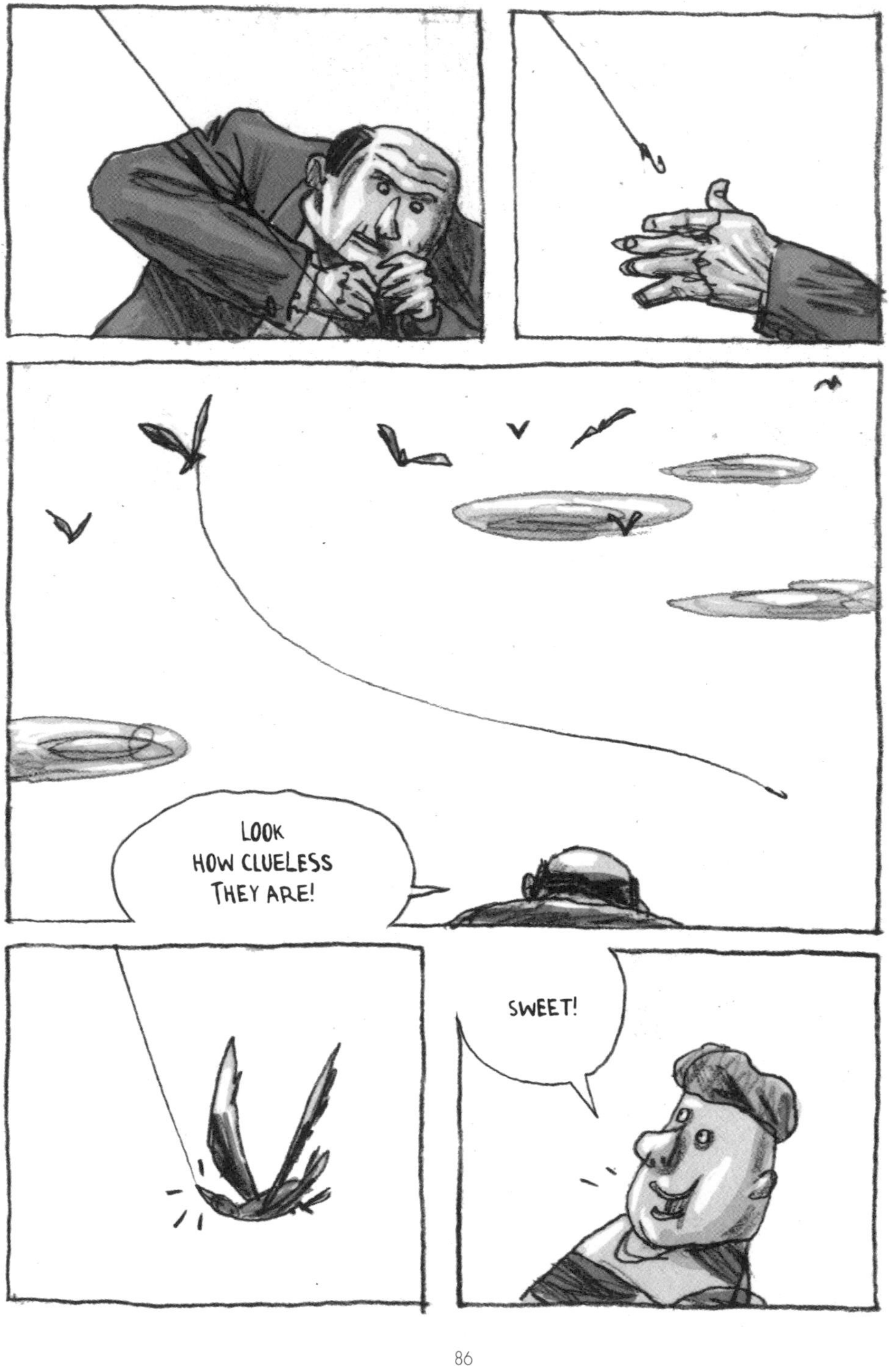
LOOK HOW CLUELESS THEY ARE!
SWEET!

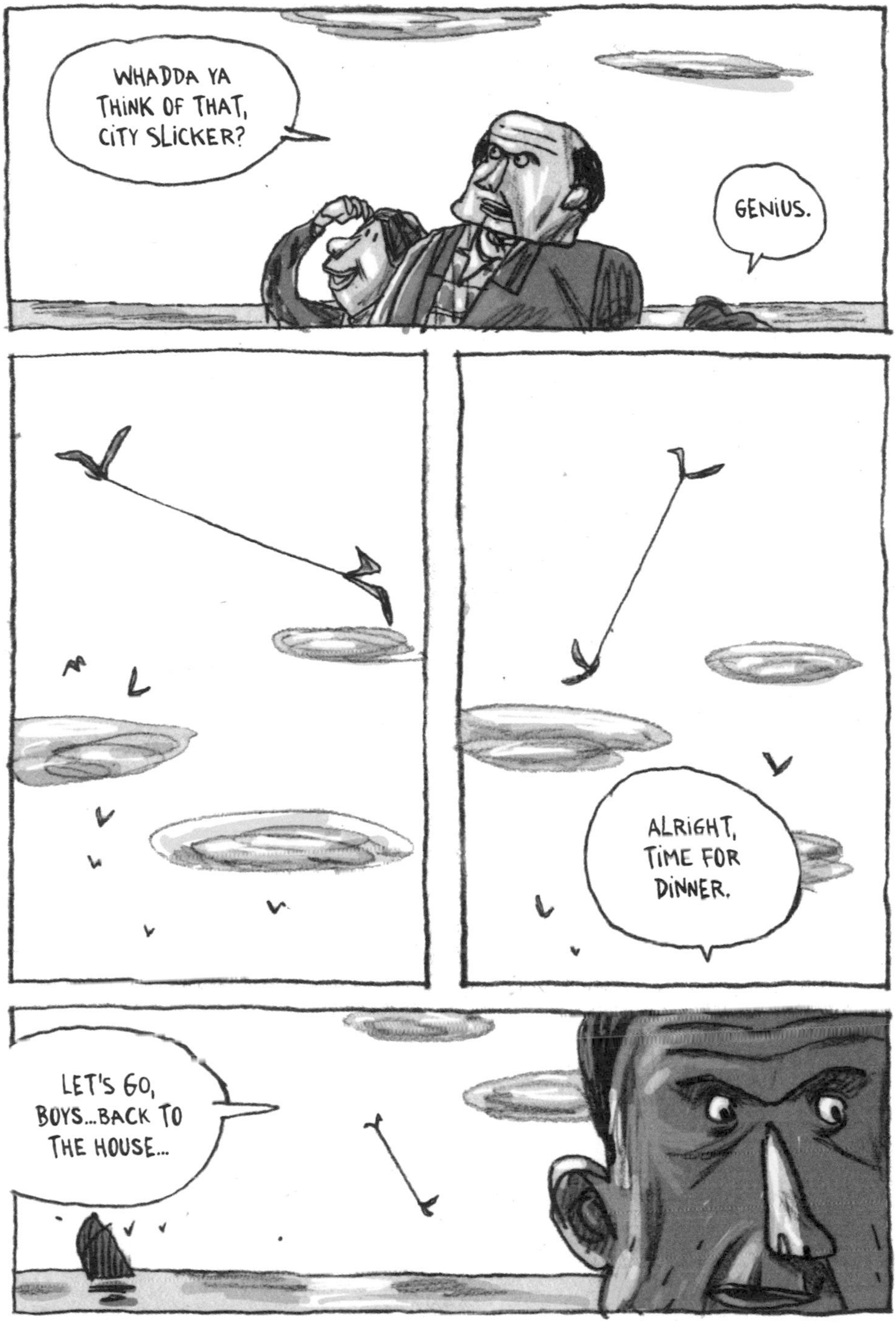
WHADDA YA THINK OF THAT, CITY SLICKER?
GENIUS.
ALRIGHT, TIME FOR DINNER.
LET'S GO, BOYS...BACK TO THE HOUSE...

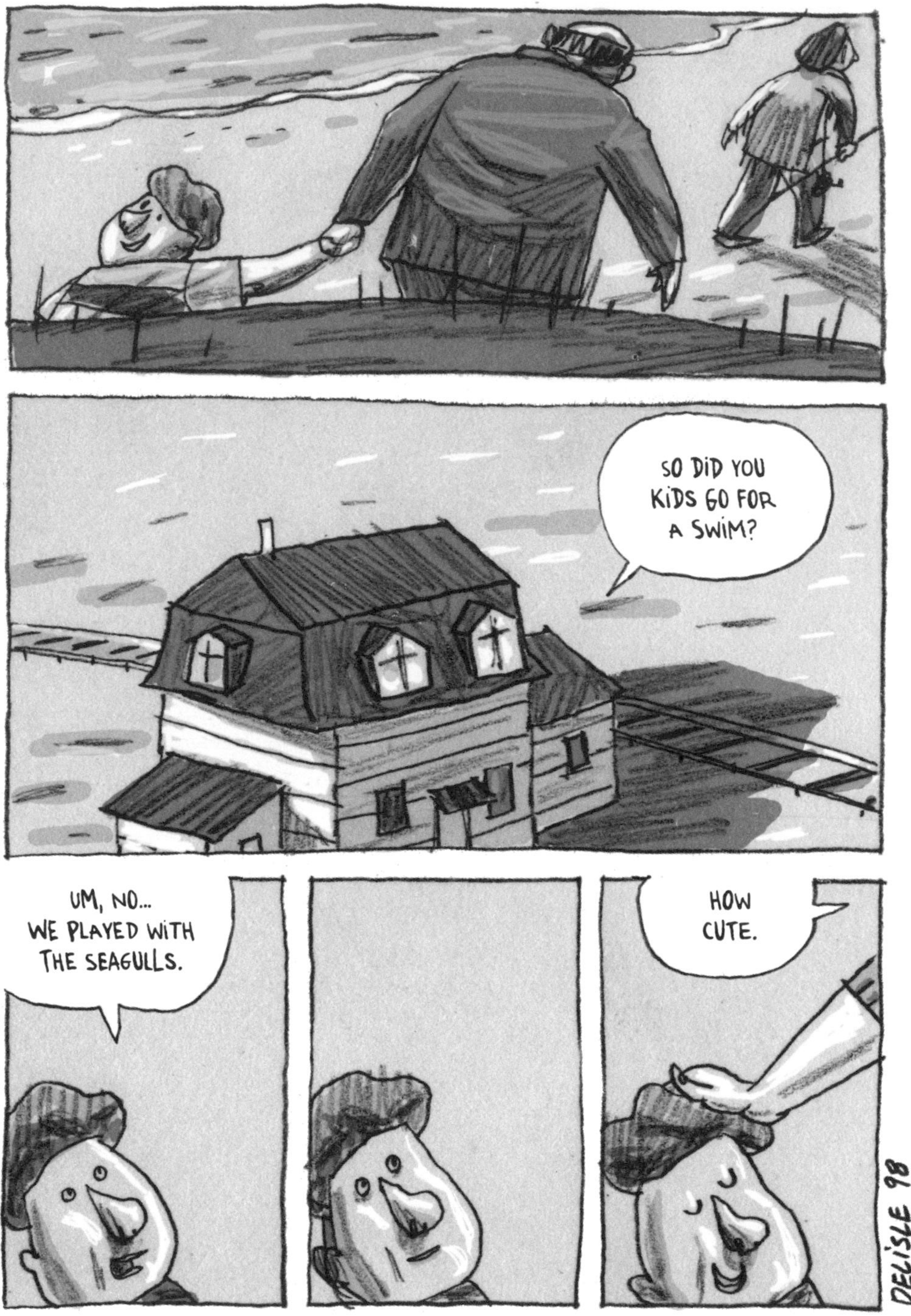
SO DID YOU KIDS GO FOR A SWIM?
UM, NO... WE PLAYED WITH THE SEAGULLS.
HOW CUTE.
DELISLE 98

THE TRAGIC DESTINY OF THE TOY FARM ANIMALS

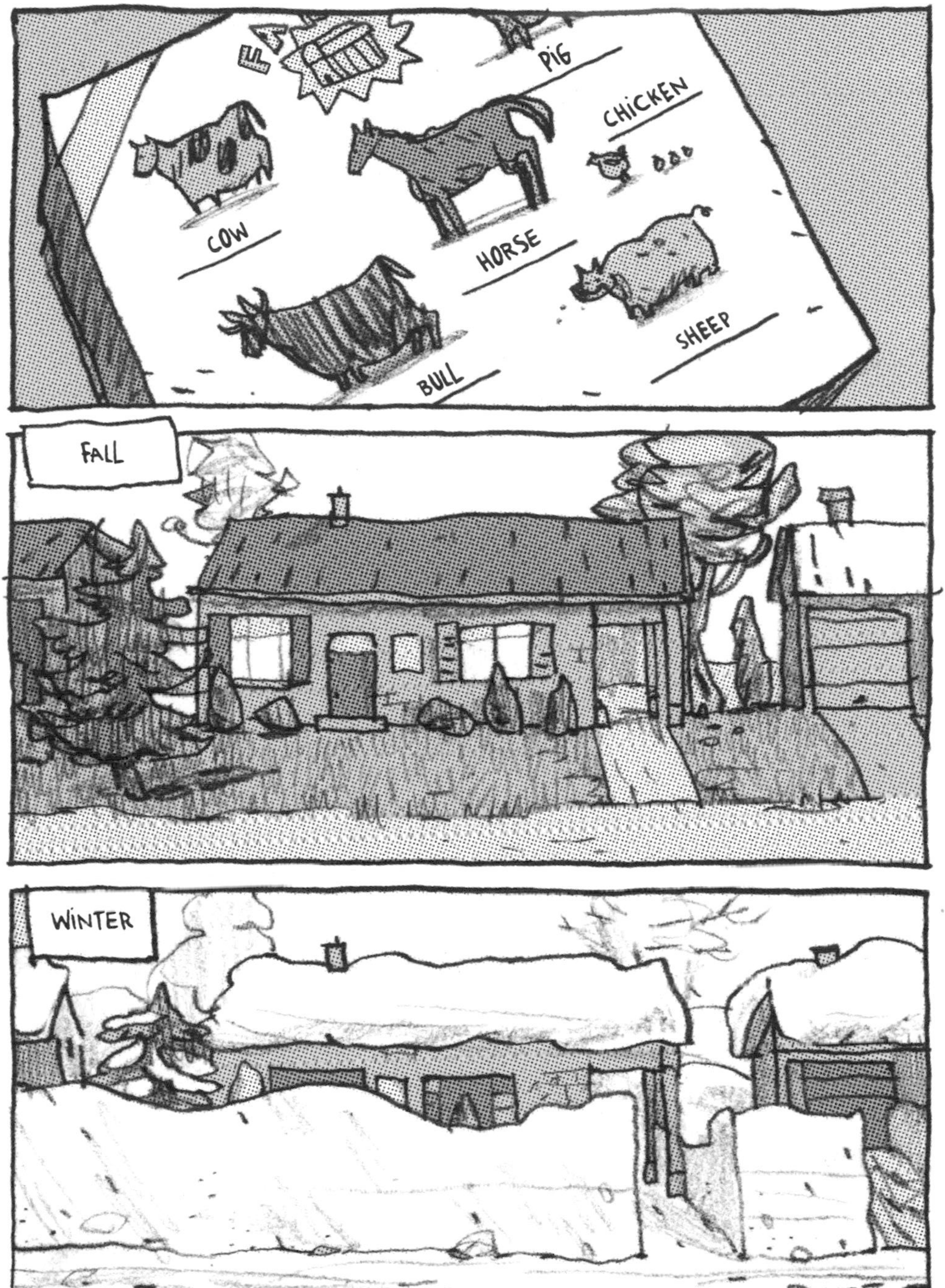
PIG
CHICKEN
COW
HORSE
BULL
SHEEP
FALL
WINTER

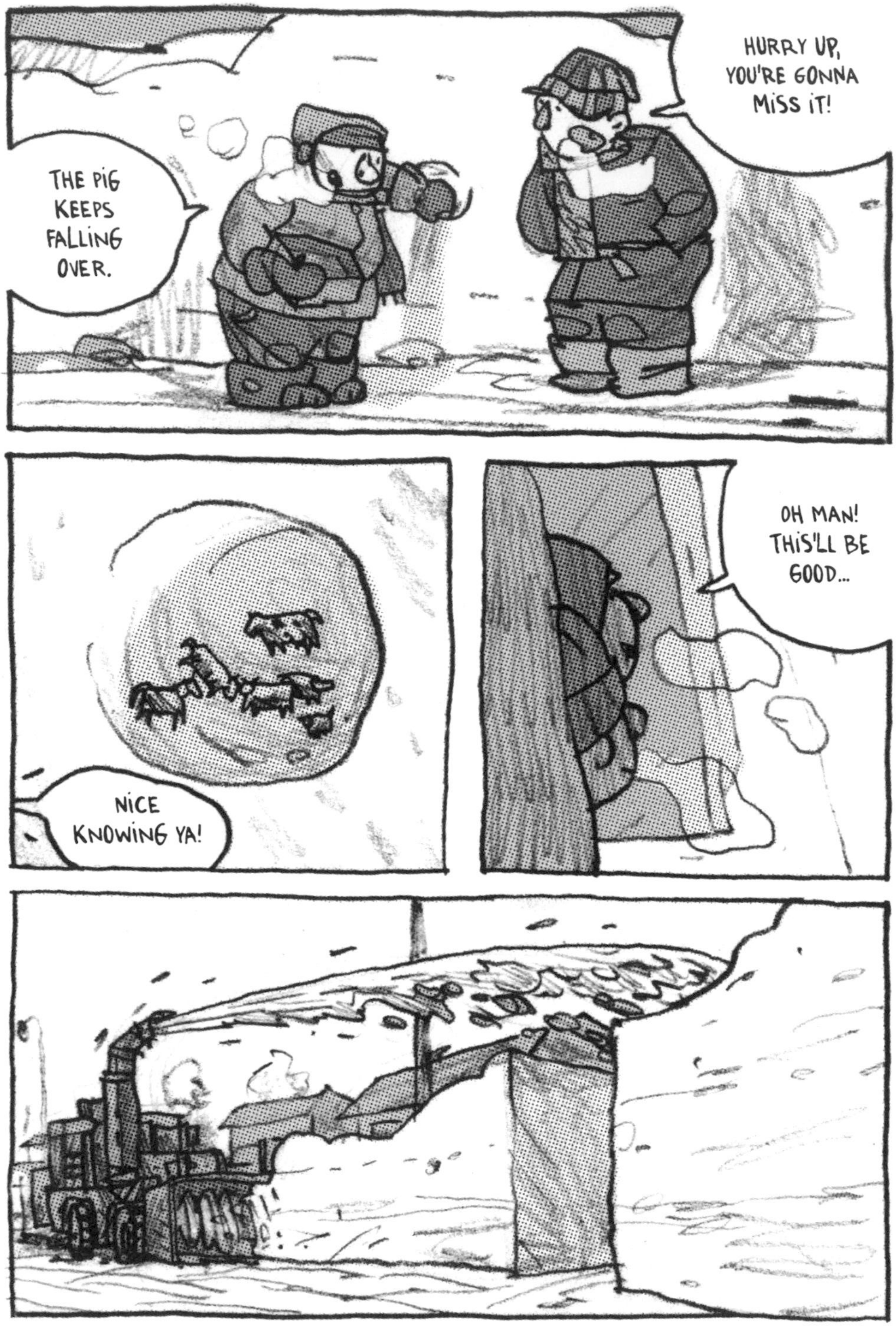
HURRY UP, YOU'RE GONNA MISS IT!
THE PIG KEEPS FALLING OVER.
NICE KNOWING YA!
OH MAN! THIS'LL BE GOOD...

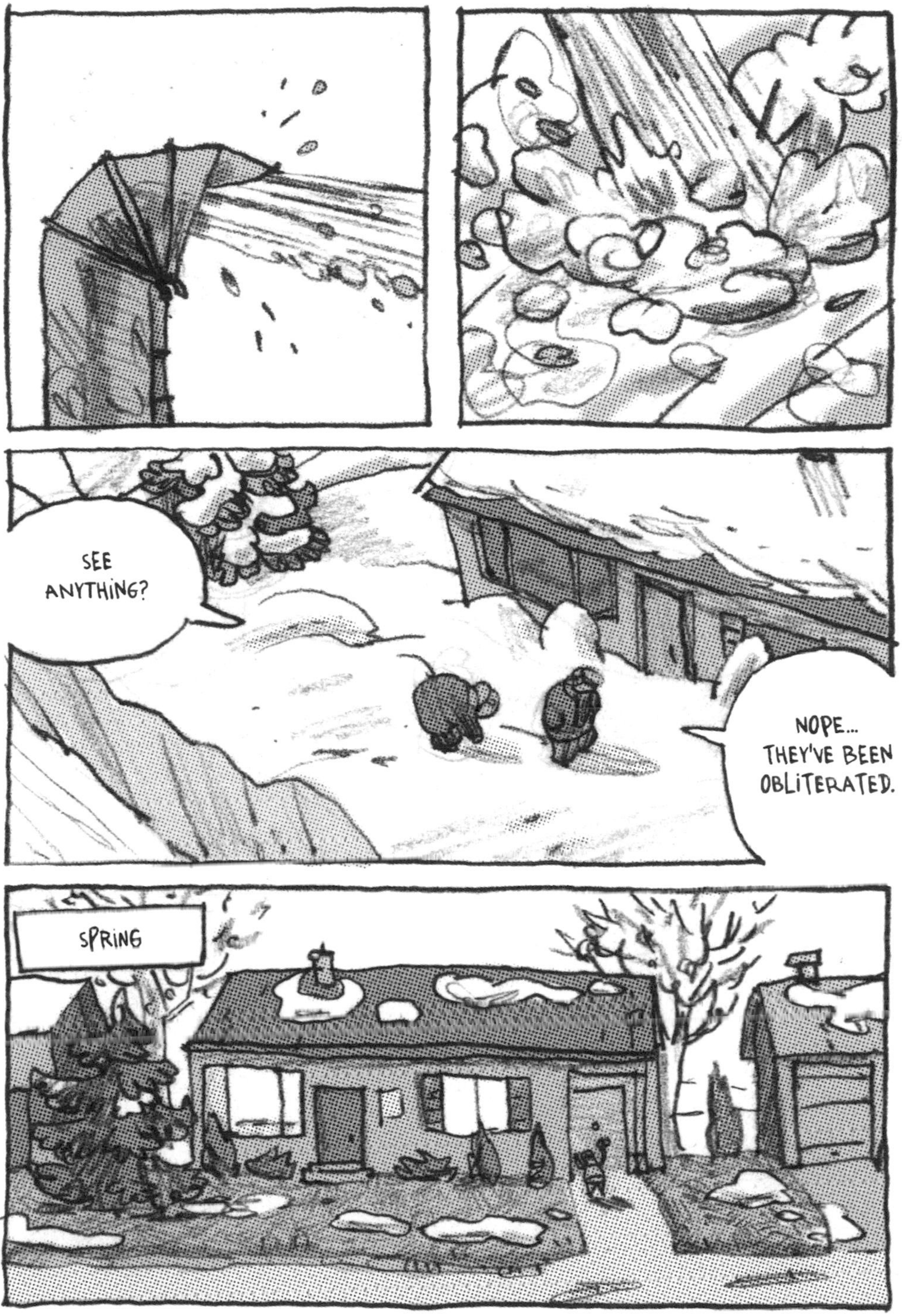
SEE ANYTHING?
NOPE... THEY'VE BEEN OBLITERATED.
SPRING

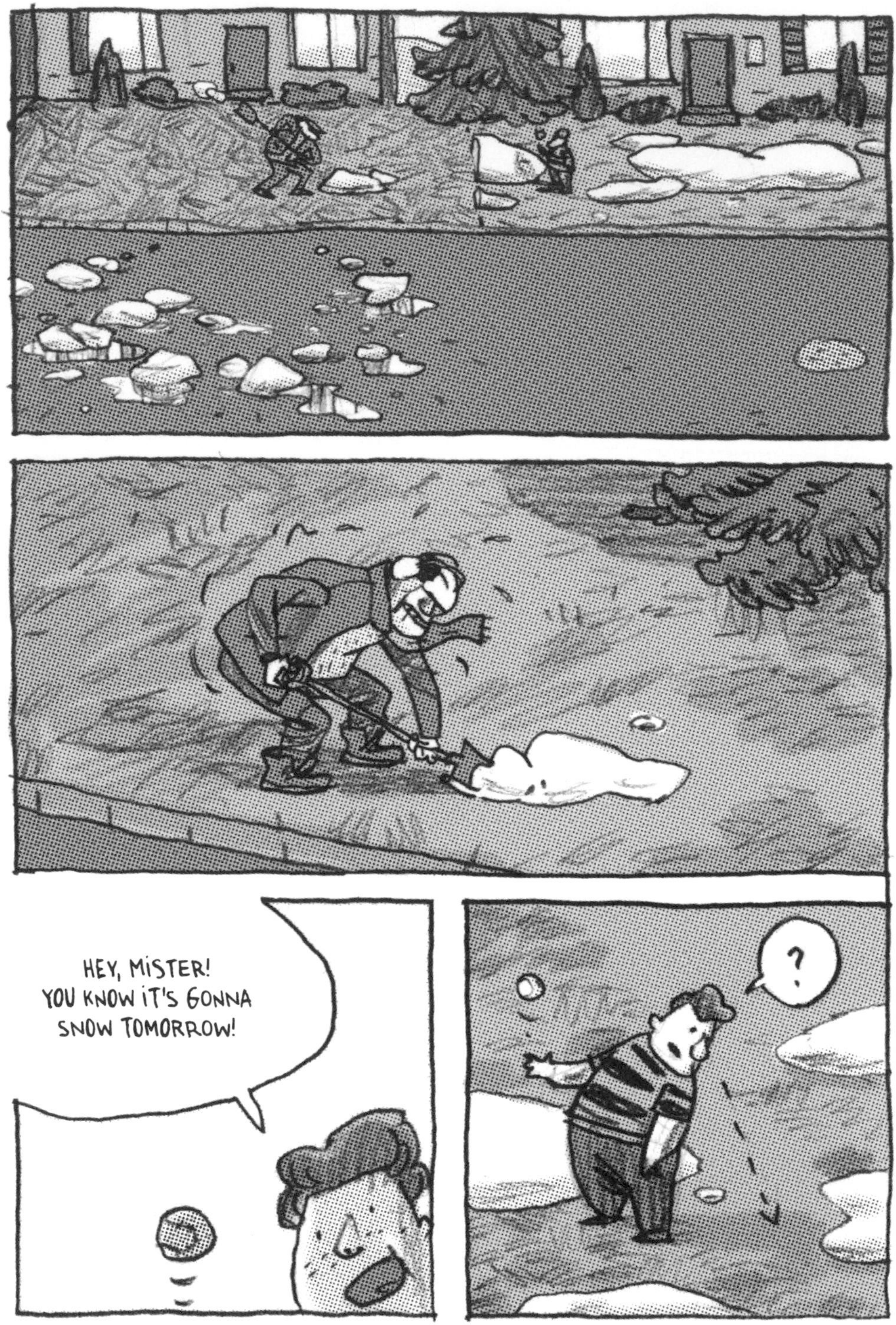
HEY, MISTER! YOU KNOW IT'S GONNA SNOW TOMORROW!
?

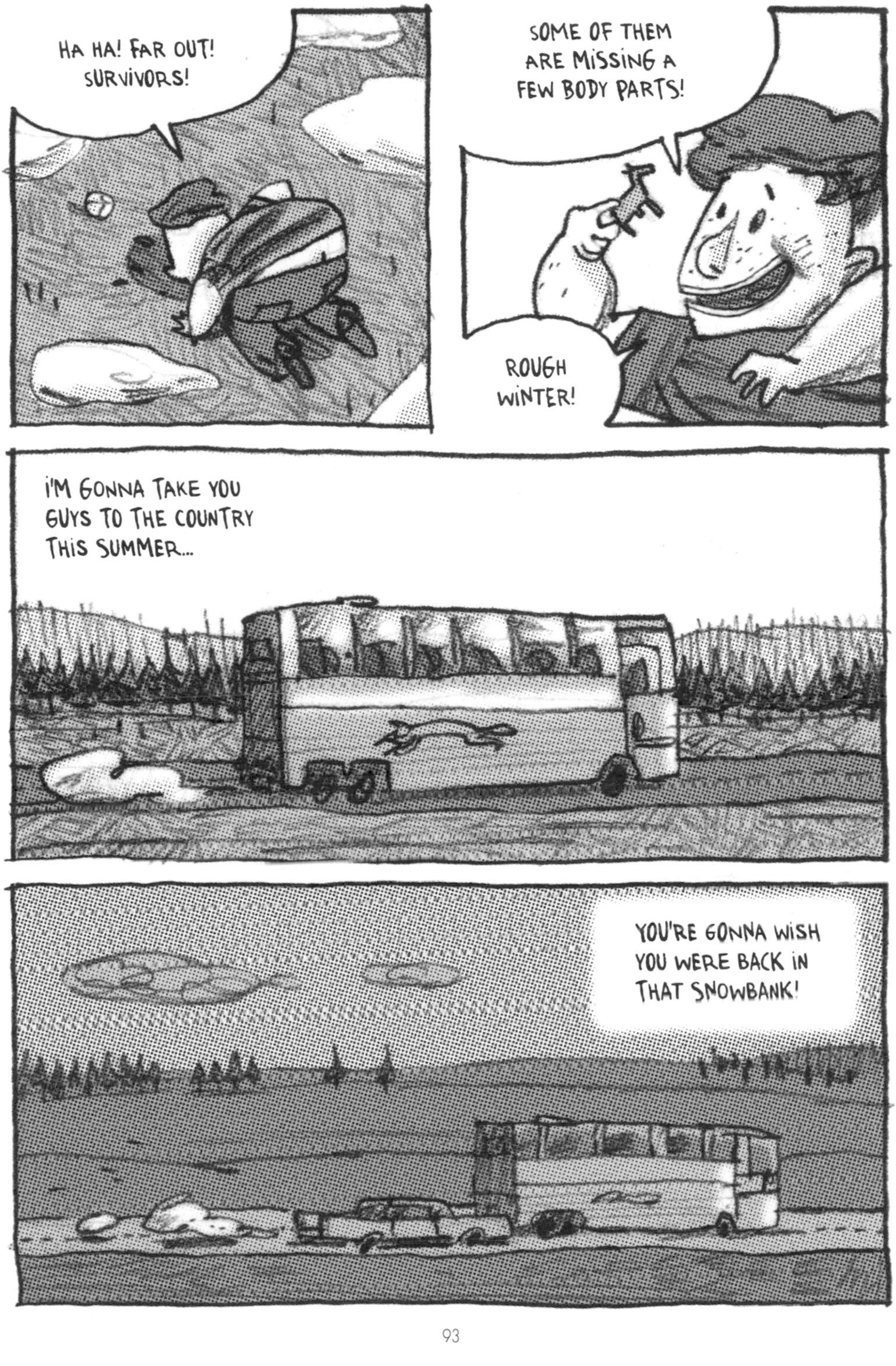
HA HA! FAR OUT! SURVIVORS!
SOME OF THEM ARE MISSING A FEW BODY PARTS!
ROUGH WINTER!
I'M GONNA TAKE YOU GUYS TO THE COUNTRY THIS SUMMER...
YOU'RE GONNA WISH YOU WERE BACK IN THAT SNOWBANK!

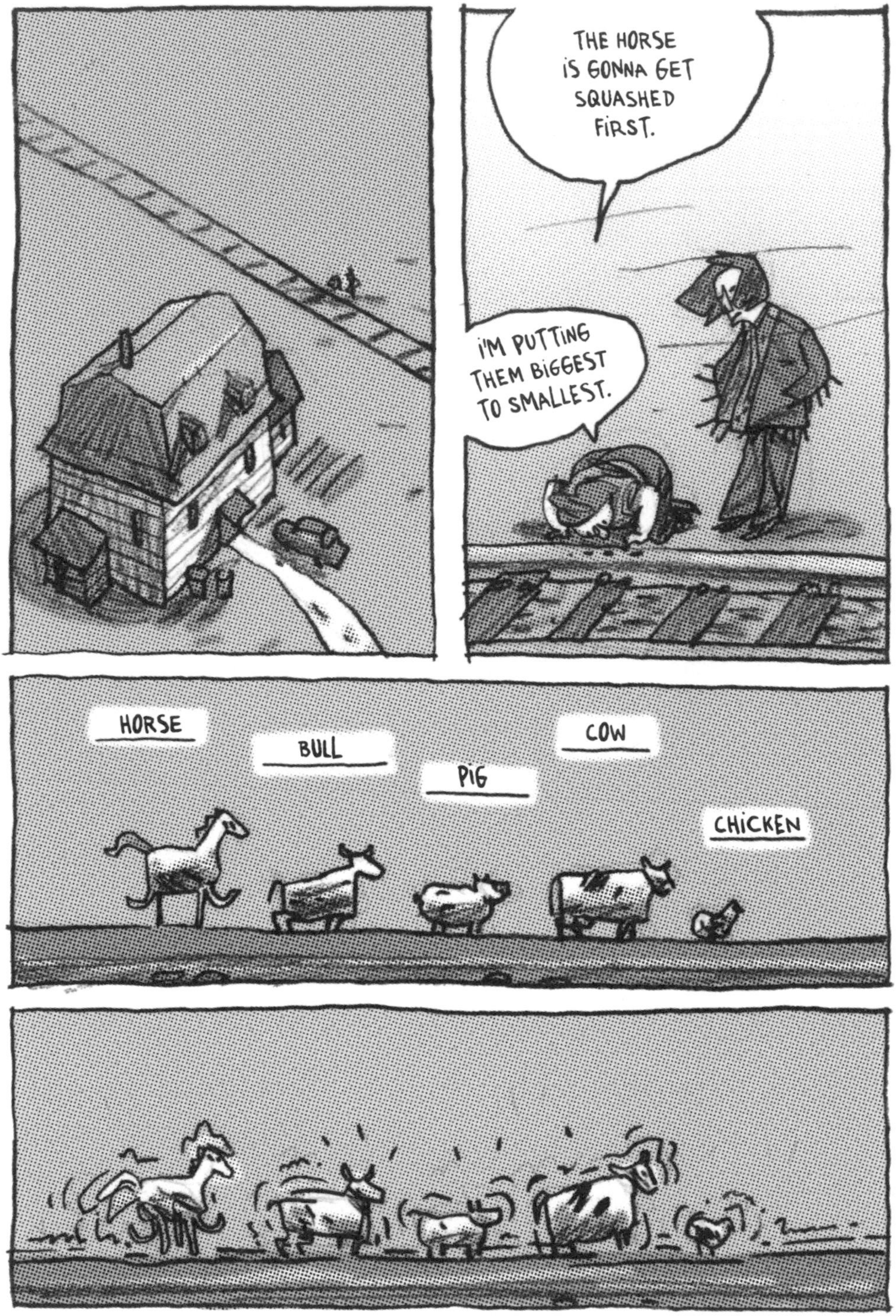
THE HORSE IS GONNA GET SQUASHED FIRST.
I'M PUTTING THEM BIGGEST TO SMALLEST.
HORSE
BULL
PIG
COW
CHICKEN

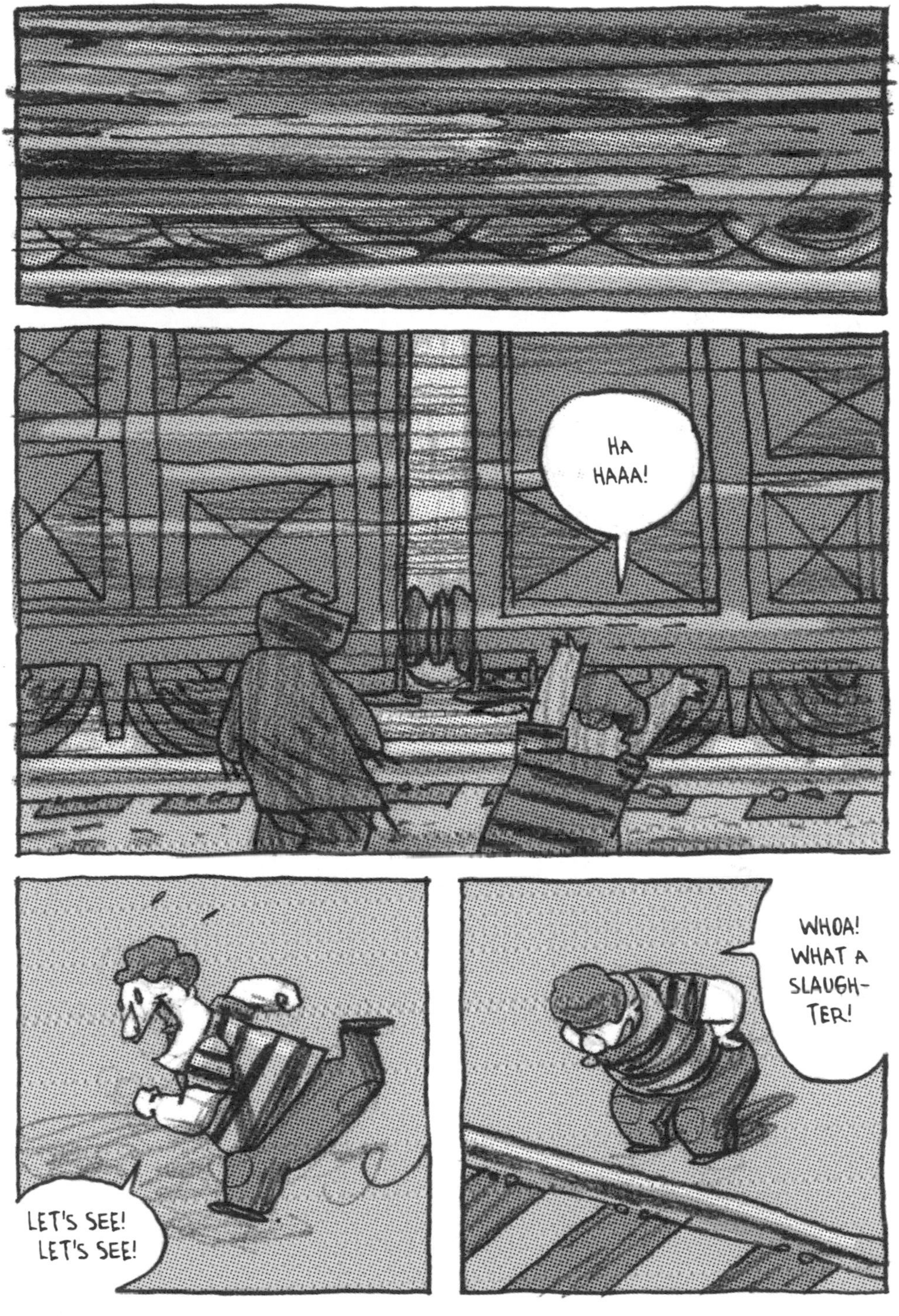
HA HAAA!
LET'S SEE! LET'S SEE!
WHOA! WHAT A SLAUGH-TER!

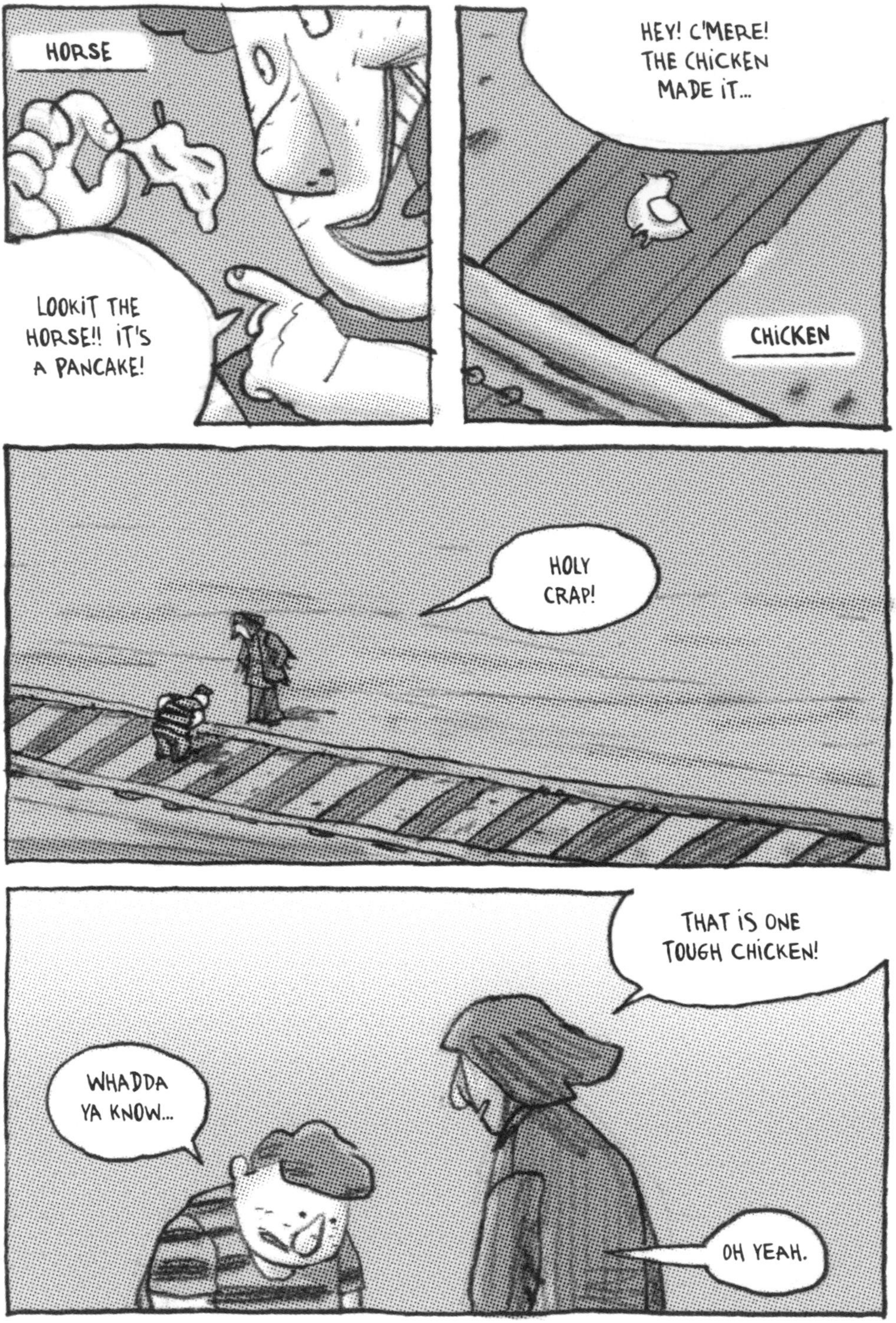
HORSE
LOOKIT THE HORSE!! IT'S A PANCAKE!
HEY! C'MERE! THE CHICKEN MADE IT...
CHICKEN
HOLY CRAP!
THAT IS ONE TOUGH CHICKEN!
WHADDA YA KNOW...
OH YEAH.

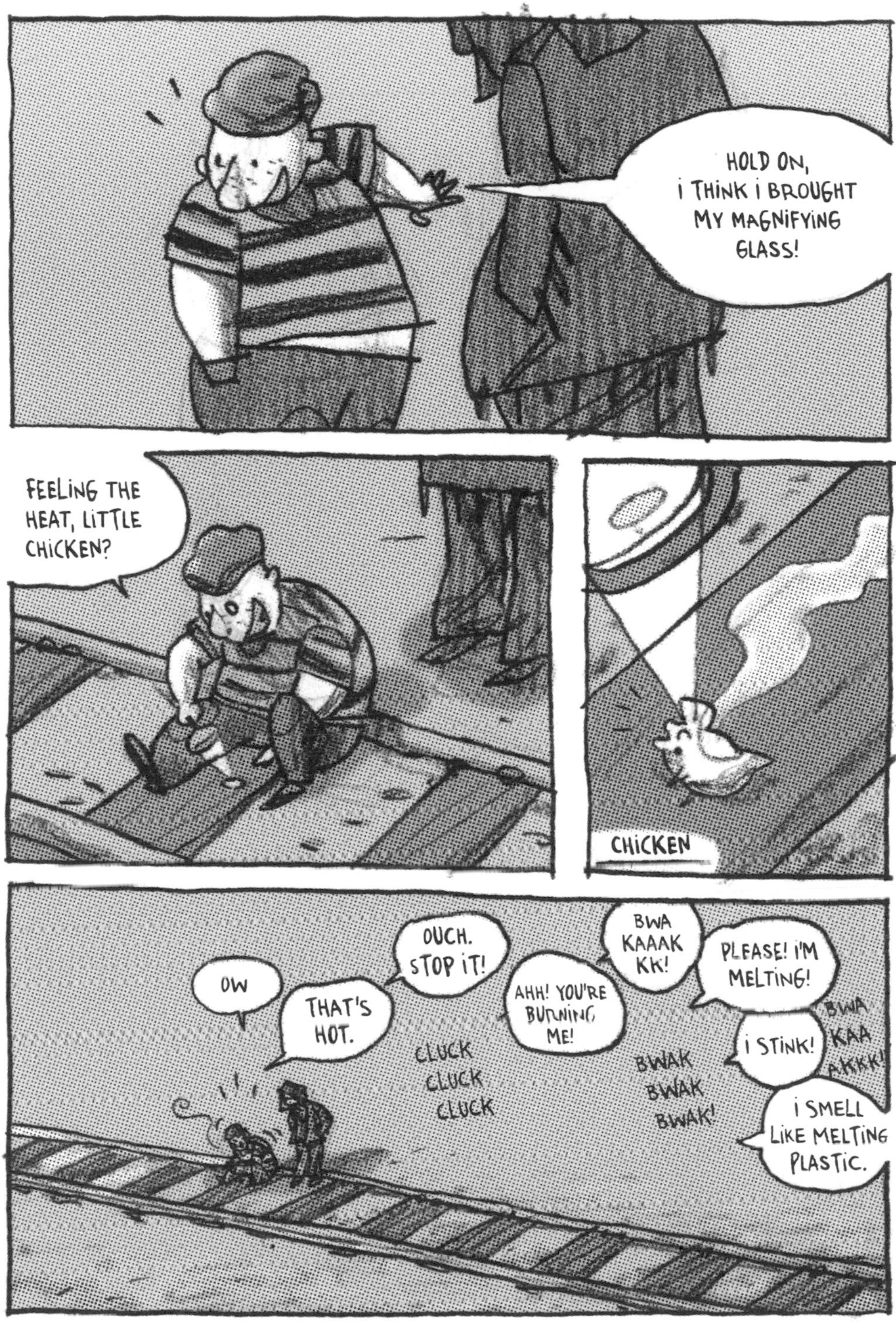
HOLD ON, I THINK I BROUGHT MY MAGNIFYING GLASS!
FEELING THE HEAT, LITTLE CHICKEN?
CHICKEN
OW
THAT'S HOT.
OUCH. STOP IT!
CLUCK CLUCK CLUCK
AHH! YOU'RE BURNING ME!
BWA KAAAK KK!
BWAK BWAK BWAK!
PLEASE! I'M MELTING!
BWA KAA AKKK!
I STINK!
I SMELL LIKE MELTING PLASTIC.
DELISLE 99

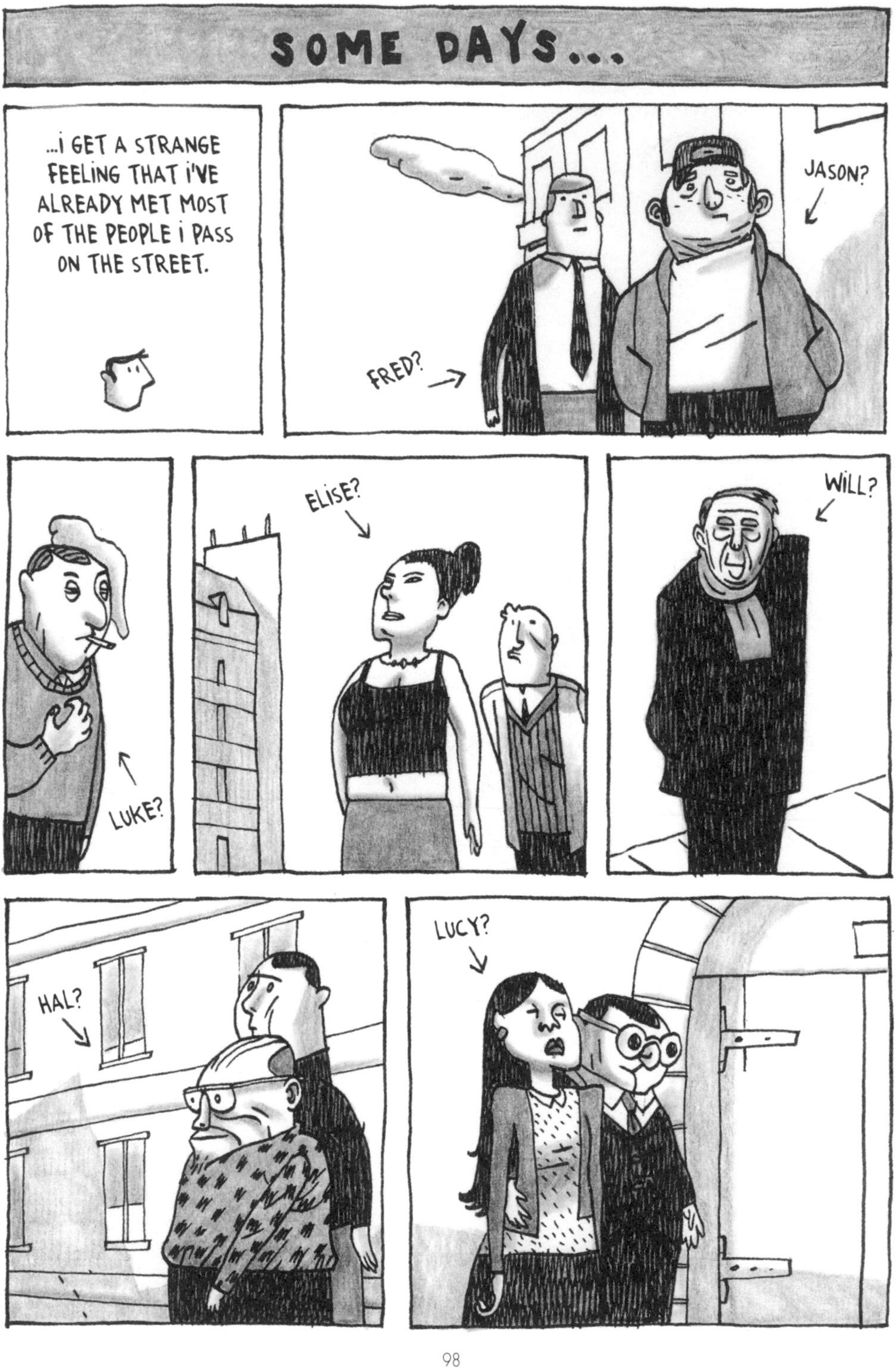
SOME DAYS...
...I GET A STRANGE FEELING THAT I'VE ALREADY MET MOST OF THE PEOPLE I PASS ON THE STREET.
JASON?
FRED?
LUKE?
ELISE?
WILL?
HAL?
LUCY?

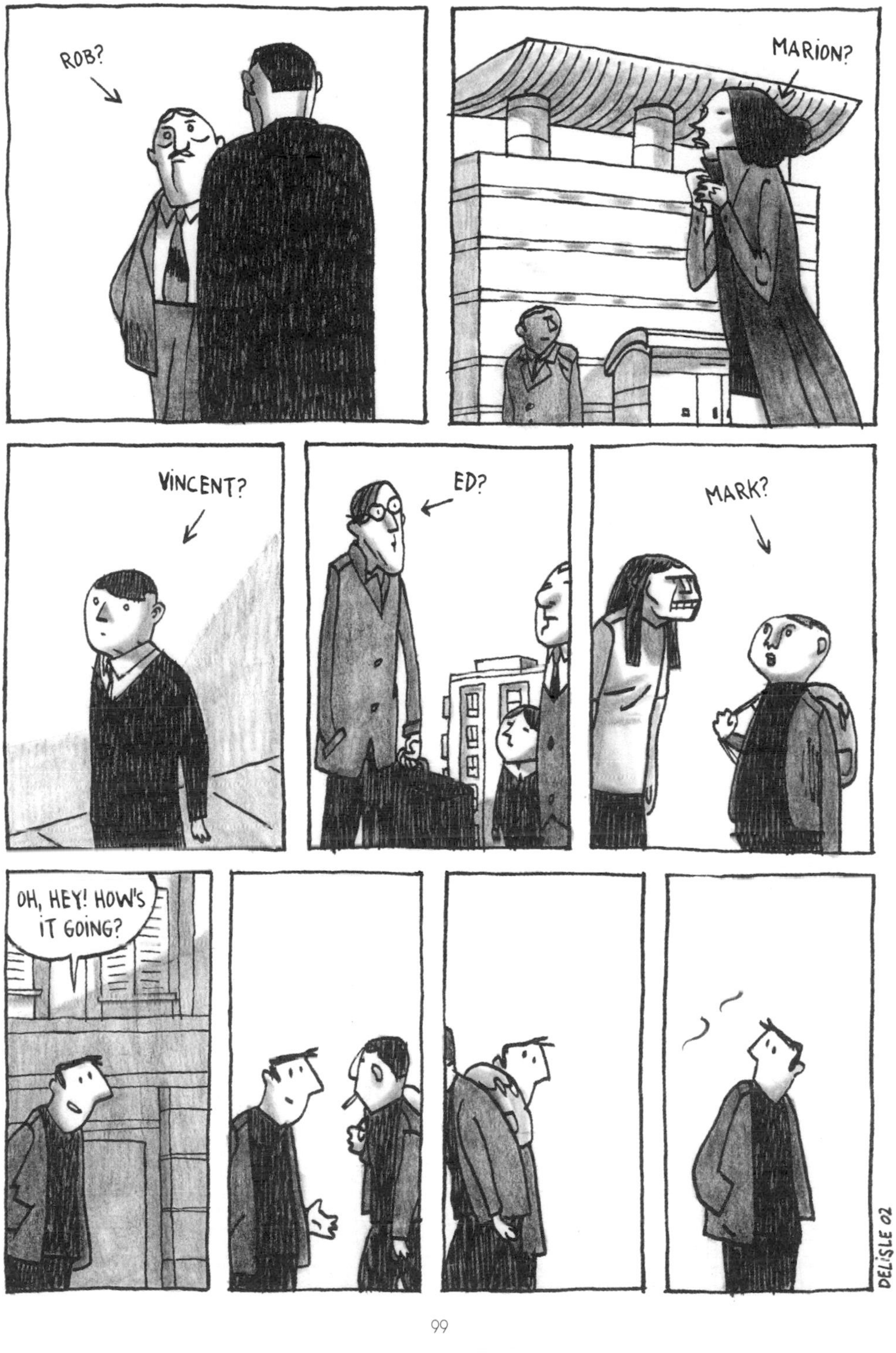
ROB?
MARION?
VINCENT?
ED?
MARK?
OH, HEY! HOW'S IT GOING?
DELISLE 02

AIRPORTED

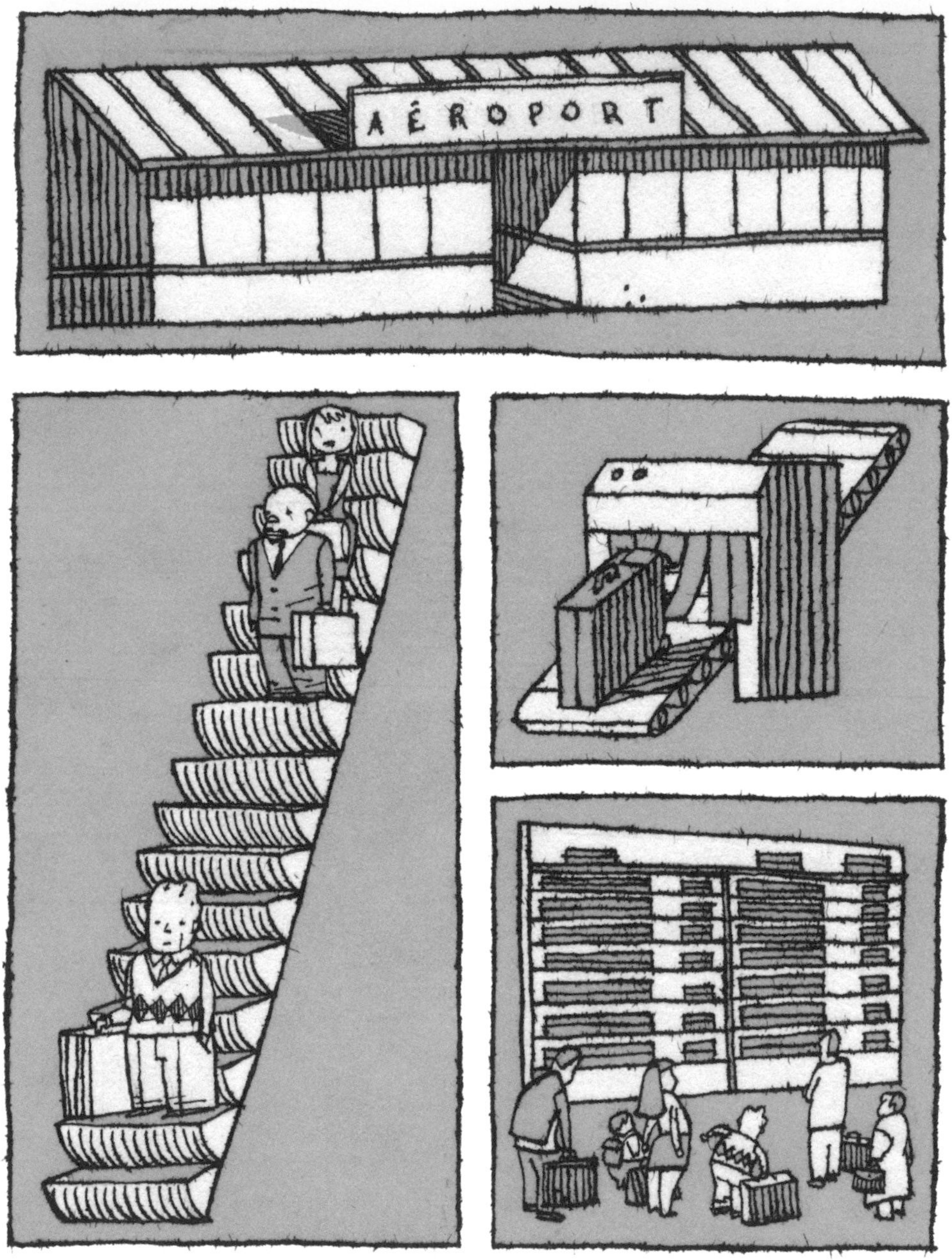
AÉROPORT

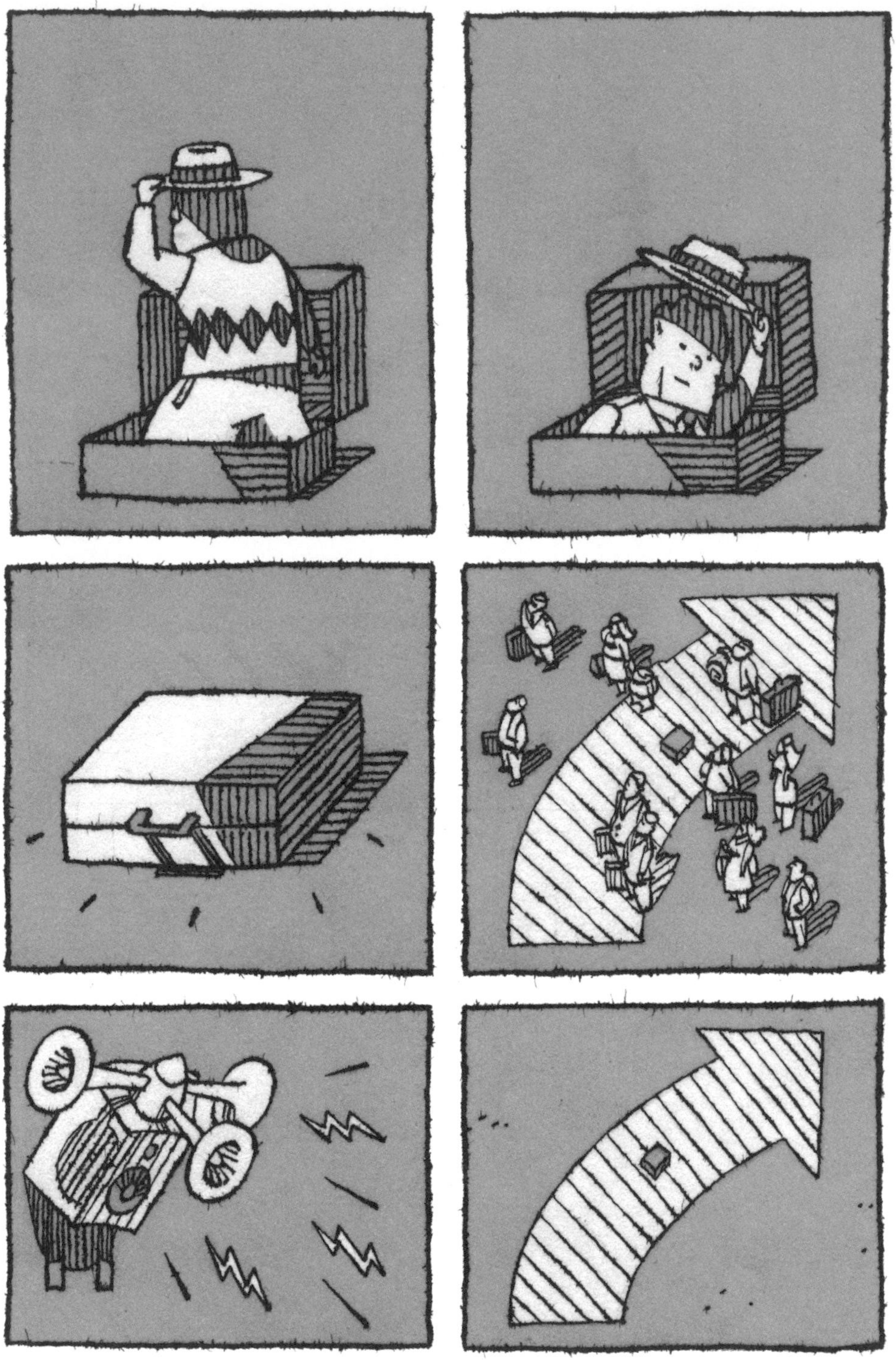

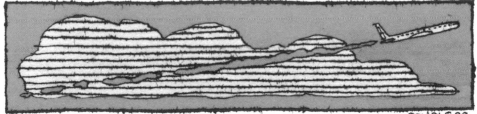

DELISLE 99

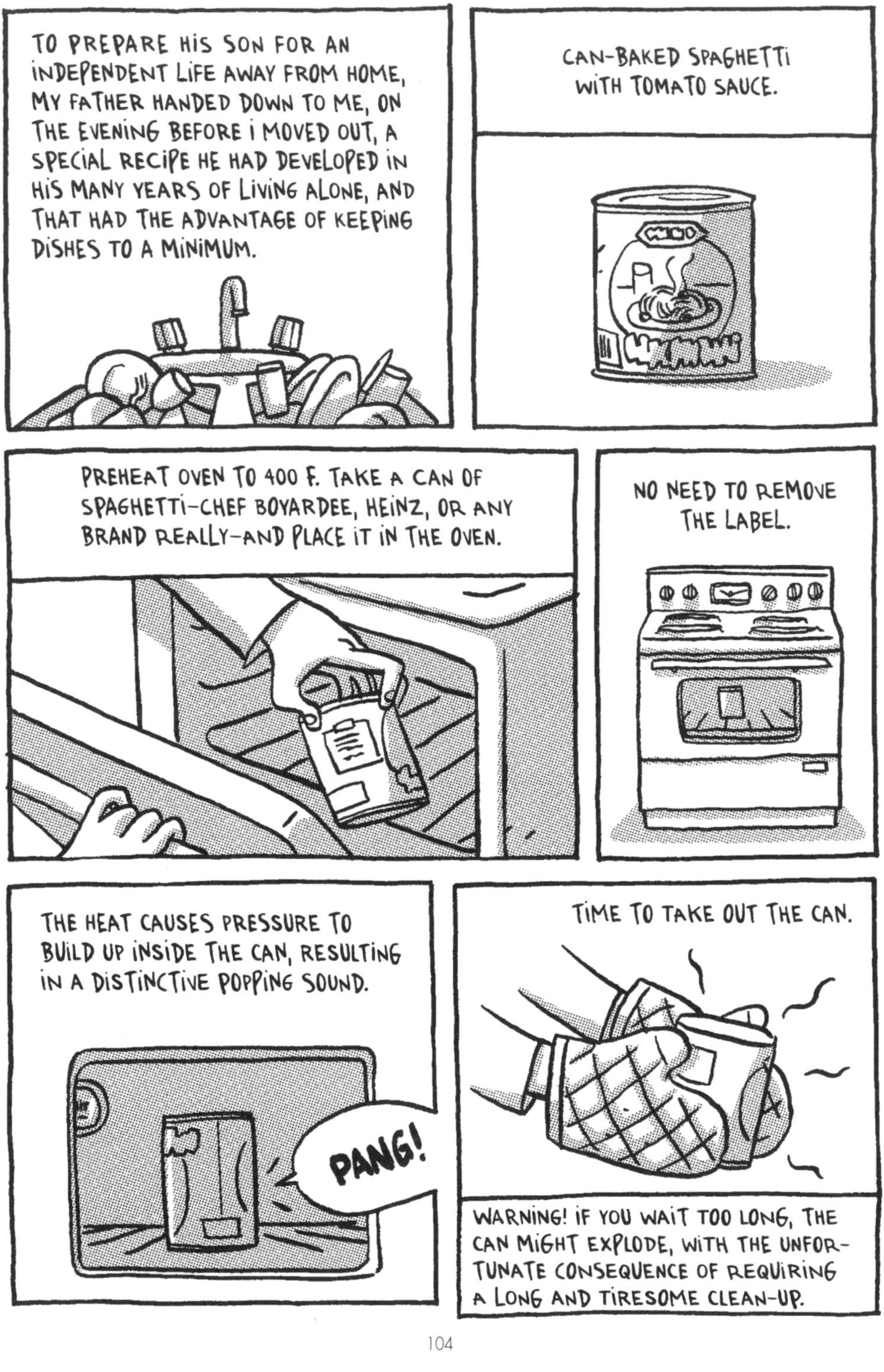
TO PREPARE HIS SON FOR AN INDEPENDENT LIFE AWAY FROM HOME, MY FATHER HANDED DOWN TO ME, ON THE EVENING BEFORE I MOVED OUT, A SPECIAL RECIPE HE HAD DEVELOPED IN HIS MANY YEARS OF LIVING ALONE, AND THAT HAD THE ADVANTAGE OF KEEPING DISHES TO A MINIMUM.
CAN-BAKED SPAGHETTI WITH TOMATO SAUCE.
PREHEAT OVEN TO 400 F. TAKE A CAN OF SPAGHETTI—CHEF BOYARDEE, HEINZ, OR ANY BRAND REALLY—AND PLACE IT IN THE OVEN.
NO NEED TO REMOVE THE LABEL.
THE HEAT CAUSES PRESSURE TO BUILD UP INSIDE THE CAN, RESULTING IN A DISTINCTIVE POPPING SOUND.
PANG!
TIME TO TAKE OUT THE CAN.
WARNING! IF YOU WAIT TOO LONG, THE CAN MIGHT EXPLODE, WITH THE UNFORTUNATE CONSEQUENCE OF REQUIRING A LONG AND TIRESOME CLEAN-UP.

AND NOW THIS IS WHERE EXPERIENCE CAN SAVE YOU A LOT OF TROUBLE.

TO AVOID THIS:

OW. SHIT!

PLACE THE CAN UNDER RUNNING COLD WATER FOR 30 TO 45 SECONDS. THIS COOLS THE CAN BUT NOT THE CONTENTS.

COLD EXTERIOR.

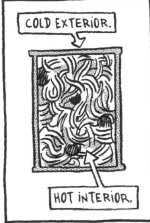

HOT INTERIOR.

OPEN IT UP AND YOUR MEAL IS READY. BON APPÉTIT!

YUM

BONUS: YOU CAN EAT IT STRAIGHT FROM THE CAN.

NOTE THE EFFICIENCY: TOSS THE CAN, WASH THE FORK AND YOU'RE DONE.

BUT...IS IT ANY GOOD?

105

DELISLE 03

Bows and Prostrations

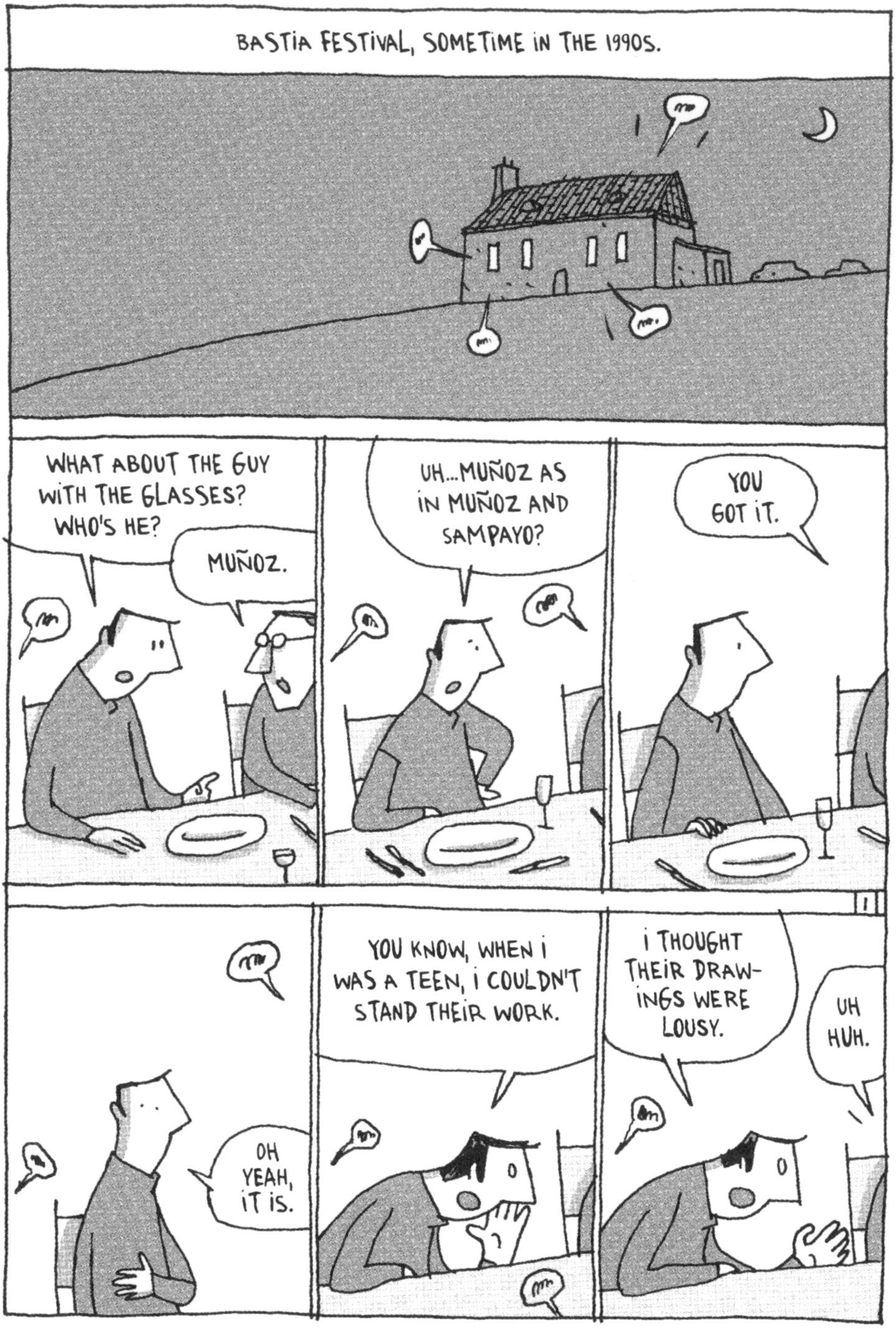

BASTIA FESTIVAL, SOMETIME IN THE 1990S.
WHAT ABOUT THE GUY WITH THE GLASSES? WHO'S HE?
MUÑOZ.
UH...MUÑOZ AS IN MUÑOZ AND SAMPAYO?
YOU GOT IT.
OH YEAH, IT IS.
YOU KNOW, WHEN I WAS A TEEN, I COULDN'T STAND THEIR WORK.
I THOUGHT THEIR DRAWINGS WERE LOUSY.
UH HUH.

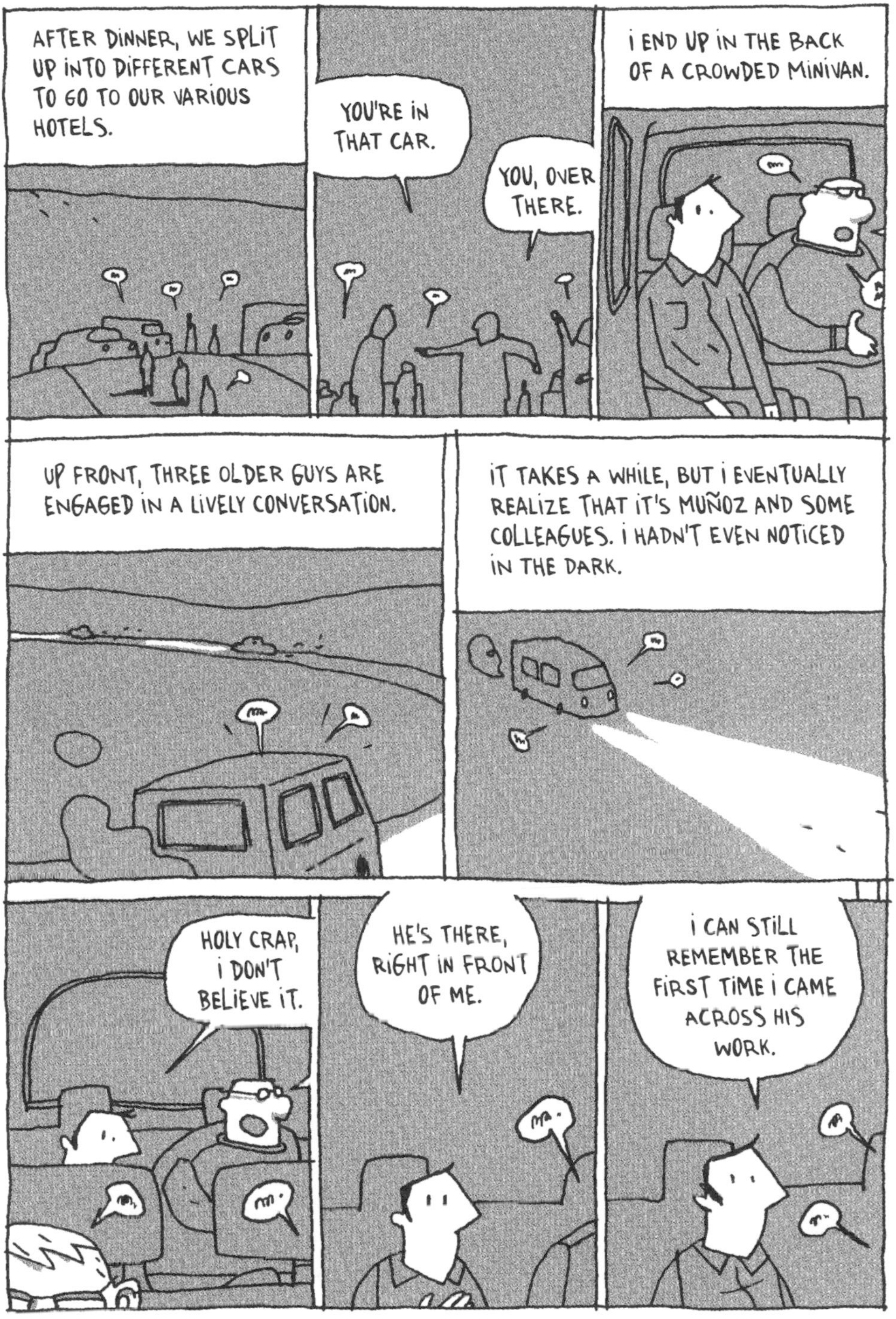
AFTER DINNER, WE SPLIT UP INTO DIFFERENT CARS TO GO TO OUR VARIOUS HOTELS.
YOU'RE IN THAT CAR.
YOU, OVER THERE.
I END UP IN THE BACK OF A CROWDED MINIVAN.
UP FRONT, THREE OLDER GUYS ARE ENGAGED IN A LIVELY CONVERSATION.
IT TAKES A WHILE, BUT I EVENTUALLY REALIZE THAT IT'S MUÑOZ AND SOME COLLEAGUES. I HADN'T EVEN NOTICED IN THE DARK.
HOLY CRAP, I DON'T BELIEVE IT.
HE'S THERE, RIGHT IN FRONT OF ME.
I CAN STILL REMEMBER THE FIRST TIME I CAME ACROSS HIS WORK.

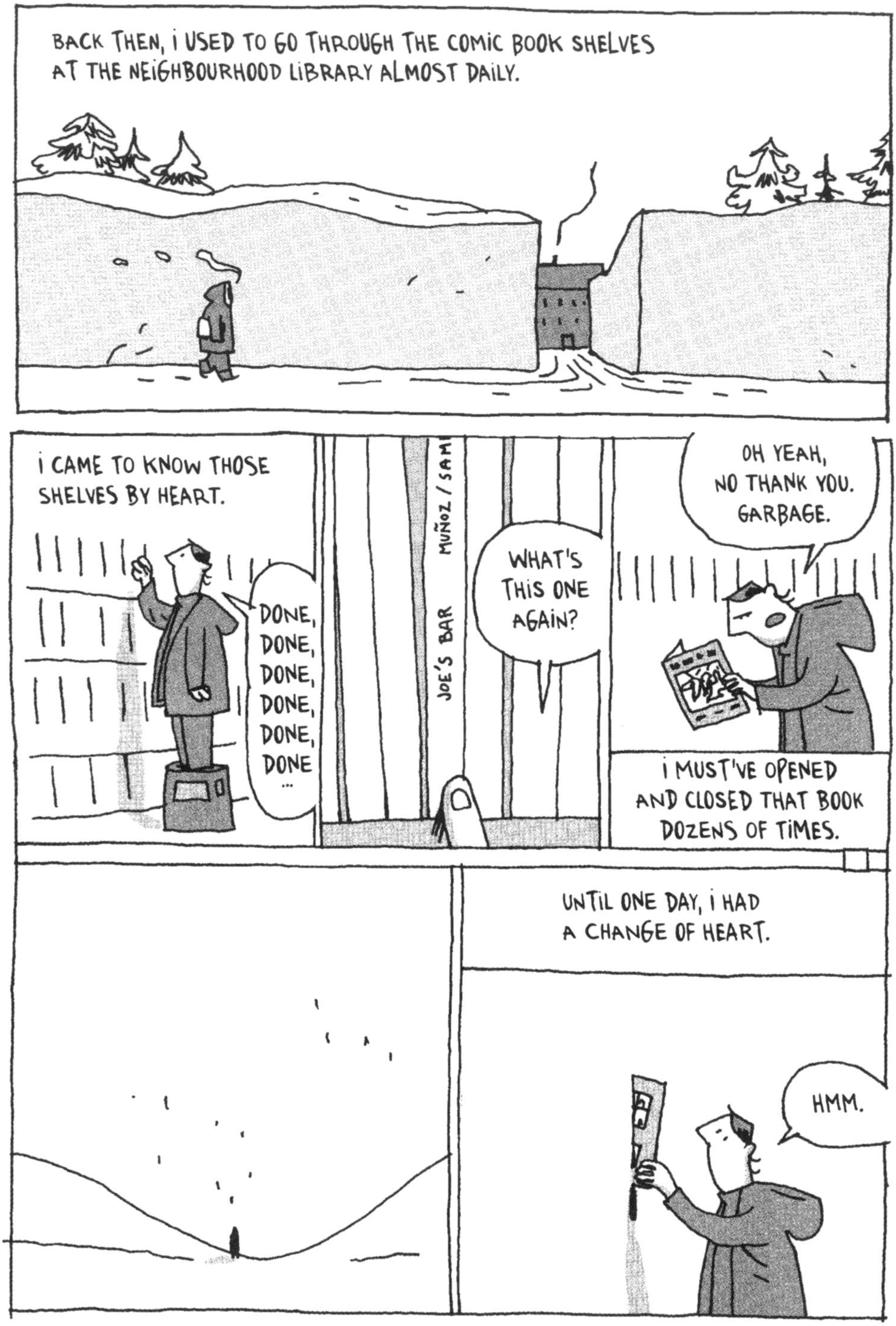
BACK THEN, i USED TO GO THROUGH THE COMIC BOOK SHELVES AT THE NEIGHBOURHOOD LIBRARY ALMOST DAILY.
i CAME TO KNOW THOSE SHELVES BY HEART.
DONE, DONE, DONE, DONE, DONE, DONE...
MUÑOZ / SAM
JOE'S BAR
WHAT'S THIS ONE AGAIN?
OH YEAH, NO THANK YOU. GARBAGE.
i MUST'VE OPENED AND CLOSED THAT BOOK DOZENS OF TiMES.
UNTiL ONE DAY, i HAD A CHANGE OF HEART.
HMM.

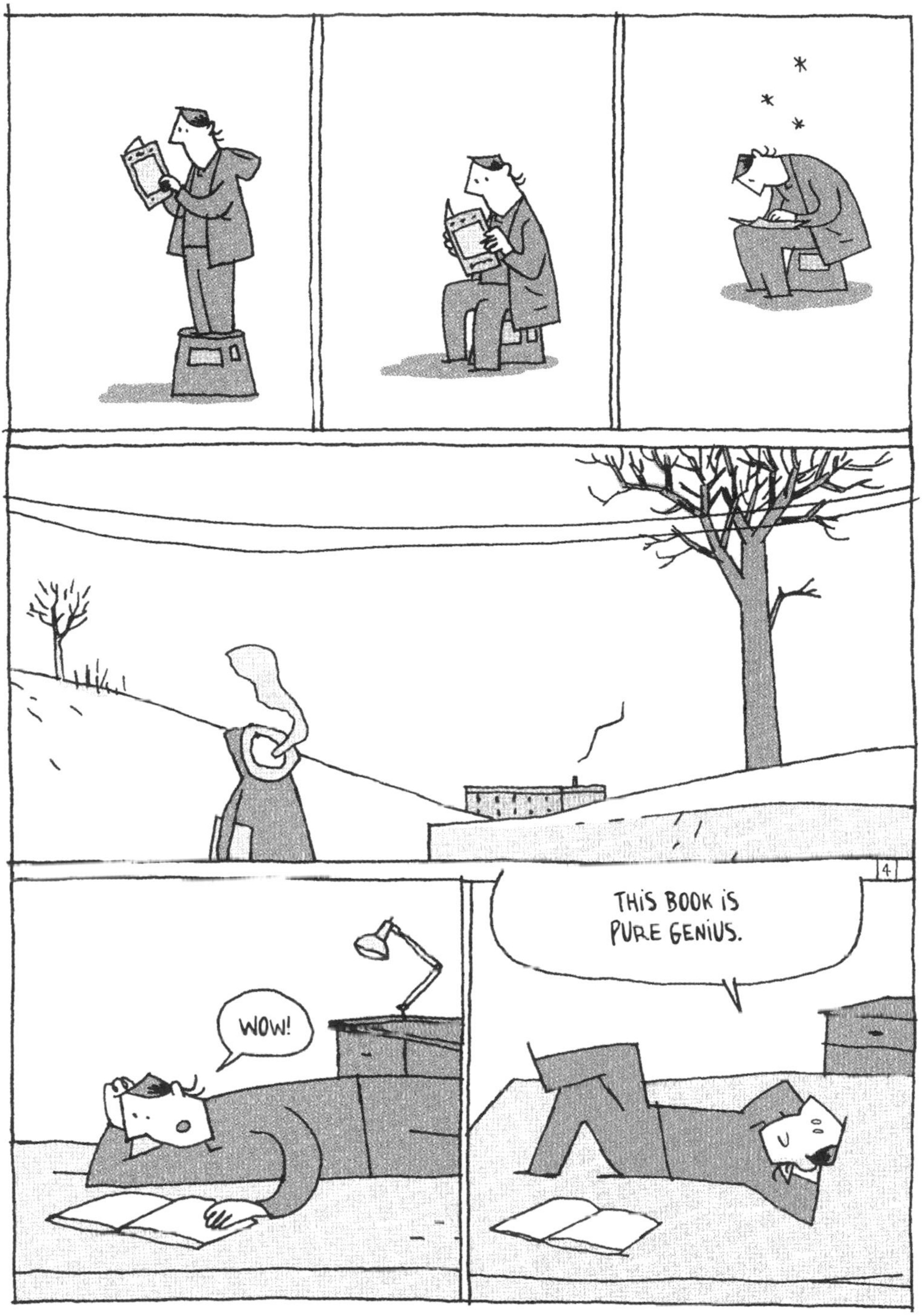
4
WOW!
THIS BOOK IS PURE GENIUS.

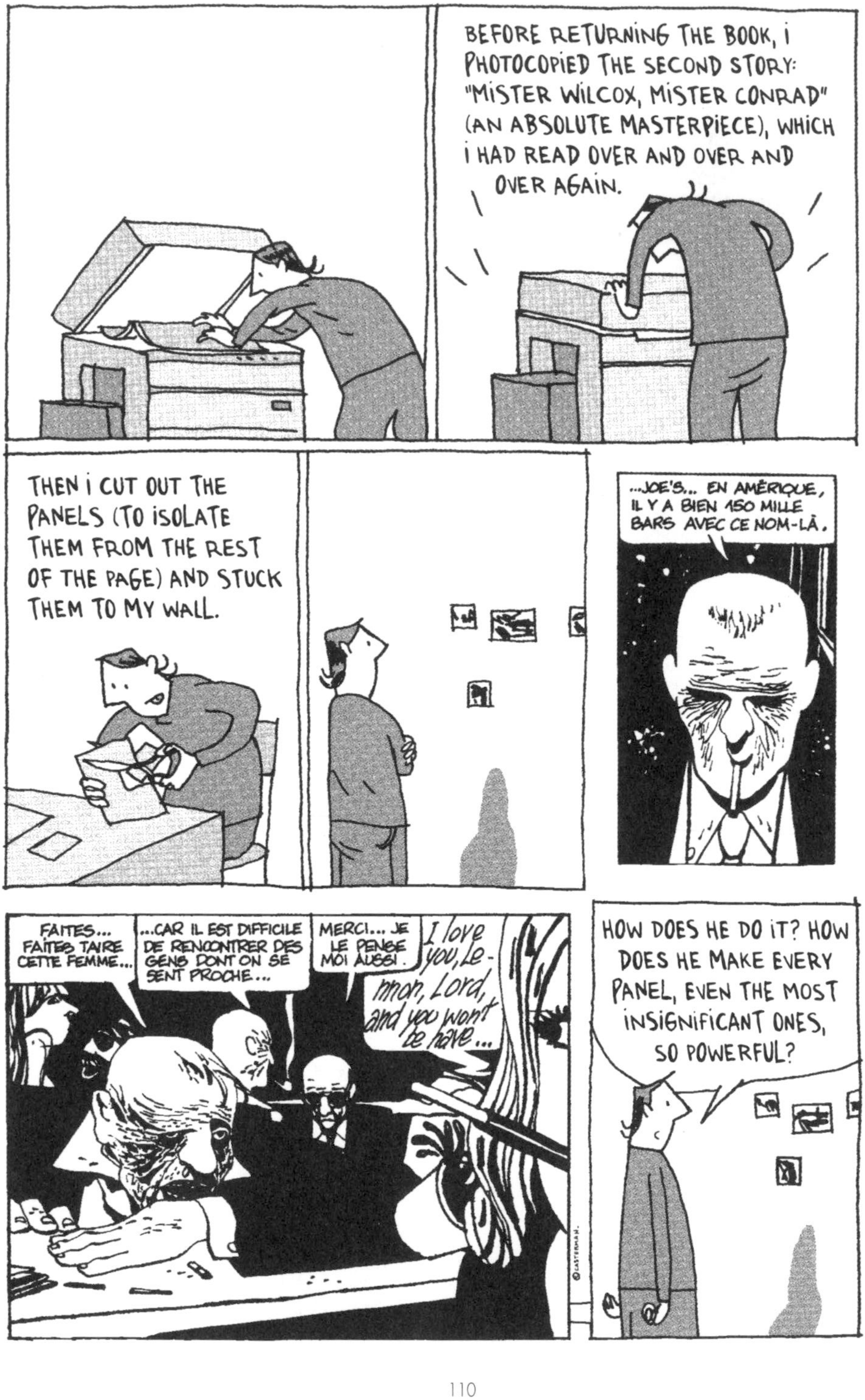
BEFORE RETURNING THE BOOK, I PHOTOCOPIED THE SECOND STORY: "MISTER WILCOX, MISTER CONRAD" (AN ABSOLUTE MASTERPIECE), WHICH I HAD READ OVER AND OVER AND OVER AGAIN.
THEN I CUT OUT THE PANELS (TO ISOLATE THEM FROM THE REST OF THE PAGE) AND STUCK THEM TO MY WALL.
...JOE'S... EN AMÉRIQUE, IL Y A BIEN 150 MILLE BARS AVEC CE NOM-LÀ.
FAITES... FAITES TAIRE CETTE FEMME...
...CAR IL EST DIFFICILE DE RENCONTRER DES GENS DONT ON SE SENT PROCHE...
MERCI... JE LE PENSE MOI AUSSI.
I love you, Lennon, Lord, and you won't be have...
©CASTERMAN
HOW DOES HE DO IT? HOW DOES HE MAKE EVERY PANEL, EVEN THE MOST INSIGNIFICANT ONES, SO POWERFUL?

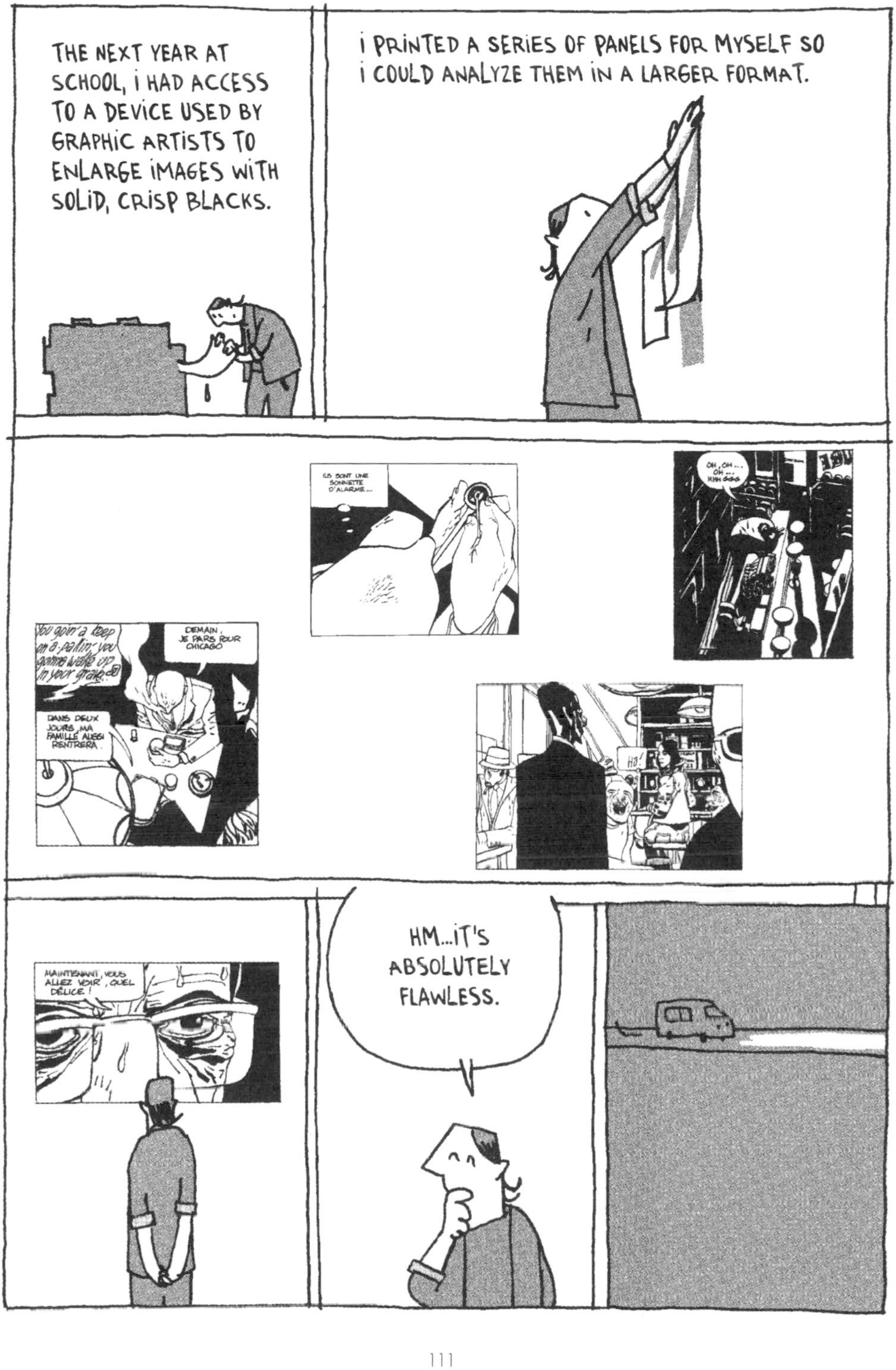
THE NEXT YEAR AT SCHOOL, I HAD ACCESS TO A DEVICE USED BY GRAPHIC ARTISTS TO ENLARGE IMAGES WITH SOLID, CRISP BLACKS.
I PRINTED A SERIES OF PANELS FOR MYSELF SO I COULD ANALYZE THEM IN A LARGER FORMAT.
ILS SONT UNE SONNETTE D'ALARME...
OH, OH... OH...
DEMAIN, JE PARS POUR CHICAGO
DANS DEUX JOURS, MA FAMILLE AUSSI RENTRERA.
HA!
MAINTENANT, VOUS ALLEZ VOIR, QUEL DÉLICE !
HM...IT'S ABSOLUTELY FLAWLESS.

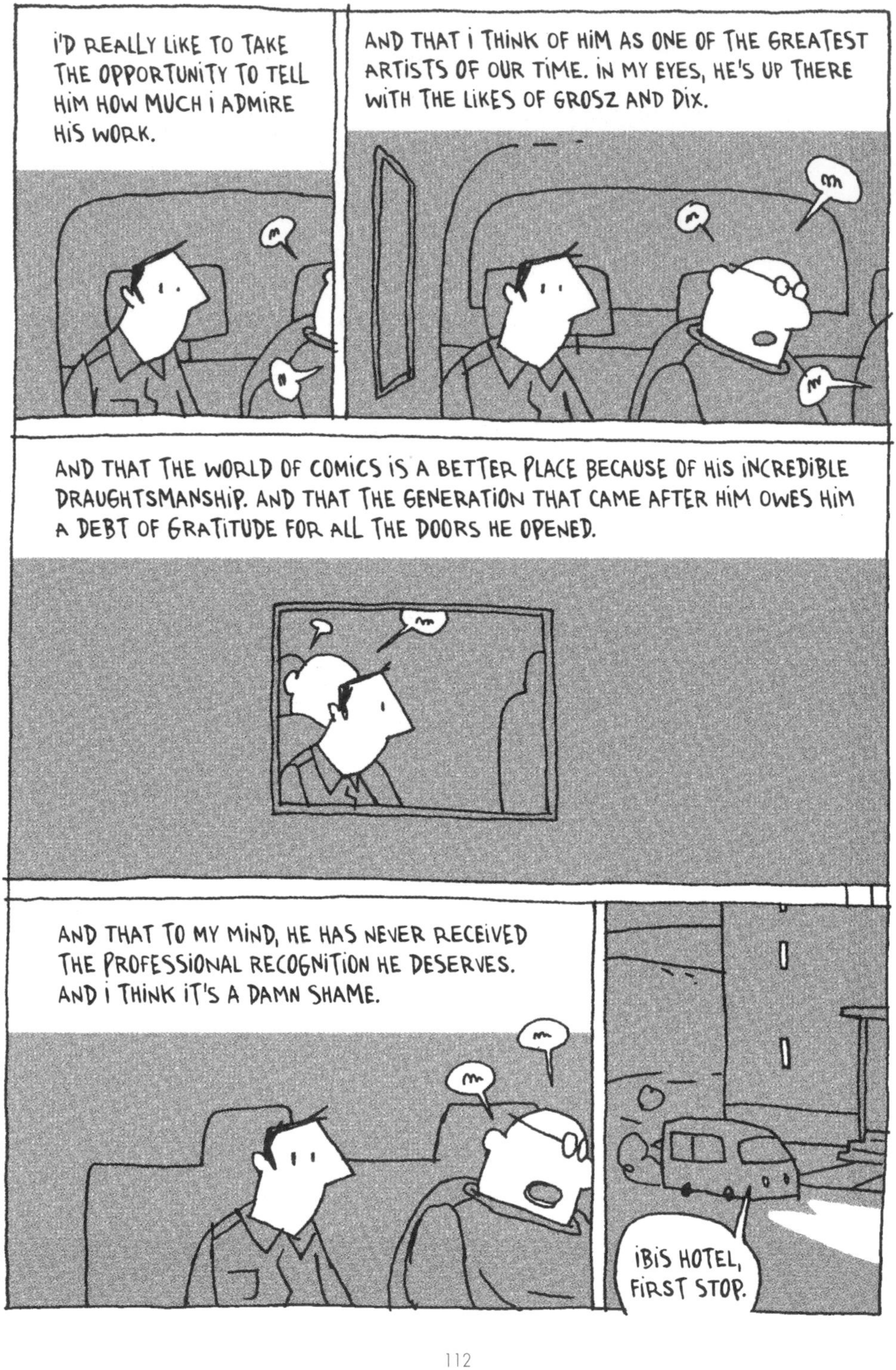
I'D REALLY LIKE TO TAKE THE OPPORTUNITY TO TELL HIM HOW MUCH I ADMIRE HIS WORK.
AND THAT I THINK OF HIM AS ONE OF THE GREATEST ARTISTS OF OUR TIME. IN MY EYES, HE'S UP THERE WITH THE LIKES OF GROSZ AND DIX.
AND THAT THE WORLD OF COMICS IS A BETTER PLACE BECAUSE OF HIS INCREDIBLE DRAUGHTSMANSHIP. AND THAT THE GENERATION THAT CAME AFTER HIM OWES HIM A DEBT OF GRATITUDE FOR ALL THE DOORS HE OPENED.
AND THAT TO MY MIND, HE HAS NEVER RECEIVED THE PROFESSIONAL RECOGNITION HE DESERVES. AND I THINK IT'S A DAMN SHAME.
IBIS HOTEL, FIRST STOP.

WHILE MUÑOZ SAYS HIS GOODBYES TO EVERYBODY, I STEP OUT TO GET A SEAT UP FRONT.

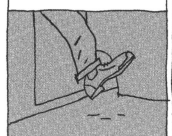

THAT'S WHEN I NOTICE SOMETHING THAT JUST DROPPED ON THE GROUND.

IT'S ONE OF THOSE BRUSH PENS THAT A LOT OF CARTOONISTS USE.

AND FOR A BRIEF MOMENT, DESPITE THE FACT THAT I'M NOT THE TYPE TO OBSESS OVER MEMORABILIA, A SERIES OF IMAGES FLASHES THROUGH MY MIND.

YEAH, THAT'S MUÑOZ'S PEN ALRIGHT. I FOUND IT AT BASTIA.

BASTIA

AMAZ-ING!

I KNOW.

UH.. MISTER MUÑOZ?

YES?

UH... I...

YOU...

YOU DROPPED YOUR PEN...

OH, THANKS.

GOOD NIGHT EVERYONE.

DELISLE 09

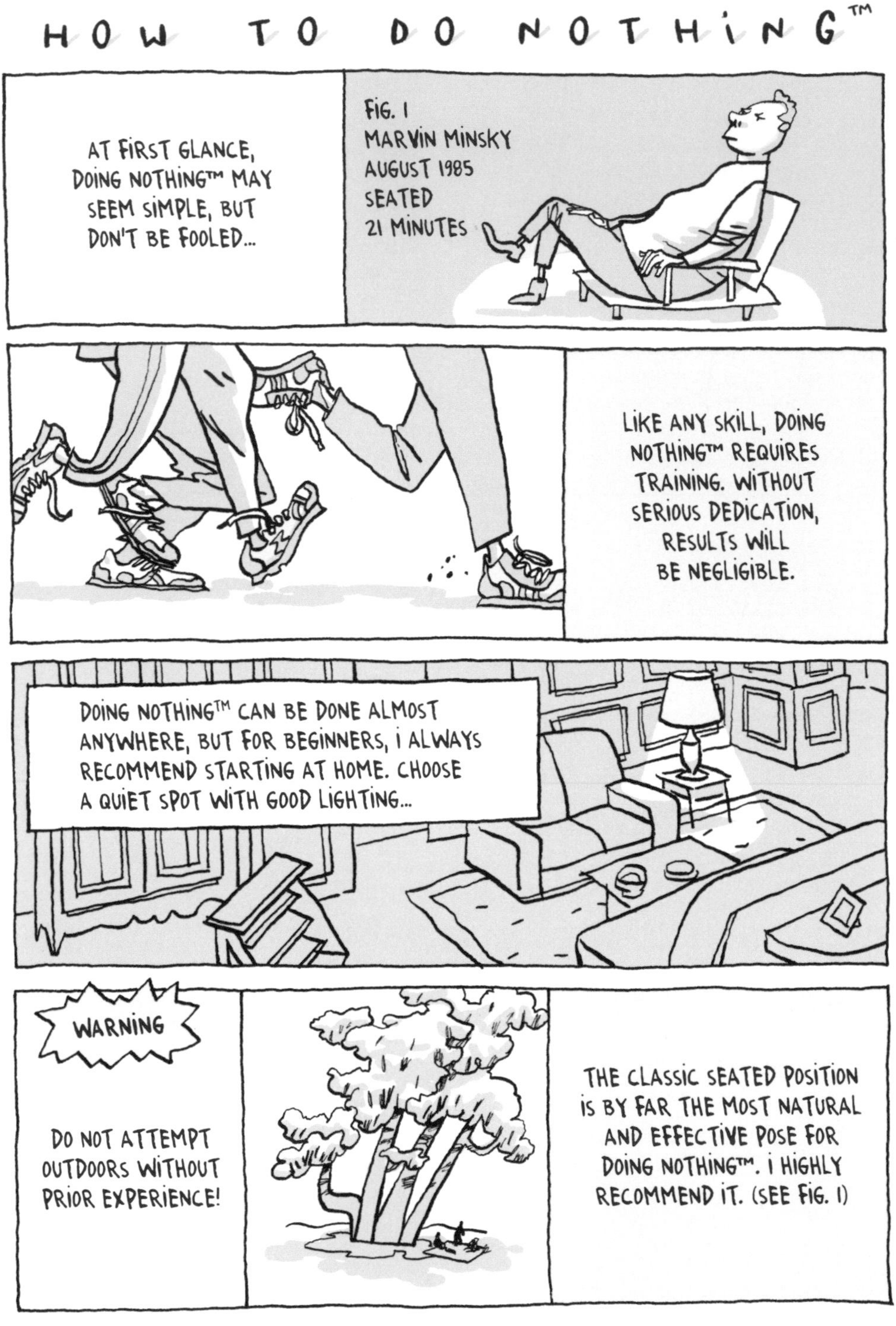
HOW TO DO NOTHING™
AT FIRST GLANCE, DOING NOTHING™ MAY SEEM SIMPLE, BUT DON'T BE FOOLED...
FIG. 1
MARVIN MINSKY
AUGUST 1985
SEATED
21 MINUTES
LIKE ANY SKILL, DOING NOTHING™ REQUIRES TRAINING. WITHOUT SERIOUS DEDICATION, RESULTS WILL BE NEGLIGIBLE.
DOING NOTHING™ CAN BE DONE ALMOST ANYWHERE, BUT FOR BEGINNERS, I ALWAYS RECOMMEND STARTING AT HOME. CHOOSE A QUIET SPOT WITH GOOD LIGHTING...
WARNING
DO NOT ATTEMPT OUTDOORS WITHOUT PRIOR EXPERIENCE!
THE CLASSIC SEATED POSITION IS BY FAR THE MOST NATURAL AND EFFECTIVE POSE FOR DOING NOTHING™. I HIGHLY RECOMMEND IT. (SEE FIG. 1)

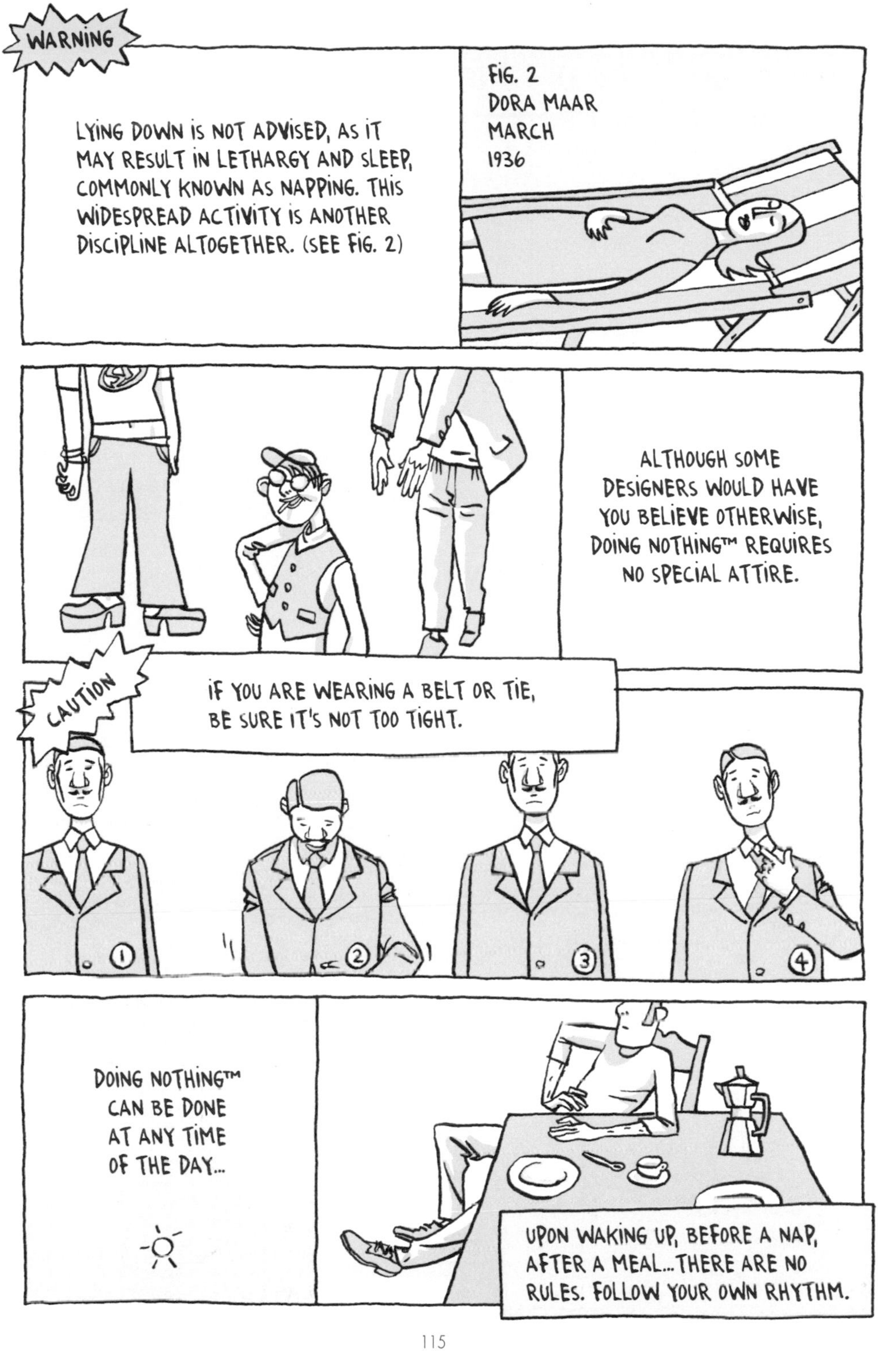
WARNING
LYING DOWN IS NOT ADVISED, AS IT MAY RESULT IN LETHARGY AND SLEEP, COMMONLY KNOWN AS NAPPING. THIS WIDESPREAD ACTIVITY IS ANOTHER DISCIPLINE ALTOGETHER. (SEE FIG. 2)
FIG. 2 DORA MAAR MARCH 1936
ALTHOUGH SOME DESIGNERS WOULD HAVE YOU BELIEVE OTHERWISE, DOING NOTHING™ REQUIRES NO SPECIAL ATTIRE.
CAUTION
IF YOU ARE WEARING A BELT OR TIE, BE SURE IT'S NOT TOO TIGHT.
1
2
3
4
DOING NOTHING™ CAN BE DONE AT ANY TIME OF THE DAY...
UPON WAKING UP, BEFORE A NAP, AFTER A MEAL... THERE ARE NO RULES. FOLLOW YOUR OWN RHYTHM.

TO IMPROVE YOUR CHANCES OF SUCCESS, IT IS BEST TO BEGIN WITH SHORT SESSIONS.

DON'T OVERESTIMATE YOUR ABILITIES. (SEE FIG. 3)

FIG. 3

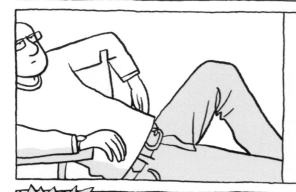

FIVE MINUTES OF DOING NOTHING™ IS AN ENTIRELY ADMIRABLE START FOR A BEGINNER. INCREASE BY A MINUTE PER SESSION TO SLOWLY BUILD UP ENDURANCE.

WARNING

NOTE THESE COMMON MISTAKES! IF YOU ARE LISTENING TO MUSIC, SMOKING OR DRINKING TEA, YOU ARE DOING SOMETHING.

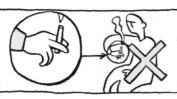

DANGER

DO NOT ATTEMPT TO DO NOTHING™ WHILE ENGAGED IN ANY OTHER ACTIVITY.

IF DURING A SESSION YOU:

- [A] BITE YOUR NAILS
- [B] FIDGET
- [C] EXPERIENCE CHEST PAIN
- [D] ARE DISTRACTED BY OBSESSIVE THOUGHTS

WARNING STOP IMMEDIATELY...

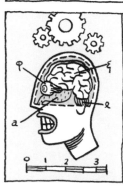

ANALYZE YOUR MINDSET: REPLAY YOUR PERFORMANCE IN SLOW MOTION AND TRY TO PINPOINT THE MOMENT YOU LOST FOCUS.

IN CERTAIN SITUATIONS, IT MAY BE ADVISABLE TO RETURN TO WORK FOR A WEEK OR TWO BEFORE RESUMING YOUR PRACTICE.

IF DURING A SESSION YOU FIND YOURSELF:

- [A] DEVELOPING A THEORY
- [B] HAVING IN-DEPTH THOUGHTS
- [C] RECREATING A MEMORY
- [D] OUTLINING A CONCEPT

KEEP IT UP! YOU'RE ON THE RIGHT PATH.

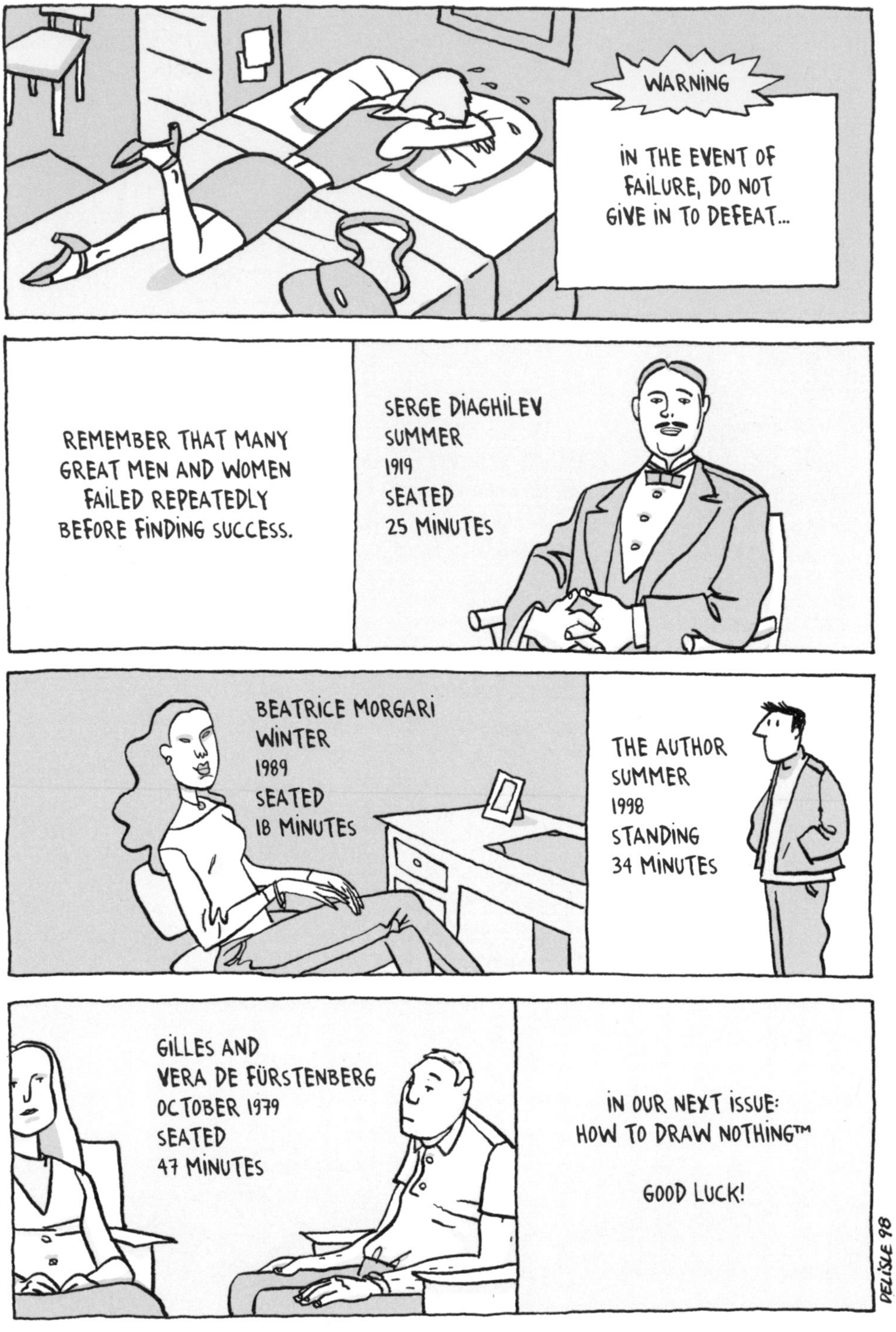
WARNING
IN THE EVENT OF FAILURE, DO NOT GIVE IN TO DEFEAT...
REMEMBER THAT MANY GREAT MEN AND WOMEN FAILED REPEATEDLY BEFORE FINDING SUCCESS.
SERGE DIAGHILEV
SUMMER
1919
SEATED
25 MINUTES
BEATRICE MORGARI
WINTER
1989
SEATED
18 MINUTES
THE AUTHOR
SUMMER
1998
STANDING
34 MINUTES
GILLES AND
VERA DE FÜRSTENBERG
OCTOBER 1979
SEATED
47 MINUTES
IN OUR NEXT ISSUE:
HOW TO DRAW NOTHING™
GOOD LUCK!
DELISLE 98

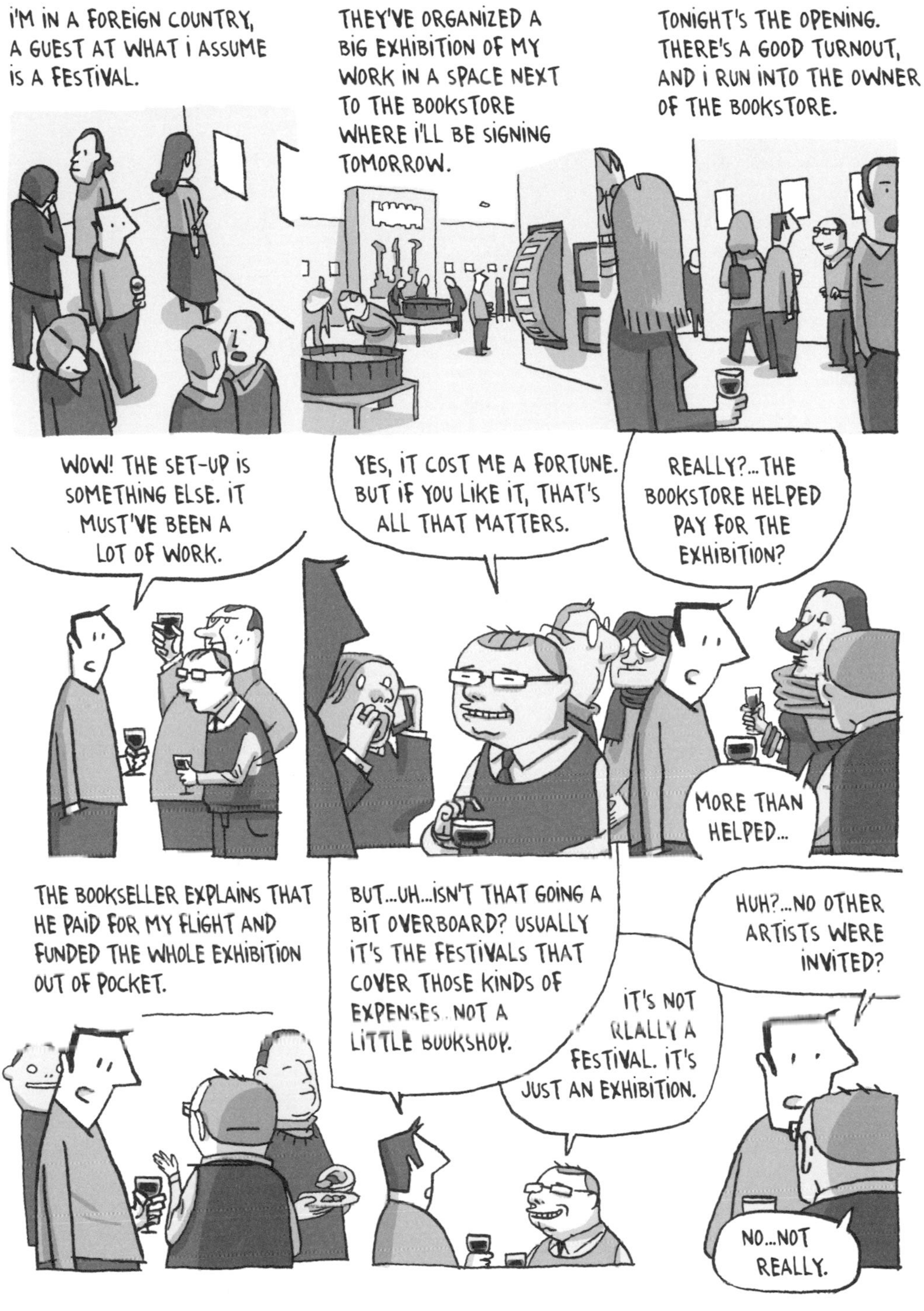
I'M IN A FOREIGN COUNTRY, A GUEST AT WHAT I ASSUME IS A FESTIVAL.
THEY'VE ORGANIZED A BIG EXHIBITION OF MY WORK IN A SPACE NEXT TO THE BOOKSTORE WHERE I'LL BE SIGNING TOMORROW.
TONIGHT'S THE OPENING. THERE'S A GOOD TURNOUT, AND I RUN INTO THE OWNER OF THE BOOKSTORE.
WOW! THE SET-UP IS SOMETHING ELSE. IT MUST'VE BEEN A LOT OF WORK.
YES, IT COST ME A FORTUNE. BUT IF YOU LIKE IT, THAT'S ALL THAT MATTERS.
REALLY?...THE BOOKSTORE HELPED PAY FOR THE EXHIBITION?
MORE THAN HELPED...
THE BOOKSELLER EXPLAINS THAT HE PAID FOR MY FLIGHT AND FUNDED THE WHOLE EXHIBITION OUT OF POCKET.
BUT...UH...ISN'T THAT GOING A BIT OVERBOARD? USUALLY IT'S THE FESTIVALS THAT COVER THOSE KINDS OF EXPENSES. NOT A LITTLE BOOKSHOP.
IT'S NOT REALLY A FESTIVAL. IT'S JUST AN EXHIBITION.
HUH?...NO OTHER ARTISTS WERE INVITED?
NO...NOT REALLY.

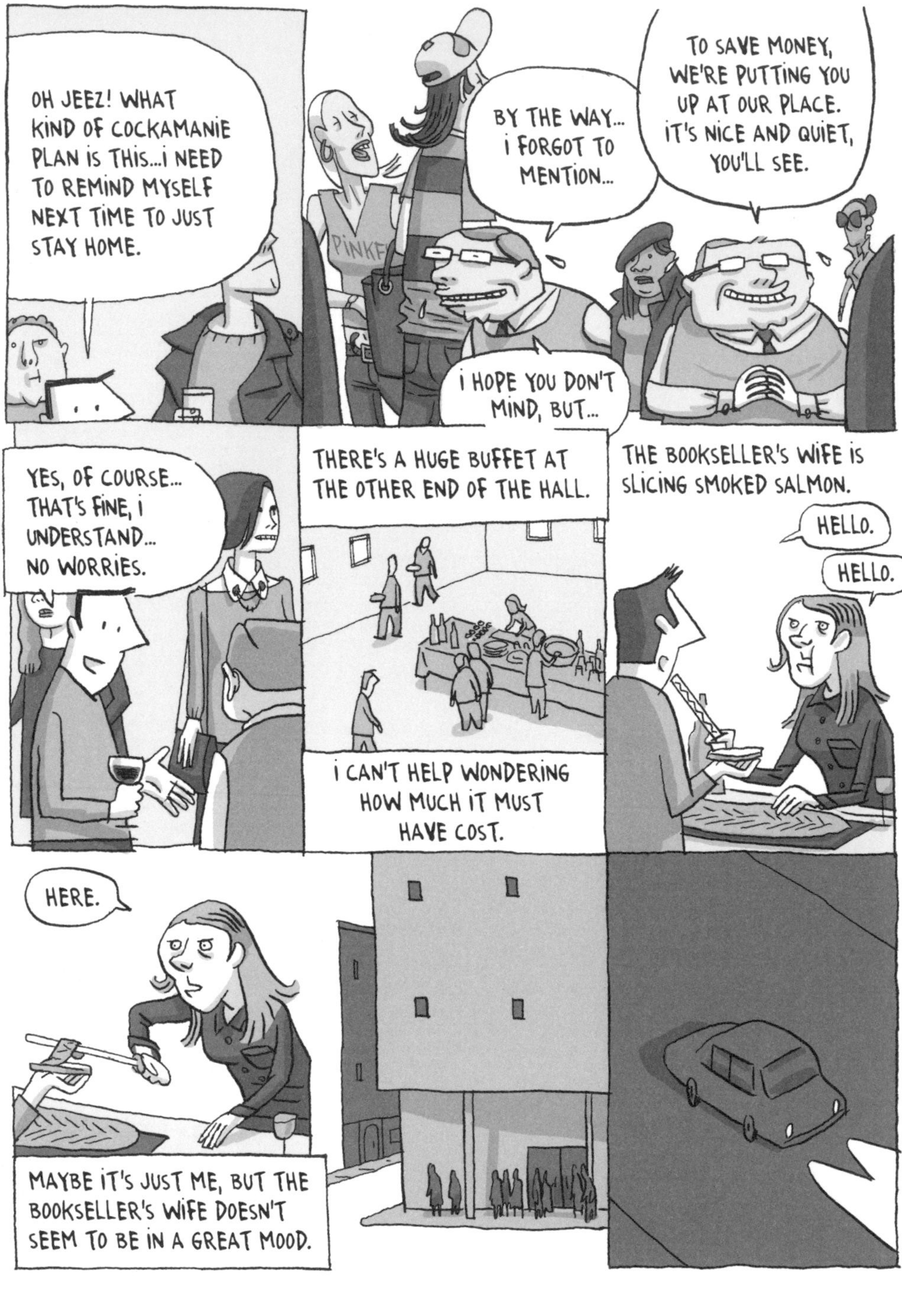

OH JEEZ! WHAT KIND OF COCKAMANIE PLAN IS THIS...I NEED TO REMIND MYSELF NEXT TIME TO JUST STAY HOME.
BY THE WAY... I FORGOT TO MENTION...
I HOPE YOU DON'T MIND, BUT...
TO SAVE MONEY, WE'RE PUTTING YOU UP AT OUR PLACE. IT'S NICE AND QUIET, YOU'LL SEE.
YES, OF COURSE... THAT'S FINE, I UNDERSTAND... NO WORRIES.
THERE'S A HUGE BUFFET AT THE OTHER END OF THE HALL.
I CAN'T HELP WONDERING HOW MUCH IT MUST HAVE COST.
THE BOOKSELLER'S WIFE IS SLICING SMOKED SALMON.
HELLO.
HELLO.
HERE.
MAYBE IT'S JUST ME, BUT THE BOOKSELLER'S WIFE DOESN'T SEEM TO BE IN A GREAT MOOD.

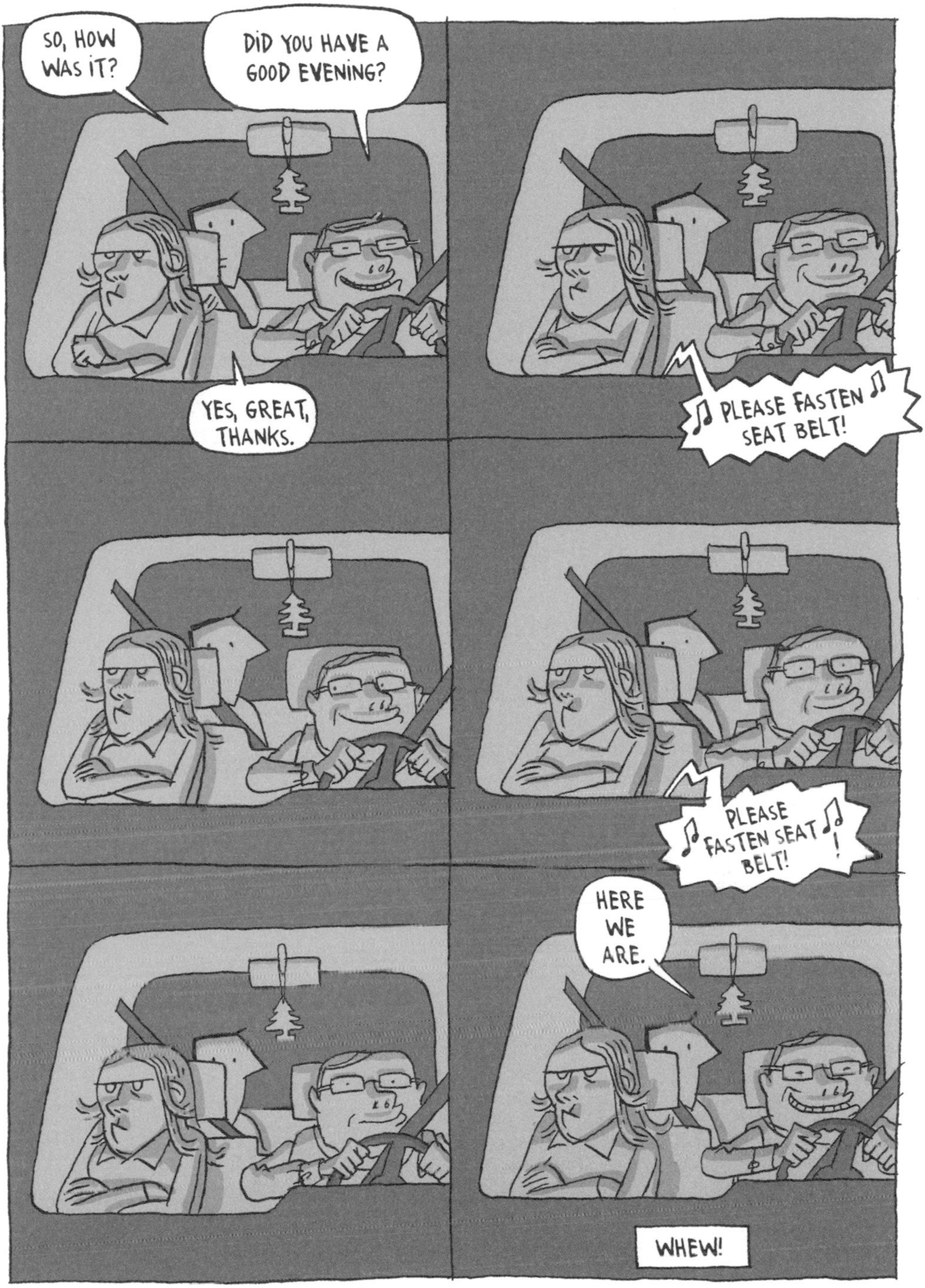
SO, HOW WAS IT?
DID YOU HAVE A GOOD EVENING?
YES, GREAT, THANKS.
♫ PLEASE FASTEN ♫ SEAT BELT!
♫ PLEASE FASTEN SEAT ♫ BELT! !
HERE WE ARE.
WHEW!

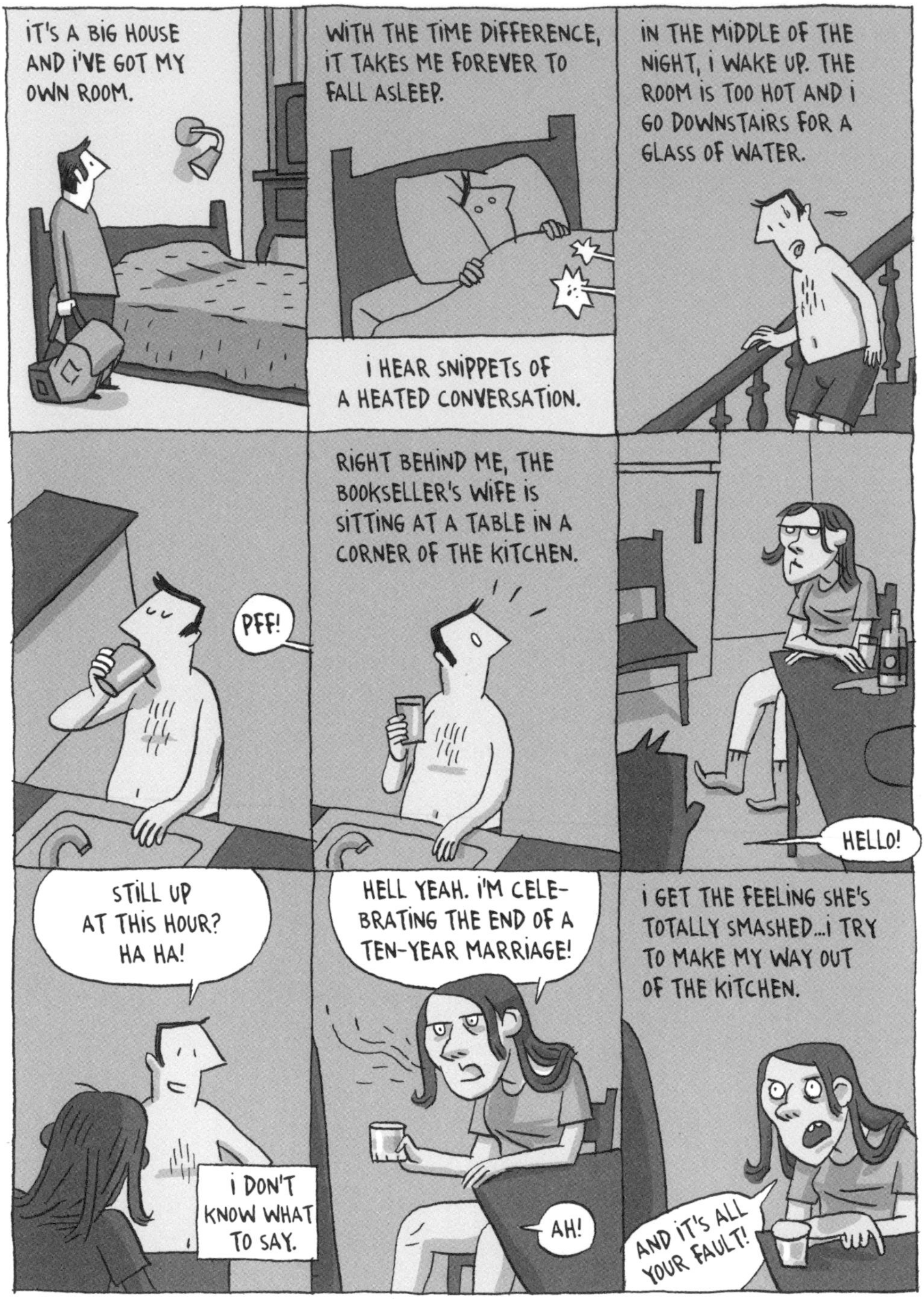
IT'S A BIG HOUSE AND I'VE GOT MY OWN ROOM.
WITH THE TIME DIFFERENCE, IT TAKES ME FOREVER TO FALL ASLEEP.
I HEAR SNIPPETS OF A HEATED CONVERSATION.
IN THE MIDDLE OF THE NIGHT, I WAKE UP. THE ROOM IS TOO HOT AND I GO DOWNSTAIRS FOR A GLASS OF WATER.
PFF!
RIGHT BEHIND ME, THE BOOKSELLER'S WIFE IS SITTING AT A TABLE IN A CORNER OF THE KITCHEN.
HELLO!
STILL UP AT THIS HOUR? HA HA!
I DON'T KNOW WHAT TO SAY.
HELL YEAH. I'M CELE-BRATING THE END OF A TEN-YEAR MARRIAGE!
AH!
I GET THE FEELING SHE'S TOTALLY SMASHED...I TRY TO MAKE MY WAY OUT OF THE KITCHEN.
AND IT'S ALL YOUR FAULT!

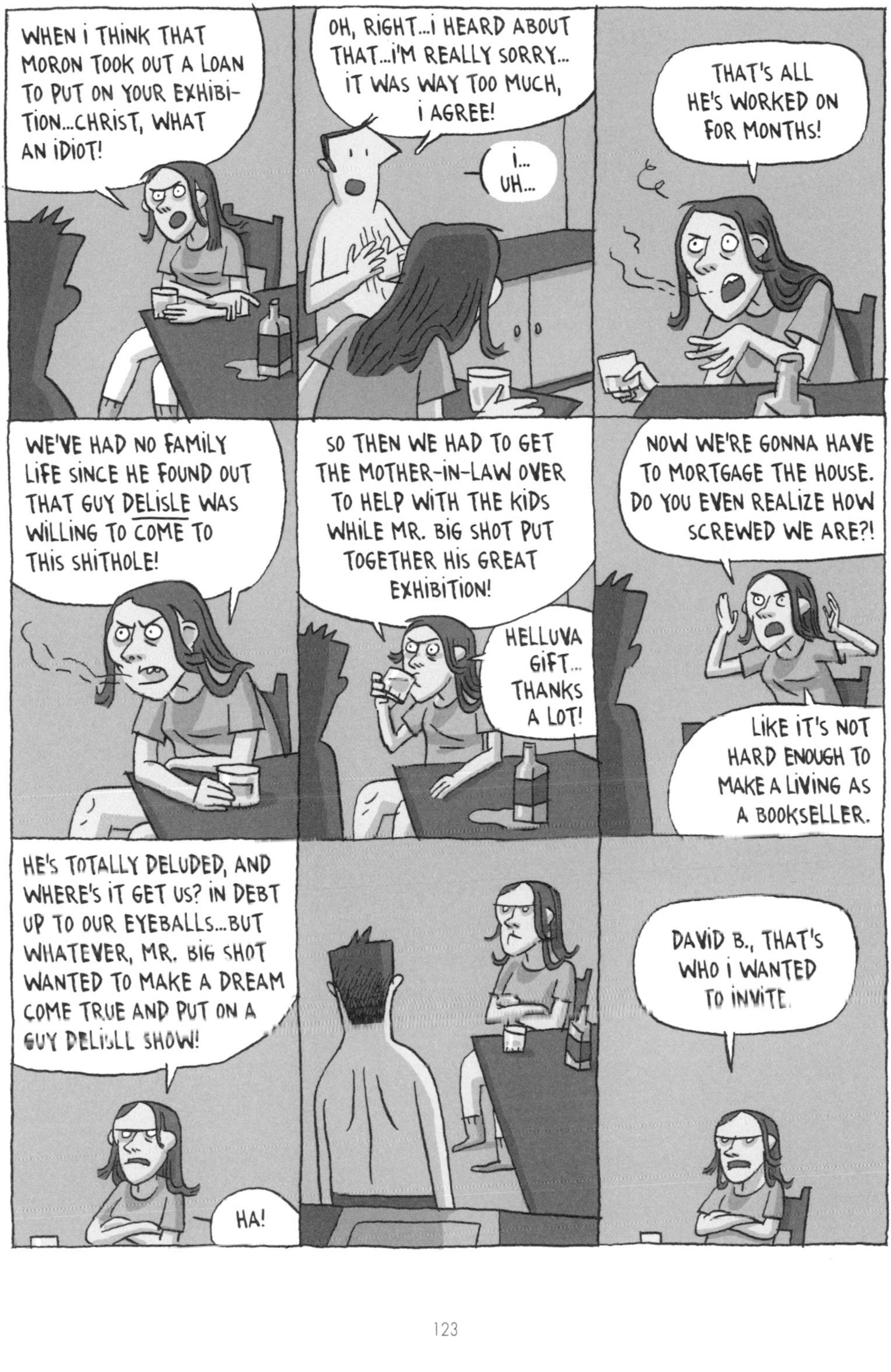
WHEN I THINK THAT MORON TOOK OUT A LOAN TO PUT ON YOUR EXHIBI-TION...CHRIST, WHAT AN IDIOT!
OH, RIGHT...I HEARD ABOUT THAT...I'M REALLY SORRY... IT WAS WAY TOO MUCH, I AGREE!
I... UH...
THAT'S ALL HE'S WORKED ON FOR MONTHS!
WE'VE HAD NO FAMILY LIFE SINCE HE FOUND OUT THAT GUY DELISLE WAS WILLING TO COME TO THIS SHITHOLE!
SO THEN WE HAD TO GET THE MOTHER-IN-LAW OVER TO HELP WITH THE KIDS WHILE MR. BIG SHOT PUT TOGETHER HIS GREAT EXHIBITION!
HELLUVA GIFT... THANKS A LOT!
NOW WE'RE GONNA HAVE TO MORTGAGE THE HOUSE. DO YOU EVEN REALIZE HOW SCREWED WE ARE?!
LIKE IT'S NOT HARD ENOUGH TO MAKE A LIVING AS A BOOKSELLER.
HE'S TOTALLY DELUDED, AND WHERE'S IT GET US? IN DEBT UP TO OUR EYEBALLS...BUT WHATEVER, MR. BIG SHOT WANTED TO MAKE A DREAM COME TRUE AND PUT ON A GUY DELISLE SHOW!
HA!
DAVID B., THAT'S WHO I WANTED TO INVITE.

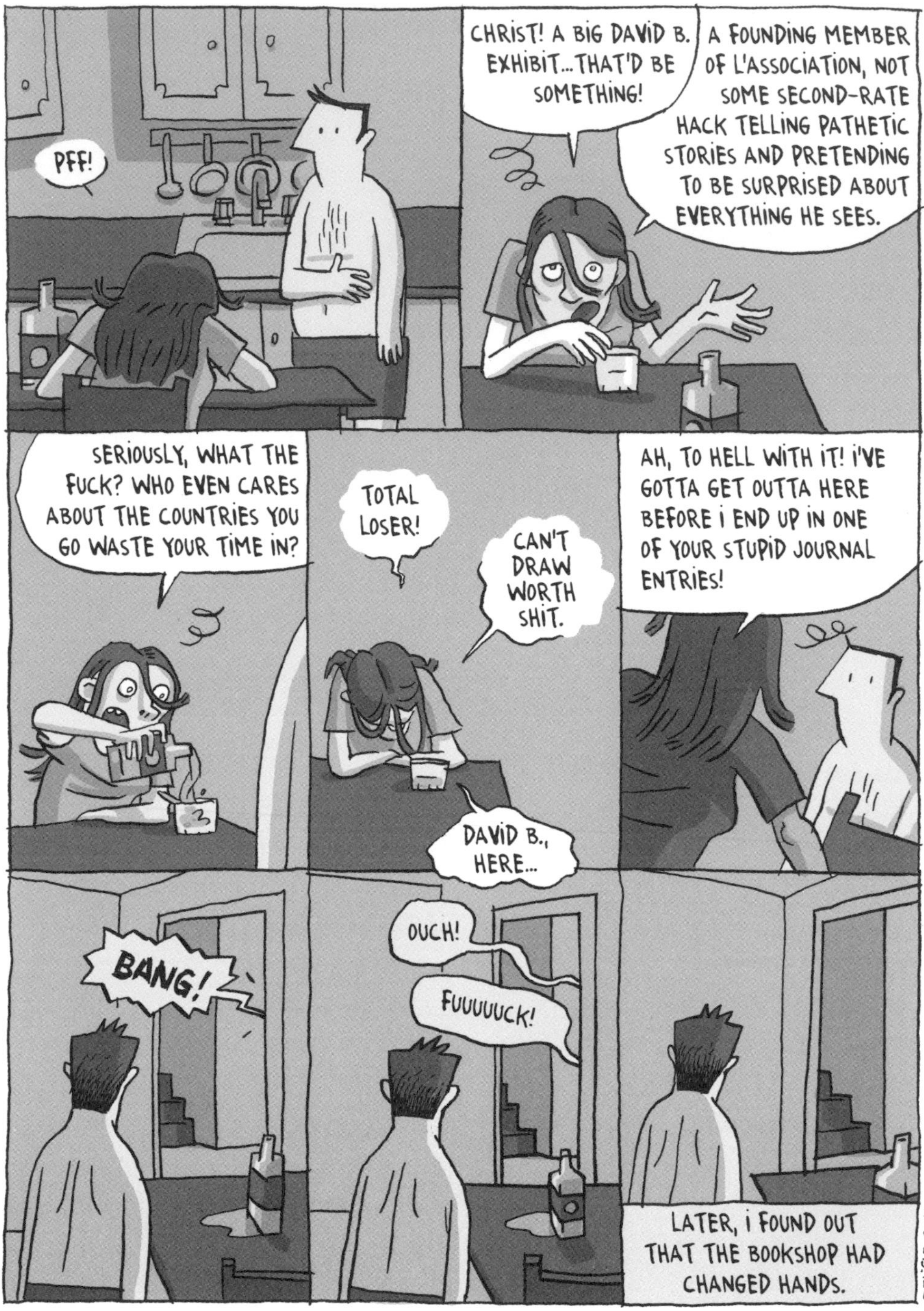
PFF!
CHRIST! A BIG DAVID B. EXHIBIT... THAT'D BE SOMETHING!
A FOUNDING MEMBER OF L'ASSOCIATION, NOT SOME SECOND-RATE HACK TELLING PATHETIC STORIES AND PRETENDING TO BE SURPRISED ABOUT EVERYTHING HE SEES.
SERIOUSLY, WHAT THE FUCK? WHO EVEN CARES ABOUT THE COUNTRIES YOU GO WASTE YOUR TIME IN?
TOTAL LOSER!
CAN'T DRAW WORTH SHIT.
DAVID B., HERE...
AH, TO HELL WITH IT! I'VE GOTTA GET OUTTA HERE BEFORE I END UP IN ONE OF YOUR STUPID JOURNAL ENTRIES!
BANG!
OUCH!
FUUUUUCK!
LATER, I FOUND OUT THAT THE BOOKSHOP HAD CHANGED HANDS.
DELISLE 2011

THE LAST PANEL

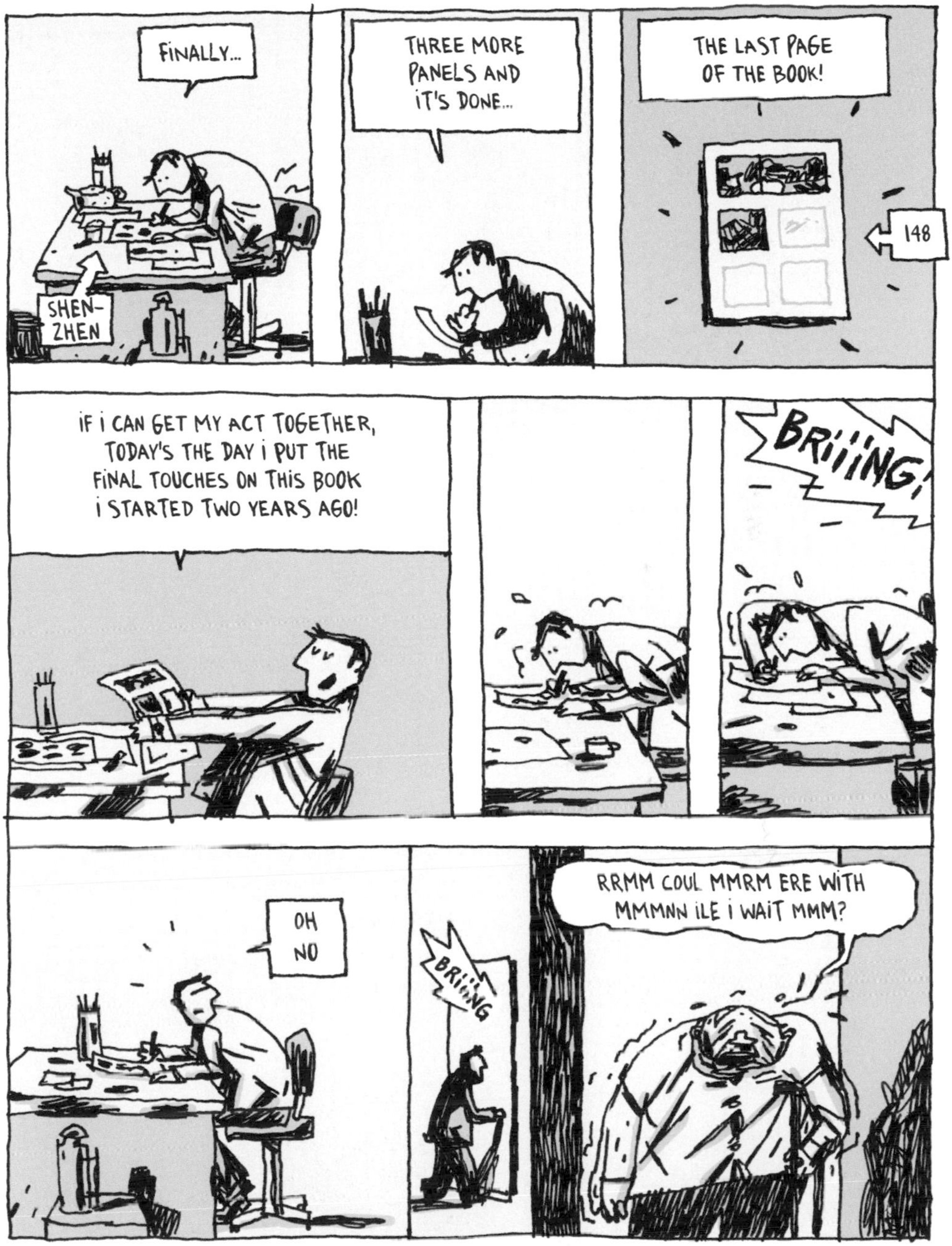
FINALLY...
SHEN-
ZHEN
THREE MORE PANELS AND IT'S DONE...
THE LAST PAGE OF THE BOOK!
148
IF I CAN GET MY ACT TOGETHER, TODAY'S THE DAY I PUT THE FINAL TOUCHES ON THIS BOOK I STARTED TWO YEARS AGO!
BRIIING!
OH NO
BRIIING
RRMM COUL MMRM ERE WITH MMMNN ILE I WAIT MMM?

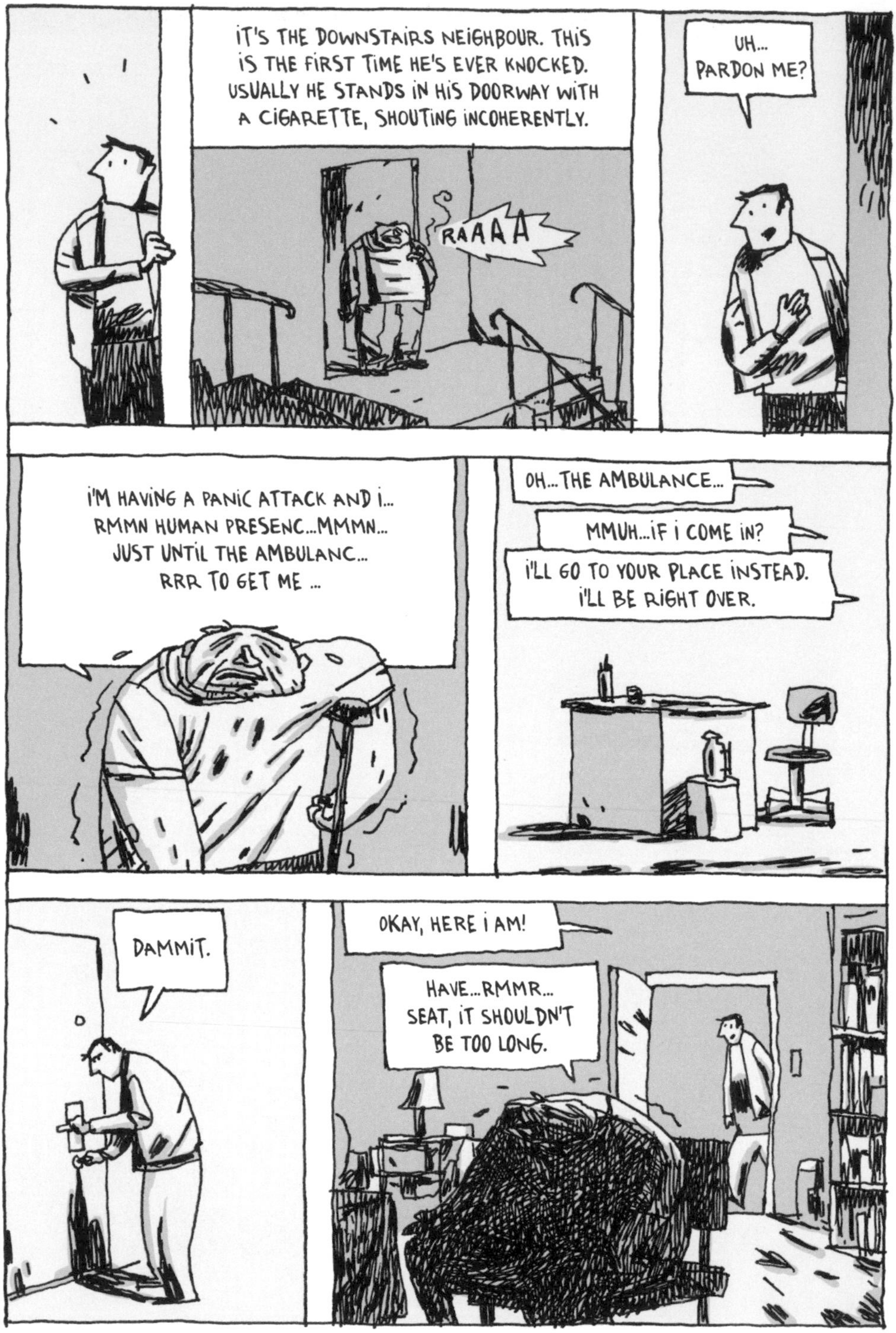
IT'S THE DOWNSTAIRS NEIGHBOUR. THIS IS THE FIRST TIME HE'S EVER KNOCKED. USUALLY HE STANDS IN HIS DOORWAY WITH A CIGARETTE, SHOUTING INCOHERENTLY.
RAAAA
UH... PARDON ME?
I'M HAVING A PANIC ATTACK AND I... RMMN HUMAN PRESENC...MMMN... JUST UNTIL THE AMBULANC... RRR TO GET ME ...
OH...THE AMBULANCE...
MMUH...IF I COME IN?
I'LL GO TO YOUR PLACE INSTEAD. I'LL BE RIGHT OVER.
DAMMIT.
OKAY, HERE I AM!
HAVE...RMMR... SEAT, IT SHOULDN'T BE TOO LONG.

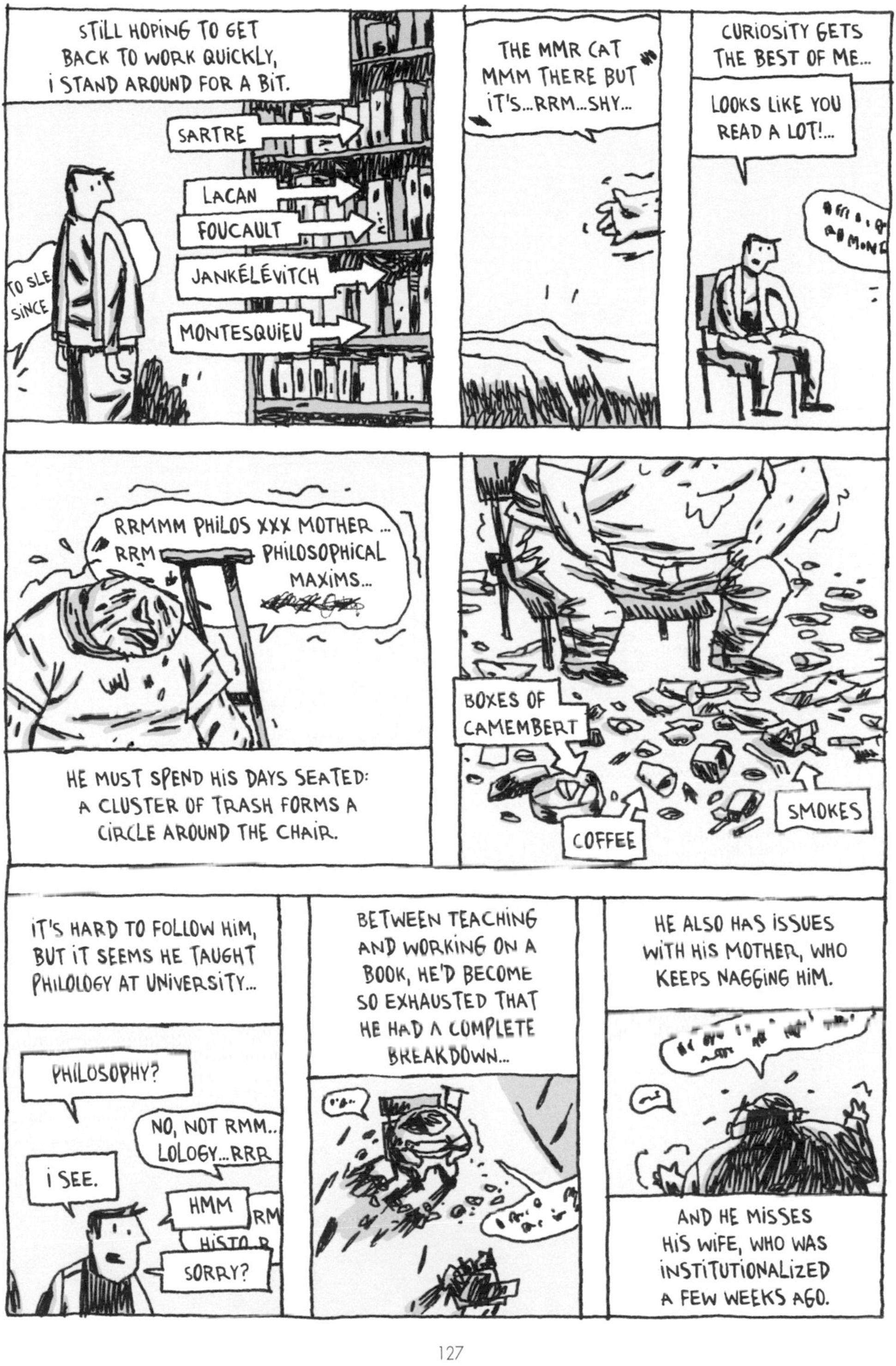
STILL HOPING TO GET BACK TO WORK QUICKLY, I STAND AROUND FOR A BIT.
SARTRE
LACAN
FOUCAULT
JANKÉLÉVITCH
MONTESQUIEU
THE MMR CAT MMM THERE BUT IT'S...RRM...SHY...
CURIOSITY GETS THE BEST OF ME...
LOOKS LIKE YOU READ A LOT!...
RRMMM PHILOS XXX MOTHER ... RRM PHILOSOPHICAL MAXIMS...
HE MUST SPEND HIS DAYS SEATED: A CLUSTER OF TRASH FORMS A CIRCLE AROUND THE CHAIR.
BOXES OF CAMEMBERT
COFFEE
SMOKES
IT'S HARD TO FOLLOW HIM, BUT IT SEEMS HE TAUGHT PHILOLOGY AT UNIVERSITY...
PHILOSOPHY?
NO, NOT RMM.. LOLOGY...RRR
I SEE.
HMM
SORRY?
BETWEEN TEACHING AND WORKING ON A BOOK, HE'D BECOME SO EXHAUSTED THAT HE HAD A COMPLETE BREAKDOWN...
HE ALSO HAS ISSUES WITH HIS MOTHER, WHO KEEPS NAGGING HIM.
AND HE MISSES HIS WIFE, WHO WAS INSTITUTIONALIZED A FEW WEEKS AGO.

THE WALLPA-
PER HAS BEEN
SHREDDED
TO PIECES.

AND YET I STILL HAVEN'T SEEN
ANY MOVEMENT ON THE BED
WHERE THE CAT IS LYING.

MAYBE IT'S DEAD?
IF SO, IT MUST HAVE
DIED RECENTLY,
BECAUSE ALL I SMELL
IS CIGARETTES AND
CAMEMBERT...

CAT
SCRATCH
MARKS.

NIGHT
FALLS...

WE CHAT A
LITTLE MORE...

OCCASIONALLY
HE DOZES OFF IN
MID-SENTENCE.

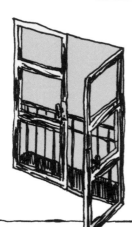

FL....

FLAUBERT...NEV

IT SEEMS TO ME THAT WHAT HE
REALLY NEEDS IS SLEEP, BUT HE GETS
UP TO MAKE HIMSELF A COFFEE.

HE CLEARED THE
SAME OBSTACLE
COURSE THREE
TIMES...BARELY
AVOIDING THE CUP-
BOARD DOOR AND
GRAZING THE BOTTLE
WITH HIS CRUTCH.

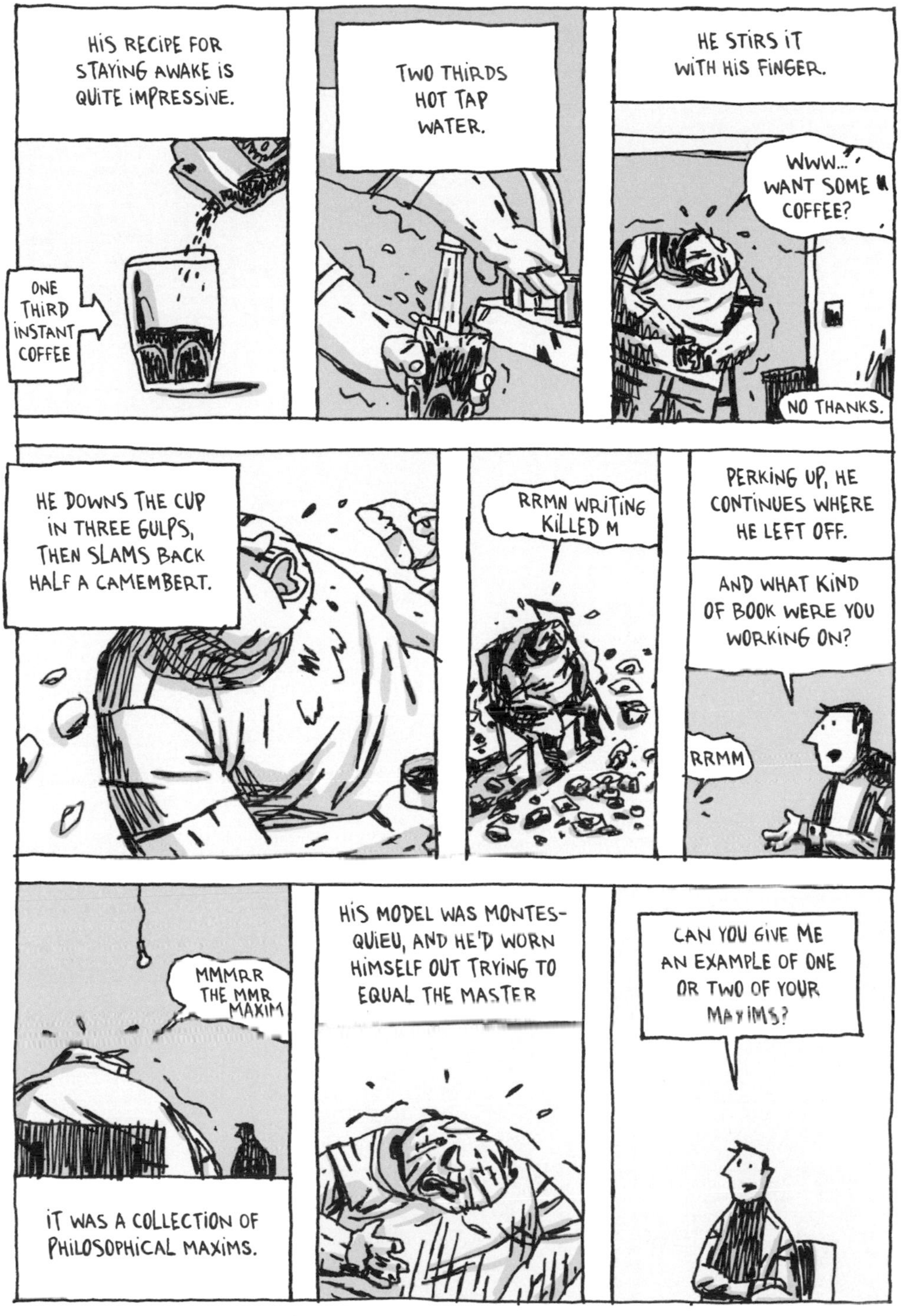

HIS RECIPE FOR STAYING AWAKE IS QUITE IMPRESSIVE.
ONE THIRD INSTANT COFFEE
TWO THIRDS HOT TAP WATER.
HE STIRS IT WITH HIS FINGER.
WWW... WANT SOME COFFEE?
NO THANKS.
HE DOWNS THE CUP IN THREE GULPS, THEN SLAMS BACK HALF A CAMEMBERT.
RRMN WRITING KILLED M
PERKING UP, HE CONTINUES WHERE HE LEFT OFF.
AND WHAT KIND OF BOOK WERE YOU WORKING ON?
RRMM
MMMRR THE MMR MAXIM
IT WAS A COLLECTION OF PHILOSOPHICAL MAXIMS.
HIS MODEL WAS MONTESQUIEU, AND HE'D WORN HIMSELF OUT TRYING TO EQUAL THE MASTER
CAN YOU GIVE ME AN EXAMPLE OF ONE OR TWO OF YOUR MAXIMS?

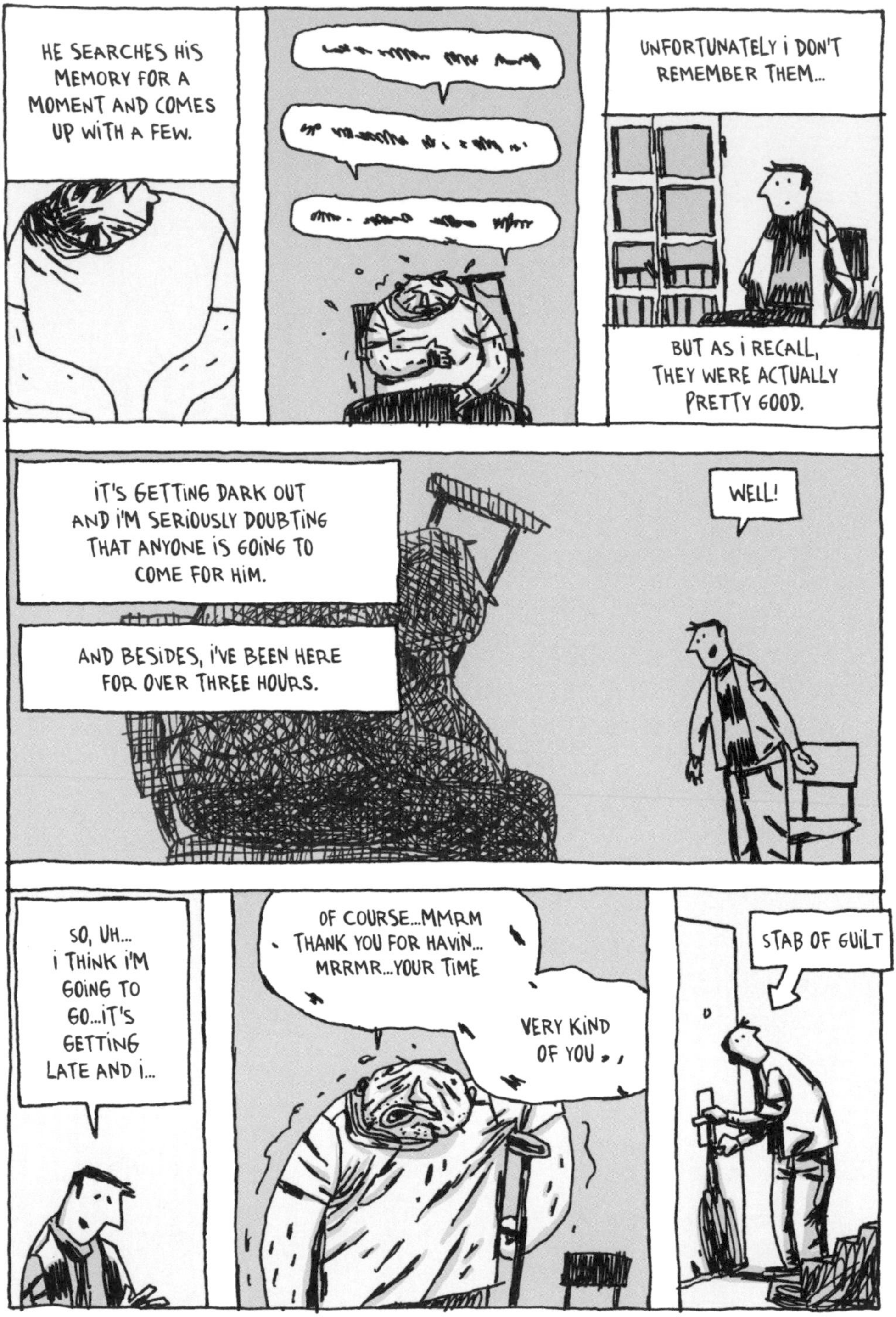
HE SEARCHES HIS MEMORY FOR A MOMENT AND COMES UP WITH A FEW.
UNFORTUNATELY I DON'T REMEMBER THEM...
BUT AS I RECALL, THEY WERE ACTUALLY PRETTY GOOD.
IT'S GETTING DARK OUT AND I'M SERIOUSLY DOUBTING THAT ANYONE IS GOING TO COME FOR HIM.
AND BESIDES, I'VE BEEN HERE FOR OVER THREE HOURS.
WELL!
SO, UH... I THINK I'M GOING TO GO...IT'S GETTING LATE AND I...
OF COURSE...MMRM THANK YOU FOR HAVIN... MRRMR...YOUR TIME
VERY KIND OF YOU
STAB OF GUILT

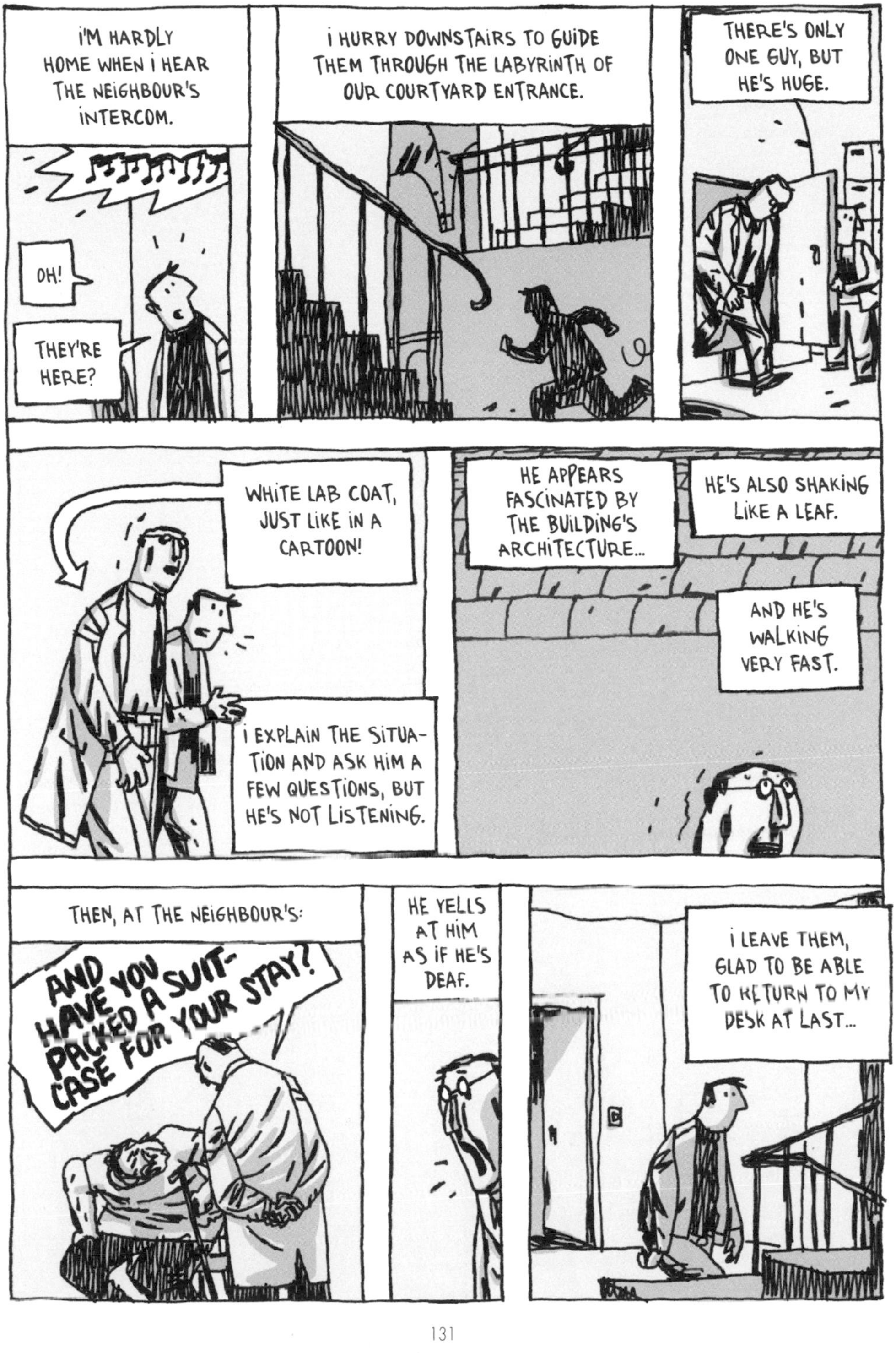

I'M HARDLY HOME WHEN I HEAR THE NEIGHBOUR'S INTERCOM.
OH!
THEY'RE HERE?
I HURRY DOWNSTAIRS TO GUIDE THEM THROUGH THE LABYRINTH OF OUR COURTYARD ENTRANCE.
THERE'S ONLY ONE GUY, BUT HE'S HUGE.
WHITE LAB COAT, JUST LIKE IN A CARTOON!
I EXPLAIN THE SITUA-TION AND ASK HIM A FEW QUESTIONS, BUT HE'S NOT LISTENING.
HE APPEARS FASCINATED BY THE BUILDING'S ARCHITECTURE...
HE'S ALSO SHAKING LIKE A LEAF.
AND HE'S WALKING VERY FAST.
THEN, AT THE NEIGHBOUR'S:
AND HAVE YOU PACKED A SUIT-CASE FOR YOUR STAY?
HE YELLS AT HIM AS IF HE'S DEAF.
I LEAVE THEM, GLAD TO BE ABLE TO RETURN TO MY DESK AT LAST...

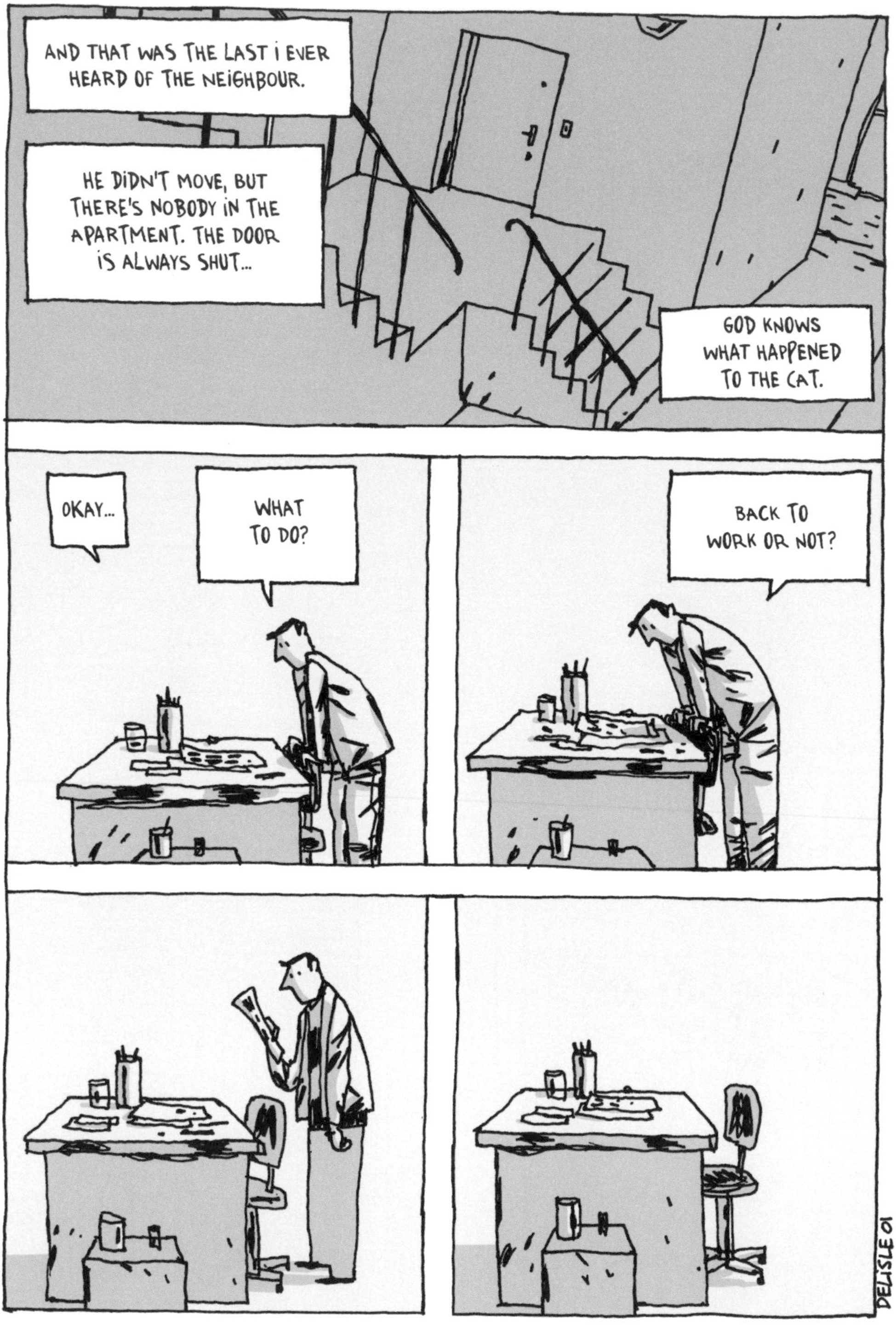
AND THAT WAS THE LAST I EVER HEARD OF THE NEIGHBOUR.
HE DIDN'T MOVE, BUT THERE'S NOBODY IN THE APARTMENT. THE DOOR IS ALWAYS SHUT...
GOD KNOWS WHAT HAPPENED TO THE CAT.
OKAY...
WHAT TO DO?
BACK TO WORK OR NOT?
DELISLE 01

Also available from Guy Delisle

Factory Summers
Hostage
Pyongyang: A Journey in North Korea
Shenzhen: A Travelogue from China
Jerusalem: Chronicles from the Holy City
Burma Chronicles

The Handbook to Lazy Parenting
The Owner's Manual to Terrible Parenting
Even More Bad Parenting Advice
A User's Guide to Neglectful Parenting

Entire contents copyright © 2022 Guy Delisle. Translation copyright © 2022 Helge Dascher and Rob Aspinall. All rights reserved. No part of this book (except small portions for review purposes) may be reproduced in any form without written permission from Guy Delisle or Drawn & Quarterly. Originally published by Les Éditions de la Pastèque © 2020.

drawnandquarterly.com | guydelisle.com

ISBN 978-1-77046-567-1 | First edition: August 2022
Printed in Turkey | 10 9 8 7 6 5 4 3 2 1
Cataloguing data available from Library and Archives Canada.

Published in the USA by Drawn & Quarterly, a client publisher of Farrar, Straus and Giroux. Published in Canada by Drawn & Quarterly, a client publisher of Raincoast Books. Published in the United Kingdom by Drawn & Quarterly, a client publisher of Publishers Group UK.

Drawn & Quarterly acknowledges the support of the Government of Canada and the Canada Council for the Arts for our publishing program.

Drawn & Quarterly reconnaît l'aide financière du gouvernement du Québec par l'entremise de la Société de développement des entreprises culturelles (SODEC) pour nos activités d'édition. Gouvernement du Québec—Programme de crédit d'impôt pour l'édition de livres—Gestion SODEC.

Index

Born in Québec City, Canada, in 1966, Guy Delisle now lives in the south of France with his wife and two children. Delisle spent ten years working in animation and is best known for his chronicles of life overseas. He is the author of numerous graphic novels and travelogues, including *Factory Summers*, *Hostage*, *Jerusalem: Chronicles from the Holy City*, and *Pyongyang: A Journey in North Korea*. In 2012, Delisle was awarded the Prize for Best Album for the French edition of *Jerusalem* at the Angoulême International Comics Festival.

World Record Holders was translated by Helge Dascher and Rob Aspinall from their respective homes in Montreal, Quebec and Guelph, Ontario. Solo and in collaboration with Aspinall, Dascher has translated all of Delisle's English graphic novels.